OXFORD WORLD'S CLASSICS

THE DEVIL
AND OTHER STORIES

COUNT LEO NIKOLAEVICH TOLSTOY, the youngest of four brothers, was born in 1828 at Yasnaya Polyana, his father's estate in Tula province, about 200 miles from Moscow. His mother died when he was 2, and his father when h̶ memory, and they were the inspiration ̶ ̶ ̶ ̶ ̶ ̶ ̶ ̶ ̶ ̶ Mary and Nicholas Rostov in *War a̶*̶ and father belonged to the Russian n̶ remained highly conscious of his ari̶s̶ towards the end of his life he embra̶c̶ Christian equality and the brotherhood

He served in the army in the Caucasus and the Crimea, where as an artillery officer at the siege of Sevastopol he wrote his first stories and impressions. After leaving the army he travelled and studied educational theories, which deeply interested him. In 1862 he married Sophie Behrs and for the next fifteen years lived a tranquil and productive life as a country gentleman and author. *War and Peace* was finished in 1869 and *Anna Karenina* in 1877. He had thirteen children. In 1879, after undergoing a severe spiritual crisis, he wrote the autobiographical *A Confession*, and from then on he became a 'Tolstoyan', seeking to propagate his views on religion, morality, non-violence, and renunciation of the flesh. He continued to write, but chiefly in the form of parables, tracts, and morality plays—written 'with the left hand of Tolstoy' as a Russian critic has put it—though he also composed a late novel, *Resurrection*, and one of his finest long tales, *Hadji Murad*. Because of his new beliefs and disciples, and his international fame as pacifist and sage, relations with his wife became strained and family life increasingly difficult. At last in 1910, at the age of 82, he left his home and died of pneumonia at a local railway station.

RICHARD F. GUSTAFSON, Professor of Russian at Barnard College, Columbia University, is a specialist in Russian literature and religious philosophy. He is the author of *Leo Tolstoy: Resident and Stranger* (1986) and has edited Tolstoy's *Resurrection* and *The Kreutzer Sonata and Other Stories* for Oxford World's Classics.

OXFORD WORLD'S CLASSICS

*For over 100 years Oxford World's Classics have brought
readers closer to the world's great literature. Now with over 700
titles—from the 4,000-year-old myths of Mesopotamia to the
twentieth century's greatest novels—the series makes available
lesser-known as well as celebrated writing.*

*The pocket-sized hardbacks of the early years contained
introductions by Virginia Woolf, T. S. Eliot, Graham Greene,
and other literary figures which enriched the experience of reading.
Today the series is recognized for its fine scholarship and
reliability in texts that span world literature, drama and poetry,
religion, philosophy and politics. Each edition includes perceptive
commentary and essential background information to meet the
changing needs of readers.*

OXFORD WORLD'S CLASSICS

═══

LEO TOLSTOY

The Devil

and Other Stories

═══

Translated by
LOUISE AND AYLMER MAUDE

Revised, with an Introduction and Notes, by
RICHARD F. GUSTAFSON

OXFORD
UNIVERSITY PRESS

OXFORD

UNIVERSITY PRESS

Great Clarendon Street, Oxford OX2 6DP

Oxford University Press is a department of the University of Oxford.
It furthers the University's objective of excellence in research, scholarship,
and education by publishing worldwide in

Oxford New York

Auckland Bangkok Buenos Aires Cape Town Chennai
Dar es Salaam Delhi Hong Kong Istanbul Karachi Kolkata
Kuala Lumpur Madrid Melbourne Mexico City Mumbai Nairobi
São Paulo Shanghai Taipei Tokyo Toronto

Oxford is a registered trade mark of Oxford University Press
in the UK and in certain other countries

Published in the United States
by Oxford University Press Inc., New York

First published as an Oxford World's Classics paperback 2003
Reissued 2009

British Library Cataloguing in Publication Data

Data available

Library of Congress Cataloging in Publication Data

Tolstoy, Leo, graf, 1828–1910.
[Short stories. English. Selections]
The devil and other stories/Leo Tolstoy; translated by Louise and Aylmer Maude;
revised, with an introduction and notes, by Richard F. Gustafson.
p. cm.—(Oxford world's classics)
Includes bibliographical references.
Contents: The snowstorm—Lucerne—Three deaths—Polikushka—Strider: the story of
a horse—God sees the truth, but waits—The notes of a madman—Where love is, God is
—The devil—Father Sergy—After the ball.
1. Tolstoy, Leo, graf, 1828–1910—Translations into English. I. Maude, Louise Shanks,
1855–1939. II. Maude, Aylmer, 1858–1938. III. Gustafson, Richard F. IV. Title. V.
Oxford world's classics (Oxford University Press)

PG3366.A13M3 2003 891.73′3—dc21 2002044698

ISBN 978-0-19-955399-0

Typeset in Ehrhardt
by RefineCatch Limited, Bungay, Suffolk
Printed in Great Britain by
Clays Ltd, Elcograf S.pA.

CONTENTS

CONTENTS

INTRODUCTION

Readers who do not wish to learn details of the stories' plots will prefer to treat the Introduction as an Epilogue

The short stories in this volume span virtually the whole of Tolstoy's literary career and represent in a number of ways the matter and method characteristic of *War and Peace* and *Anna Karenina*. What is striking about this group of stories is that while they reflect many of Tolstoy's central themes, such as love, sexuality, and death, issues of justice both human and divine, and the difficulties of the pursuit of moral life, they are to the one unique in form. True, Tolstoy's verbal style can be seen throughout these pages, but what is equally evident is his sensitivity to the possibilities and significance of literary structure. What makes these stories so accomplished is the way Tolstoy uses these possibilities to give expression to his complex moral and religious world view.

By the time Tolstoy published 'The Snow Storm' in 1856, he had already established himself as an important young author with the publication of two parts of his trilogy, his first extended fiction, the *Bildungsroman* entitled *Childhood, Boyhood, Youth,* and several of his Sevastopol sketches. 'The Snow Storm' recalls *Childhood* in that so much of it is built around 'recollections and pictures of the distant past' (p. 14). This story shares with the trilogy a sensitivity to the beauty of nature, often depicted in detail, and a narrator who recalls his youth and need for attention: 'Everything around me is beautiful, and that beauty affects me so powerfully that it seems to me that I myself am good, and the one thing that vexes me is that nobody is there to admire me' (p. 15). The theme of self-conscious vanity is most striking at the culmination of the central recollection, when as a peasant drowns the narrator stands by wishing he could save him in order that others would admire his heroic deed (p. 16). The narrator does not seem to be proud of this vanity he recalls from his youth, but the potential for a moralistic stance yields to the telling of the tale. In form 'The Snow Storm' uses what will become one of Tolstoy's major tropes, the journey of discovery. In this early work what the narrator discovers, however, is not quite clear. As a journey through a snow storm it recalls Tolstoy's famous late story 'Master and Man', where the whole point of the tale is the moral and metaphysical discovery made at the end of the journey. As is characteristic of Tolstoy, the later story is highly emblematic with a fairly clear religious subtext. The journey in 'The Snow Storm' is not so much a discovery as a recovery, a remembrance of things past.

The representation of the psychic state of recollection is the most extraordinary accomplishment of this early story. Tolstoy had already explored the representation of altered states of consciousness, most memorably in his representation of the dying of Praskukhin in 'Sevastopol in May'. Of this and comparable scenes the Russian critic Nikolay Chernyshevsky wrote in 1856 that Tolstoy had created a new form he termed both the 'dialectic of the soul' and 'interior monologue'. In 'The Snow Storm' the altered state of awareness is especially marked by complex verbal play. The journey through the snow storm is punctuated by sounds, in the beginning the sound of the beating of the swingletree (*valyok*) against the front of the sledge (p. 13) and throughout the sounds of the troika bells, singly, in thirds, and in fifths. These sounds lull the narrator into a state of drowsiness, even as he begins to feel that his feet are getting cold from the frost. As he falls into a sleepy reverie, he recalls a scene from his childhood at his 'favourite place by the lake' (p. 15). From that lake comes the sound of a 'beetle' (*valyok*), that is, a wooden paddle, which is 'beating wet linen, and the sound reverberates and is borne down along the lake' (p. 15). The moment when the dead body of the drowned peasant is dragged from the lake—the most horrible scene in the recollection—is accompanied by 'the strokes (*udary*) of a beetle (*valyok* also means the loom of an oar) reverberating over the lake' (p. 19). The narrator then comments: 'But this beetle sounds as if two beetles were beating together in thirds, and that sound torments and worries me, the more so because I know that this beetle is a bell, that Fyodor Filippych will not make it stop. Then this beetle, like an instrument of torture, presses my foot which is freezing, and I fall asleep.' Later, as the narrator falls into a deeper sleep, this bell is transformed into recollected church bells (p. 26). Thus the whole state of recollecting consciousness is marked by the intruding sound of the troika bells (which recall church bells) and three apparently different sounds, the beating *swingletree* on the sledge, the *beetle* beating wet linen heard in the distance, and the strokes of the *loom* of an oar on the lake, all three expressed by the one word with three meanings, *valyok*. Such verbal play used to express the meandering of the mind in varied states of semi-sleep reaches its height in the representation of Nikolay Rostov's vision of the 'white spot' in *War and Peace* (1. iii. 13).

'Lucerne', published in 1857, one year after 'The Snow Storm', shares with this work it so clearly does not resemble one important thing: both works are grounded in specific experiences in Tolstoy's own life. 'The Snow Storm' was inspired by a night journey through a snow storm in the Caucasus, as Tolstoy was on his way back to Russia in 1854. 'Lucerne' is based on Tolstoy's impressions of Europe on his first trip there in 1857 and presented as if it were a diary entry for 8 July of that year. As a result of this diary form, this story also shares with 'The Snow Storm' the first-person narrative. The diary form itself is underlined by the full title 'From the Notes of Prince D. Nekhlyudov. Lucerne'. This generic marker allows Tolstoy to give the first-person narrator a name. This is significant since this Prince Nekhlyudov is the one character who appears in several of Tolstoy's fictions, from the early trilogy to the late novel *Resurrection* of which he is the central male protagonist. In all these fictions the character named Nekhlyudov reflects in one way or another his creator. The use of this name marks the autobiographical origin as well as the autopsychological status of the fiction.

Unlike 'The Snow Storm' 'Lucerne' has a clear moral focus. Nekhlyudov sees Lucerne and the English tourists there as emblematic of a modern 'four-cornered, five-storeyed' (p. 32) world inhabited by isolated, alienated, self-absorbed, and self-interested strangers. He contrasts this City of Man with the wonder of nature in which he sees harmony in all the variety and which he experiences as 'tranquillity, softness, unity, and the inevitability of the beautiful' (p. 33). This experience of nature arouses in him 'a need to express an excess of something' and 'a desire to embrace someone, to hug him closely'. The irony is that he experiences this wonderful harmony and desire for human contact when he is isolated in his room, wrapped up in himself as he stares out of the window. With others he just becomes depressed. But then when he happens to hear the song of a wandering singer, 'instead of the weariness, dullness, and indifference towards everything in the world that I had felt a moment before, I suddenly experienced a need for love, a fullness of hope, and a spontaneous joy of life' (p. 37). Like the beauty of nature, the beauty of art arouses in him a desire to unite with all who are separate, a feeling that is the nucleus of the definition of art Tolstoy articulated many years later in his famous work *What Is Art?* (1898). Much of the story is then devoted to Nekhlyudov's rage at the Englishmen who do not share his 'excess of something' and at the waiters at the hotel who ridicule his misguided attempts to befriend the 'little man'. To the reader it becomes clear that Nekhlyudov is still wrapped up in himself, for in all his efforts to draw close to the singer, his interest is always the demonstration of his love for others to others and himself.

The 'little man' leaves and Nekhlyudov, left all alone, turns inward and to himself delivers a long, angry harangue against the cruelty and injustice of all these people who take pleasure from the poetry but care not for the human needs and dignity of the poet. In this response he sees the evil of all modern, Western culture with its progress and advanced governments and laws. He cannot understand how these advanced people do 'not find in their souls the simple, primordial feeling of one human being for another' (p. 52). To him it is clear that 'we have one unerring guide, and only one, the universal Spirit, which, penetrating each separately and all of us together, implants in every individual a striving for what ought to be, that same Spirit which in the tree bids it grow towards the sun, in the flower bids it shed its seeds in the autumn, and in us bids us huddle instinctively closer to each other' (p. 53). This sense of the indwelling Spirit of life in all, which recalls Coleridge's 'one Life within us and abroad', became the foundation for Tolstoy's later theological beliefs. But then, hearing the voice of the singer in the distance, Nekhlyudov turns his attention to himself and sees the contradiction in his enraged and spiteful tirade. It is his own anger that has separated him from others, although he now would believe that even with his spite he is somehow answering 'the harmonious need of the eternal and infinite' (p. 54). Prince Nekhlyudov's journey to Switzerland has turned out to be a journey of discovery.

'Three Deaths', published two years later in 1859, begins with a journey which is neither of recovery nor discovery. This short tale does resemble 'Lucerne' in its moral and religious focus, but in its form it represents another of the master tropes of Tolstoy's fiction, the juxtaposition of delineated segments which are simultaneously similar and different, the structure that governs both *War and Peace* and *Anna Karenina*. This text juxtaposes the deaths of a 'lady' named Marya Dmitrevna Shirkina, a peasant referred to as 'Uncle Khvyodor', and a tree. Marya Dmitrevna is depicted in great detail, down to the 'dry and deathly . . . whiteness of the skin' of the parting in her hair (p. 55). Sick unto death, she knows, but does not want to know, that she is about to die. She is on a journey to Italy to get well, the grand illusion she uses to hide from the fact of her own mortality. Even when very near death, she blames her husband for her illness, and when her cousin leans over to kiss her hand, she exclaims, 'No, kiss me here! Only dead people are kissed on the hand' (p. 65). She claims to be a Christian and to understand that she is about to die, but she rebels at her own mortality and to the end is completely self-absorbed.

Uncle Khvyodor is also sick unto death, a fact he simply accepts. Furthermore when Marya Dmitrevna's driver, who has stopped at the station where Uncle Khvyodor is lying on top of the stove to keep his dying body warm, asks the dying peasant for the boots he will never wear again, Uncle Khvyodor gladly gives the lad what he desires. In Tolstoy's own reading of this story, Uncle Khvyodor, who has lived a life of sowing and reaping and raising and killing sheep, is a man who has lived 'in harmony with the whole world' while Marya Dmitrevna has spent her life in 'discord'.[1] Thus the one knows that all mortal life is a process of dying and the other refuses, like Ivan Ilyich, to '*respice finem*', that is, to remember that we all die. Because he does remember this, Uncle Khvyodor dies, according to Tolstoy's reading, 'calmly', representing 'happiness and beauty'.

Uncle Khvyodor's last act is an act of charity, but this is charity for a price, since Uncle Khvyodor wants the young driver to put a stone on his grave, a humble marker of remembrance that signals not self-absorption but the all too familiar fear of being forgotten. This is his single flaw, but it is a failing significant enough for Tolstoy to underline the difference between the death of the two humans and the tree. The humans are depicted in the season of dying. The whole story opens with the sentence 'It was autumn'. The second half of the work opens with an announcement of the season of rebirth,

---

[1] L. N. Tolstoi, *Polnoe sobranie sochinenii* (Complete Works), 90 vols. (Moscow, 1928–58), lx. 266; 1858. Henceforth all citations from Tolstoy's non-fiction will be given parenthetically from this edition, the first number referring to the volume, the second to the page, and the third, after the semicolon, to the date.

'Spring had come' (p. 62), followed by a sumptuous description of burgeoning nature. This second half is then devoted to the final moments in the life of Marya Dmitrevna and her death in bad faith juxtaposed to the death of the tree. This death is the result of Uncle Khvyodor's flaw, for the young driver chops it down to make a cross as a temporary marker of the old peasant's grave. As the tree falls onto the 'damp earth' (p. 67), which in Russian folklore is a complex symbol of the renewing cycle of life and death, space is cleared for the other trees that now 'flaunt their beauty still more joyously'. The final paragraph depicts the joy and peace that reign over the dead tree. In Tolstoy's own reading this beauty and peace are signs of the moral honesty of the dead tree which 'does not lie, does not put on airs, does not fear, does not regret'. Thus this short piece details responses to one's dying that will be further explored in the major novels and most famously in 'The Death of Ivan Ilyich'.

'Polikushka', published in 1863 just before Tolstoy began writing *War and Peace*, is unique in Tolstoy's fiction because it portrays the life not of the upper classes, but of the peasants, a focus it shares among the major works only with the play *The Power of Darkness* (1886). It is unique also in its complex and even ironic representation of the moral issues involved. Furthermore, the third-person narration in this case allows for a more rounded presentation of character that works against Tolstoy's tendency to express his sympathy or satirical criticism of a particular class, group, or character, as for example in 'Three Deaths'. This long short story is an extraordinary accomplishment with a highly nuanced view of human character and fate. No wonder the renowned writer Ivan Turgenev exclaimed upon reading it: 'I was amazed at the power of this great talent . . . A master, a master!'[2]

The story is built from two intertwined events, the necessity required by law to select for military service a recruit from the peasant commune and Polikushka's central journey of recovery. Both events revolve around money, and the stakes are high. The recruit who will ultimately be sent is in fact sentenced to death, since peasant soldiers rarely returned home from military service alive. Money makes escape from this death sentence possible, since the law allows those who have the requisite 300 roubles to buy a substitute recruit.

[2] I. S. Turgenev, *Polnoe sobranie sochinenii i pisem* (Complete Works and Letters), 25 vols. (Moscow–Leningrad, 1960–8), v (*Pis'ma*). 216.

Polikushka's journey, ostensibly to collect some money for his mistress in whose house he works as a servant, is in fact a journey to recover his spoiled reputation, indeed his own belief in his own worth, in order to earn the right not to be sent as a recruit. The success of this journey is all the more important because the commune, contrary to the mistress's wishes, would prefer to send the house servant Polikushka as the recruit, rather than any of the sons of the established commune families from whom they must choose. 'Polikushka' is at one level a highly ironic tale about the role of money in deciding one's fate.

The story of Polikushka can be summed up in two sentences: 'God had given him good luck' and 'Everything went wrong' (pp. 73–4). As a person Polikushka is hardly the idealized peasant one has come to associate with Tolstoy, whether it be Platon Karataev in *War and Peace* or the happy peasants Levin encounters in *Anna Karenina*. Whereas Tolstoy uses these peasants as emblems of the moral good, Polikushka is a flawed human being, not evil, but still a petty thief, a fake horse doctor, and a bit of a drunkard. His mistress believes in him despite all this and sends him on his journey of recovery to prove to all that she is right. And the irony of this journey is that she is right. Polikushka does everything in his power to make use of this 'good fortune' his mistress has given him. He steadfastly avoids every tavern along the way, collects the money, and secures it in his cap. On the way back he conscientiously keeps track of the money, making sure that it stays put in its safe hiding place. But despite his 'good fortune' and his honest attempt to live up to it, 'everything went wrong'. And 'everything went wrong' because he tried to be conscientious. The hand that kept on checking the safety of the money in his cap was the hand that accidentally widened the opening through which the money, unbeknownst to him, fell out. The sincere attempt to prove himself undoes him. The lost money seals his fate, and he hangs himself in despair over his failure.

Polikushka's story is not a tragedy in the classic mode, for he is not undone by a tragic flaw. Rather it is an ironic tragedy in which he is undone by honestly and nobly trying to overcome his tragic failings. In such a world there seems to be no justice. The people believe it is the work of the 'evil spirit', but the narrator would have us focus on the terrifying truth, in typical Tolstoyan fashion, embodied in one compelling image:

if some bold fellow had taken a candle or lantern that terrible night, and crossing himself . . . had gone up into the loft—slowly dispelling before him the horror of the night with the candle, lighting up the rafters, the sand, the cobweb-covered flue-pipe, and the dress left behind by the carpenter's wife—till he came to Ilyich, and, conquering his fears, had raised the lantern to the level of the face, he would have beheld the familiar thin body bending lifelessly to one side . . . no cross visible under the open shirt, the head drooping on the breast, the good-natured face with open sightless eyes, and the meek, guilty smile, and a solemn calmness and silence over all. (p. 106)

This one sentence enacts the process of discovering the truth, a truth which makes psychological sense, but reveals a world beyond human understanding.

The second event that is woven into 'Polikushka', the selection of a recruit for conscription, would seem to allow Tolstoy to explore his negative view of war and the system of governmental violence embodied in the military, ideas that he began developing during his own service in the Crimean War in 1854–5 and explored first in his Sevastopol sketches as well as *War and Peace* and later much more explicitly in many tracts, most fully in *The Kingdom of God Is Within You* (1893). But this story is not a diatribe against conscription. Rather it explores the self-centred and self-interested attitudes of the mistress, the owner of the serfs, and especially of Dutlov, the well-off peasant from the commune whose nephew becomes the commune's candidate for military service. Shown in their psychological complexity, they resemble each other because each expresses concern for a potential recruit, the mistress for Polikushka, Dutlov for his nephew. As the issue comes to the fore the text marks the parallelism by the similarity of the recruits' names: Ilyich (Polikushka's patronym used as his name) and Ilya. Yet while having the monetary means to buy a substitute neither the mistress nor Dutlov gives it a thought. To each, it would seem, money means more than a human life.

The drama of the selection of the recruit focuses mainly on Dutlov and his nephew Ilyushka. That Dutlov is a kind man is made clear by the very presence of his nephew in his household, for upon his brother's death, Dutlov took in his children. However, Dutlov's kindness, like the mistress's, evaporates in the face of a possible financial cost. To Ilyushka Dutlov's refusal to pay for a substitute is devastating, for it feels like a betrayal and another loss of a father, even as it condemns him and his wife to a hard and meaningless future. But then the story takes another ironic turn. On his return from taking Ilyushka to be conscripted, Dutlov finds the envelope with the money Polikushka had lost and brings it to the mistress, who in her confusion and guilt simply tells Dutlov to keep it. Astounded, Dutlov starts out for home. While it is assumed that the found money will enable him to buy a substitute, Dutlov denies this, but Polikushka's suicide, of which he has just learned, begins to weigh upon his conscience: he has a dream in which Polikushka attempts to strangle him, while shouting 'The money's mine' (p. 117). This dream is the turning point in Dutlov's moral life. He awakens from his penury, buys a substitute for Ilyushka, and bowing to the ground before him begs his nephew's forgiveness. ' "You have been as my own son to me, and if I have wronged you in any way, well, we all live in sin! Is it not so, good Orthodox folk?" he said, turning to the peasants who were standing round' (p. 121). This conversion shows that Dutlov is like Polikushka, a 'good man, not a bad one, but just weak' (p. 74).

The drama of the selection of the recruit does not end on this note of moral conversion. Rather the main point of this drama turns on the central theme of the whole work: 'One man's sorrow is another man's good fortune' (p. 110). Of course it is this theme that links the stories of Polikushka and both Dutlov and Ilyushka. It is at the end of the tale, however, that the real significance of this theme is brought into tragic focus. The recruit Alyokha, who has been bought to replace Ilyushka, drinks himself into a dancing rage, and shouts at the whole Dutlov family, 'Go to the Devil' (p. 123). Dutlov falls asleep, Ilyushka and his cousin Ignat down a bottle of vodka, and they all drive off. The story ends with one final compelling image:

Ilya began a song, the women joined in, and Ignat shouted merrily in time with the song. A post-chaise drove merrily towards them. The driver called lustily to his horses as he passed the two festive carts, and the post-boy turned round and winked at the red faces of the peasant men and women who sat being jolted around while singing their jovial song. (p. 124)

In this image we see the irony of the whole work. Dutlov's conversion has brought ruin to Alyokha, but by falling asleep Dutlov remains unaware of this. Ilyushka's salvation likewise results in Alyokha's damnation, but Ilyushka chooses to hide from his awareness of this in drink. The 'jovial song' masks a tragedy in which the law that gives those with money power to ruin the lives of others turns the converted Dutlov into a virtual murderer and the innocent victim Ilyushka into a victimizer. While Dutlov sleeps in a state of denial, the vodka and the 'jovial song' tell us that Ilyushka is aware of this momentous moral change. All 'good fortune' turns into someone's 'sorrow', but no one seems to be at fault.

Tolstoy published 'Strider: The Story of a Horse' in 1885, three years after completing *A Confession*, the work that marked his turn toward a more concentrated, perhaps even obsessive concern with the social, moral, and especially religious issues that had dogged him from his earliest days. He first had the idea for this story, however, in 1856 and actually wrote a draft of it before he began *War and Peace* in 1863. The final text turns out to be the only work of fiction that spans the two main periods of Tolstoy's writing career and thus occupies a special place in his oeuvre. In form likewise this is the only work with an extended third-person narrative that has embedded in it a long first-person confession.

When in 1856 Tolstoy told Turgenev the first idea for 'the story of a horse', Turgenev was so impressed with Tolstoy's feeling for horse-life that he exclaimed that Tolstoy must have been a horse in some other life. Be that as it may, 'Strider' is a work that feels autobiographical and is highly autopsychological, in this sense a work like 'Lucerne'. The Strider we meet in the third-person narrative is an old discarded piebald gelding who bears up under the insults from the other horses who feel superior to him in looks and worth. From his own confession, however, we learn that he claims there is 'no more thoroughbred horse in the world' than he and that his name 'Strider' encodes his reputation for 'my long and sweeping strides' (p. 135). With such statements Tolstoy marks the complex emblematic nature of the story. Throughout his life Tolstoy tended to alienate or isolate himself from the very people who would most appreciate his art, even as he ranted at those who criticized his work. He was in many ways a stranger in the world in which he resided, an 'alien resident' (p. 133) like Strider. Furthermore, from his own diaries we know that Tolstoy believed himself neither attractive nor lovable. To be loved by others became his major paradoxical psychological pursuit, even as his quest for fame from his 'long and sweeping' narratives became one of the 'sins' for which he most chastised himself.

Tolstoy also gives Strider the same central psychological wound from which he himself suffered. At the age of 2 Tolstoy's mother died, making him an orphan, at least by Russian definition. It is most telling that virtually all Tolstoy's central characters are or become orphans, including among others the young hero from his early trilogy, as well as Prince Andrey, Pierre, Anna Karenina, Levin, and Nekhlyudov. Strider is not technically an orphan, but he too experiences the loss of his mother, which he considers the 'cause' of 'the first sorrow of my life' (p. 137). What is most striking is that this loss is not due to death, but sex. Strider's mother is taken from him to be bred to Kindly I, and Strider believes that 'I had lost my mother's love for ever' (p. 138). Furthermore, like most children, Strider believes that he himself is the real cause of the loss of his mother's love: 'And it's all because I am piebald!' Nowhere in Tolstoy's fiction do we peer more movingly into the depths of Tolstoy's own unconscious. What is more, the very next 'dreadful' thing that happens to Strider is that he himself discovers sexual attraction which, because he is a piebald and therefore not a desirable breeder, results in his castration: 'I became what I am now' (p. 139). By nature tending toward seriousness and deep thought, Strider now 'pondered over the injustice of men, who blamed me for being piebald' as well as 'over the inconstancy of maternal love and feminine love in general and on its dependence on physical conditions' (p. 140). Thus Tolstoy gives Strider his own most deep-seated anxiety over sexuality, an anxiety which plays itself out in his life, his moral and religious worldview, and in a great deal of his fiction, both before and after his announced conversion in *A Confession*.

In his first-person narrative Strider reveals that he is a proud aristocrat originally named Muzhik I (i.e. 'peasant'), the son of Affable I and Baba (i.e. 'peasant woman'). 'There is no more thoroughbred horse in the world' than he (p. 135). This revelation opens up the second layer in this emblematic story, where the psychological self-probing yields to social and moral criticism. Tolstoy's identification with the Russian peasantry is well known. But what Tolstoy focuses on here is the injustice of serfdom and of property owning in general: the reader of Proudhon's *Property Is Theft* questions the human need for possession. Now Strider's voice is used for Tolstoy's favourite device of defamiliarization: 'The words *"my* horse" applied to me, a live horse, seemed to me as strange as to say "my land", "my air", or "my water" ' (p. 141). Strider is so puzzled by this concept of ownership expressed in 'these strange words' that he develops a whole theory of language.

Men are guided in life not by deeds but by words. They like not so much the ability to do or not do something, as the ability to speak of various objects in conventionally agreed-upon words. Such words, considered very important among them, are *my* and *mine* . . . and he who in this game of theirs may use that conventional word about the greatest number of things is considered the happiest.

That Strider's words here ventriloquize the voice not only of the Russian peasant but also of Tolstoy himself becomes clear in this verbal slippage: 'I became convinced that not only as applied to us horses, but in regard to other things, the idea of *mine* has no other foundation than a base, *animal* [italics added] instinct in men, which they call the feeling or right of property' (p. 142). In Tolstoy's philosophical anthropology, already well developed at this time, humans are dichotomous beings composed of a 'spiritual' and 'animal' (or sometimes 'personal') self. His major fictions show male protagonists who lead an 'animal' or 'personal' life until in some central epiphanic moment they discover their 'spiritual' self. The third and final layer of 'Strider' explores the life of a man, Strider's favourite owner and master, who leads a 'personal' life unto death without any redeeming discovery of the spiritual.

Nikita Serpukhovskoy, a hussar officer, 'never loved anything or anyone', and because 'he was handsome, happy, rich, and therefore never loved anybody' (p. 145), Strider paradoxically liked him most of all. Furthermore, Strider adds that 'his coldness, his cruelty, and my dependence on him gave special strength to my love for him'. What draws Strider to Serpukhovskoy is the hussar's lack of love so familiar to Strider's psychological experience and his high status as a handsome hussar with a beautiful mistress. He who was not loved can accept love only when it is not really shown him. And most importantly Strider acquires status through his master, for as he uses his talents to outrun the other horses, he gains the respect and admiration he never had, but felt entitled to. The peak moment in his life is reached when his master refuses an offer to sell him, because he 'isn't a horse, but a friend' (p. 148). This 'happiest event of my life' is immediately followed by 'my greatest misfortune' (p. 148). The master's mistress leaves him for another man, and upon discovering this Serpukhovskoy drives off in a rage, for the first time ever striking Strider with his whip. Strider misses his step, gets whipped again, and bangs his foot against the iron front of the sledge. Neither Strider nor Serpukhovskoy recover from their wounds. Strider is sold off and Serpukhovskoy goes into a depression that destroys his life. Like Polikushka they are granted good fortune, only to have everything go wrong.

The story draws to a close the 'evening after' Strider's last monologue with the sudden and ironic reappearance of Serpukhovskoy as a 'flabby, old man' embittered by life. Strider's young master receives him as an old acquaintance. The two men are completely absorbed in their own worlds, the young master proud of his mistress and his fine horses, Serpukhovskoy angry and resentful of this mirror image of himself before his fall from good fortune. The scene ends with a compelling image of what Serpukhovskoy had become:

He sat down, took off his coat and waistcoat and somehow managed to kick off his trousers, but for a long time could not get his boots off, his soft stomach being in the way. He got one off at last, and struggled for a long time with the other, panting and becoming exhausted. And so with his foot in the boot-top he rolled over and began to snore, filling the room with the smell of tobacco, wine, and slovenly old age. (p. 158)

This image of the body in decay is then swiftly followed in the narrative by the death of Strider, whose body—skin, flesh, and bones—gets put to use so that his sorrow is another's good fortune. Recalling 'Three Deaths', Strider's death is then juxtaposed with Serpukhovskoy's, represented in the final compelling image that closes the whole work:

the dead who bury their dead found it necessary to clothe that swollen body, which at once began to decompose, in a good uniform and good boots and put it into a new and expensive coffin with new tassels at its four corners, and then to place that new coffin in another lead one, to take it to Moscow and there dig up some long-buried human bones and right in that spot hide this decomposing maggoty body in its new uniform and polished boots and cover it all up with earth. (p. 160)

The satirical tone of this sentence, marked by characteristic verbal repetition, here of 'good' and especially 'new', reveals Tolstoy's contempt for the useless lives of the upper classes in comparison with the peasants, the class he considered the real Russian people.

Tolstoy manifested his concern for the peasantry, the overwhelming majority of the population in nineteenth-century Russia, in various ways throughout his adult life: he wrote about them, he established special schools with an innovative pedagogy appropriate for them, in time of famine he helped organize relief for them, and above all in the 1870s and 1880s he reinvented himself as a writer in order to produce a body of literature for them. His main work, written just before he began *Anna Karenina*, was a series of primers to be used in schools, a series that became popular in Russia for many years. In these primers he retold in simple language folk epics, fables, and fairy tales, wrote delightful and instructive little pieces such as 'What Is the Wind For?', 'The Senses', and 'What Is the Dew on the Grass?', and composed stories based on religious themes, often borrowing his plots from already existing texts both secular and religious. 'God Sees the Truth, But Waits', published in 1872 and later incorporated into one of the primers, is actually a reworking of a tale Platon Karataev tells to Pierre in *War and Peace* (IV. iii. 13). The story clearly demonstrates Tolstoy's interest in religious, even theological issues long before the publication of *A Confession*.

'God Sees the Truth, But Waits' tells the story of the merchant Ivan Dmitrich Aksyonov who is unjustly accused of a murder and sentenced to Siberia. At this level it illustrates one of Platon Karataev's sayings, 'Where there is judgement, there is injustice' (IV. iii. 12). But the real theme of the story is forgiveness. By chance after twenty-six years a man namd Makar Semyonov, who turns out to be the real murderer, shows up in the same prison camp. Makar immediately begins digging a tunnel in an attempt to escape. Aksyonov, who suspects who the man really is, happens upon the would-be tunnel, and Makar tells him of his plan for escape, promising to get him out too. The authorities soon find the tunnel and interrogate the prisoners. When Aksyonov is asked what he knows, he first thinks, 'If I do cover for him, still why should I forgive him, when he ruined my life? Let him pay for what I have suffered. But if I tell on him, they will probably flog the life out of him, and what if I suspect him wrongly? And, after all, what good would it be to me?' (p. 166).

So Aksyonov tells the strict truth: 'I didn't see and don't know.' That night, obviously moved, Makar asks Aksyonov to forgive him, confessing the truth and promising to tell the authorities: 'You will be forgiven and can go to your home' (p. 167). But Aksyonov no longer has a home to go to, and although he 'took pity' on Makar in not telling on him, he will not forgive him. Makar, clearly a changed man as a result of Aksyonov's 'pity', is so distraught that he breaks down in tears. 'When Aksyonov heard him sobbing he too began to weep.' Thus Aksyonov identifies with Makar in his suffering and, when he admits, 'maybe I am a hundred times worse than you', even in his sin. Aksyonov cannot love and forgive his enemy until he has removed the barriers he has placed between them, his resentment and failure to admit his own sinfulness. Like Prince Andrey in *War and Peace* Aksyonov moves from a human to a divine conception of love. As he pronounces 'God will forgive you', Aksyonov's 'heart suddenly grew light' and he was released, again like Prince Andrey, from all desire except the desire to die. By the time justice is re-established through Makar's confession, Aksyonov's wish has been granted. Aksyonov learns what Karataev, who loves to tell this story, already knows. In Tolstoy's theological worldview one suffers from one's own sins, not for one's own good but for the good of others, but because one suffers for others even as a result of one's own sin, one will be granted God's forgiveness. All humans are united in their potential for sin and for that forgiveness called love.

'The Notes of a Madman' is the first work of fiction Tolstoy wrote (although never really finished) after *A Confession*. It resembles 'Lucerne' in two ways, first in genre and second in origin. The genre of 'notes' is common in Russian literature, most famous from Dostoevsky's 'Notes from the Underground' (1864). Here, however, Tolstoy actually borrows the title from another and very different Russian work, a story by Nikolay Gogol written fifty years earlier. The genre of 'notes' frees the author from the limitations of narrative expectation, even as they give a semblance of verisimilitude. For Tolstoy they are a fine example of the 'deviation from European forms', which he claimed in his 'Some Words about the Book *War and Peace*' was characteristic of all works of Russian literature that rose above mediocrity (xvi. 7; 1868). In Tolstoy's story, as in his earlier 'Lucerne', the genre of 'notes' is connected to the origin of the work: in each case the story is based on a biographical event of which we have an actual written record, for 'Lucerne' in Tolstoy's own diary (xli. 140–1; 1857) and for 'The Notes of a Madman' in a letter to his wife (lxxxiii. 167; 1869). The experience that lies behind 'The Notes of a Madman', for example, was a journey Tolstoy himself took to buy an estate in the Penza province: on a stopover in Arzamas at two in the morning he was overcome with an anxiety attack which consisted of an overwhelming sense of 'depression, terror, and horror'. These biographical records of the original event that sparked the literary work reveal the fundamental rhythm of Tolstoy's creative life, which moved from experience to image and then later to some philosophical or religious idea. These two stories show the movement from experience to image; in its very structure *War and Peace* illustrates the movement from image to idea.

The unnamed first-person narrator of these 'notes' tells us that he had lived like everyone else till the age of 35, the age when Tolstoy believed the 'development and growth of the body is coming to an end and the development and growth of the spirit should begin' (lvii. 93; 1909). Significantly, however, in childhood the narrator had had moments 'resembling my present condition' (p. 168): empathetic despair over the suffering of others and a sense of love of all for all. The 'madness' of which Tolstoy writes in this autopsychological work is clearly the root experience that grew into Tolstoy's own moral and religious ideas. We should note that these childhood experiences disappeared when the madman discovered his sexuality, first in masturbation and then with prostitutes, a sexuality aroused by excess of food and lack of physical labour. In Tolstoy bodily needs and desires compete with spiritual urges. The bulk of the story is built around three journeys of discovery, each leading to a fuller understanding of what becomes the madman's new view of life, of which he had inklings, like the narrator of *A Confession*, in his early days. On these journeys the narrator is 'suddenly' overcome with the ultimate existential questions Who am I?, Why do I exist?, Where am I going?, What is death?—the very questions Pierre had asked himself in *War and Peace* (II. ii. 1), which Tolstoy finished just before his own experience of the 'Arzamas horror'. What the narrator of this story discovers, both in his moments of existential crisis and through reading the Gospels and saints' lives, is the relationship between a belief in the divine and in the fundamental humanity of the suffering peasants to whose welfare he now devotes himself. In this expression of love for others he overcomes the anxiety of death that had haunted him, even as it haunted his creator. The meaninglessness of one's personal, physical life the end of which is death is a theme that recurs in Tolstoy's major fictions as well as such different stories as 'Three Deaths', 'Strider', and this moving, if unfinished, piece.

While working on 'The Notes of a Madman' and his most accomplished piece of fiction from this period, 'The Death of Ivan Ilyich', Tolstoy published (in 1885) 'Where Love Is, God Is'. This work resembles 'God Sees the Truth, But Waits' in style and its intended audience, even though it was not included in any of the primers. Also like many of the works in those collections it is not an original piece, but a reworked translation of a French short story by the prominent French evangelical pastor and hymnist Ruben Saillens (1855–1942), entitled 'Le Père Martine'. The French work, which Tolstoy praised highly in a letter to the author (lxiv. 189; 1888), can be traced back to earlier Christian literature in the Western tradition and comparable themes can be found in works of medieval Russian literature. Tolstoy's version of the story illustrates a theme we have seen runs throughout his work, the opposition between living for oneself (the 'animal' or 'personal' self) and living 'for God' (the 'divine' or 'spiritual self'). In *Anna Karenina*, for example, Levin learns from a peasant the difference between living 'for one's belly' and living 'for God' (viii. 12), although how Levin's life would be reordered to live 'for God' remains beyond the borders of the novel.

'Where Love Is, God Is' goes beyond the borders into a representation of a life lived 'for God'. It tells of a simple cobbler named Martyn Avdeich who in a moment of despair encounters a 'wanderer' who chastises him for his loss of faith, repeating another of Platon Karataev's folk sayings, 'Not by our reasoning, but by God's judgement' (p. 179; see *War and Peace*, IV. i. xii). He explains to Martyn that his despair arises from his life lived for himself and not 'for God' and advises him to read the Gospels in order to find out how to live. What he reads in the scriptures begins the process of change which culminates in a miraculous moment in an altered state of awareness (is it a dream?) when he hears what is apparently the voice of Christ saying, 'Martyn, Martyn! Look out into the street tomorrow, for I shall come' (p. 182). What follows the next day is a series of encounters, with an old soldier, a poor woman with a baby in her arms, and an old woman selling apples. In each case Martyn, following the scriptural advice to see Christ in everyone, gives the people what they need: the illiterate old soldier gets hot tea and Christian teachings based on the Sermon on the Mount, the poor woman food, clothing, and help with care for her baby, and the street vendor the central message of the story. She is angry at a young boy who has stolen an apple from her cart. When she strikes out to punish the boy, Martyn gets him to beg her forgiveness and then gives the boy an apple, promising to pay her for it. She is outraged that the boy will go unpunished. Martyn exclaims, 'If he should be whipped for stealing an apple, what should be done to us for our sins?' (p. 188). He then begins instructing them both, concluding that 'God bids us forgive . . . or else we shall not be forgiven. Forgive everyone' (p. 188). What allows the old street vendor to forgive the boy, however, is her realization that he is but a child like her own grandchildren, a realization that softens her heart. The boy responds to this softening by offering to help her, an offer she accepts, even as she forgets about the money owed her for the apple. The old woman and the boy are both transformed by their acts of forgiveness. Like Martyn himself, they no longer live 'for their belly' but 'for God'.

Tolstoy wrote 'The Devil' in 1889, the year in which he published 'The Kreutzer Sonata' and began work on his last novel, *Resurrection*. All three works bring to the fore the theme of sexuality which we have already seen runs throughout Tolstoy's oeuvre. 'The Devil' and *Resurrection*, however, share a similar origin: both were stimulated by real-life stories of sexual misadventure Tolstoy heard, stories which in each case resonated with particular sexual involvements Tolstoy himself had. It is most telling that Tolstoy chooses to name the hero of 'The Devil' Irtenev, virtually the same name as the hero of his early autopsychological trilogy (Irten'ev) whose best friend Nekhlyudov surfaces as the hero of *Resurrection*: the very names of the characters return us to the time of Tolstoy's youthful days of sexual indiscretion. 'The Devil' was written thus at a time when Tolstoy seems to have been overcome with guilt over his sexual past.

'The Devil' is based on the real-life story of N. N. Friderikhs who fell in love with a peasant woman named Stepanida and then shot her dead three months after his marriage to a woman of his own social class. The 'Friderikhs story', as Tolstoy referred to 'The Devil' in his diary, obviously reverberated with his own two-year relationship with the 23-year-old Aksin'ya Bazykina, which he terminated before he married. This relationship was apparently the most emotionally involved one Tolstoy had with a peasant woman; in 1860 he even claimed that 'it's even beginning to terrify me that she feels so close . . . no longer the feeling of a stag, but of a husband for a wife' (xlviii. 25; 1860). While 'The Devil' shares with 'The Snow Storm', 'Lucerne', and 'The Notes of a Madman' an origin in autobiographical experience, it is unique in its autopsychological exploration of the terror felt in sexual attraction.

'The Devil' tells the story of Yevgeny Irtenev who moves to the country to take over the family estate, begins to have sexual encounters with a peasant woman named Stepanida, eventually gets married, but then cannot get rid of his attraction to the peasant woman. The bulk of the story is devoted to the conflict that the continuing attraction presents to him. This conflict comes to the fore in the unresolved ending of the work. In the first variant the hero resolves his conflict by killing himself. He thus considers himself guilty for not being able to resist the attraction of 'a devil' (*chert*). Upon reading this version of the story in February 1890, Tolstoy's close friend V. G. Chertkov urged him to publish it immediately. Tolstoy looked over the piece and in that very same month rewrote the ending, making it conform more to the 'Friderikhs story'. In this version he shifts the burden of guilt onto Stepanida, who becomes 'the devil' (*d'yavol*) incarnate. He may be weak, but she is the evil source of the temptation. Thus Tolstoy placed the story in intertextual relationship to Christian hagiographical literature in which the devil appears in the form of a woman. But even this did not satisfy his psychological discomfort with this story, which he hid from his wife and family and never published.

What makes this story so autopsychologically revealing is the representation of the experience of sexual attraction. For Irtenev this attraction is felt as a loss of self-control and thus of freedom, something that happens 'against his will' (p. 194). In this he resembles most Pierre in *War and Peace*, who is overwhelmed by the very physical presence of Hélène's body. When 'terrifyingly close to him', this body comes to have a 'power (*vlast*') over him' which despite his serious reservations his 'will' ultimately cannot resist (I. iii. 1). Despite all his more serious reservations, Irtenev likewise has no resistance to his attraction. 'Above all he felt that he was conquered, that he did not have his own will but that there was another power (*sila*) moving him' (p. 216). This representation of sexual attraction is particularly remarkable because it is expressed in the very terms Tolstoy came to use about the paradoxical relationship between our 'free will' and the 'will of God'. 'Free will', Tolstoy claimed, 'is the possibility of acting not by some external, alien will, but by one's own will in accord or not in accord with the law of the All' (lvi. 101; 1908), which he defined a year after 'The Devil' as 'the law according to which everything big and small is accomplished . . . the only real and certain thing, the will of God' (lii. 8; 1891). Of course the paradox is that if 'everything big and small is accomplished' by the 'will of God', then what happens to our freedom? Indeed in that very same year, Tolstoy asserted that 'free will is the action of the divine power (*sila*) in man' (lii. 50; 1891). What is important here is not Tolstoy's resolution of this ancient theological paradox, but the implied connection between the sexual and the religious experience, both of which entail a 'will' that while both seeming to be and not to be our own has the power to move us to do something. Traditionally religious literature has treated sexual love as a metaphor for our love for God. With Tolstoy sexual attraction is seen as the negative version of the positive desire to do God's will, which is always understood as the establishment of the good, that is, peace and harmony among all on earth. In Tolstoy's work—and this is especially true of his three major novels—sexuality is feared not so much because it is an evil in itself as because it creates evil, that is, discontent and discord among people.

After his final reworking of 'The Devil' in 1890, Tolstoy began 'Father Sergy', which he laboured over for eight years, while simultaneously writing his last novel, *Resurrection*. 'Father Sergy' shares with 'The Devil' the theme of sexuality, but for the monk the indulgence in sexual activity is itself an evil, a violation of the vow of chastity. Thus while he feels that he has 'two different foes', doubt and lust, they are in fact 'one and the same' (p. 251). The high point of Father Sergy's life is his resistance to the advances of the adventurous Makovkina, whom Sergy, well acquainted with hagiographical literature, fears as the devil incarnate. He accomplishes this feat of asceticism by the gruesome act of chopping off a finger to stay his passion, a feat suggested to him by his reading of a rather less severe act of self-mutilation in the life of a saint (p. 257), an act Irtenev also read of and imitated more literally, but to no avail (p. 217). The fall that leads to Father Sergy's resurrection is likewise related to sexual attraction, in this case his failure to resist a sexual temptation. This failure leads him to consider suicide and doubt the existence of God (p. 269), just as Irtenev commits suicide in the first variant ending and doubts the existence of God in the second. Both works represent heroes attempting to gain freedom from their sexual urges, but 'Father Sergy' is not a story about sexual passion.

'Father Sergy' tells of a man driven to succeed. 'From early childhood . . . he tried in everything he took up to attain . . . success and perfection' (p. 239). For Prince Stepan Kasatsky this need to be the best in everything he did became an unsatisfiable obsession, so that 'having mastered one thing, he took up another'. Furthermore the motivation for this success was twofold: to attain 'people's praise and astonishment' and to achieve fame and power. This need for fame and power follows Kasatsky into the monastery, where Father Sergy's desire to live for God is undermined by these same two psychological needs. Furthermore, Father Sergy's need to be superior is accompanied by a need for some ideal or perfect being whose image serves him as a guide. In life he thus looks simultaneously 'down from above' (p. 243) and 'up . . . from below' (p. 241). When his ideal fails him, as with Tsar Nikolay I, or he fails it, as in his sexual fall, he is thrust out of his role in search of a new one. Both success and failure spur him on.

'Father Sergy' is a psychologized *vita*. This form provides Tolstoy with a distancing mechanism which he lacked in 'The Devil'. This psychologized *vita* represents Father Sergy's quest for fame as a movement through a series of styles of piety characteristic of Russian Orthodoxy, from a monk in the hesychast tradition, a yoga-style meditative regime based on the inner repetition of the mantra-like Jesus Prayer in order to attain inner silence (Gr. *hesychia*), then to hermit, elder (*starets*), 'saintly type' (*ugodnik*), miracle worker, and finally to wanderer. As it was for Tolstoy, it is his quest for fame that undermines Father Sergy's sincere quest to 'live for God'. His obsession eventually thrusts him into the paradoxical state of seeing himself as a saint, even as he is aware that he is but playing the role of a saint to acquire the fame and glory he needs. He knows it all comes from mere vanity, the very vice that plagued Tolstoy himself throughout his life, even early on in such works as the trilogy and 'The Snow Storm'. Father Sergy's fall occurs at the height of this desperately needed fame and glory. But the fall spurs him on to his final success, his return to Pashenka who reveals to him the real way to 'live for God'. 'I lived for men on the pretext of living for God, while she lives for God imagining that she lives for men' (p. 277). Pashenka's message that only a humble disregard for self enables one truly to live for others and for God was one Tolstoy often reminded himself of in his diaries.

'After the Ball' was written in 1903, some five years after the completion of 'Father Sergy' and *Resurrection*. Like 'The Kreutzer Sonata', it has a peculiar form of dual narration: a faceless third-person narrator reports an event which in the main consists of a first-person narrator, Ivan Vasilyevich, telling of a critical episode in his life. The third-person narrator is thus able both to show the telling of a story and represent the audience that hears it. The present time is somewhere in the last quarter of the nineteenth century, while Ivan Vasilyevich's recollected story is set in the 1840s, a complex period in which the militaristic ethos of Nikolay I's reign coincided with the rise of idealism in student philosophical circles and an idealistic view of life among the educated class. Ivan Vasilyevich's tale is presented as an argument against the prevailing belief of his present audience that one's understanding of good and evil is 'all a matter of the environment' (p. 280). While Ivan Vasilyevich's tale is intended to prove that his life is shaped by chance, the reader may end up feeling that however critical the chance episode is for his life, it is not the chance event, but his reaction to it, that shapes his life. This seems to be a psychological study in the guise of a philosophical tale.

'After the Ball' is a story of lost illusions. Ivan Vasilyevich attends a ball where he dances the evening away with Varenka, the young woman with whom he is in love. This love is not like Irtenev's sexual obsession with Stepanida, for the attraction seems more spiritual than physical. At the height of his love, sounding like Natasha in love with Prince Andrey in *War and Peace* (II. iii. xvii), he exclaims, 'I was happy, blessed, I was good, I was not me, but some unearthly being that knew no evil and was capable only of the good' (p. 283). He is especially taken by Varenka's father as he watches him dance with his daughter. Tolstoy conveys the feel of the narrator's experience of this dance with his characteristic imitative syntax:

As soon as the mazurka began, he smartly stamped with one foot, thrust the other forward, and his tall, stout figure began, now softly and smoothly, now loudly and quickly, to move through the room with the thumping of boot soles and of foot against foot. (p. 284)

Ivan Vasilyevich is especially touched by the affection the father shows for his daughter. The moment magically transforms his love for Varenka:

the love for Varenka in my soul released all the pent-up potential for love in my soul. I loved the hostess . . . her husband and her guests and her servants, and I even loved the engineer Anisimov who was now feeling a bit peeved with me. And towards Varenka's father . . . I experienced at that moment a certain rapturously tender feeling. (pp. 284–5)

At the height of his innocent love Ivan Vasilyevich resembles Levin in his moment of rapturous love in *Anna Karenina* (iv. 14–15).

It is the illusion of this innocent love for all that is lost 'by chance'. The morning after the ball Ivan Vasilyevich happened on a scene of military discipline. He saw a Tatar soldier being beaten for desertion, a scene he represents with this compelling image:

His whole body twitching, his feet tramping through the melting snow, and with blows raining upon him from both sides, the man being punished started to move toward me, now toppling over backwards, with the non-commissioned officers who were leading him by their rifles pushing him up, now falling forward, with the non-commissioned officers who were trying to keep him from falling pushing him back. (p. 287)

What makes this scene even more terrifying and especially horrible for Ivan Vasilyevich is that the commanding officer presiding over this punishment is Varenka's father, who while 'walking right alongside, and, now looking down at his own feet, now at the man being punished . . . took in deep gulps of air, puffing out his cheeks and then slowly letting the air out through his protruding lips'. Seen thus close up, Varenka's affectionate father becomes a monster of a man intoxicated with his punishing power. He strikes a 'frightened, puny, weak soldier in the face with his powerful, suede-gloved hand, because the soldier had not struck the Tatar's red back powerfully enough with his stick' (p. 288) and then calls for fresh willow sticks to make sure the Tatar is appropriately beaten. This chance encounter changed Ivan Vasilyevich's whole life: his plans to enter the military or civil service faded along with his love for Varenka, and he became 'useless' to society. But precisely why he was so psychologically devastated by this chance encounter we never learn.

'After the Ball' is in fact a philosophical tale, but not the one it purports to be. Rather than an argument against environmental determinism in favour of the nebulous notion of 'chance', this story uses the pretext of this argument to present the basic dichotomy that shapes Tolstoy's political and religious world view. Ivan Vasilyevich's chance encounter with a scene of violence immediately after his experience of rapturous love for all encodes the essence of Tolstoy's anarchistic version of Christianity. The story is an emblematic representation of the opposition of the fundamental human self which is always understood as a conduit of the divine 'force' (*sila*) of love and the human self distorted by such institutions of civilization as schools, churches, governments, and the military, all of which are understood to be grounded in 'violence' and 'coercion' (*nasilie* translates both). Ivan Vasilyevich turns out useless because he fails to confront the violence with his love. He makes no 'effort' (*usilie*) at all. And 'effort' is what is at the centre of Tolstoy's moral as well as political theology. Ivan Vasilyevich fails, precisely where Nekhlyudov, Polikushka, Irtenev, and Father Sergy do not, for these characters at least try to overcome their moral weaknesses. This effort is their success, a success they share with their creator Leo Tolstoy, who spent his prophetic life attempting to overcome moral failings, both his own and those of the world in which he lived.

NOTE ON THE TEXTS

The stories in this edition were first published as follows: 'The Snow Storm' in 1856, 'From the Notes of Prince D. Nekhlyudov: Lucerne' in 1857, 'Three Deaths' in 1859, 'Polikushka' in 1863, 'Strider' in 1885, 'God Sees the Truth, But Waits' in 1872, 'The Notes of a Madman' posthumously in 1912, 'Where Love Is, God Is' in 1885, 'The Devil' posthumously in 1911, 'Father Sergy' posthumously in 1911, and 'After the Ball' in 1903.

Aylmer Maude was personally acquainted with Tolstoy and he and his wife together translated most of his major work. Tolstoy often expressed his gratitude for their services, and their translations have achieved classic status. For this edition the translations have been correlated with the established Russian texts. Personal names have been given in their Russian forms throughout, inconsistencies and errors have been corrected, where possible Tolstoy's style has been rendered closely, and, when necessary, certain phrases and expressions have been modernized.

'After the Ball' was translated for this volume by Richard F. Gustafson.

SELECT BIBLIOGRAPHY

Biographies

Maude, Aylmer, *The Life of Tolstoy*, 2 vols. (London, 1929–30).

Noyes, George Rapall, *Tolstoy* (New York, 1918).

Rolland, Romain, *The Life of Tolstoy*, trans. from French (New York, 1911).

Shklovsky, Victor, *Leo Tolstoy*, trans. from Russian (Moscow, 1978).

Simmons, Ernest J., *Leo Tolstoy* (Boston, 1946).

Troyat, Henri, *Tolstoy*, trans from French (Garden City, NY, 1967).

Wilson, A. N., *Tolstoy* (London, 1988).

General Studies

Bayley, John, *Tolstoy and the Novel* (London, 1966).

Berlin, Isaiah, *The Hedgehog and the Fox: An Essay on Tolstoy's View of History* (London, 1954).

Christian, R. F., *Tolstoy: A Critical Introduction* (Cambridge, 1969).

Ciatati, Pietro, *Tolstoy*, trans. from Italian (New York, 1986).

Gustafson, Richard F., *Leo Tolstoy, Resident and Stranger* (Princeton, 1986).

Hayman, Ronald, *Tolstoy* (New York, 1970).

Merejkowski, Dmitri, *Tolstoy as Man and Artist, with an Essay on Dostoievski* (New York, 1902).

Orwin, Donna Tussing, *Tolstoy's Art and Thought, 1847–1880* (Princeton, 1993).

Simmons, Ernest J., *Introduction to Tolstoy's Writings* (Chicago, 1968).

Wasiolek, Edward, *Tolstoy's Major Fiction* (Chicago, 1978).

Useful Collections

Christian, R. F., *Tolstoy's Diaries*, 2 vols. (New York, 1985).

—— (ed.), *Tolstoy's Letters*, 2 vols. (New York, 1978).

Gifford, Henry (ed.), *Leo Tolstoy: A Critical Anthology* (Harmondsworth, 1971).

Knowles, A. V., *Tolstoy: The Critical Heritage* (London, 1978).

Matlaw, Ralph E., *Tolstoy: A Collection of Critical Essays* (Englewood Cliffs, NJ, 1967).

Further Reading in Oxford World's Classics

Chekhov, Anton, *Early Stories*, ed. and trans. Patrick Miles and Harvey Pitcher.

—— *The Princess and Other Stories*, ed. and trans. Ronald Hingley.

—— *The Russian Master and Other Stories*, ed. and trans. Ronald Hingley.

—— *The Steppe and Other Stories*, ed. and trans. Ronald Hingley.

—— *Ward Number Six and Other Stories*, ed. and trans. Ronald Hingley.

Dostoevsky, Fyodor, *A Gentle Creature and Other Stories*, trans. Alan Myers, introduction by W. J. Leatherbarrow.

Gogol, Nikolai, *Plays and Petersburg Tales*, trans. Christopher English, introduction by Richard Peace.

Tolstoy, Leo, *Anna Karenina*, trans. Louise and Aylmer Maude, introduction by Gareth Jones.

—— *The Kreutzer Sonata and Other Stories*, trans. Louise and Aylmer Maude, ed. Richard F. Gustafson.

—— *The Raid and Other Stories*, trans. Louise and Aylmer Maude, ed. P. N. Furbank.

—— *Resurrection*, trans. Louise Maude, ed. Richard F. Gustafson.

—— *War and Peace*, trans. Louise and Aylmer Maude, ed. Henry Gifford.

A CHRONOLOGY OF LEO TOLSTOY

1828   28 August (os): born at Yasnaya Polyana, province of Tula, fourth son of Count Nikolay Tolstoy. Mother dies 1830, father 1837.

1844–7 Studies at University of Kazan (Oriental Languages, then Law). Leaves without graduating.

1851   Goes to Caucasus with elder brother. Participates in army raid on local village. Begins to write *Childhood* (pub. 1852).

1854   Commissioned. *Boyhood*.[1] Active Service on Danube; gets posting to Sevastopol.

1855   After its fall returns to Petersburg, already famous for his first two *Sevastopol Sketches*. Literary and social life in the capital.

1856   Leaves army. *A Landlord's Morning*.

1857   Visits Western Europe. August: returns to Yasnaya Polyana.

1859   His interest and success in literature wane. Founds on his estate a school for peasant children. *Three Deaths*; *Family Happiness*.

1860–1 Second visit to Western Europe, in order to study educational methods.

1861   Serves as Arbiter of the Peace, to negotiate land settlements after Emancipation of Serfs.

1862   Death of two brothers. Marries Sophia Behrs, daughter of a Moscow physician. There were to be thirteen children of the marriage, only eight growing up. Publishes educational magazine *Yasnaya Polyana*.

1863   *The Cossacks, Polikushka*. Begins *War and Peace*.

1865–6 *1805* (first part of *War and Peace*).

1866   Unsuccessfully defends at court martial soldier who had struck officer.

1869   *War and Peace* completed; final vols. published.

1870   Studies drama and Greek.

1871–2 Working on *Primer* for children.

1872   *A Prisoner in the Caucasus*.

---

[1] Tolstoy's works are dated, unless otherwise indicated, according to the year of publication.

1873   Goes with family to visit new estate in Samara. Publicizes Samara famine. Begins *Anna Karenina* (completed 1877).

1877   His growing religious problems. Dismay over Russo–Turkish War.

1879   Begins *A Confession* (completed 1882).

1881   Letter to new tsar asking for clemency towards assassins of Alexander II.

1882   *What Men Live By.* Begins *Death of Ivan Ilych* and *What Then Must We Do?* (completed 1886).

1883   Meets Chertkov, afterwards his leading disciple.

1885   Founds with Chertkov's help the *Intermediary*, to publish edifying popular works, including his own stories. Vegetarian, gives up hunting.

1886   *The Death of Ivan Ilych.* Writes play *The Power of Darkness.*

1889   *The Kreutzer Sonata* completed. Begins *Resurrection.*

1891–2   Organizes famine relief.

1893   *The Kingdom of God is Within You* pub. abroad.

1897   Begins *What is Art?* (pub. 1898) and *Hadji Murad.*

1899   *Resurrection.*

1901   Excommunicated from Orthodox Church. Seriously ill. In Crimea meets Chekhov and Gorky.

1902   *What is Religion?* completed. Working on play *The Light Shineth in Darkness.*

1903   Denounces pogroms against Jews.

1904   *Shakespeare and the Drama* completed. Also *Hadji Murad* (pub. after his death). Pamphlet on Russo–Japanese War, *Bethink Yourselves!*

1906   Death of favourite daughter Masha. Increasing tension with wife.

1908   *I Cannot Be Silent*, opposing capital punishment. 28 August: celebrations for eightieth birthday.

1909   Frequent disputes with wife. Draws up will relinquishing copyrights. His secretary Gusev arrested and exiled.

1910   Flight from home, followed by death at Astapovo railway station, 7 November (OS).

THE DEVIL
AND OTHER STORIES

THE SNOW STORM

A TALE

I

Towards seven o'clock in the evening, after having drunk my tea, I left a station, the name of which I do not remember, though I do remember it was somewhere in the district of the Don Cossack Army near Novocherkassk.* It was already dark when, having wrapped myself in my fur coat and blanket, I took my seat beside Alyoshka in the sledge. Beyond the post-station it seemed mild and calm. Though no snow was falling, not a star was visible overhead and the sky looked extremely low and black, in contrast to the pure snowy plain spread out before us.

We had hardly passed the dark shapes of the windmills, one of which was clumsily turning its large vanes, and left the settlement behind us, when I noticed that the road had become deeper in snow and more difficult to pass, that the wind began blowing more fiercely on the left, tossing the horses' tails and manes sideways, and that it kept carrying away the snow stirred up by the hoofs and sledge-runners. The sound of the bell began to die down, and through some opening in my sleeve a stream of cold air forced its way behind my back, and I recalled the stationmaster's advice, not to start for fear of going astray all night and being frozen on the road.

'Might we not lose our way?' I said to the driver, and not receiving an answer I put my question more definitely: 'I say, driver, do you think we shall reach the next station without losing our way?'

'God only knows,' he answered without turning his head. 'Just see how the snow is drifting along the ground! The road can't be seen at all. O Lord!'

'Yes, but you'd better tell me whether you expect to get me to the next station or not?' I insisted. 'Will we get there?'

'We ought to manage it,' said the driver, and went on to add something the wind prevented my hearing.

I did not feel inclined to turn back, but the idea of straying about all night in the frost and snow storm on the perfectly bare steppe

which made up that part of the Don Army district was also far from
pleasant. Moreover, though I could not see my driver very well in the
dark, I did not much like the look of him and he did not inspire me
with confidence. He sat exactly in the middle of his seat with his legs
in, instead of to one side; he was too big, he spoke lazily, his cap, not
like those usually worn by drivers, was too big and flopped from side
to side; besides, he did not urge the horses on properly, but held the
reins in both hands, like a footman who had taken the coachman's
place on the box. But my chief reason for not believing in him was
because he had a kerchief tied over his ears. In a word he did not
please me, and his solemn, stooping back looming in front of me
seemed to bode no good.

'In my opinion we'd better turn back,' remarked Alyoshka.
'There's no sense in getting lost!'

'O Lord! Just look how the snow is blowing, the road can't be seen
at all, my eyes are all stuck with snow . . . O Lord!' muttered the
driver.

We had not been going a quarter of an hour before the driver
handed the reins to Alyoshka, clumsily freed his legs, and went off
to look for the track, making the snow crunch with his big boots.

'What is it? Where are you going? Are we off the road?' I asked. But
the driver did not answer and, turning his face away from the wind
which was beating into his eyes, he walked away from the sledge.

'Well, is the road there?' I asked when he returned.

'No, there's nothing,' he answered with sudden impatience and
irritation, as if I were to blame that he had strayed off the track, and
having slowly thrust his big legs again into the front of the sledge he
began arranging the reins with his frozen gloves.

'What are we to do?' I asked when we had started again.

'What are we to do? We'll drive where God sends us.'

And we took off at the same slow trot, though quite evidently not
following a road, now through dry snow five inches deep, and now
over brittle crusts of frozen snow.

Though it was cold, the snow on my fur collar melted very
quickly; the drift along the ground grew worse and worse, and a few
dry flakes began to fall from above.

It was plain that we were going heaven knows where, for having
driven for another quarter of an hour we had not seen a single
verst-post.*

'Well, what do you think?' I asked the driver again. 'Will we get to the station?'

'Which station? We will get back, if we give the horses the lead they will take us there. But hardly to the next station—we would just perish,'

'Well then, let us just go back,' I said.

'Then I am to turn back?' said the driver.

'Yes, yes, turn back!'

The driver gave the horses the reins. They began to run faster, and though I did not notice that we were turning, I felt the wind blowing from a different quarter, and we soon saw the windmills appearing through the snow. The driver cheered up and began to talk.

'The other day the return sledges from the other station spent the whole night in a snow storm among haystacks and did not get in till the morning. Lucky that they got among those stacks, else they'd have all been frozen, it was so cold. As it is, one of them had his feet frozen, and was at death's door for three weeks with them.'

'But it's not cold now, and it seems calmer,' I said, 'we might perhaps go on?'

'It's warm enough, that's true, but the snow is drifting. Now that we have it at our back it seems easier, but the snow is driving strongly. I might go if it were on courier-duty or something of the kind, on my own. But it's no joke if a passenger gets frozen. How am I to answer for your honour afterwards?'

II

Just then we heard behind us the bells of several troikas* which were rapidly overtaking us.

'It's the courier's bell,' said my driver. 'There's no other like it in the district.'

And in fact the bell of the front troika, the sound of which was already clearly borne to us by the wind, was exceedingly fine: clear, sonorous, deep, and slightly quivering. As I learnt afterwards it was a connoisseur's bell. It had three bells—a large one in the middle with what is called a *crimson* tone, and two small ones tuned to a third. The ringing of that third and of the quivering fifth echoing in the air was extraordinarily effective and strangely beautiful in that silent and deserted steppe.

'The post is running,' said my driver, when the first of the three troikas overtook us. 'How is the road? Is it usable?' he called out to the driver of the last sledge, but the man only shouted at his horses and did not reply.

The sound of the bells was quickly lost in the wind as soon as the post sledges had passed us.

I suppose my driver felt ashamed.

'Well, let us try it again, sir!' he said to me. 'Others have made their way through and their tracks will be fresh.'

I agreed, and we turned again, facing the wind and struggling forward through the deep snow. I kept my eyes on the side of the road so as not to lose the track left by the troikas. For some two versts the track was plainly visible, then only a slight unevenness where the runners had gone, and soon I was quite unable to tell whether it was a track or only a layer of driven snow. My eyes were dimmed by looking at the snow monotonously receding under the runners, and I began to look straight ahead. We saw the third verst-post, but were quite unable to find a fourth. As before we drove against the wind, and with the wind, and to the right and to the left, and at last we came to such a pass that the driver said we must have turned off to the right, I said we had gone to the left, and Alyoshka was sure we had turned right back. Again we stopped several times and the driver disengaged his big feet and climbed out to look for the road, but all in vain. I too once went to see whether something I caught a glimpse of might not be the road, but hardly had I taken some six steps with difficulty against the wind before I became convinced that the same monotonous white layers of snow lay everywhere, and that I had seen the road only in my imagination. When I could no longer see in the sledge I cried out: 'Driver! Alyoshka!' but I felt how the wind caught my voice straight from my mouth and bore it instantly somewhere away from me. I set off to where the sledge had been—but it was not there; I set off to the right, it was not there either. I am ashamed to remember in what a loud, piercing, and even rather despairing voice I again shouted 'Driver!' and there he was within two steps of me. His black figure with the little whip and enormous cap pushed to one side, suddenly loomed up before me. He led me to the sledge.

'Thank the Lord, it's still warm,' he said, 'if the frost were to get us it would be terrible . . . O Lord!'

'Give the horses the lead: let them take us back,' I said, having seated myself in the sledge. 'They will take us back, driver, eh?'

'They ought to.'

He let go of the reins, struck the harness-pad of the middle horse with the whip, and we again took off for somewhere. We had travelled on for about half an hour when suddenly ahead of us we recognized the connoisseur's bell and the other two, but this time they were coming towards us. There were the same three troikas, which having delivered the mail were now returning to the station with relay horses attached. The courier's troika with its big horses and musical bells ran quickly in front, with one driver on the driver's seat shouting vigorously. Two drivers were sitting in the middle of each of the empty sledges that followed, and one could hear their loud and merry voices. One of them was smoking a pipe, and the spark that flared up in the wind showed part of his face.

Looking at them I felt ashamed that I had been afraid to go on, and my driver probably shared the same feeling, for we both said at once: 'Let's follow them!'

III

Before the third troika had passed, my driver began turning so clumsily that his shafts hit the horses attached behind it. The three houses shied, broke their strap, and galloped aside.

'You cross-eyed devil! Can't you see when you're turning into someone, you devil?' one of the drivers began to curse in hoarse, quivering tones. The short old man, who was, as far as I could judge by his voice and figure, seated in the last sledge, quickly jumped out of the sledge and ran after the horses, still continuing his coarse and harsh abuse of my driver.

But the horses did not stop. The driver followed them, and in a moment both he and they were lost in the white mist of driving snow.

'Vasi-i-ly! Get the dun horse! I can't catch them without it,' his voice shouted.

One of the other drivers, a very tall man, got out of his sledge, silently unfastened his three horses, climbed on one of them by its breeching, and disappeared at a clumsy gallop in the direction of the first driver.

Though there was no road, and the other two troikas started off, following the courier's troika, which with its bell ringing went along at full trot.

'Catch them! Not likely!' said my driver of the one who had run after the horses. 'If a horse won't come to other horses, that shows it's bewitched and will take you somewhere you'll never return from.'

From the time he began following the others my driver seemed more cheerful and talkative, a fact of which I naturally took advantage, as I did not yet feel sleepy. I began asking where he came from, and why, and who he was, and it turned out that like myself he was from Tula province, a serf from Kirpichnoe village, where they were short of land and had had bad harvests since the cholera year. He was one of two brothers in the family, the third having gone as a soldier, and still they had not enough grain to last till Christmas and had to live on outside earnings. His youngest brother was head of the house, being married, while he himself was a widower. An *artel** of drivers came from their village to these parts every year. Though he had not driven before, he had taken the job to help his brother, and lived, thank God, quite well, earning a hundred and twenty roubles a year, of which he sent a hundred home to the family; and that life would be quite good 'if only the couriers were not such beasts, and the people hereabouts not so abusive'.

'Now why did that driver scold me so? O Lord! Did I set his horses loose on purpose? Do I mean harm to anybody? And why did he go galloping after them? They'd have come back of themselves, and now he'll only tire out the horses and get lost himself,' said the God-fearing peasant.

'And what is that black thing there?' I asked, noticing several black objects in front of us.

'Why, a train of carts. That's pleasant driving!' he went on, when we had come abreast of the huge mat-covered wagons on wheels, following one another. 'Look, you can't see a single soul—they're all asleep. A wise horse knows by itself . . . you can't make it miss the way anyhow . . . We've driven that way on contract work ourselves,' he added, 'so we know.'

It really was strange to see those huge wagons covered with snow from their matted tops to their very wheels, and moving along all alone. Only in the front corner of the wagon did the matting, covered two inches thick with snow, lift a bit and a cap appear for a moment from under it as our bells tinkled past. The large pie-bald horse, stretching its neck and straining its back, went evenly along the completely snow-hidden road, monotonously shaking its shaggy head under the whitened harness-bow, and pricking one snow-covered ear when we overtook it.

When we had gone on for another half-hour the driver again turned to me.

'What d'you think, sir, are we going right?'

'I don't know,' I answered.

'At first there was wind, but now we are going right under it. No, we are not going where we ought, we are going astray again,' he said quite calmly.

You could see that, though he was inclined to be a coward, yet 'even death itself is pleasant in company' as the saying goes, and he had become quite tranquil now that there were several of us and he no longer had to lead and be responsible. He made remarks on the blunders of the driver in front with the greatest coolness, as if it were none of his business. And in fact I noticed that we sometimes saw the front troika on the left and sometimes on the right; it even seemed to me that we were going round in a very small circle. However, that might be an optical illusion, like the impression that the leading troika was sometimes going uphill, and then along a slope, or downhill, whereas I knew that the steppe was perfectly level.

After we had gone on again for some time, I saw a long way off, on the very horizon as it seemed to me, a long, black, moving stripe; and a moment later it became clear that it was the same train of wagons we had passed before. The snow was still covering their creaking wheels, some of which did not even turn any longer, the men were still asleep as before under the matting, and the piebald horse in front blew out its nostrils as before, sniffed at the road, and pricked its ears.

'There, we've turned and turned and come back to the same wagons!' exclaimed my driver in a dissatisfied voice. 'The courier's horses are good ones, that's why he's driving them so recklessly, but ours will stop altogether if we go on like this all night.'

He cleared his throat.

'Let us turn back, sir, before we get into trouble!'

'No! Why? We shall get somewhere.'

'Where shall we get to? We shall spend the night in the steppe. See how it is blowing! . . . O Lord!'

Though I was surprised that the driver of the front troika, having evidently lost the road and the direction, went on at a fast trot without looking for the road, and cheerfully shouting, I did not want to lag behind them.

'Follow them!' I said.

My driver obeyed, whipping up his horses more reluctantly than before, and did not turn to talk to me any more.

IV

The storm grew more and more violent, and the snow fell dry and fine. I thought it was beginning to freeze: my cheeks and nose felt colder than before, and streams of cold air made their way more frequently under my fur coat, so that I had to wrap it closer around me. Sometimes the sledge bumped on the bare ice-glazed ground from which the wind had swept the snow. As I had already travelled more than five hundred versts without stopping anywhere for the night, I involuntarily kept closing my eyes and dozing off, although I was much interested to know how our wandering would end. Once when I opened my eyes I was struck for a moment by what seemed to me a bright light falling on the white plain; the horizon had widened considerably, the low black sky had suddenly vanished, and on all sides slanting white streaks of falling snow could be seen. The outlines of the front troikas were more distinct, and as I looked up it seemed for a minute as though the clouds had dispersed, and that only the falling snow veiled the sky. While I was dozing the moon had risen and was casting its cold bright light through the tenuous clouds and the falling snow. The only things I saw clearly were my sledge, the horses, my driver, and the three troikas in front of us: the courier's sledge in which a driver still sat, as before, driving at a fast trot; the second, in which two drivers having laid down the reins and made a shelter for themselves out of a coat sat smoking their pipes all the time, as could be seen by the sparks that flew from them; and the third in which no one was visible, as probably the driver was lying asleep in the body of the sledge. The driver of the first troika, however, at the time I awoke, occasionally stopped his horses and sought for the road. As soon as we stopped the howling of the wind sounded louder and the vast quantity of snow borne through the air became more apparent. In the snow-shrouded moonlight I could see the driver's short figure probing the snow in front of him with the handle of his whip, moving backwards and forwards in the white dimness, again returning to his sledge and jumping sideways onto his seat, and again amid the monotonous whistling of the wind I heard his dexterous, resonant cries urging on the horses, and the ringing of the bells. Whenever the driver of the front troika got out to search for some sign of a road or haystacks, there came from the second troika the bold, self-confident voice of one of the drivers shouting to him:

'Hey, Ignashka, you've gone quite to the left! Bear to the right, facing the wind!' Or: 'What are you twisting about for, quite uselessly? Follow the snow, see how the drifts lie, and we'll come out just right.' Or: 'Take to the right, to the right, mate! See, there's something black—it must be a post.' Or: 'What are you straying about for? Unhitch the piebald and let him run in front, he'll lead you right out onto the road. That would be better.'

But the man who was giving this advice not only did not unhitch one of his own side-horses or get out to look for the road, but did not show his nose from under his sheltering coat, and when Ignashka, the leader, shouted in reply to one of his counsels that he should take on the lead himself if he knew which way to go, the advice-giver replied that if he were driving the courier's troika he would take the lead and take us right onto the road. 'But our horses won't take the lead in a snow storm!' he shouted—'they're not that kind of horse!'

'Then don't bother me!' Ignashka replied, whistling cheerfully to his horses.

The other driver in the second sledge did not speak to Ignashka at all, and in general took no part in the matter, though he was not asleep, as I concluded from his pipe being always alight, and because, whenever we stopped, I heard the even and continuous sound of his voice. He was telling a folk tale. Only once, when Ignashka stopped for the sixth or seventh time, he apparently grew vexed at being interrupted during the pleasure of his drive, and shouted to him:

'Hey, why have you stopped again? Just look, he wants to find the road! He's been told there's a snow storm! Even that surveyor himself couldn't find the road now. You should drive on as long as the horses will go, and then maybe we won't freeze to death . . . Go on, now!'

'I daresay! Didn't a postilion freeze to death last year?' my driver remarked.

The driver of the third sledge did not wake up all this time. Once when we had stopped the advice-giver shouted:

'Filipp! Hey, Filipp!' and receiving no reply remarked: 'Has he frozen, perhaps? . . . Go and have a look, Ignashka.'

Ignashka, who found time for everything, walked up to the sledge and began to shake the sleeping man.

'Just see what half a bottle of vodka has done! Talk about freezing!' he said, shaking him.

The sleeper grunted something and cursed.

'He's alive, all right,' said Ignashka, and ran forward again. We drove on, and so fast that the little sorrel on my side of the troika, which my driver continually touched with the whip near his tail, now and then broke into an awkward little gallop.

V

It was I think already near midnight when the little old man and Vasily, who had gone after the runaway horses, rode up to us. They had managed to catch the horses and to find and overtake us; but how they had managed to do this in the thick blinding snow storm amid the bare steppe will always remain a mystery to me. The old man, swinging his elbows and legs, was riding the shaft-horse at a trot (the two side-horses were attached to its collar: one dare not let horses loose in a snow storm). When he came abreast of us he again began to scold my driver.

'Look at the cross-eyed devil, really . . .'

'Eh, Uncle Mitrich!' the folk-tale teller in the second sledge called out: 'Are you alive? Get in here with us.'

But the old man did not reply and continued his abuse. When he thought he had said enough he rode up to the second sledge.

'Have you caught them all?' someone in it asked.

'What do you think?'

His small figure threw itself forward on the back of the trotting horse, then jumped down on the snow, and without stopping he ran after the sledge and tumbled in, his legs sticking out over its side. The tall Vasily silently took his old place in the front sledge beside Ignashka, and the two began to look for the road together.

'How the old man nags . . . O Lord!' muttered my driver.

For a long time after that we drove on without stopping over the white wasteland, in the cold, pellucid, and quivering light of the snow storm. I'd open my eyes and the same clumsy snow-covered cap and back would be jolting before me: the same low shaft-bow, under which, between the taut leather reins and always at the same distance from me, the head of our shaft-horse kept bobbing with its black mane blown to one side by the wind, while looking across its back I could see the same little piebald horse on the right, with its tail tied up short, and the swingletree which sometimes knocked against the front of the sledge. I'd look down and there was the same scurrying snow through which our runners were cutting, and which the wind resolutely bore away to one side. In front, always at the same distance away, glided the first troika, while to right and left everything glimmered white and dim. Vainly did my eye look for any new object: neither post, nor haystack, nor fence was to be seen. Everywhere all was white and shifting: now the horizon seemed immeasurably distant, now it closed in on all sides to within two paces of me; suddenly a high white wall would seem to rise up on the right and run beside the sledge, then it would suddenly vanish and rise again in front, only to glide on further and further away and again disappear. I'd look up and it would seem lighter for a moment, as if I might see the stars through the haze, but the stars would run away higher and higher from my sight and only the snow would be visible, falling past my eyes onto my face and the collar of my fur cloak. The sky everywhere remained equally light, equally white, monotonous, colourless, and constantly shifting. The wind seemed to be changing: now it blew in my face and the snow plastered my eyes, now it blew from one side and annoyingly tossed the fur collar of my cloak against my head and mockingly flapped my face with it; now it howled through some opening. I heard the soft incessant crunching of the hoofs and the runners on the snow, and the clang of the bells dying down when we drove through deep drifts. Only now and then, when we drove against the snow and glided over bare frozen ground, did Ignashka's energetic whistling and the sonorous sound of the bell with its accompanying bare fifth reach me and give sudden relief to the dismal character of the wasteland; and then again the bells would sound monotonous, playing always with insufferable precision the same tune, which I involuntarily imagined I was hearing. One of my feet began to feel the frost, and when I turned to wrap myself up better, the snow that had settled on my collar and cap sifted down my neck and made me shiver, but on the whole I still felt warm in my fur coat, and drowsiness overcame me.

VI

Recollections and pictures of the distant past superseded one another with increasing rapidity in my imagination.

'That advice-giver who is always calling out from the second sledge—what sort of fellow can he be?' I thought. 'Probably red-haired, thick-set, and with short legs, like Fyodor Filippych, our old butler.' And I saw the staircase of our big house and five domestic serfs with heavy steps bringing a piano from the wing on slings made of towels, and Fyodor Filippych with the sleeves of his nankeen coat turned up, holding one of the pedals, running forward, lifting a latch, pulling here at the slings, pushing there, crawling between people's legs, getting into everybody's way, and shouting incessantly in an anxious voice:

'Lean it against yourselves, you there in front, you in front! That's the way—the tail end up, up, up! Turn into the door! That's the way.'

'Just let us do it, Fyodor Filippych! We can manage it alone,' timidly remarks the gardener, quite red with straining, as he is pressed against the bannisters, with great effort holding up one corner of the grand piano.

But Fyodor Filippych will not be quiet.

'What does it mean?' I reflect. 'Does he think he is useful or necessary for the work in hand, or is he simply glad God has given him this self-confident persuasive eloquence, and enjoys dispensing it? That must be it.' And then somehow I see the lake, and tired domestic serfs up to their knees in the water dragging a fishing-net, and again Fyodor Filippych with a watering can, shouting at everybody as he runs up and down on the bank, now and then approaching the brink to empty out some turbid water and to take up fresh, while holding back the golden carp with his hand. But now it is a July noon. I am going somewhere over the freshly mown grass in the garden, under the burning, vertical rays of the sun; I am still very young, and I feel a lack of something and a desire to fill that lack. I go to my favourite place by the lake, between the briar-rose bed and the birch-lined lane, and lie down to sleep. I remember the feeling with which, lying down, I looked across between the prickly red stems of the rose trees at the dark, dry, crumbly earth, and at the bright blue mirror of the lake. It is a feeling of naive self-satisfaction and melancholy. Everything around me is beautiful, and that beauty affects me so powerfully that it seems to me that I myself am good, and the one thing that vexes me is that nobody is there to admire me. It is hot. I try to sleep so as to console myself, but the flies, the unendurable flies, give me no peace here either: they gather round me and, with a kind of dull persistence, hard as cherry-stones, jump from my forehead onto my hands. A bee buzzes not far from me in the blazing sunlight; yellow-winged butterflies fly from one blade of grass to another as if exhausted by the heat. I look up: my eyes hurt as the sun glitters too brightly through the light foliage of the curly birch tree whose branches sway softly high above me, and it seems hotter than ever. I cover my face with my handkerchief: it feels stifling, and the flies seem to stick to my hands which begin to perspire. In the very centre of the wild rose bush sparrows begin to bustle about. One of them hops to the ground about two feet from me, energetically pretends to peck at the ground a couple of times, flies back into the bush, rustling the twigs, and chirping merrily flies away. Another also hops down, jerks his little tail, looks about him, chirps, and flies off quick as an arrow after the first one. From the lake comes a sound of a beetle* beating wet linen, and the sound reverberates and is borne down along the lake. Sounds of laughter and the voices and splashing of bathers are heard. A gust of wind rustles the crowns of the birch trees, still far from me; now it comes nearer and I hear it stir the grass, and now the leaves of the wild roses begin to flutter, pressed against their stems, and at last a fresh stream of air reaches me, lifting a corner of my handkerchief and tickling my moist face. Through the gap where the corner of the kerchief was lifted a fly comes in and flutters with fright close to my moist mouth. A dry twig presses against my back. No, I can't lie still: I had better go and have a bathe. But just then, close to the rose bush, I hear hurried steps and a woman's frightened voice:

'O God! How could such a thing happen! And none of the men are here!'

'What is it? What is it?' running out into the sunshine I ask a woman serf who hurries past me groaning. She only looks round, waves her arms, and runs on. But here comes seventy-year-old Matryona hurrying to the lake, holding down with one hand the kerchief which is slipping off her head, and hopping and dragging one of her feet in its worsted stocking. Two little girls come running up hand in hand, and a ten-year-old boy, wearing his father's coat and clutching the homespun skirt of one of the girls, keeps close behind them.

'What has happened?' I ask them.

'A peasant is drowning.'

'Where?'

'In the lake.'

'Who is he? One of ours?'

'No, a stranger.'

Ivan the coachman, dragging his heavy boots through the newly mown grass, and the fat clerk Yakov, all out of breath, run to the pond and I after them.

I remember the feeling which said to me: 'There you are, plunge in and pull out the peasant and save him, and everyone will admire you,' which was exactly what I wanted.

'Where is he? Where?' I ask the throng of domestic serfs gathered on the bank.

'Out there, in the very deepest part near the other bank, almost at the boathouse,' says the washerwoman, hanging the wet linen on her wooden yoke. 'I look, and see him dive; he just comes up and is gone, then comes up again and calls out: "I'm drowning, help!" and goes down again, and nothing but bubbles come up. Then I see that the man is drowning, so I give a yell: "Hey, everybody! A peasant's drowning!" '

And lifting the yoke to her shoulder the laundress waddles sideways along the path away from the lake.

'Oh gracious, what a business!' says Yakov Ivanov, the office-clerk, in a despairing tone. 'What a bother there'll be with the rural court. We'll never get through with it!'

A peasant carrying a scythe pushes his way through the throng of women, children, and old men who have gathered on the further shore, and hanging his scythe on the branch of a willow slowly begins to take off his boots.

'Where? Where did he go down?' I keep asking, wishing to rush there and do something extraordinary.

But they point to the smooth surface of the lake which is occasionally rippled by the passing breeze. I do not understand how he came to drown; the water is still so smooth, lovely, and calm above him, shining golden in the midday sun, and it seems that I can do nothing and can astonish no one, especially as I am a very poor swimmer and the peasant is already pulling his shirt over his head and ready to plunge in. Everybody looks at him hopefully and with bated breath, but after going in up to his shoulders he slowly turns back and puts his shirt on again—he cannot swim.

People still keep on gathering and the throng grows and grows; the women cling to one another, but nobody does anything to help. Those who have just come give advice, and sigh, and their faces express fear and despair; but of those who have been there awhile, some, tired with standing, sit down on the grass, while some go away. Old Matryona asks her daughter whether she shut the oven door, and the boy who is wearing his father's coat diligently throws small stones into the water.

But now Fyodor Filippych's dog Tresorka, barking and looking back in perplexity, comes running down the hill, and then Fyodor himself, running downhill and shouting, appears from behind the briar-rose bushes:

'What are you standing there for?' he cries, taking off his coat as he runs. 'A man drowning, and they stand there! . . . Get me a rope!'

Everybody looks at Fyodor Filippych with hope and fear as, leaning his hand on the shoulder of an obliging domestic serf, he pries off his right boot with the toe of the left.

'Over there, where the people are, a little to the right of the willow, Fyodor Filippych, just there!' someone says to him.

'I know,' he replies, and knitting his brows, in response, no doubt, to the signs of shame among the crowd of women, he pulls off his shirt, removes the cross from his neck and hands it to the gardener's boy who stands obsequiously before him, and then, stepping energetically over the cut grass, approaches the lake.

Tresorka, perplexed by the quickness of his master's movements, has stopped near the crowd and with a smack of his lips eats a few blades of grass near the bank, then looks at his master intently and with a joyful yelp suddenly plunges with him into the water. For a moment nothing can be seen but foam and spray, which even reaches to us; but now Fyodor Filippych, gracefully swinging his arms and rhythmically raising and lowering his back, swims briskly with long strokes to the opposite shore. Tresorka, having swallowed some water, returns hurriedly, shakes himself near the throng, and rubs his back on the grass. Just as Fyodor Filippych reaches the opposite shore two coachmen come running up to the willow with a fishing-net wrapped round a pole. Fyodor Filippych for some unknown reason lifts his arms, dives down once and then a second and a third time, on each occasion squirting a jet of water from his mouth, and gracefully tosses back his hair without answering the questions that are hurled at him from all sides. At last he comes out onto the bank, and as far as I can see only gives instructions as to spreading out the net. The net is drawn in, but there is nothing in it except ooze with a few small carp entangled in it. While the net is being lowered again I go round to that side.

The only sounds to be heard are Fyodor Filippych's voice giving orders, the plashing of the wet rope on the water, and sighs of terror. The wet rope attached to the right side of the net, more and more covered by grass, comes further and further out of the water.

'Now then, pull together, harder, all together!' shouts Fyodor Filippych.

The floats appear dripping with water.

'Hey, there is something. It's heavy to pull!' someone calls out.

But now the net, in which two or three little carp are struggling, is dragged right onto the bank, wetting and pressing down the grass. And in the extended wings of the net, through a thin swaying layer of turbid water, something white comes right into sight. Amid dead silence an impressive, though not loud, gasp of horror passes through the crowd.

'Pull harder, onto the land!' comes Fyodor Filippych's resolute voice, and the drowned body is dragged over the stubble of burdock and thistle, way out to the willow.

And now I see my good old aunt in her silk dress, with her face ready to burst into tears. I see her lilac parasol with its fringe, which seems somehow incongruous in this scene of death, so terrible in its simplicity. I remember the disappointment her face expressed because arnica* could be of no use, and I also remember the painful feeling of annoyance I experienced when, with the naive egotism of love, she said: 'Come away my dear. Oh, how dreadful it is! And you always go bathing and swimming by yourself.'

I remember how bright and hot the sun was as it baked the powdery earth underfoot; how it sparkled and mirrored in the lake; how the plump carp plashed near the banks and shoals of little fish rippled the water in the middle; how a hawk hovering high in the air circled over the ducklings, which quacking and splashing had come swimming out through the reeds into the middle of the lake; how curling white thunder-clouds gathered on the horizon; how the mud drawn out onto the bank by the net gradually receded; and how as I crossed the dyke I again heard the strokes of a beetle reverberating over the lake.

But this beetle sounds as if two beetles were beating together in thirds, and that sound torments and worries me, the more so because I know that this beetle is a bell, and that Fyodor Filippych will not make it stop. Then this beetle, like an instrument of torture, presses my foot which is freezing, and I fall asleep.

I am awakened, as it seems to me, by our galloping very fast and by two voices calling out quite close to me:

'I say, Ignat! Eh, Ignat!' my driver is saying. 'You take my passenger. You have to go on anyhow, but what's the use of my goading my horses uselessly? You take him!'

Ignat's voice quite close to me replies:

'And what do I get for making myself responsible for the passenger? Will you stand me a bottle?'

'Oh, come, a bottle . . . say half a bottle.'

'Half a bottle, indeed!' shouts another voice. 'Wear out the horses for half a bottle!'

I open my eyes. Before them still flickers the same intolerable swaying snow, the same drivers and horses, but now we are abreast of another sledge. My driver has overtaken Ignat, and we drive side by side for some time. Though the voice from the other sledge advises him not to accept less than a bottle, Ignat suddenly reins in his troika.

'Well, shift over. So be it! It's your luck. You'll stand half a bottle when we return tomorrow. Is there much luggage?'

My driver jumps out into the snow with unusual alacrity for him, bows to me, and begs me to change over into Ignat's sledge. I am quite willing to, but evidently the God-fearing peasant is so pleased that he has to pour out his gratitude and delight to someone. He bows and thanks me, Alyoshka, and Ignat.

'There now, the Lord be praised! What has it been like . . . O Lord! We've been driving half the night and didn't know where we were going. He'll get you there, dear sir, but my horses are quite worn out.'

And he shifts my things with increased zeal.

While my things were being transferred I went to the second sledge, following the wind, which almost lifted me off my feet. That sledge was more than six inches deep in snow, especially from the side where a coat had been arranged on the two men's heads to shelter them from the wind, but behind the coat it was quiet and comfortable. The old man still lay with his legs sticking out, and the storyteller was still going on with his tale:

'Well, when the general comes to Mary in prison, in the King's name, you know, Mary at once says to him: "General, I don't need you and can't love you, and so, you see, you are not my lover, but my lover is the prince himself . . ." '

'And just then . . .' he went on, but seeing me he stopped for a moment and began filling his pipe.

'Well, sir, have you come to listen to the tale?' asked the other whom I called the advice-giver.

'Yes, you're well off here, quite merry,' I said.

'Why not? It whiles away the time, anyhow it keeps one from thinking.'

'And do you know where we are now?'

This question did not seem to please the drivers.

'Who can make out where we are? Maybe we've driven into Kalmyk territory,'* answered the advice-giver.

'Then what are we going to do?' I asked.

'What can we do? We'll go on, and maybe we'll get somewhere,' he said in a dissatisfied tone.

'But suppose we don't get anywhere, and the horses stick in the snow, what then?'

'What then? Why, nothing.'

'But we might freeze.'

'Of course we might, because one can't even see any haystacks: that means we have got right among the Kalmyks. The chief thing is to watch the snow.'

'And you seem afraid of getting frozen, sir,' remarked the old man in a shaky voice.

Though he seemed to be chaffing me, it was evident that he was chilled to his very bones.

'Yes, it is getting very cold,' I said.

'Eh, sir, you should do as I do, take a run now and then, that will warm you up.'

'Yes, the chief thing is to have a run behind the sledge,' said the advice-giver.

VII

'We're ready, your honour!' shouted Alyoshka from the front sledge.

The storm was so violent that, though I bent almost in two and clutched the skirts of my cloak with both hands, I was hardly able to walk over the drifting snow which the wind swept from under my feet, or even take the few steps that separated me from the sledge. My former driver was already kneeling in the middle of his empty sledge, but when he saw me going he took off his big cap (whereupon the wind lifted his hair furiously) and asked for a tip. Evidently he did not expect me to give him one, for my refusal did not grieve him in the least. He thanked me anyway, put his cap on again, and said: 'God keep you, sir . . .' and jerking his reins and clicking his tongue, turned away from us. Then Ignat swayed his whole back and shouted to the horses, and the sound of the snow crunching under their hoofs, the cries, and the bells, replaced the howling of the wind which had been peculiarly noticeable while we stood still.

For a quarter of an hour after my transfer I kept awake and amused myself watching my new driver and his horses. Ignat sat like a mettlesome fellow, continually rising in his seat, flourishing over the horses the arm from which his whip was hung, shouting, beating one foot against the other, and bending forward to adjust the breeching of the shaft-horse, which kept slipping to the right. He was not tall, but seemed to be well built. Over his sheepskin he wore a large, loose cloak without a belt, the collar of which was turned down so that his neck was bare. He wore not felt but leather boots, and a small cap which he kept taking off and putting straight. His ears were only protected by his hair. In all his movements one was aware not only of energy, but even more, as it seemed to me, of a desire to arouse that energy in himself. And the further we went the more often he straightened himself out, rose in his seat, beat his feet together, and addressed himself to Alyoshka and me. It seemed to me that he was afraid of losing courage. And there was good reason for it: though the horses were good the road grew more and more difficult at every step, and it was plain that they were running less willingly: it was already necessary to touch them up with the whip, and the shaft-horse, a good, big, shaggy animal, stumbled more than once, though immediately, as if frightened, it jerked forward again and tossed its shaggy head almost as high as the bell hanging from the bow above it. The right-side horse, which I could not help watching, with a long leather tassel to its breeching which shook and jerked on its off side, noticeably let its traces slacken and required the whip, but from habit as a good and even mettlesome horse seemed vexed at its own weakness, and angrily lowered and tossed its head at the reins. It was terrible to realize that the snow storm and the frost were increasing, the horses growing weaker, the road becoming worse, and that we did not at all know where we were, or where we were going, or whether we should reach a station or even a shelter of any sort; it seemed strange and ridiculous to hear the bells ringing so easily and cheerfully, and Ignat shouting as lustily and pleasantly as if we were out for a drive along a village street on a frosty noon during a Twelfth Night holiday, but it was stranger still that we were always driving and driving fast somewhere from where we were. Ignat began to sing some song in a horrid falsetto, but so loud and with such intervals, during which he whistled, that it seemed strange to be afraid while one heard him.

'Hey there, what are you splitting your throat for, Ignat?' came the advice-giver's voice. 'Stop a minute!'

'What?'

'Sto-o-op!'

Ignat stopped. Again all became silent, and the wind howled and whined, and the whirling snow fell still more thickly into the sledge. The advice-giver came up to us.

'Well, what now?'

'What now? Where are we going?'

'Who can tell?'

'Are your feet freezing, that you knock them together so?'

'Quite numb!'

'You should go over there: look, where there's something glimmering. It must be a Kalmyk camp. It would warm your feet too.'

'All right. Hold the reins . . . here you are.'

And Ignat ran in the direction indicated.

'You always have to go about a bit and look, then you find the way, or else what's the good of driving about like a fool?' the advice-giver said to me. 'See how the horses are steaming.'

All the time Ignat was gone—and that lasted so long that I even began to fear he might have lost his way—the advice-giver kept telling me in a self-confident and calm tone how one should behave in a snow storm, that it was best to unharness a horse and let it go, and, as God is holy, it would be sure to lead one out, and how it is sometimes possible to find the way by the stars, and that had he been driving in front we should long ago have reached the station.

'Well, is there anything?' he asked Ignat when the latter came back, stepping with difficulty through the knee-deep snow.

'There is, there is a camp of some sort,' replied Ignat, gasping for breath, 'but I can't tell what it is. We must have strayed right into the Prologov estate. We must bear off to the left.'

'What's he jabbering about? It's our camp that's behind the Cossack village,' rejoined the advice-giver.

'I tell you it's not!'

'Well, I've had a look too, and I know: that's what it is, and if it isn't, then it's Tamyshevsk. Anyhow we must bear to the right, and then we'll come right out to the big bridge at the eighth verst.'

'I tell you it's nothing of the sort. Haven't I looked?' said Ignat with annoyance.

'Yah, brother, and you call yourself a driver!'

'Yes, a driver! . . . Go and look for yourself.'

'Why should I go? I know without going.'

Ignat had evidently grown angry: he jumped into the sledge without replying and drove on.

'How numb my legs have got! I can't warm them up,' he said to Alyoshka, knocking his feet together oftener and oftener, and scooping up and emptying out the snow that had got into his boot-legs.

I felt dreadfully sleepy.

VIII

'Can it be that I am freezing to death?' I thought, half asleep. 'They say it always begins with drowsiness. It would be better to drown than to freeze, let them drag me out with a net; but it does not matter much whether I freeze or drown if only that stick, or whatever it is, would not prod me in the back and I could forget myself!'

I did so for a few seconds.

'But how will all this end?' I suddenly asked myself, opening my eyes for a moment and peering into the white expanse before me. 'How will it all end? If we don't find any haystacks and the horses stop, as they seem likely to do soon, we shall all freeze to death.' I confess that, though I was a little afraid, the desire that something extraordinary, something rather tragic, should happen to us, was stronger in me than that fear. It seemed to me that it would not be bad if towards morning the horses brought us of their own accord, half-frozen, to some far-off unknown village, or if some of us were even to perish of the cold. Fancies of this kind presented themselves to me with extraordinary clearness and rapidity. The horses stop, the snow drifts higher and higher, and now nothing is seen of the horses but their ears and the bows above their heads, but suddenly Ignat appears above us with his troika, and drives past. We entreat him, we shout that he should take us, but the wind carries our voices away and we have no voices left. Ignat grins, shouts to his horses, whistles, and disappears into some deep, snow-covered ravine. The little old man jumps astride a horse, flourishes his elbows and tries to gallop away, but cannot stir from the spot; my former driver with the big cap rushes at him, drags him to the ground and tramples him into the snow. 'You're a wizard!' he shouts. 'You're a scolder! We shall all be lost together!' But the old man breaks through the heap of snow with his head; and now he is not so much an old man as a hare, and leaps away from us. All the dogs bound after him. The advice-giver, who is Fyodor Filippych, tells us all to sit round in a circle, that if the snow covers us it will be all right, we shall be warm that way. And really we are warm and cosy, only I want a drink. I fetch out my lunch-basket, and treat everybody to rum and sugar, and enjoy a drink myself. The storyteller spins a tale about a rainbow, and now there is a ceiling of snow and a rainbow above us. 'Now let us each make himself a room in the snow and let us go to sleep!' I say. The snow is soft and warm, like fur. I make myself a room and want to enter it, but Fyodor Filippych, who has seen the money in my lunch-basket, says: 'Stop! Give me your money, you have to die anyway!' And he grabs me by the leg. I hand over the money and only ask him to let me go; but they won't believe it is all the money I have and want to kill me. I seize the old man's hand and begin to kiss it with inexpressible pleasure: his hand is tender and sweet. At first he snatches it from me, but afterwards lets me have it, and even caresses me with his other hand. Then Fyodor Filippych comes near and threatens me. I run away into my room: it is, however, no longer a room but a long white corridor, and someone is holding my legs. I wrench myself free. My clothes and part of my skin remain in the hands of the man who was holding me, but I only feel cold and ashamed, all the more ashamed because my aunt with her parasol and homoeopathic medicine-chest under her arm is coming towards me arm in arm with the drowned man. They are laughing and do not understand the signs I make to them. I throw myself into the sledge, my feet trail behind me in the snow, but the old man rushes after me flapping his elbows. He is already near, but I hear two church bells ringing in front of me, and know that I shall be saved when I get to them. The church bells sound nearer and nearer; but the little old man has caught up with me and falls with his stomach on my face, so that I can scarcely hear the bells. I again grasp his hand and begin to kiss it, but the little old man is no longer the little old man, he is the man who was drowned . . . and he shouts: 'Ignat, stop! There are the Akhmetkins' stacks, I think! Go and have a look at them!' This is too terrible. No, I had better wake up.

I open my eyes. The wind has thrown the flap of Alyoshka's cloak over my face, my knee is uncovered, we are going over the bare frozen road, and the bells with their quivering third can be distinctly heard.

I look to see the haystacks, but now that my eyes are open I see no stacks, but a house with a balcony and the crenellated wall of a fortress. I am not interested enough to scrutinize this house and fortress: I am chiefly anxious to see the white corridor along which I ran, to hear the sound of the church bells, and to kiss the little old man's hand. I close my eyes again and fall asleep.

IX

I slept soundly, but heard the ringing of the bells all the time. They appeared to me in my dream now in the guise of a dog that barked and attacked me, now of an organ in which I was one of the pipes, and now of some French verses I was composing. Sometimes those bells seemed to be an instrument of torture which kept squeezing my right heel. I felt that so strongly that I woke up and opened my eyes, rubbing my foot. It was getting frost-bitten. The night was still light, misty, and white. The same motion was still shaking me and the sledge; the same Ignat sat sideways, knocking his feet together; the same side-horse with outstretched neck ran at a trot over the deep snow without lifting its feet much, while the tassel on the breeching bobbed and flapped against its belly. The head of the shaft-horse with its flying mane stooped and rose rhythmically as it alternately drew the reins tight and loosened them. But all this was covered with snow even more than before. The snow whirled about in front, at the side it covered the horses' legs knee-deep, and the runners of the sledge, while it fell from above on our collars and caps. The wind blew now from the right, now from the left, playing with Ignat's collar, the skirt of his cloak, the mane of the side-horse, and howling between the shafts and above the bow over the shaft-horse's head.

It was growing terribly cold, and hardly had I stuck my head out of my coat collar before the frosty, crisp, whirling snow covered my eyelashes, got into my nose and mouth, and penetrated behind my neck. When I looked round, everything was white, light, and snowy, there was nothing to be seen but the dull light and the snow. I became really terrified. Alyoshka was asleep at my feet at the bottom of the sledge, his whole back covered by a thick layer of snow. Ignat did not lose courage: he kept pulling at the reins, shouting, and clapping his feet together. The bell went on ringing just as wonderfully. The horses snorted a little, but ran more slowly and stumbled more and more often. Ignat again leaped up, waved his mitten, and again began singing in his strained falsetto. Before finishing the song he stopped the troika, threw down the reins on the front of the sledge, and got out. The wind howled furiously; the snow poured on the skirts of our cloaks as out of a scoop. I turned round: the third troika was not to be seen (it had lagged behind somewhere). Near the second sledge, in the snowy mist, I saw the little old man jumping from foot to foot. Ignat went some three steps from the sledge, and sitting down in the snow undid his belt and pulled off his boots.

'What are you doing?' I asked.

'I must change, or my feet will be quite frozen,' he replied, and went on with what he was doing.

It was too cold to keep my neck out of my collar to watch what he was doing. I sat up straight, looking at the side-horse, which with one leg wearily stretched out, painfully whisked its tail that was tied in a knot and covered with snow. The thump Ignat gave the sledge as he jumped onto his seat roused me.

'Where are we now?' I asked. 'Shall we get anywhere, say by daybreak?'

'Don't worry, we'll get you there,' he replied. 'Now that I have changed, my feet are much warmer.'

And he drove on, the bell began to ring, the sledged swayed again, and the wind whistled under the runners. We again started to swim over the limitless sea of snow.

X

I fell soundly asleep. When Alyoshka woke me up by pushing me with his foot, and I opened my eyes, it was already morning. It seemed even colder than in the night. No more snow was falling from above, but a stiff dry wind continued to sweep the powdery snow across the plain, and especially under the hoofs of the horses and the runners of the sledge. In the east, to our right, the sky was heavy and of a dark bluish colour, but bright orange oblique streaks were growing more and more defined in it. Overhead, through flying white clouds as yet scarcely tinged, gleamed the pale blue of the sky; on the left, bright, light clouds were drifting. Everywhere, as far as eye could see, deep snow lay over the plain in sharply defined layers. Here and there could be seen greyish mounds, over which fine, crisp, powdery snow swept steadily. No track either of sledge, man, or beast could be seen. The outlines and colour of the driver's back and of the horses were clearly and sharply visible even on the white background. The rim of Ignat's dark-blue cap, his collar, his hair, and even his boots were white. The sledge was completely covered with snow. The right side and forelock of the grey shaft-horse were thick with snow, the legs of the horse on my side were covered with it up to the knee, and its curly sweating flank was covered and frozen to a rough surface. The tassel still bobbed up and down in tune to any rhythm you liked to imagine, and the side-horse itself kept running in the same way, only the sunken, heaving belly and drooping ears showing how exhausted it was. The one novel object that attracted my attention was a verst-post from which the snow was falling to the ground, and near which to the right the snow was swept into a mound by the wind, which still kept raging and throwing the crisp snow from side to side. I was very much surprised that we had travelled all night, twelve hours, with the same horses, without knowing where, and had arrived after all. Our bell seemed to tinkle yet more cheerfully. Ignat kept wrapping his cloak around him and shouting; the horses behind us snorted, and the bells of the little old man's and the advice-giver's troika tinkled, but the driver who had been asleep had certainly strayed from us in the steppe. After going another half-mile we came across the fresh, only partly obliterated, traces of a three-horsed sledge, and here and there pink spots of blood, probably from a horse that had overreached itself.

'That's Filipp. Fancy his being ahead of us!' said Ignat.

But here by the roadside a lonely little house with a signboard was seen in the midst of the snow, which covered it almost to the top of the windows and to the roof. Near the inn stood a troika of grey horses, their coats curly with sweat, their legs outstretched and their heads drooping wearily. At the door there was a shovel and the snow had been cleared away, but the howling wind continued to sweep and whirl snow off the roof.

At the sound of our bells, a tall, ruddy-faced, red-haired peasant came out with a glass of vodka in his hand, and shouted something. Ignat turned to me and asked permission to stop. Then for the first time I saw his mug.

XI

His face was not swarthy and lean with a straight nose, as I had expected judging by his hair and figure. It was a round, jolly, very snub-nosed mug, with a large mouth and bright light-blue eyes. His cheeks and neck were red, as if rubbed with flannel; his eyebrows, his long eyelashes, and the down that smoothly covered the bottom of his face, were plastered with snow and were quite white. We were only half a mile from our station and we stopped.

'Only be quick about it!' I said.

'Just one moment,' replied Ignat, springing down and walking over to Filipp.

'Let's have it, brother,' he said, taking the mitten from his right hand and throwing it down with his whip on the snow, and tossing back his head he emptied at a gulp the glass that was handed to him.

The innkeeper, probably a discharged Cossack, came out with a half-bottle in his hand.

'Who shall I serve?' said he.

Tall Vasily, a thin, brown-haired peasant, with a goatee beard, and the advice-giver, a stout, light-haired man with a thick beard framing his red face, came forward and also drank a glass each. The little old man too went over to the drinkers, but was not served, and he went back to his horses, which were fastened behind the sledge, and began stroking one of them on the back and croup.

The little old man's appearance was just what I had imagined it to be: small, thin, with a wrinkled livid face, a scanty beard, sharp little nose, and worn yellow teeth. He had a new driver's cap on, but his coat was shabby, worn, smeared with tar, torn on one shoulder, had holes in the skirt, and did not cover his knees, or the homespun trousers which were tucked into his huge felt boots. He himself was bent over, puckered up, his face and knees trembled, and he tramped about near the sledge evidently trying to get warm.

'Come, Mitrich, you should have a glass; you'd warm right up,' said the advice-giver.

Mitrich's face twitched. He adjusted the harness of one of his horses, straightened the bow above its head, and came over to me.

'Well, sir,' he said, taking the cap off his grey head and bending low, 'we have been wandering about together all night, looking for the road: won't you give me enough for a small glass? Really sir, your honour! I haven't anything to get warm on,' he added with an ingratiating smile.

I gave him a quarter-rouble. The innkeeper brought out a small glass and handed it to the old man. He took off his mitten, together with the whip that hung on it, and put out his small, dark, rough, and rather livid hand towards the glass; but his thumb refused to obey him, as though it did not belong to him. He was unable to hold the glass and dropped it on the snow, spilling the wine.

All the drivers burst out laughing.

'See how frozen Mitrich is, he can't even hold the wine.'

But Mitrich was greatly grieved at having spilt the wine.

However, they filled another glass for him and poured it into his mouth. He became cheerful in a moment, ran into the inn, lit his pipe, showed his worn yellow teeth, and began to swear with every word he spoke. Having drained the last glass, the drivers returned to their troikas and we started again.

The snow kept growing whiter and brighter so that it hurt one's eyes to look at it. The orange-tinted reddish streaks rose higher and higher, and growing brighter and brighter spread upwards over the sky; even the red disc of the sun became visible on the horizon through the blue-grey clouds; the sky grew more brilliant and of a deeper blue. On the road near the settlement the sledge tracks were clear, distinct, and yellowish, and here and there we were jolted by pot-holes in the road; one could feel a pleasant lightness and freshness in the tense, frosty air.

My troika went very fast. The head of the shaft-horse, and its neck with its mane fluttering around the bow, swayed swiftly from side to side almost in one place under the special bell, the tongue of which no longer struck the sides but scraped against them. The good side-horses tugged together at the frozen and twisted braces, and sprang energetically, while the tassel bobbed from right under the horse's belly to the breeching. Now and then a side-horse would stumble from the beaten track into the snowdrift, throwing up the snow into our eyes as it briskly got out again. Ignat shouted in his merry tenor; the dry frosty snow squeaked under the runners; behind us two little bells were ringing resonantly and festively, and I could hear the tipsy shouting of the drivers. I looked back. The grey shaggy side-horses, with their necks outstretched and breathing evenly, their bits awry, were leaping over the snow. Filipp, flourishing his whip, was adjusting his cap; the little old man, with his legs hanging out, lay in the middle of the sledge as before.

Two minutes later my sledge scraped over the boards before the clean-swept entrance of the station house, and Ignat turned to me his snow-covered merry face, smelling of frost.

'We've got you here after all, sir!' he said.

LUCERNE

FROM THE NOTES OF PRINCE D. NEKHLYUDOV

8 July

Last night I arrived at Lucerne, and put up at the best hotel here, the Schweizerhof.

'Lucerne, an ancient town and the capital of the canton, situated on the shore of the Lake of Lucerne,' says Murray,* 'is one of the most romantic places in Switzerland: here three important high roads meet, and it is only one hour by steam-boat to Mount Rigi, from which one of the most magnificent views in the world can be seen.'

Whether this be right or not, other guide-books say the same, and so tourists of all nationalities, especially the English, flock here.

The magnificent five-storeyed Schweizerhof Hotel was recently erected on the quay, close to the lake at the very place where of old there had been a roofed and crooked bridge* with chapels at its corners and carvings on its beams. Now, thanks to the enormous influx of English people, their needs, their tastes, and their money, the old bridge has been torn down and a granite quay, as straight as a stick, erected, on which straight, four-cornered, five-storeyed houses have been built, in front of which two rows of little lindens with stakes to them have been planted, between which the usual small green benches have been placed. This is a promenade, and here Englishwomen wearing Swiss straw hats, and Englishmen in stout and comfortable clothes, walk about enjoying what has been produced for them. Perhaps such quays and houses and lime trees and Englishmen are all very well in some places, but not here amid this strangely majestic and yet inexpressibly harmonious and gentle nature.

When I went up to my room and opened the window facing the lake I was at first literally blinded and shaken by the beauty of that water, those mountains, and the sky. I felt an inward restlessness and a need to express somehow that excess of something which suddenly filled my soul to overflowing. At that moment I felt a desire to embrace someone, to hug him closely, to tickle and pinch him, in general to do something extraordinary to him and to myself.

It was past six and had rained all day, but was now beginning to clear up. The lake, light-blue like burning sulphur, and dotted with little boats which left vanishing tracks behind them, seemed motionless, smooth, and convex before my windows, while it spread out between its variegated green shores, then passed into the distance where it narrowed between two enormous promontories, and, darkening, leaned against and disappeared among the pile of mountains, clouds, and glaciers that towered one above the other. In the foreground were the moist, fresh-green, far-stretching shores with their reeds, meadows, gardens, and chalets; further off were dark-green wooded promontories crowned by ruined castles; in the background was the rugged, purple-white distance with its fantastic, rocky, dull-white, snow-covered mountain crests, the whole bathed in the delicate, transparent azure of the air and lit up by warm sunset rays that pierced the torn clouds. Neither on the lake nor on the mountains, nor in the sky, was there a single precise line, or one precise colour, or one unchanging moment: everywhere was motion, irregularity, fantastic shapes, an endless intermingling and variety of shades and lines, and over it all lay tranquillity, softness, unity, and the inevitability of the beautiful. And here, before my very window, amid this undefined, confused, unfettered beauty, the straight white line of the quay stretched stupidly and artificially, with its lime trees, their supports, and the green benches—miserable, vulgar human productions which did not blend with the general harmony of the beauty as did the distant chalets and ruins, but on the contrary clashed coarsely with it. My eyes continually encountered that dreadfully straight quay, and I felt a desire to push it away or demolish it, as I would wipe off a black smudge I could see on my nose. But the embankment with the English people walking about on it remained where it was, and I instinctively tried to find a point of view from which it would not be visible. I found a way to do this, and sat till dinner-time all alone, enjoying the incomplete, but all the more tormentingly sweet feeling one experiences when one gazes in solitude on the beauty of nature.

At half-past seven I was called to dinner. In the large, splendidly decorated room on the ground floor two tables were laid for at least a hundred persons. For about three minutes the silent movement of assembling visitors continued, the rustle of women's dresses, light footsteps, whispered discussions with the very polite and elegant waiters, but at last all the seats were occupied by men and women very well and even richly and in general extraordinarily immaculately dressed. As usual in Switzerland the majority of the visitors were English, and therefore the chief characteristics of the common table were the strict decorum they regard as a law, a reserve not based on pride, but on the absence of any necessity for intimacy, and on the lonely contentment with the comfortable and agreeable satisfaction of their needs. On all sides gleamed the whitest of laces, the whitest of collars, the whitest of natural and artificial teeth, and the whitest of complexions and hands. But the faces, many of them very handsome, expressed only a consciousness of their own well-being and a complete lack of interest in all that surrounded them unless it directly concerned themselves; and the whitest of hands in gloves with rings on moved only to adjust a collar, to cut up beef, or to lift a wine glass: no heartfelt emotion was reflected in their movements. Occasionally families would exchange a few words among themselves in subdued voices about the pleasant flavour of this or that dish or wine, or the lovely view from Mount Rigi. Individual tourists, men and women, sat beside one another lonely, silent, not even exchanging a look. If occasionally some two among these hundred people spoke to one another it was sure to be about the weather and the ascent of Mount Rigi. Knives and forks moved on the plates with scarcely any sound, food was taken a little at a time, peas and other vegetables were invariably eaten with a fork. The waiters, involuntarily subdued by the general silence, asked in a whisper what wine you would take. At such dinners I always feel depressed, uncomfortable, and in the end melancholy. I always feel as if I were guilty of something and am being punished, as I used to be when, as a child, I was put in a chair when I had been naughty, and ironically told: 'Rest yourself, my dear!' while my youthful blood surged in my veins and I heard the merry shouts of my brothers in the next room. Formerly I tried to rebel against the feeling of oppression I experienced during such dinners, but in vain: all those dead faces have an insuperable effect on me and I become just as dead myself. I desire nothing, think nothing, and do not even observe. At first I used to try to talk to my neighbours; but except for phrases apparently repeated a hundred thousand times in the same place and by the same people I got no response. And yet not all these frozen people are stupid and unfeeling, on the contrary many of them, no doubt, have an inner life just such as my own, and in many of them it may be much more complex and interesting. Then why do they deprive themselves of one of life's greatest pleasures—the enjoyment of each other, the enjoyment of a human being?

How different it was in our Paris *pension*, where some twenty of us, of various nationalities, professions, and dispositions, under the influence of French sociability used to meet at the common table for amusement! There, from one end of the table to the other, conversation, interspersed with jests and puns, even if in broken language, at once became general. There everyone, not troubling how it would sound, said anything that came into his head; there we had our philosopher, our debater, our *bel esprit*,[1] and our victim, everything was in common. There immediately after dinner we pushed away the table and on the dusty carpet danced the polka, in time or out, till late in the evening. There, even if we were inclined to flirt and were not very clever or respectable, we were human beings. The Spanish countess with her romantic adventures, the Italian abbé who declaimed the *Divine Comedy* after dinner, the American doctor who had the entrée to the Tuileries,* the young playwright with long hair, and the pianist who, according to her account, had composed the best polka in the world, the unhappy widow who was a beauty and had three rings on every finger—we all treated one another like human beings, in a friendly if superficial manner, and carried away, some of us light, and others sincere and cordial memories. But seated at those English *tables d'hôte*,[2] I often think, as I look at all these silk dresses, laces, ribbons, rings, and pomaded locks, how many live women would be happy and make others happy with these adornments. It is strange to think how many potential friends and lovers, very happy friends and lovers, may be sitting there side by side without knowing it, and, God knows why, will never know it and never give one another the happiness which they might so easily give and which they desire so much.

I began to feel melancholy, as always after such a dinner, and without finishing my dessert went in very low spirits to stroll about the town. The narrow, dirty, unlighted streets, the shops closing, the

---

[1] 'Wit'.   [2] 'Hotel dining-room tables'.

encounters I had with tipsy workmen and with women going bare-headed to fetch water, or others wearing hats who flitted along the walls of the side-streets and continually glanced round, not only did not dispel my ill humour but even increased it. It had already grown quite dark in the streets when, without looking around me and without any thought in my head, I turned back to the hotel hoping by sleep to rid myself of my dismal frame of mind. I was feeling terribly chilled at heart, lonely and depressed, as sometimes happens without apparent cause upon arrival at a new place.

Looking at nothing but the ground at my feet I walked along the quay towards the Schweizerhof, when I was suddenly struck by the sound of some strange but exceedingly sweet and agreeable music. These sounds had an immediately vivifying effect on me, as if a bright cheerful light had penetrated my soul. I felt myself happy and cheerful. My dormant attention was again alive to all the objects surrounding me. The beauty of the night and of the lake, to which I had been feeling indifferent, suddenly struck me joyfully like a novelty. In an instant I involuntarily noticed both the heavy grey patches of cloud on the dark blue of the sky lit up by the rising moon, the smooth dark-green lake with the little lights reflected on it, and the mist-covered mountains in the distance; I heard the croaking of the frogs from Freschenburg, and the fresh limpid whistle of quails on the opposite shore. But directly in front of me, on the spot whence the sounds to which my attention was chiefly directed came, I saw amid the semi-darkness a throng of people collected in a half-circle in the middle of the road, and at some short distance from them a tiny man in black clothes. Behind the people and the man the black poplars in the garden were gracefully silhouetted on the dark grey and blue ragged sky, and the severe spires on each side of the ancient cathedral towered majestically.

I drew nearer, the sounds became more distinct, and at some distance I could clearly distinguish the full chords of a guitar which vibrated sweetly in the evening air and several voices, which intercepting one another did not actually sing the melody but indicated it by chiming in at the chief passages. The tune was something in the nature of a charming and graceful mazurka. The voices sometimes seemed nearer and sometimes farther away; now you could hear a tenor, now a bass, and now a guttural falsetto with a warbling Tyrolese* yodel. It was not a song, but the light, masterly sketch of a song. I could not make out what it was, but it was beautiful. The passionate soft chords of the guitar, that sweet gentle melody, and the lonely little figure of the man in black against the fantastic background of the dark lake, the gleaming moon, the two tall spires silently stretching upwards, and the black poplars in the garden, were all strangely but inexpressibly beautiful, or so it seemed to me.

All the confused and arbitrary impressions of life suddenly received meaning and charm. It was as if a fresh and fragrant flower had bloomed within me. Instead of the weariness, dullness, and indifference towards everything in the world that I had felt a moment before, I suddenly experienced a need for love, a fullness of hope, and a spontaneous joy of life. 'What can I possibly want, or desire?' I involuntarily thought. 'Here it is, beauty and poetry surround me on all sides. Inhale full deep draughts of it with all the strength that is in you, enjoy it. What more do you need? It is all yours, and all good.'

I went nearer. The little man seemed to be an itinerant singer from the Tyrol. He stood before the windows of the hotel with one foot advanced, his head thrown back, and while thrumming his guitar was singing his graceful song in those different voices. I immediately felt an affection for him, and gratitude for the change he had brought about in me. As far as I could see, he was dressed in an old black coat, had short black hair, and wore a very ordinary old cap on his head. There was nothing artistic about his attire, but his jaunty, childishly merry pose and movements, with his diminutive stature, produced a touching yet amusing effect. On the steps, at the windows, and on the balconies of the brilliantly lighted hotel, stood ladies resplendent in full-skirted dresses, gentlemen with the whitest of collars, a porter and footmen in gold-embroidered liveries; in the street, in the semicircle of the crowd, and further along the boulevard among the lime trees, elegantly dressed waiters, cooks in the whitest of caps and blouses, girls with their arms around one another, and passers-by, had gathered and stopped. They all seemed to experience the same sensation that I did, and stood in silence round the singer, listening attentively. Everything was quiet, only at intervals in the singing, from far away across the water came the rhythmic sound of a hammer, and from the Freschenburg shore the staccato trills of the frogs intermingling with the fresh, monotonous whistle of the quails.

In the darkness of the street the little man warbled like a nightingale, couplet after couplet and song after song. Though I had drawn close to him, his singing continued to give me great pleasure. His small voice was extremely pleasing, and the delicacy, the taste, and the sense of proportion with which he managed that voice were extraordinary, and showed immense natural gifts. He sang the refrain differently after each couplet and it was evident that all these graceful variations came to him freely and instantaneously.

Among the throng, above in the Schweizerhof and below on the boulevard, appreciative whispers could often be heard, and a respectful silence reigned. The balconies and windows kept filling, and by the hotel lights more and more elegantly dressed men and women could be seen leaning out picturesquely. The passers-by stopped and everywhere in the shadows on the embankment groups of men and women stood under the lime trees. Near me, separated from the rest of the crowd and smoking cigars, stood an aristocratic waiter and the chef. The chef seemed to feel the charm of the music strongly and at every high falsetto note rapturously winked, nodded, and nudged the waiter in ecstatic perplexity, with a look that said: 'How he sings, eh?' The waiter, by whose broad smile I detected the pleasure the singing gave him, replied to the chef's nudgings by shrugging his shoulders to show that it was hard to surprise him, and that he had heard much better things than this.

In an interval in the song, while the singer was clearing his throat, I asked the waiter who the man was and whether he came there often.

'Well, he comes about twice a summer,' replied the waiter. 'He is from Aargau*—just a beggar.'

'And are there many like him about?' I asked.

'Oh, yes,' replied the man not having at first understood what I was asking, but having afterwards made it out, he added: 'Oh no, he is the only one I know of. There are no others.'

Just then the little man, having finished his first song, briskly turned his guitar over and said something in his German patois, which I could not understand but which caused the crowd to laugh.

'What did he say?' I asked.

'He says his throat is dry and he would like some wine,' replied the waiter near me.

'Well, I suppose he is fond of drink.'

'Yes, such people are all like that,' answered the waiter with a deprecatory gesture of his hand.

The singer took off his cap and with a flourish of the guitar went up to the hotel. Throwing back his head he addressed the people at the windows and on the balconies: '*Messieurs et Mesdames*,' he said with a half-Italian and half-German accent and the intonation conjurors employ when addressing their audience: '*Si vous croyez que je gagne quelque chose, vous vous trompez; je ne suis qu'un pauvre tiable.*'[1] He paused and waited a moment in silence, but as no one gave him anything, he again jerked his guitar and said: '*A présent messieurs et mesdames, je vous chanterais l'air du Righi.*'[2]

The audience up above kept silent, but continued to stand in expectation of the next song; below, among the throng, there was laughter, probably because he expressed himself so queerly and because no one had given him anything. I gave him a few centimes, which he threw nimbly from one hand to the other, and put into his waistcoat pocket. Then putting on his cap again he began to sing a sweet and graceful Tyrolese song which he called '*l'air du Righi*'. This song, which he had left to the last, was even better than the others, and on all sides among the now increased crowd one heard sounds of appreciation. He finished the song. Again he flourished his guitar, took off his cap, held it out, made two steps towards the windows, and again repeated his incomprehensible phrase: '*Messieurs et Mesdames. si vous croyez que je gagne quelque chose—*' which he evidently considered very smart and witty, but in his voice and movements I now detected a certain hesitation and childlike timidity which were the more noticeable on account of his small figure. The elegant audience still stood just as picturesquely grouped in the windows and on the balconies, the lights shining on their rich attire. A few of them talked in decorously subdued voices, apparently about the singer who was standing before them with outstretched hand, others looked with attentive curiosity down at the little black figure; on one balcony could be heard a young girl's merry laughter.

In the crowd below the talking and laughter grew louder and louder. The singer repeated his phrase a third time, in a still feebler voice, and this time he did not even finish it, but again held out his cap, and then drew it back immediately. And for the second time not

---

[1] 'If you think I earn anything you are mistaken. I am only a poor devil.'

[2] 'Now, gentlemen and ladies, I will sing you the Rigi song.'

one of those hundreds of brilliantly dressed people who had come to hear him threw him a single penny. The crowd laughed unmercifully. The little singer seemed to me to shrink still more into himself. He took the guitar in his other hand, lifted his cap above his head, and said: '*Messieurs et Mesdames, je vous remercie, et je vous souhaite une bonne nuit.*'[1] Then he replaced his cap. The crowd roared with merry laughter. The handsome men and women, quietly conversing, gradually disappeared from the balconies. The strolls on the boulevard were resumed. The street that had been quiet during the singing again became animated, only a few persons looked at the singer from a distance and laughed. I heard the little man mutter something to himself. He turned and, seeming to grow still smaller, took off quickly towards the town. The merry strollers, still watching him, followed him at a certain distance, and laughed.

My mind was in a whirl. I was at a loss to understand what it all meant, and without moving from the spot where I had been, I senselessly gazed into the darkness after the tiny retreating figure of the man as he went striding rapidly towards the town and at the laughing strollers who followed him. I felt pained, grieved, and above all ashamed for the little man, for the crowd, and for myself, as if it were I who had been asking for money and had received nothing, and had been laughed at. I, too, without looking back and with an aching heart, moved off with rapid steps and went to the entrance of the Schweizerhof. I could not yet account for my emotions, but only knew that something heavy and unsolved filled my heart and oppressed me.

At the brilliantly lit entrance I met the hall porter who politely stepped aside, and an English family. A tall, portly, handsome man with black side-whiskers worn in the English fashion, a black hat on his head, a plaid over his arm, and an expensive cane in his hand, was walking with lazy self-confidence arm in arm with a lady in a grey silk gown, and a cap trimmed with bright ribbons and exquisite lace. Beside them walked a pretty, fresh-complexioned girl wearing a graceful Swiss hat trimmed with a feather *à la Mousquetaire*,* and with charming long soft flaxen curls that fell over her fair face. In front of them skipped a ten-year-old girl with rosy cheeks and plump white knees showing from under the finest embroideries.

---

[1] 'Thank you, ladies and gentlemen. I wish you good-night.'

'A lovely night!' said the lady in a tender, happy voice, just as I passed them.

'Ohe!' lazily muttered the Englishman, for whom life was so comfortable that he did not even feel like talking. To all of them life in this world was so comfortable, convenient, clean, and easy; their movements and faces expressed such indifference to any other kind of life than their own, such assurance that the porter would step aside for them and bow, and that on returning they would find comfortable rooms and beds, that it all must be so and that they had a right to it all, that I involuntarily contrasted them with the vagrant singer who, tired and perhaps hungry, was escaping ashamed from the laughing crowd, and I realized what it was that weighed on my heart like a stone, and I felt indescribable anger against these people. Twice I walked to and fro past the Englishman, and each time with inexpressible pleasure avoided making way for him and pushed him with my elbow; then darting down the steps I hastened through the darkness in the direction of the town, where the little man had disappeared.

Having overtaken three men who were walking together, I asked them where the singer was. They laughed and pointed straight ahead. He was walking quickly, by himself. No one went near him, and he seemed to me to be angrily muttering something to himself. I caught up with him and proposed that we go somewhere and drink a bottle of wine. He went on walking just as fast and looked disconsolately at me, but when he had made out what I wanted, he stopped.

'Well, I won't refuse it, if you are so kind,' he said. 'There is a small café here, we could go in there. It's a plain place,' he added, pointing to a pub which was still open.

The word 'plain' involuntarily suggested to me the idea of not going to the plain café but to the Schweizerhof, where the people were who had listened to him. Though in timid agitation he several times declined to go to the Schweizerhof, saying that it was too fine there, I insisted on it and he walked back along the quay with me pretending not to be at all abashed, and gaily swinging his guitar. Several idle strollers drew near as soon as I went up to the singer and listened to what I was saying: and now, after arguing among themselves, they followed us to the hotel entrance, probably expecting some further performance from the Tyrolese.

I met a waiter in the vestibule and asked him for a bottle of wine, but he merely looked at us with a smile and ran past. The head waiter, to whom I addressed the same request, listened to me seriously, and having scanned the tiny figure of the timid singer from head to foot, sternly told the porter to take us to the room on the left. This room was a bar for common people, the whole furniture consisted of bare wooden tables and benches, and a hunchbacked woman was washing up dishes in a corner. The waiter who came to take our order looked at us with a mildly supercilious smile and, thrusting his hands in his pockets, exchanged remarks with the hunchbacked dish-washer. He evidently wished to let us know that, feeling himself immeasurably superior to the singer in social standing as well as on his own merits, he was not at all offended, but even quite amused, to be waiting on us.

'Will you have *vin ordinaire*?' he asked with a knowing look, winking towards my companion and shifting his napkin from one arm to the other.

'Champagne, and your very best!' I said, trying to assume a haughty and imposing air. But neither the champagne nor my endeavour to look haughty and imposing had any effect on the waiter: he grinned, stood awhile gazing at us, looked deliberately at his gold watch, and went leisurely and with soft steps out of the room as if he were out for a stroll. He soon returned with the wine and with two other waiters. The two waiters sat down near the dish-washer and gazed at us with the amused attention and bland smiles with which parents watch their dear children when they play nicely. Only the hunchbacked dish-washer seemed to look at us with sympathy rather than irony. Though I felt it very uncomfortable and awkward to talk with the singer and entertain him under the fire of those eyes, I tried to do my part with as little constraint as possible. In the lighted room I could see him better. He was a tiny, well-proportioned, wiry man, almost a midget, with bristly black hair, large tearful black eyes without lashes, and a thoroughly pleasant and attractively shaped little mouth. He had short side-whiskers, rather short hair, and his clothes were simple and poor. He was dingy, tattered, sunburnt, and had in general the look of a labourer. He was more like a poor pedlar than an artist. Only in his moist, shining eyes and puckering mouth was there something original and touching. Judging by his appearance he might have been anything from twenty-five to forty years old; he was in fact thirty-eight.

This is what he told me, with good-natured readiness and evident sincerity, about his life. He was from Aargau. While still a child he had lost his father and mother and had no other relations. He had never had any means of his own. He had been apprenticed to a joiner, but twenty-two years ago a bone of his finger had begun to decay, which made it impossible for him to work. He had been fond of music from his childhood and began to go round singing. Foreigners occasionally gave him money. He made a profession of it, bought a guitar, and for eighteen years had wandered through Switzerland and Italy singing in front of hotels. His whole belongings were the guitar and a purse, in which he now had only a franc and a half, which he would have to spend that night on food and lodging. He had gone every year to all the best and most frequented places in Switzerland: Zurich, Lucerne, Interlaken, Chamonix, and so on; and was now going round for the eighteenth time. He passed over the St Bernard into Italy and returned by St Gotthard or through Savoy. It was getting hard for him to walk now, because a pain in his feet which he called *Gliederzucht* (rheumatism) got worse every year when he caught cold, and his eyes and his voice were growing weaker. In spite of this he was now on his way to Interlaken, Aix-les-Bains, and over the little St Bernard to Italy, of which country he was particularly fond; in general he seemed to be very well satisfied with his life. When I asked him why he was going home and whether he had any relations there, or a house and land, his mouth puckered into a merry smile and he replied: '*Oui, le sucre est bon, il est doux pour les enfants!*'[1] and winked at the waiters.

I did not understand what he meant, but the group of waiters burst out laughing.

'I've got nothing, or would I be going about like this?' he explained. 'I go home because, after all, something draws me back to my native land.'

And he again repeated, with a sly self-satisfied smile, the phrase: '*Oui, le sucre est bon!*' and laughed good-naturedly. The waiters were very pleased and laughed heartily. Only the hunchbacked dish-washer looked at the little man seriously with her large kindly eyes and picked up the cap he had dropped from the bench during our conversation. I had noticed that wandering singers, acrobats, and

[1] 'Yes, sugar is good: it is sweet for children.'

even jugglers, like to call themselves artists, and so I hinted several times to my companion that he was an artist; but he did not at all acknowledge that quality in himself, and considered his occupation simply as a means of subsistence. When I asked him whether he did not himself compose the songs he sang, he was surprised at so strange a question, and answered: 'How could I? They are all old Tyrolese songs.'

'But what about the Rigi song—that is not old, is it?' I said.

'No, that was composed about fifteen years ago,' he said. 'There was a German in Basle, a very clever man. He composed it. It's a splendid song! You see, he composed it for the tourists.'

And, translating them into French as he went along, he began repeating to me the words of the Rigi song, which he liked so much:

> 'If you would go up the Rigi
> You need no shoes as far as Weggis
>   (Because you go that far by steamer)
> But in Weggis take a big stick,
> And upon your arm a maiden.
> Drink a glass of wine at starting,
>   Only do not drink too much.
> For he who wants to have a drink
>   Should first have earned . . .

'Oh, it's a splendid song!' he said, as he finished.

The waiters, too, probably considered the song very good, for they came nearer to us.

'Yes, but who composed the music?' I asked.

'Oh, nobody! It comes of itself, you know—one must have something new to sing to the foreigners.'

When the ice was brought and I had poured out a glass of champagne for my companion, he seemed to feel ill at ease, and glancing round at the waiters shifted uneasily in his seat. We clinked glasses to the health of artists; he drank half a glass, and then found it necessary to raise his eyebrows in profound thought.

'It's a long time since I drank such wine, *je ne vous dis que ça.*[1] In Italy the d'Asti wine is good, but this is better still. Ah, Italy! It's splendid to be there!' he added.

---

[1] 'I only say that to you.'

'Yes, there they know how to appreciate music and artists,' I said, wishing to lead him back to the subject of his failure that evening before the Schweizerhof.

'No,' he replied. 'There, as far as music is concerned, I cannot give anyone pleasure. The Italians are themselves musicians like none others in the world: I sing only Tyrolese songs—that at any rate is a novelty for them.'

'And are the people more generous there?' I went on, wishing to make him share my resentment against the guests at the Schweizerhof. 'It couldn't happen there, could it, as it did here, that in an immense hotel frequented by rich people, out of a hundred who listen to an artist not one gives him anything?'

My question had quite a different effect on him from what I had expected. It did not enter his head to be indignant with them: on the contrary he detected in my remark a reflection on his talent, which had failed to elicit any reward, and he tried to justify himself to me.

'One does not get much every time,' he replied. 'Sometimes my voice fails or I am tired. Today, you know, I have been walking for nine hours and singing almost all the time. That is hard. And the great people, the aristocrats, don't always care to hear Tyrolese songs.'

'But still, how could they give nothing at all?' I insisted.

He did not understand my remark.

'It's not that,' he said, 'the chief thing here is, *on est très serré pour la police*,[1] that's where the trouble is. Here under their republican laws* you are not allowed to sing, but in Italy you may go about as much as you please, and no one will say a word to you. Here they allow it only when they please, and if they don't please, they may put you in prison.'

'How is that? Is it possible?'

'Yes, if they caution you once and you sing again they may imprison you. I was there for three months,' he said smiling, as though this were one of his pleasantest recollections.

'Oh, that's dreadful!' I said. 'What for?'

'That is so under the new republican laws,' he continued, growing animated. 'They don't want to understand that a poor fellow must live somehow. If I were not a cripple, I would work. But does my

---

[1] 'One is much cramped by the police.'

singing hurt anyone? What does it mean? The rich can live as they please, but *un pauvre tiable* like myself cannot even live. Are these the laws a republic should have? If so, we don't want a republic— isn't that so, dear sir? We don't want a republic, but we want—we simply want . . . we want'—he hesitated awhile—'we want natural laws.'

I filled up his glass.

'You are not drinking,' I said to him.

He took the glass in his hand and bowed to me.

'I know what you want,' he said, screwing up his eyes and shaking his finger at me. 'You want to make me drunk, so as to see what will happen to me; but no, you won't succeed!'

'Why should I want to make you drunk?' I said. 'I only want to give you pleasure.'

Probably he was sorry to have offended me by interpreting my intention wrongly, for he grew confused, got up, and pressed my elbow.

'No, no, I was only joking!' he said, looking at me with a beseeching expression in his moist eyes.

Then he uttered some fearfully intricate, complicated sentence intended to imply that I was a good fellow after all.

'*Je ne vous dis que ça!*' he concluded.

So we continued drinking and talking and the waiters continued to watch us unceremoniously and, as it seemed, to make fun of us. Despite my interest in our conversation I could not help noticing them and, I confess, I grew more and more angry. One of them got up, came over to the little man, looked down on the crown of his head, and began to smile. I had accumulated a store of anger for the guests at the Schweizerhof which I had not yet been able to vent on anyone, and I own that this audience of waiters irritated me beyond endurance. Then, without taking off his cap, the porter came in and, leaning his elbows on the table, sat down beside me. This last cir- cumstance, having stung my self-esteem or vanity, finally caused the oppressive rage that had been smouldering in me all the evening to explode. Why when I was alone at the entrance did he humbly bow to me, and now that I am sitting with an itinerant singer, why does he sprawl near me so rudely? I was filled with a boiling rage of indigna- tion which I like in myself and even stimulate when it besets me, because it has a tranquillizing effect, and gives, at least for a short time, an unusual suppleness, energy, and power to all my physical and mental faculties.

I jumped up.

'What are you laughing at?' I shouted at the waiter, feeling that I was growing pale and that my lips were involuntarily twitching.

'I am not laughing; it's nothing!' said the waiter stepping back.

'No, you are laughing at this gentleman. . . . And what right have you to be here and to be sitting down, when there are visitors here? Don't dare to sit here!' I cried.

The porter got up with a growl and moved towards the door.

'What right have you to laugh at this gentleman and to sit near him, when he is a visitor and you are a lackey? Why didn't you laugh at me or sit beside me at dinner this evening? Is it because he is poorly dressed and sings in the street, while I wear good clothes, is that it? He is poor, but I am convinced that he is a thousand times better than you, for he insults no one, while you are insulting him!'

'But I am not doing anything!' replied my enemy the waiter, timidly. 'Do I prevent his sitting here?'

The waiter did not understand me and my German speech was lost on him. The rude porter tried to take the waiter's part, but I attacked him so vehemently that he pretended that he, too, did not understand me, and waved his arm. The hunchbacked dish-washer, either noticing my heated condition and afraid of a scandal, or because she really shared my views, took my part and, trying to interpose herself between me and the porter, began to persuade him to be quiet, saying that I was right and asking me to calm myself. '*Der Herr hat recht; Sie haben recht!*'[1] she said firmly. The singer presented a most piteous, frightened appearance and, evidently without understanding why I was excited or what I was aiming at, begged me to go away quickly. But my angry loquacity burned stronger and stronger in me. I recalled everything: the crowd that had laughed at him, and the audience that had given him nothing—and I would not quiet down on any account. I think that if the waiters and the porter had not been so yielding I should have enjoyed a fight with them, or could have whacked the defenceless young English lady on the head with a stick. Had I been at

---

[1] 'The gentleman is right; you are right.'

Sevastopol* at that moment I would gladly have rushed into an English trench to hack and slash at them.

'And why did you show me and this gentleman into this room, and not the other, eh?' I asked the porter, seizing his arm to prevent his going away. 'What right had you to decide from his appearance that this gentleman must be in this and not in the other room? Are not all who pay on an equal footing in an hotel—not only in a republic, but all over the world? Yours is a lousy republic! . . . This is your equality! You dare not show those English people into this room, the very Englishmen who listened to this gentleman without paying him, that is, who each stole from him the few centimes they ought to have given him. How dared you show us in here?'

'The other room is closed,' replied the porter.

'No!' I cried. 'That's not true, it's not closed.'

'You know better then.'

'I know! I know that you are lying.'

The porter turned his shoulder away from me.

'What is the use of talking?' he muttered.

'No, not "what is the use . . ." ' I shouted. 'Take us to the other room at once!'

Despite the hunchbacked woman's and the singer's entreaties that we should go away, I had the head waiter called and went into the other room with my companion. When the head waiter heard my angry voice and saw my excited face he did not argue with me, but told me with contemptuous civility that I might go where I liked. I could not convict the porter of his lie, as he had disappeared before I went into the other room.

The room was really open and lighted up, and at one of the tables the Englishman with the lady was having supper. Though we were shown to another table, I sat down with the dirty singer close to the Englishman, and ordered the unfinished bottle to be brought to us.

The Englishman and the lady looked first with surprise and then with anger at the little man who sat beside me more dead than alive. They exchanged some words, and the lady pushed away her plate, and rustled her silk dress as they both went away. Through the panes in the door I could see the Englishman speaking angrily to the waiter, pointing in our direction all the time. The waiter thrust his head in at the door and looked towards us. I waited with pleasure for them to come to turn us out, and to be able at last to vent my whole indignation on them—but fortunately, though I then regretted it, they left us in peace.

The singer, who had before refused the wine, now hastened to empty the bottle in order to get away as soon as possible. However, he thanked me, feelingly I thought, for his entertainment. His moist eyes became still more tearful and shining, and he expressed his gratitude in a most curious and confused little speech. But that speech, in which he said that if everyone respected artists as I did he would be well off and that he wished me all happiness, was very pleasant to me. We went out into the vestibule. The waiters were there and my enemy the porter who seemed to be complaining of me to them. They all looked on me, I think, as insane. I let the little man come up to them all, and then, with all the respect I could show, I took off my hat and pressed his hand with its ossified and withered finger. The waiters pretended not to take any notice of me, but one of them burst into a sardonic laugh.

After bowing to me, the singer disappeared into the darkness, and I went up to my room, wishing to sleep off all these impressions and the foolish, childish anger which had so unexpectedly beset me. Feeling too agitated however for sleep, I went out again into the street to walk about till I calmed down, and also I must admit with a vague hope of finding an opportunity to come across the porter, the waiter, or the Englishman, to prove to them how cruel and above all how unjust they had been. But I met no one except the porter, who turned his back on seeing me, and I paced up and down the embankment all alone.

'This is the strange fate of art!' I reflected, having grown a little calmer. 'All seek it and love it, it is the one thing everybody wants and tries to find in life, yet nobody acknowledges its power, nobody values this greatest blessing in the world, nor esteems or is grateful to those who give it to mankind. Ask anyone you like of all these guests at the Schweizerhof what is the greatest blessing in the world, and everyone, or ninety-nine out of a hundred, assuming a sardonic expression, will say that the best thing in the world is money! "Maybe this idea does not please you and does not conform to your lofty ideas," he will tell you, "but what is to be done if human life is so constituted that money alone gives people happiness? I cannot help letting my reason see the world as it is," he will add, "that is— see the truth."

'Pitiful is your reason, pitiful the happiness you desire, and you are a miserable being who does not know what you want. Why have you all left your country, your relations, your occupations, and your financial affairs, and congregated here in this small Swiss town of Lucerne? Why did you all come out onto the balcony this evening and listen in respectful silence to the songs of that poor little mendicant? And had he chosen to go on singing you would still have remained silent and listened. What money, even millions of it, could have driven you all from your country and assembled you in this little corner, Lucerne? Could money have gathered you all on those balconies and made you stand for half an hour silent and motionless? No! One thing alone causes you to act, and will always influence you more strongly than any other motive power in life, and that is the need for poetry, which you do not acknowledge, but which you feel and will always feel as long as there is anything human left in you. The word "poetry" seems ridiculous to you. You use it as a scornful reproach; you perhaps allow love of the poetic in children and in silly girls, but even then you laugh at them; but for yourselves you require something positive. But children see life healthily, they love and know what men should love, and what gives happiness, but life has so enmeshed and depraved you that you laugh at the one thing you love, and seek only that which you hate and which causes you unhappiness. You are so enmeshed that you do not understand your obligation to this poor Tyrolese who has afforded you pure enjoyment, yet you feel yourselves bound to humble yourselves gratuitously before a lord, without advantage or pleasure, and for some reason sacrifice for him your comfort and convenience. What nonsense! What incomprehensible senselessness! But it was not this that struck me most this evening. This ignorance of what gives happiness, this unconsciousness of poetic enjoyment, I almost understand, or have become used to, having often met it in my life; nor was the coarse, unconscious cruelty of the crowd new to me. Whatever the advocates of the popular spirit may say, a crowd is a combination possibly of good people, but of people who have come in touch merely on their base, animal sides, and it expresses only the weakness and cruelty of human nature. How could you, children of a free, humane nation, as Christians or simply as human beings, respond with coldness and ridicule to the pure enjoyment afforded you by an unfortunate mendicant? But no, in your country there are institutions for the needy.

There are no beggars and must be none, nor must there be any compassion, on which mendicancy is based. But this man had laboured, he gave you pleasure, he implored you to give him something from your superabundance for his pains, of which you availed yourselves. But you, from your lofty, brilliant palace, regarded him with a cold smile and there was not one among you hundred, happy, rich people who threw him anything. He went away humiliated, and the senseless crowd followed him laughing, and insulted not you but him, because you were cold, cruel, and dishonest; because you stole the enjoyment he had afforded you, they insulted *him*.'

'*On the seventh of July 1857, in Lucerne, in front of the Hotel Schweizerhof in which the richest people stay, an itinerant beggar singer sang and played the guitar for half an hour. About a hundred people listened to him. The singer asked them all three times to give him something. Not one of them gave him anything, and many people laughed at him.*'

This is not fiction, but a positive fact, which can be verified by anyone who likes from the permanent residents at the Hotel Schweizerhof, after ascertaining from the papers who the foreigners were who were staying at the Schweizerhof on the 7th of July.

Here is an event the historians of our time ought to record in indelible letters of fire. This event is more significant, more serious, and has a profounder meaning, than the facts usually printed in newspapers and histories. That the English have killed another thousand Chinamen* because the Chinese buy nothing for money while their country absorbs metal coins, that the French have killed another thousand Arabs* because corn grows easily in Africa and constant warfare is useful for training armies; that the Turkish Ambassador in Naples must not be a Jew,* and that the Emperor Napoleon walks on foot at Plombières* and assures the people in print that he reigns only by the will of the whole nation—all these are words that conceal or reveal what has long been known; but the event that took place at Lucerne on 7 July appears to me to be something quite new and strange, and relates not to the eternally evil side of human nature, but to a certain epoch in social evolution. This is a fact not for the history of human actions, but for the history of progress and civilization.

Why is this inhuman fact, which would be impossible in any German, French, or Italian village, possible here where civilization, liberty, and equality have been brought to the highest point, and where the most civilized travellers from the most civilized nations congregate? Why have these developed, humane people, who collectively are capable of any honourable and humane action, no human, heartfelt feeling for a kindly personal deed? Why do these people, who in their parliaments, meetings, and societies are warmly concerned about the condition of the celibate Chinese in India,* about propagating Christianity and education in Africa,* about the establishment of societies for the betterment of the whole human race,* not find in their souls the simple, primordial feeling of one human being for another? Is it possible that they do not possess that feeling, and that its place has been occupied by the vanity, ambition, and cupidity governing these men in their parliaments, meetings, and societies? Can it be that the spread of the sensible and selfish association of men called civilization destroys and contradicts the need for instinctive, loving association? And is it possible that this is the equality for which so much innocent blood has been shed and so many crimes committed? Is it possible that nations, like children, can be made happy by the mere sound of the word 'equality'?

Equality before the law? But does the whole life of man take place in the sphere of law? Only a thousandth part of it depends on law, the rest takes place outside, in the sphere of social customs and conceptions. In this society the waiter is better dressed than the singer and insults him with impunity. I am better dressed than the waiter and insult him with impunity. The porter regards me as superior, and the singer as inferior, to himself; when I joined the singer he considered himself our equal and became rude. I grew insolent to the porter and he felt himself inferior to me. The waiter was insolent to the singer and the latter felt himself inferior to him. Can a country be free— 'positively free' as people say—in which there is a single citizen who, without having caused harm to anyone, is put in prison for doing the only thing he can do to save himself from starvation?

What an unfortunate, pitiful creature is man, with his desire for positive decisions, thrown into this ever moving, limitless ocean of good and evil, of facts, conceptions, and contradictions! For ages men have struggled and laboured to place good on one side and evil on the other. Centuries pass, and whenever an impartial mind places good and evil on the scales, the balance remains even, and the proportion of good and evil remains unaltered. If only man would learn not to judge, not to think sharply and positively, and not to answer questions presented to him only because they are for ever unanswerable! If only he understood that every idea is both false and true! False by one-sidedness resulting from man's inability to embrace the whole of truth, and true as an expression of one fact of human endeavour.

Men have made subdivisions for themselves in this eternally moving, unending, intermingled chaos of good and evil; they have traced imaginary lines on that ocean, and expect the ocean to divide itself accordingly, as if there were not millions of other subdivisions made from quite other points of view on another plane. It is true that fresh subdivisions are worked out from century to century, but millions of centuries have passed and millions more will pass. Civilization is good, barbarianism is bad. Freedom is good, captivity is bad. This imaginary knowledge destroys the instinctive, most blessed, primordial needs for kindliness in human nature. And who will define for me what is freedom, what is despotism, what is civilization, and what barbarianism? Where does the boundary lie between the one and the other? Whose soul possesses so absolute a standard of good and evil that he can measure all the confused and fleeting facts? Whose mind is so great that it can comprehend and measure even the facts of the unchanging past? And who has seen a condition in which good and evil did not exist together? And how do I know that it is not my point of view which decides whether I see more of the one than of the other? Who is capable, even for a moment, of severing himself so completely from life as to look down on it with complete detachment? We have one unerring guide, and only one, the universal Spirit, which, penetrating each separately and all of us together, implants in every individual a striving for what ought to be, that same Spirit which in the tree bids it grow towards the sun, in the flower bids it shed its seeds in the autumn, and in us bids us huddle instinctively closer to each other.

And it is that one blissful and impeccable voice that the noisy, hasty development of civilization stifles. Who is more a man and less a barbarian: that lord who, seeing the threadbare clothes of the singer, angrily left the table, and for his efforts did not give him a millionth part of his wealth, and who now sits, well fed, in a bright comfortable room, calmly discussing the affairs in China and finding the massacres committed there quite justified, or the little singer, who risking imprisonment and with a franc in his pocket has for twenty years been going over mountains and valleys doing no one any harm, but bringing consolation to them by his singing, and who was today insulted and almost driven out and, tired, hungry, and humiliated, has gone to sleep somewhere on rotting straw?

At that moment, in the dead stillness of the night, I heard somewhere in the far distance the little man's guitar and voice.

'No,' I said to myself involuntarily, 'you have no right to pity him and to be indignant at the lord's well-being. Who has weighed the inner happiness to be found in the soul of each of them? He is now sitting somewhere on a dirty door-step, gazing at the gleaming moonlit sky and gaily singing in the calm of the fragrant night; in his heart there is no reproach, or malice, or regret. And who knows what is now going on in the souls of all the people within these palatial walls? Who can tell whether among them all there is as much care-free, meek joy of life and harmony with the world as lives in the soul of that little man? Endless is the mercy and wisdom of him who has allowed and ordained that all these contradictions should exist. Only to you, insignificant worm, who rashly and wrongly try to penetrate his laws and his intentions, only to you do they seem contradictions. He looks down benignly from his bright immeasurable height and rejoices in the infinite harmony in which you move ever contradictorily and endlessly. In your pride you thought you could separate yourself from the universal law. But you, too, with your mean and petty indignation at the waiters, have responded to the harmonious need of the eternal and infinite . . .'

18 July 1857

THREE DEATHS

A TALE

I

It was autumn. Two vehicles were going along the highway at a quick
pace. In the first sat two women. One was a lady, thin and pale. The
other was a maidservant, glowingly rosy and plump. Her short dry
hair kept slipping out from under her faded bonnet and her red hand
in its torn glove kept pushing it back by fits and starts. Her full
bosom, covered by a woollen shawl, breathed health, her quick black
eyes now watched the fields as they glided past the window, now
glanced timidly at her mistress, and now restlessly scanned the
corners of the carriage. In front of her nose dangled her mistress's
bonnet, pinned to the luggage carrier, on her lap lay a puppy, her feet
were raised on the boxes standing on the floor and just audibly
tapped against them to the creaking of the coach-springs and the
clatter of the window-panes.

Having folded her hands on her knees and closed her eyes, the
lady swayed feebly against the pillows placed at her back, and, frowning slightly, coughed inwardly. On her head she had a white nightcap,
and a blue kerchief was tied round her delicate white throat. A
straight line receding under the cap parted her light brown,
extremely flat, pomaded hair, and there was something dry and
deathly about the whiteness of the skin of that wide parting. Her
flabby, rather sallow skin loosely covered the delicate and handsome
features of her face, which had a flush on the cheeks. Her lips were
dry and restless, her scanty eyelashes had no curl in them, and her
cloth travelling coat fell in straight folds over her sunken breast.
Though her eyes were closed, the lady's face bore an expression of
weariness, irritation, and habitual suffering.

A footman, leaning on the arms of his seat, was dozing on the box,
the mail-coach driver, shouting lustily, urged on his four big sweating horses, occasionally turning to the other driver who called to him
from the calèche* behind. The broad parallel tracks of the tyres
spread themselves evenly and fast on the muddy, chalky surface of

the road. The sky was grey and cold and a damp mist was settling on the fields and road. It was stuffy in the coach and there was a smell of eau-de-cologne and dust. The sick woman drew back her head and slowly opened her eyes. Her large eyes were brilliant and of a beautiful, dark colour.

'Again,' she said, nervously pushing away with her beautiful thin hand an end of her maid's cloak which had lightly touched her foot, and her mouth twitched painfully. Matryosha gathered up her cloak with both hands, rose on her strong legs, and seated herself further away. Her fresh face grew scarlet. The lady, leaning with both hands on the seat, also tried to raise herself so as to sit up higher, but her strength failed her. Her mouth twisted, and her whole face became distorted by a look of impotent, malevolent irony. 'You might at least help me! Oh, don't bother! I can do it myself, only don't put your bags or anything behind me, for goodness' sake! No, better not touch me since you don't know how to!' The lady closed her eyes and then, again quickly raising her eyelids, glared at the maid. Matryosha, looking at her, bit her red lower lip. A deep sigh rose from the sick woman's chest and turned into a cough before it was completed. She turned away, puckered her face, and clutched her chest with both hands. When the coughing fit was over she once more closed her eyes and continued to sit motionless. The carriage and calèche entered a village. Matryosha stretched out her thick hand from under her shawl and crossed herself.

'What is it?' asked her mistress.

'A post-station, madam.'

'I am asking why you crossed yourself.'

'There's a church, madam.'

The invalid turned to the window and began slowly to cross herself, looking with large wide-open eyes at the big village church her carriage was passing.

The carriage and calèche both stopped at the post-station and the sick woman's husband and doctor stepped out of the calèche and went up to the coach.

'How are you feeling?' asked the doctor, taking her pulse.

'Well, my dear, how are you? Are you tired?' asked the husband in French. 'Wouldn't you like to get out?'

Matryosha gathered up the bundles and squeezed herself into a corner so as not to interfere with their conversation.

'So-so, just the same,' replied the sick woman. 'I won't get out.'

Her husband after standing there a while went into the station house, and Matryosha, too, jumped out of the carriage and ran on tiptoe across the mud and in at the gate.

'If I feel ill, it's no reason for you not to have lunch,' said the sick woman with a slight smile to the doctor, who was standing at her window.

'None of them has any thought for me,' she added to herself as soon as the doctor, having slowly walked away from her, ran quickly up the steps to the station house. 'They are well, so they don't care. Oh, my God!'

'Well, Eduard Ivanovich?' said the husband, rubbing his hands as he met the doctor with a merry smile. 'I have ordered a lunch-basket to be brought in. What do you think about it?'

'That's fine,' replied the doctor.

'Well, how is she?' asked the husband with a sigh, lowering his voice and lifting his eyebrows.

'As I told you: it is not only impossible for her to reach Italy, but God grant that she gets even as far as Moscow, especially in this weather.'

'But what are we to do? Oh, my God, my God!' The husband covered his eyes with his hand. 'Bring it here!' he said to the man who had brought in the lunch-basket.

'She ought to have stayed at home,' said the doctor, shrugging his shoulders.

'But what could I do?' rejoined the husband. 'You know I used every possible means to get her to stay. I spoke of the expense, of our children whom we had to leave behind, and of my business affairs, but she would not listen to anything. She is making plans for life abroad as if she were in good health. To tell her of her condition would be to kill her.'

'But she is killed already, you must know that, Vasily Dmitrich. A person can't live without lungs, and new lungs won't grow. It is sad and hard, but what is to be done? My business and yours is to see that her end is made as peaceful as possible. It's a priest who is needed for that.'

'Oh, my God! Think of my condition, having to remind her about her will. Come what may I can't tell her that, you know how good she is . . .'

'Still, try to persuade her to wait till the roads are fit for sledging,' said the doctor, shaking his head significantly, 'or something bad may happen on the journey.'

'Aksyusha, hey Aksyusha!' yelled the stationmaster's daughter, throwing her jacket over her head and stamping her feet on the muddy back porch. 'Come and let's have a look at the Shirkin lady: they say she is being taken abroad for chest trouble, and I've never seen what consumptive people look like!'

Aksyusha jumped onto the threshold, and seizing one another by the hand the two girls ran out of the gate. Checking their pace, they passed by the coach and looked in at the open window. The sick woman turned her head towards them but, noticing their curiosity, frowned and turned away.

'De-arie me!' said the stationmaster's daughter, quickly turning her head away. 'What a wonderful beauty she was, and see what she's like now! It's dreadful. Did you see, did you, Aksyusha?'

'Yes, how thin!' Aksyusha agreed. 'Let's go and look again, as if we were going to the well. See, she turned away, and I hadn't seen her yet. What a pity, Masha!'

'Yes, and what mud!' said Masha, and they both ran through the gate.

'Evidently I look frightful,' thought the sick woman. 'If only I could get abroad quicker, quicker. I should soon recover there.'

'Well, my dear, how are you?' said her husband, approaching her and still chewing.

'Always the same question,' thought the sick woman, 'and he himself is eating.'

'So-so,' she murmured through her closed teeth.

'You know, my dear, I'm afraid you'll get worse travelling in this weather, and Eduard Ivanovich says so too. Don't you think we'd better turn back?'

She remained angrily silent.

'The weather will perhaps improve and the roads be fit for sledging; you will get better meanwhile, and we will all go together.'

'Excuse me. If I had not listened to you for so long, I would now at least have reached Berlin, and have been quite well.'

'What could be done, my angel? You know it was impossible. But now if you stayed another month you would get nicely better, I should have finished my business, and we could take the children with us.'

'The children are well, but I am not.'

'But do understand, my dear, that if in this weather you should get worse on the road. . . . At least you would be at home.'

'Well, what's at home? To die at home?' answered the sick woman, flaring up. But the word 'die' evidently frightened her, and she looked imploringly and questioningly at her husband. He hung his head and was silent. The sick woman's mouth suddenly widened like a child's, and tears rolled down her cheeks. Her husband hid his face in his handkerchief and stepped silently away from the carriage.

'No, I will go on,' said the sick woman, and lifting her eyes to the sky she folded her hands and began whispering incoherent words: 'Oh, my God, what is this for?' she said, and her tears flowed faster. She prayed long and fervently, but her chest ached and felt as tight as before; the sky, the fields, and the road were just as grey and gloomy, and the autumnal mist fell, neither thickening nor lifting, and settled on the muddy road, the roofs, the carriage, and the sheepskin coats of the drivers, who talking in their strong merry voices were greasing the wheels and getting the carriage ready.

II

The carriage was ready but the driver still loitered. He had gone into the drivers' room at the station. It was hot, stuffy, and dark there, with an oppressive smell of human habitation, baked bread, cabbage, and sheepskin garments. Several drivers were sitting in the room, and a cook was busy at the oven, on the top of which, wrapped in sheepskins, lay a sick man.

'Uncle Khvyodor! Uncle Khvyodor!' said the young driver, entering the room in his sheepskin coat with a whip stuck in his belt, and addressing the sick man.

'What do you want Khvyodor for, lazybones?' asked one of the drivers. 'Your carriage is waiting for you.'

'I want to ask for his boots; mine are quite worn out,' answered the young fellow, tossing back his hair and straightening the mittens tucked in his belt. 'Is he asleep? Uncle Khvyodor!' he repeated, walking over to the oven.

'What is it?' a weak voice was heard, and a lean face with a red beard looked down from the oven, while a broad, emaciated, pale, and hairy hand pulled up the coat over the dirty shirt covering his angular shoulder.

'Give me a drink, lad. What is it you want?'

The lad handed him up a dipper with water.

'Well, you see, Fedya,' he said, shifting from foot to foot, 'I expect you don't need your new boots now; won't you let me have them? I don't suppose you'll go about any more.'

The sick man, lowering his weary head to the shiny dipper and immersing his sparse drooping moustache in the turbid water, drank feebly but eagerly. His matted beard was dirty, and his sunken clouded eyes had difficulty in looking up at the lad's face. Having finished drinking he tried to lift his hand to wipe his wet lips, but he could not do so, and rubbed them on the sleeve of his coat instead. Silently, and breathing heavily through his nose, he looked straight into the lad's eyes, collecting his strength.

'But perhaps you have promised them to someone else?' asked the lad. 'If so, it's all right. The worst of it is, it's wet outside and I have to go about my work, so I said to myself: "Suppose I ask Fedka* for his boots; I expect he doesn't need them." If you need them yourself—just say so.'

Something began to rumble and gurgle in the sick man's chest; he doubled up and began to choke with an abortive cough in his throat.

'Need them indeed!' the cook snapped out unexpectedly so as to be heard by the whole room. 'He hasn't come down from the oven for more than a month! Hear how he's choking, it makes me ache inside just to hear him. What does he want with boots? They won't bury him in new boots. And it was time long ago, God forgive me the sin! See how he chokes. He ought to be taken into the other room or somewhere. They say there are hospitals in the town. Is it right that he should take up the whole corner? There's no more to be said. I've no room at all, and yet they expect cleanliness!'

'Hey, Seryoga! Come along and take your place, the gentlefolk are waiting!' shouted the drivers' overseer, looking in at the door.

Seryoga was about to go without waiting for a reply, but the sick man, while coughing, let him understand by a look that he wanted to give him an answer.

'Take my boots, Seryoga,' he said when he had mastered the

cough and rested a moment. 'But listen, buy a stone for me when I die,' he added hoarsely.

'Thank you, uncle. Then I'll take them, and I'll buy a stone for sure.'

'There, lads, you heard that?' the sick man managed to utter, and then bent double again and began to choke.

'All right, we heard,' said one of the drivers. 'Go and take your seat, Seryoga, there's the overseer running back. The Shirkin lady is ill, you know.'

Seryoga quickly pulled off his unduly big, dilapidated boots and threw them under a bench, Uncle Khvyodor's new boots just fitted him, and having put them on he went to the carriage with his eyes fixed on his feet.

'What fine boots! Let me grease them,' said a driver, who was holding some axle-grease in his hand, as Seryoga climbed onto the box and gathered up the reins. 'Did he give them to you for nothing?'

'Why, are you envious?' Seryoga replied, rising and wrapping the skirts of his coat under his legs. 'Off with you! Gee up, my beauties!' he shouted to the horses, flourishing the whip, and the carriage and calèche with their occupants, portmanteaux, and trunks rolled rapidly along the wet road and disappeared in the grey autumnal mist.

The sick driver was left on the top of the oven in the stuffy room and, unable to gain any relief by coughing, turned with an effort onto his other side and became silent.

Till late in the evening people came in and out of the room and dined there. The sick man made no sound. When night came, the cook climbed up onto the oven and stretched over his legs to get down her sheepskin coat.

'Don't be cross with me, Nastasya,' said the sick man. 'I shall soon leave your corner empty.'

'All right, all right, never mind,' muttered Nastasya. 'But what is it that hurts you? Tell me, uncle.'

'My whole inside has wasted away. God knows what it is!'

'I suppose your throat hurts when you cough?'

'Everything hurts. My death has come, that's how it is. Oh, oh, oh!' moaned the sick man.

'Cover up your feet like this,' said Nastasya, drawing his coat over him as she climbed down from the oven.

A night-light burnt dimly in the room. Nastasya and some ten drivers slept on the floor or on the benches, loudly snoring. The sick man groaned feebly, coughed, and turned about on the oven. Towards morning he grew quite quiet.

'I had a queer dream last night,' said Nastasya next morning, stretching herself in the dim light. 'I dreamt that Uncle Khvyodor got down from the oven and went out to chop wood. "Come, Nastasya," he says, "I'll help you!" and I say, "How can you chop wood now?", but he just seizes the axe and begins chopping quickly, quickly, so that the chips fly all about. "Why," I say, "haven't you been ill?" "No," he says, "I am well," and he swings the axe so that I was quite frightened. I gave a cry and woke up. I wonder whether he is dead! Uncle Khvyodor! Uncle Khvyodor!'

Khvyodor did not answer.

'True enough, he may have died. I'll go and see,' said one of the drivers, waking up.

The lean hand covered with reddish hair that hung down from the oven was pale and cold.

'I'll go and tell the stationmaster,' said the driver. 'I think he is dead.'

Khvyodor had no relatives: he was from some distant place. They buried him next day in the new cemetery beyond the wood, and Nastasya went on for days telling everybody of her dream, and of having been the first to discover that Uncle Khvyodor was dead.

III

Spring had come. Rivulets of water hurried down the wet streets of the city, gurgling between lumps of frozen manure; the colours of the people's clothes as they moved along the streets looked vivid and their voices sounded shrill. Behind the garden-fences the buds on the trees were swelling and their branches were just audibly swaying in the fresh breeze. Everywhere transparent drops were forming and falling. The sparrows chirped and fluttered awkwardly with their little wings. On the sunny side of the street, on the fences, houses, and trees, everything was in motion and sparkling. There was joy and youth in the sky, on the earth, and in the hearts of men.

In one of the chief streets fresh straw had been strewn on the road before a large manor-house, where the sick woman who had been in a hurry to go abroad lay dying.

At the closed door of her room stood the sick woman's husband and an elderly woman. On the sofa a priest sat with bowed head, holding something wrapped in his stole. In a corner of the room the sick woman's old mother lay on a lounge chair weeping bitterly: beside her stood one maidservant holding a clean handkerchief, waiting for her to ask for it, while another was rubbing her temples with something and blowing under the old lady's cap onto her grey head.

'Well, may Christ be with you, dear friend,' the husband said to the elderly woman who stood near him at the door. 'She has such confidence in you and you know so well how to talk to her, persuade her as well as you can, my dear, go to her.' He was about to open the door for her, but his cousin stopped him, pressing her handkerchief several times to her eyes and giving her head a shake.

'There now, I don't think I look as if I had been crying,' she said and, opening the door herself, went in.

The husband was in great agitation and seemed quite distracted. He walked towards the old woman, but while still several steps from her turned back, walked about the room, and went up to the priest. The priest looked at him, raised his eyebrows to heaven, and sighed. His thick, greyish beard also rose as he sighed and then came down again.

'My God, my God!' said the husband.

'What is to be done?' said the priest with a sigh, and again his eyebrows and beard rose and fell.

'And her mother is here!' said the husband almost in despair. 'She won't be able to bear it, so loving her. I just don't know! If you would only try to comfort her, Father, and persuade her to leave.'

The priest got up and went to the old woman.

'It is true, no one can appreciate a mother's heart,' he said—'but God is merciful.'

The old woman's face suddenly twitched all over, and she began to hiccup hysterically.

'God is merciful,' the priest continued when she grew a little calmer. 'Let me tell you of a patient in my parish who was much worse than Marya Dmitrevna, and a simple tradesman cured her in a short time with various herbs. That tradesman is even now in

Moscow. I told Vasily Dmitrich—we might try him. . . . It would at any rate comfort her. To God all is possible.'

'No, she will not live,' said the old woman. 'God is taking her instead of me,' and the hysterical hiccuping grew so violent that she fainted.

The sick woman's husband hid his face in his hands and ran out of the room.

In the passage the first person he met was his six-year-old son, who was running full speed after his younger sister.

'Won't you let the children be taken to their mamma?' asked the nurse.

'No, she doesn't want to see them, it would upset her.'

The boy stopped a moment, looked intently into his father's face, then gave a kick and ran on, shouting merrily.

'She is pretending to be the black horse, Papa!' he shouted, pointing to his sister.

Meanwhile in the other room the cousin sat down beside the sick woman and tried by skilful conversation to prepare her for the thought of death. At one of the windows the doctor was mixing a potion.

The patient, in a white dressing gown, sat up in bed supported all round by pillows, and looked at her cousin in silence.

'Ah, my dear friend,' she said, unexpectedly interrupting her, 'don't prepare me! Don't treat me like a child. I am a Christian. I know it all. I know I have not long to live, and know that if my husband had listened to me sooner I should now have been in Italy and perhaps—no, certainly—should have been well. Everybody told him so. But what is to be done? Evidently this is God's wish. We have all sinned heavily. I know that, but I trust in God's mercy everybody will be forgiven, probably all will be forgiven. I try to understand myself. I have many sins to answer for, dear friend, but then how much I have had to suffer! I try to bear my sufferings patiently.'

'Then shall I call the priest, my dear? You will feel still more comfortable after receiving communion,' said her cousin.

The sick woman bent her head in assent.

'God forgive me, sinner that I am!' she whispered.

The cousin went out and signalled with her eyes to the priest.

'She is an angel!' she said to the husband, with tears in her eyes.

The husband burst into tears; the priest went into the room; the sick woman's mother was still unconscious, and all was silent there. Five minutes later he came out again, and after taking off his stole, straightened out his hair.

'Thank God she is calmer now,' he said, 'and wishes to see you.'

The cousin and the husband went in. The sick woman was silently weeping, gazing at an icon.

'I congratulate you, my dear,'* said her husband.

'Thank you! How well I feel now, what inexpressible sweetness I feel!' said the sick woman, and a soft smile played on her thin lips. 'How merciful God is! Is he not? Merciful and all powerful!' and again she looked at the icon with eager entreaty and her eyes full of tears.

Then suddenly, as if she remembered something, she beckoned to her husband to come closer.

'You never want to do what I ask,' she said in a feeble and dissatisfied voice.

The husband, craning his neck, listened to her humbly.

'What is it, my dear?'

'How many times have I not said that these doctors don't know anything; there are simple women who can heal and who do cure. The priest was saying . . . a tradesman . . . Send!'

'For whom, my dear?'

'O God, he doesn't want to understand anything!' And the sick woman's face puckered and she closed her eyes.

The doctor came up and took her hand. Her pulse was beating more and more feebly. He glanced at the husband. The sick woman noticed that gesture and looked round in affright. The cousin turned away and began to cry.

'Don't cry, don't torture yourself and me,' said the sick woman. 'Don't take from me the last of my tranquillity.'

'You are an angel,' said the cousin, kissing her hand.

'No, kiss me here! Only dead people are kissed on the hand. My God, my God!'

That same evening the sick woman was a corpse, and the body lay in a coffin in the music room of the large house. A deacon sat alone in that big room reading the psalms of David through his nose in a monotonous voice. A bright light from the wax candles in their tall silver candlesticks fell on the pale brow of the dead woman, on her heavy waxlike hands, on the stiff folds of the pall which brought out in awesome relief her knees and toes. The deacon without understanding the words read on monotonously, and in the quiet room the words sounded strangely and died away. Now and then from a distant room came the sounds of children's voices and the patter of their feet.

'Thou hidest thy face, they are troubled,' the psalter proclaimed. 'Thou takest away their breath, they die and return to their dust. Thou sendest forth thy spirit, they are created: and thou renewest the face of the earth. May the glory of the Lord endure for ever.'*

The dead woman's face looked stern and majestic. Neither in the clear cold brow nor in the firmly closed lips was there any movement. She seemed all attention. But had she even now understood those solemn words?

IV

A month later a stone chapel was being erected over the grave of the deceased woman. Over the driver's tomb there was still no stone, and only the light green grass sprouted on the mound which served as the only token of the past existence of a man.

'It will be a sin, Seryoga,' said the cook at the station house one day, 'if you don't buy a stone for Khvyodor. You kept saying "It's winter, it's winter!" but why don't you keep your word now? You know I was there. He has already come back once to ask you to do it; if you don't buy him one, he'll come again and choke you.'

'But why? I'm not backing out of it,' replied Seryoga. 'I'll buy a stone as I said I would, and give a rouble and a half for it. I haven't forgotten it, but it has to be fetched. When I happen to be in town I'll buy one.'

'You might at least put up a cross, you really should, else it's quite wrong,' interposed an old driver. 'You know you are wearing his boots.'

'Where can I get a cross? I can't cut one out of a log.'

'What do you mean, can't cut one out of a log? You take an axe and go into the forest as early as possible, and you can cut one there. Cut down a young ash or something like that, and you can make a cross of it, or else you may have to treat the forester to vodka. One can't afford to treat him for every trifle. Now, I broke my splinter-bar and went and cut a new one, and nobody said a word.'

Early in the morning, as soon as it was daybreak, Seryoga took an axe and went into the wood.

A cold white cover of dew, which was still falling untouched by the sun, lay on everything. The east was imperceptibly growing brighter, reflecting its pale light on the vault of heaven still veiled by a covering of clouds. Not a blade of grass below, nor a leaf on the topmost branches of the trees, stirred. Only occasionally a sound of wings amid the brushwood, or a rustling on the ground, broke the silence of the forest. Suddenly a strange sound, foreign to nature, resounded and died away at the outskirts of the forest. Again the sound was heard, and was rhythmically repeated at the foot of the trunk of one of the motionless trees. A treetop began to tremble in an unwonted manner, its lush leaves whispered something, and the robin who had been sitting in one of its branches fluttered twice from place to place with a whistle, and jerking its tail sat down on another tree.

The axe at the bottom gave off a more and more muffled sound, sappy white chips were scattered on the dewy grass and a slight creaking was heard above the sound of the blows. The tree, shudder-ing through its whole body, bent down and quickly rose again, vibrating with fear on its roots. For an instant all was still, but the tree bent again, a crashing sound came from its trunk, and with its branches breaking and its boughs hanging down it fell with its crown onto the damp earth.

The sounds of the axe and of the footsteps were silenced. The robin whistled and flitted higher. A twig which it brushed with its wings shook a little and then with all its foliage grew still like the rest. The trees flaunted the beauty of their motionless branches still more joyously in the newly cleared space.

The first sunbeams, piercing the translucent cloud, shone out and spread over earth and sky. The mist began to quiver like waves in the hollows, the dew sparkled and played on the verdure, the transparent cloudlets grew whiter and hurriedly dispersed over the deepening azure vault of the sky. The birds stirred in the thicket and, as though bewildered, twittered joyfully about something; the lush leaves whispered joyfully and peacefully on the heights, and the branches of the living trees began to rustle slowly and majestically over the dead, prostrate tree.

POLIKUSHKA

I

'As you wish, ma'am! Only it's a pity for the Dutlovs. They're all good men and if we don't send at least one of the house-serfs, one of them must go,' said the steward. 'As it is now, everyone is suggesting them. But as you like, ma'am!'

And he placed his right hand over his left in front of him, inclined his head towards his right shoulder, drew in his thin lips almost with a smack, turned up his eyes, and said no more, evidently intending to keep silent for a long time and to listen without reply to all that nonsense his mistress was sure to utter.

The steward, a domestic serf, clean-shaven and dressed in a long coat of a peculiar steward-like cut, had come that autumn evening to give a report to his proprietress. The report from the mistress's point of view meant listening to a statement of the business done on her estate and giving instructions for further business. From Yegor Mikhaylovich's (the steward's) point of view, a report was a ceremony of standing straight on both feet with out-turned toes in a corner facing the sofa listening to all sorts of irrelevant chatter, and by various ways and means getting the mistress into a state of mind in which she would quickly and impatiently say, 'All right, all right!' to all that Yegor Mikhaylovich proposed.

The business under consideration was the conscription. The estate of Pokrovskoe had to supply three recruits. Fate itself seemed to have selected two of them by a coincidence of domestic, moral, and economic circumstances. As far as they were concerned there could be no hesitation or dispute either on the part of the commune,* the mistress, or public opinion. But who the third was to be was a debatable point. The steward was anxious to save the three Dutlov men and to send Polikushka, a married house-serf with a very bad reputation, who had been caught more than once stealing sacks, harnessing, and hay; but the mistress, who had often petted Polikushka's ragged children and improved his morals by exhortations from the Bible, did not wish to give him up. At the same time she did not wish to injure the Dutlovs, whom she did not know and had never even seen. But for some reason she did not seem able to grasp the situation, and the steward could not make up his mind to tell her straight out, that if Polikushka did not go one of the Dutlovs would have to. 'But I don't wish the Dutlovs any ill!' she said feelingly. 'If you don't, then pay three hundred roubles for a substitute,' should have been the steward's reply. But policy did not allow that.

So Yegor Mikhaylovich took up a comfortable position, and even leaned imperceptibly against the door-post, while keeping a servile expression on his face and watching the movements of the mistress's lips and the flutter of the frills of her cap and their shadow on the wall beneath a picture. But he did not consider it at all necessary to attend to the meaning of her words. The mistress spoke long and said much. A desire to yawn gave him a cramp behind his ears, but he adroitly turned the spasm into a cough, holding his hand to his mouth and faking the sound. Not long ago I saw Lord Palmerston sit with his hat over his face while a member of the opposition was storming at the ministry and then suddenly rise and in a three hours' speech answer his opponent point by point. I saw it without surprise, because I had seen the same kind of thing going on between Yegor Mikhaylovich and his mistress a thousand times. Whether he was afraid of falling asleep or thought she was letting herself go too far, he switched the weight of his body from his left to his right foot and began, as he always did, with an unctuous preface:

'As you like, ma'am, only . . . only there is a gathering of the commune now being held in front of my office window and we must come to some decision. The order says that the recruits are to be in town before the feast of Pokrov.* Among the peasants the Dutlovs are being suggested, and no one else. The commune does not share your interests. What does it care if we ruin the Dutlovs? I know what a hard time they've been having! Ever since I first had the steward-ship they have been living in want. The old man's youngest nephew has scarcely had time to grow up to be a help, and now they're to be ruined again! And I, as you well know, am as careful of your property as of my own. It's a pity, ma'am, whatever you're pleased to think! They're neither kith nor kin to me, and I've received nothing from them.'

'Why, Yegor, as if I ever thought of such a thing!' interrupted the mistress and at once suspected him of having been bribed by the Dutlovs.

'Only theirs is the best-kept homestead in the whole of Pokrovskoe. They're God-fearing, hard-working peasants. The old man has been church elder for thirty years; he doesn't drink or swear, and he goes to church' (the steward well knew with what to bait the hook). 'But the chief thing that I would like to report to you is that he has only two sons, the others are adopted nephews. The commune claims that lots should be cast for the two-men families. Many families have split up because of their own improvidence and their sons have separated from them, and so they are safe now, while these will have to suffer just because they have been charitable.'

Here the mistress could not follow at all. She did not understand what he meant by 'two-men families' or 'charitableness'. She only heard sounds and observed the nankeen buttons on the steward's coat. The top one, which he probably did not button up so often, was firmly fixed on, the middle one was hanging loose and ought long ago to have been sewn on again. But it is a well-known fact that in a conversation, especially a business conversation, it is not at all necessary to understand what is being said, but only to remember what you yourself want to say. The mistress acted accordingly.

'How is it you won't understand, Yegor Mikhaylovich?' she said. 'I have not the least desire that a Dutlov should become a soldier. One would think that knowing me as you do you might credit me with the wish to do everything in my power to help my serfs, and that I don't want any harm to come to them. You know that I would sacrifice all I possess to escape from this sad necessity and to send neither Dutlov nor Polikushka.' (I don't know whether it occurred to the steward that to escape the sad necessity there was no need to sacrifice everything, for three hundred roubles* would have sufficed; but this thought might well have crossed his mind.) 'I will only tell you this: that I will not give up Polikushka on any account. When he confessed to me of his own accord after that affair with the clock, and wept, and gave his word to amend, I talked to him for a long time and saw that he was touched and sincerely penitent.' ('There! She's off now!' thought Yegor Mikhaylovich, and began to scrutinize the jam she had in a glass of water: 'Is it orange or lemon? Slightly bitter, I expect,' he thought.) 'That is seven months ago now, and he has not once been drunk, and has behaved splendidly. His wife tells me he is a different man. How can you wish me to punish him now that he has reformed? Besides it would be inhuman to make a soldier of a man who has five children, and only he to keep them. No, you'd better not say any more about it, Yegor!'

And the mistress took a sip from her glass.

Yegor Mikhaylovich watched the motion of her throat as the liquid passed down it and then replied shortly and dryly:

'Then you have decided to choose Dutlov?'

The lady clasped her hands together.

'How is it you don't understand? Do I wish Dutlov ill? Have I anything against him? God is my witness I am prepared to do anything for them.' (She glanced at a picture in the corner, but remembered it was not an icon. 'Well, never mind ... that's not to the point,' she thought. And again, strange to say, the idea of the three hundred roubles did not occur to her.) 'Well, what can I do? What do I know about it? It's impossible for me to know. Well then, I rely on you, you know my wishes. Act so as to satisfy everybody and according to the law. What's to be done? They are not the only ones: everyone has difficult times. Only Polikushka can't be sent. You must understand that it would be dreadful of me to do such a thing.'

She was roused and would have continued to speak for a long time had not one of her maidservants entered the room at that moment.

'What is it, Dunyasha?'

'A peasant has come to ask Yegor Mikhaylovich if the meeting is to wait for him,' said Dunyasha, and glanced angrily at Yegor Mikhaylovich. ('Oh, that steward!' she thought; 'he's upset the mistress. Now she won't let me get a wink of sleep till two in the morning!')

'Well then, Yegor, go and do the best you can.'

'Yes, ma'am.' (He did not say anything more about Dutlov.) 'And who is to go to the gardener to fetch the money?'

'Hasn't Pyotr returned from town?'

'No, ma'am.'

'Couldn't Nikolay go?'

'Father is down with backache,' remarked Dunyasha.

'Shall I go myself tomorrow, ma'am?' asked the steward.

'No, Yegor, you are wanted here.' (The mistress pondered.) 'How much is it?'

'Four hundred and sixty-two roubles.'

'Send Polikey,'* said the mistress with a determined glance at
Yegor Mikhaylovich's face.

Yegor Mikhaylovich stretched his lips into the semblance of a
smile but without parting his teeth, and the expression on his face
did not change.

'Yes, ma'am.'

'Send him to me.'

'Yes, ma'am;' and Yegor Mikhaylovich went to his office.

II

Polikey, as a man of little importance, of tarnished reputation, and
not even a native of the village, had no influence either with the
housekeeper, the butler, the steward, or the maid, and his *corner* was
the very worst, though there were seven in his family. The late
master had had these *corners* built in the following manner: in the
middle of a brick building, about twenty-three feet square, there was
a large brick baking-oven surrounded by a *colidor* (as the servants
called it), and the four corners of the building were separated from
this *colidor* by wooden partitions. So there was not much room in
these *corners*, especially in Polikey's, which was nearest to the door.
The conjugal couch, with a print quilt and pillow-cases, a cradle
with a baby in it, a small three-legged table (on which the cooking
and washing were done and all sorts of domestic articles placed, and
at which Polikey, who was a horse-doctor, worked), tubs, clothing,
some chickens, a calf, and the seven members of the family, filled the
whole *corner*, and could not have stirred in it had it not been for their
quarter of the brick stove, on which both people and things could lie,
and for the possibility of going out onto the steps. That, however,
was hardly possible, for it is cold in October and the seven of them
only possessed one sheepskin cloak between them; but on the other
hand the children could keep warm by running about and the
grown-ups by working, and both the one and the other could climb
on the top of the stove where the temperature rose as high as 120
degrees Fahrenheit. It may seem dreadful to live in such conditions,
but they did not mind: one could live. Akulina washed and sewed her
husband's and her children's clothes, spun, wove, and bleached her
linen, cooked and baked in the common oven, and quarrelled and

gossiped with her neighbours. The monthly rations sufficed not only for the children, but for an addition to the cow's food. Firewood was free, as was fodder for the cattle, and a little hay from the stables sometimes came their way. They had a strip of kitchen-garden. Their cow had calved, and they had their own fowls. Polikey was employed in the stables to look after two stallions; he bled horses and cattle, cleaned their hoofs, lanced their sores, administered ointments of his own invention, and for this was paid in money and in kind. Also some of the master's oats used to find their way into his possession, and for two measures of them a peasant in the village gave twenty pounds of mutton regularly every month. Life would have been possible had there been no trouble at heart. But the whole family had a great trouble. Polikey in his youth had lived at a stud farm in another village. The groom into whose hands he happened to fall was the greatest thief in the whole district, and got exiled to Siberia. Under this man Polikey served his apprenticeship, and in his youth became so used to *these trifles* that in later life, though he would willingly have left off, he could not rid himself of the habit. He was a young man and weak; he had neither father nor mother nor anyone else to teach him. Polikey liked drink, and did not like to see anything lying about loose. Whether it was a strap, a piece of harness, a padlock, a bolt, or a thing of greater value, Polikey Ilyich found some use for everything. There were people everywhere who would take these things and pay for them in drink or in money, by agreement. Such earnings, so people say, are the easiest to get: no apprenticeship is required, no labour or anything, and he who has once tried that kind of work does not care for any other. It has only one drawback: although you get things cheap and easily and live pleasantly, yet all of a sudden through somebody's malice things go all wrong, the trade fails, everything has to be accounted for at once, and you rue the day you were born.

And so it happened to Polikey. Polikey had married and God had given him good luck. His wife, the herdsman's daughter, turned out to be a healthy, intelligent, hard-working woman, who bore him one fine baby after another. Polikey stuck to his trade and all went well. Suddenly one fine day a failing overtook him and he was caught. And he was caught because of a trifle: he had hidden away some peasant's leather reins. They were found, he was beaten, the mistress was told of it, and he was watched. He was caught a second and a third time.

People began to taunt him, the steward threatened to have him conscripted, the mistress gave him a scolding, and his wife wept and was broken-hearted. Everything went wrong. He was a good man, not a bad one, but just weak, fond of drink and so in the habit of it that he could not leave it alone. Sometimes his wife would scold him and even beat him when he came home drunk, and he would weep, saying: 'Unfortunate man that I am, what shall I do? Damn it, I'll give it up! Never again!' A month would go by, he would leave home, get drunk, and not be seen for a couple of days. And his neighbours would say: 'He must get that money to carouse with from somewhere!' His latest trouble had been with the office clock. There was an old wall-clock there that had not been in working order for a long time. He happened to go into the open office by himself and the clock tempted him. He took it and got rid of it in the town. As ill luck would have it the shopman to whom he sold the clock was related to one of the house-serfs, and coming to see her one holiday he spoke about the clock. People began making enquiries, just as if it were anyone's concern! Especially the steward, who disliked Polikey. It was all found out and reported to the mistress, and she sent for Polikey. He fell at her feet at once and pathetically confessed everything, just as his wife had told him to do. He carried out her instructions very well. The mistress began admonishing him; she talked and talked and wailed and wailed, about God and about virtue and about the future life and about his wife and children, and at last moved him to tears. The mistress said:

'I forgive you; only you must promise me never to do it again!'

'Never in all my life. May I be damned! May my bowels be torn out!' said Polikey, and wept touchingly.

Polikey went home and for the rest of the day lay on the stove blubbering like a calf. Since then nothing more had been traced to him. But his life was no longer pleasant; he was looked on as a thief, and when the time of the conscription drew near everybody started suggesting him.

As already mentioned, Polikey was a horse-doctor. How he had suddenly become one nobody knew, himself least of all. At the stud farm, when he worked under the head keeper who got exiled, his only duties were to clean out the dung from the stables, sometimes to groom the horses, and to carry water. He could not have learned it there. Then he became a weaver; after that he worked in a garden, weeding the paths; then he was condemned to break bricks for some offence; then he took a place as yard-porter for a merchant, paying a yearly sum to his mistress for leave to do so. So evidently he could not have had any experience as a veterinary there either; yet somehow during his last stay at home his reputation as a wonderfully and even a rather supernaturally clever horse-doctor began gradually to spread. He bled a horse once or twice. Then once he threw a horse down and prodded about in its thigh, and then once demanded that a horse should be placed in a trave,* where he began cutting the sole of its hoof till it bled, though the horse struggled and even squealed, and he said this meant 'letting off the sub-hoof blood'! Then he once explained to a peasant that it was absolutely necessary to let the blood from both veins, 'for greater ease', and began to strike his dull lancet with a mallet. Then he once bandaged the innkeeper's horse under its belly with a scrap torn from his wife's shawl. In the end he began to sprinkle all sorts of sores with vitriol, to drench them with something out of a bottle, and sometimes to give internally whatever came into his head. And the more horses he tormented and did to death, the more he was believed in and the more of them were brought to him.

I feel that for us educated people it is hardly the thing to laugh at Polikey. The methods he employed to inspire confidence are the same that influenced our fathers, that influence us, and will influence our children. The peasant lying prone on the head of his only mare (which not only constitutes his whole wealth but is almost one of his family) and gazing with faith and horror at Polikey's significantly frowning face and at his thin arms with upturned sleeves, as he presses upon the very spot that is sore and boldly cuts into the living flesh (with the secret thought, 'The bow-legged brute will be sure to get over it!'), and pretends to know where is blood and where pus, where is a tendon and where a vein, while holding a healing rag or a bottle of vitriol between his teeth—that peasant cannot conceive that Polikey could lift his hand to cut without knowing where to do it. He himself could not do so. And once the thing is done he will not reproach himself with having cut unnecessarily. I don't know how you feel about it, but I have gone through just the same experience with a doctor who, at my request, was tormenting those dear to me. The lancet, the mysterious whitish bottle of sublimate, and the words, 'the staggers, the glanders, to let blood, or matter', and so on, do they not come to the same thing as 'neurosis, rheumatism, organisms', and so forth? *Wage du zu irren und zu träumen** refers not so much to poets as to doctors and veterinary surgeons.

III

On the evening when the village meeting, in the cold darkness of an October night, was choosing the recruits and vociferating in front of the office, Polikey was sitting on the edge of his bed pounding some horse medicine on the table with a bottle, but what it was he himself did not know. There was corrosive sublimate, sulphur, Glauber's salts, and a herb which Polikey had gathered, having suddenly imagined it to be good for broken wind and then considered it not amiss for other disorders. The children were already lying down, two on the stove, two on the bed, and one in the cradle beside which Akulina sat spinning. The candle-end, one of the mistress's candles which had not been put away carefully enough, was burning in a wooden candlestick on the window-sill and Akulina every now and then got up to straighten it out with her fingers, so that her husband should not have to break off his important occupation. There were some free-thinkers who regarded Polikey as a worthless veterinary and a worthless man. Others, the majority, considered him a worthless man but a great master of his art; but Akulina, though she often scolded and even beat her husband, thought him undoubtedly the first of horse-doctors and the best of men. Polikey sprinkled some kind of medicinal spice on the palm of his hand (he never used scales, and spoke ironically of the Germans who use them: 'This,' he used to say, 'is not an apothecary!'). Polikey weighed the spice on his hand and tossed it up, but there did not seem enough of it and he poured in ten times more. 'I'll put in the lot,' he said to himself. 'It will pick 'em up better.' Akulina quickly turned round at the sound of her lord and master's voice, expecting some command, but seeing that the business did not concern her she shrugged her shoulders. 'What knowledge! Where does he get it?' she thought, and went on spinning. The paper which had held the spice fell to the floor. Akulina did not overlook this.

'Anyutka,' she cried, 'look! Father has dropped something. Pick it up!'

Anyutka put out her thin little bare legs from under the cloak with which she was covered, slid down under the table like a kitten, and got the paper.

'Here, daddy,' she said, and darted back into bed with her chilled little feet.

'Don't puth!' squeaked her lisping younger sister sleepily.

'I'll give it you!' muttered Akulina, and both heads disappeared again under the cloak.

'He'll give me three roubles,' said Polikey, corking up the bottle. 'I'll cure the horse. It's even too cheap,' he added, 'brain-splitting work! . . . Akulina, go and ask Nikita for a little 'baccy. I'll pay him back tomorrow.'

Polikey took out of his trouser-pocket a limewood pipe-stem, which had once been painted and had a mouthpiece made of sealing-wax, and began fixing it onto the bowl.

Akulina left her spindle and went out, managing to steer clear of everything, though this was very difficult. Polikey opened the cupboard and put away the medicine, then tilted a vodka bottle into his mouth, but it was empty. He made a grimace, but when his wife brought the tobacco he filled the bowl, began to smoke, sat down on the edge of the bed, and his face beamed with the content and pride of a man who has completed his day's task. Perhaps he was thinking how on the morrow he would catch hold of the horse's tongue and pour his wonderful mixture down its throat or reflecting that a useful person never gets a refusal and that Nikita really had sent him the tobacco. He felt happy. Suddenly the door, which hung on one hinge, was thrown open and a maidservant from *up there*, not the second maid but the third, the little one that was kept to run errands, entered their *corner*. (*Up there*, as everyone knows, means the master's house, even if it stands on lower ground.) Aksyutka, that was the girl's name, always flew like a bullet, and did it without bending her arms, which keeping time with the speed of her flight swung like pendulums, not at her sides but in front of her. Her cheeks were always redder than her pink dress, and her tongue moved as fast as her legs. She flew into the room, and for some reason catching hold of the stove, began to sway to and fro, then as if intent on not emitting more than two or three words at once, she suddenly addressed Akulina breathlessly as follows:

'The mistress has given orders that Polikey Ilyich should come this minute up there, she has given orders . . .' (She stopped, drawing breath with difficulty.) 'Yegor Mikhaylovich has been with the mistress, they talked about *rickruits*, they mentioned Polikey Ilyich. Avdotya Mikolavna has ordered him to come this minute. Avdotya Mikolavna has ordered him' (again a sigh) 'to come this minute.'

For half a minute Aksyutka looked round at Polikey, at Akulina, and the children who had put out their heads from under their coverlets and picked up a nutshell that lay on the stove and threw it at little Anyutka. Then she repeated: 'To come this minute! . . .' and rushed out of the room like a whirlwind, the pendulums swinging as usual across her line of flight.

Akulina again rose and got her husband his boots, abominable soldier's boots with holes in them, and took down his coat from the stove and handed it to him without looking at him.

'Won't you change your shirt, Ilyich?'*

'No,' he answered.

Akulina never once looked at his face while he silently put on his boots and coat, and she did well not to look. Polikey's face was pale, his lower jaw twitched, and in his eyes there was that tearful, submissive, and deeply unhappy look one only sees in the eyes of kindly, weak, and guilty people. He combed his hair and was going out, but his wife stopped him, tucked in the edge of his shirt that hung down from under his coat, and put his cap on for him.

'What's that, Polikey Ilyich? Has the mistress sent for you?' came the voice of the carpenter's wife from behind the partition.

Only that very morning the carpenter's wife had had heated words with Akulina about her pot of lye that Polikey's children had upset in her *corner*, and at first she was pleased to hear Polikey being summoned to the mistress, most likely for no good. She was a subtle, diplomatic lady, with a biting tongue. Nobody knew better than she how to cut one with a word: so at least she imagined.

'I expect you'll be sent to town to buy things,' she continued. 'I suppose a trusty person is wanted for that job so she is sending you! You might buy me a quarter of a pound of tea there, Polikey Ilyich.'

Akulina forced back her tears, and an angry expression distorted her lips. She felt as if she could have clutched that vixen, the joiner's wife, by her mangy hair. But as she looked at her children and thought that they would be left fatherless and she herself be a soldier's wife and as good as widowed, she forgot the sharp-tongued carpenter's wife, hid her face in her hands, sat down on the bed, and let her head sink in the pillows.

'Mummy, you're cwushing me!' lisped the little girl, pulling the cloak with which she was covered from under her mother's elbow.

'If only you'd die, all of you! I've brought you into the world for nothing but sorrow!' cried Akulina, and sobbed aloud, to the delight of the carpenter's wife who had not yet forgotten the lye spilt that morning.

IV

Half an hour passed. The baby began to cry. Akulina got up and gave it the breast. Weeping no longer, but resting her thin though still handsome face on her hand and fixing her eyes on the last flickerings of the candle, she sat thinking why she had married, wondering why so many soldiers were needed, and also how she could repay the carpenter's wife.

She heard her husband's footsteps and, wiping her tears, got up to let him pass. Polikey entered like a conqueror, threw his cap on the bed, sighed, and undid his belt.

'Well, what did she want you for?'

'H'm! As usual! Polikushka is the least of men, but when there's business to be done, who's wanted? Polikushka.'

'What business?'

Polikey was in no hurry to reply. He lit his pipe and spat.

'To go and fetch money from a merchant.'

'To fetch money?' Akulina asked.

Polikey chuckled and nodded his head.

'Ah! Ain't she clever at words? "You have been regarded," she says, "as an untrustworthy man, but I trust you more than any other" ' (Polikey spoke loud that the neighbours might hear). ' "You promised me you'd reform, so here", she says, "is the first proof that I believe you. Go", she says, "to the merchant, fetch the money he owes, and bring it back to me." And I say: "We are all your serfs, ma'am," I say, "and must serve you as we serve God, so I feel that I can do anything for your honour and cannot refuse any kind of work; whatever you order I will do, because I am your slave." ' (He again smiled that peculiar smile of a weak, kindly, and guilty man.) ' "Well, then," she says, "you will do it faithfully? You understand," she says, "that your fate depends on it?" "How could I fail to understand that I can do it all? If they have told tales about me, well, anyone can tell tales about another, but I never in any way, I believe, have even had a thought against your honour." In a word, I buttered her up till my mistress was quite softened. "I shall think highly of you," she says.' (He kept silent a minute, then the smile again appeared on his face.) 'I know very well how to talk to the likes of them! Formerly, when I used to go out to work on my own, at times someone would come down hard on me; but only let me get in a word or two and I'd butter him up till he'd be as smooth as silk!'

'Is it much money?' Akulina asked.

'Fifteen hundred roubles,' replied Polikey casually.

She shook her head.

'When are you to go?'

' "Tomorrow," she says. "Take any horse you like," she says, "call at the office, and then start and God be with you!" '

'The Lord be praised!' said Akulina, rising and crossing herself. 'May God help you, Ilyich,' she added in a whisper, so that she might not be heard beyond the partition and holding him by his shirt-sleeve. 'Ilyich, listen to me! I beseech you in the name of Christ our God: kiss the cross when you start out and promise that not a drop shall pass your lips.'

'A likely thing!' he snorted; 'to drink when carrying all that money! Ah! how somebody was playing the piano up there! Awfully nice!' he said, after a pause, and smiled. 'I suppose it was the young mistress. I was standing like this in front of the mistress, beside the whatnot, and the young lady was rattling away behind the door. She rattled and rattled on, fitting it together so neatly! O my! Wouldn't I like to play a tune! I'd soon master it, I would. I'm awfully good at that sort of thing. Let me have a clean shirt tomorrow!'

And they went to bed happy.

V

Meanwhile the meeting in front of the office had been noisy. The business before them was no trifle. Almost all the peasants were present. While the steward was with the mistress they kept their caps on, more voices were heard, and they talked more loudly. The hum of deep voices, interrupted at rare intervals by breathless, husky, and shrill tones, filled the air and, entering through the windows of the mistress's house, sounded like the noise of a distant sea, making her feel a nervous agitation like that produced by a heavy thunderstorm. She felt something between terror and discomfort. It seemed to her that the voices might at any moment grow yet louder and faster and that something would happen. 'As if it could not all be done quietly, peaceably, without disputing and shouting,' she thought, 'according to the Christian law of brotherly love and meekness!'

Many voices were speaking at once, but Fyodor Rezun, the carpenter, shouted loudest. There were two grown-up young men in his family and he was attacking the Dutlovs. Old Dutlov was defending himself: he stepped forward from the crowd behind which he had at first been standing. Now spreading out his arms, now clutching his little beard, he sputtered and snuffled in such a way that it would have been hard for him to understand what he himself was saying. His sons and nephews, splendid fellows all of them, stood huddled behind him, and the old man resembled the mother-hen in the game of hawk and chicks. The hawk was Rezun, as were all the men who had only one or two grown sons in the family, almost the whole gathering, and they were attacking Dutlov. The point was that Dutlov's brother had been recruited thirty years before, and that Dutlov wished therefore to be excused from taking his turn with the families in which there were three eligible young men, and wanted his brother's service in the army to be reckoned to the credit of his family, so that it should be given the same chance as those in which there were only two young men, and that these families should all draw lots equally and the third recruit be chosen from among all of them. Besides Dutlov's family there were four others in which there were three young men, but one was the village elder's family and the mistress had exempted him. From the second a recruit had been taken the year before, and from each of the two remaining families a recruit was now being taken. One of them had not even come to this meeting, but his wife stood sorrowfully behind all the others, vaguely hoping that the wheel of fortune might somehow turn her way. The red-haired Roman, the father of the other recruit, in a tattered coat, though he was not poor, hung his head and silently leaned against the porch, only now and then looking up attentively at anyone who raised his voice, and then hanging his head again. Misery seemed to breathe from his whole figure. Old Semyon Dutlov was a man to whose keeping anyone who knew anything of him would have trusted hundreds and thousands of roubles. He was a steady, God-fearing, reliable man, and was the church elder. Therefore the excitement he was now in was all the more striking.

Rezun the carpenter, a tall dark man, was, on the contrary, a riotous drunkard, very smart in a dispute and in arguing at meetings and fairs with workmen, tradespeople, peasants, or gentlefolk. Now he was calm and sarcastic, and from his superior height with the whole strength of his ringing voice and oratorical talent he was crushing down the spluttering church elder who was exasperated out of his usual sober groove. Besides these, the youngish, round-faced, square-headed, curly-bearded, thick-set Garaska Kopylov, one of the speakers of the younger generation, followed Rezun and took part in the dispute. He had already gained some weight at village meetings, having distinguished himself by his trenchant speeches. Then there was Fyodor Melnichny, a tall, thin, yellow-faced, round-shouldered man, also young, with a scanty beard and small eyes, always embittered and gloomy, seeing the dark side of everything and often bewildering the meeting by unexpected and abrupt questions and remarks. Both these speakers sided with Rezun. Besides these there were two babblers who now and then joined in: one, called Khrapkov, with a most good-humoured face and flowing brown beard, who kept repeating the words, 'Oh, my dearest friend!', the other, Zhidkov, a little fellow with a birdlike face who also kept remarking at every opportunity, 'It'll work out, brothers!' addressing himself to everybody and speaking fluently but never to the point. Both of these sided first with one and then with the other party, but no one listened to them. There were others like them, but these two, who kept moving through the crowd and shouting louder than anybody and frightening the mistress, were listened to less than anyone else. Intoxicated by the noise and shouting, they gave themselves up entirely to the pleasure of letting their tongues wag. There were many other characters among the members of the commune, stern, respectable, indifferent, or depressed; and there were women standing behind the men with sticks in their hands, but, God willing, I'll speak of them some other time. The greater part of the crowd, however, consisted of peasants who stood as if they were in church, whispering behind each other's backs about home affairs, or of when to cut firewood in the forest, or silently awaiting the end of the jabber. There were also rich peasants whose well-being the meeting could not add to nor diminish. Such was Yermil, with his broad shiny face, whom the peasants called the 'big-bellied', because he was rich. Such too was Starostin, whose face showed a self-satisfied expression of power that seemed to say, 'You may talk away, but no one will touch me! I have four sons, but not one of them will have to go.' Now and then these two were attacked by some independent thinker such as Kopylov and Rezun, but they replied quietly and firmly and with a consciousness of their own inviolability. If Dutlov was like the mother-hen in the game of hawk and chicks, his lads did not much resemble the chicks. They did not flutter about and squeak, but stood quietly behind him. His eldest son, Ignat, was already thirty; the second, Vasily, was also a married man and more-over not fit for a recruit; the third, his nephew Ilyushka, who had just got married—a fair, rosy young man in a smart sheepskin coat (he was a post-chaise driver)—stood looking at the crowd, sometimes scratching his head under his hat, as if the whole matter was no concern of his, though it was just on him that the hawks wished to swoop down.

'If it comes to that, my grandfather was a soldier,' said Pezun, 'and so I might refuse to draw lots in just the same way! There's no such law, friend. Last recruiting, Mikheichev was taken though his uncle had not even returned from service then.'

'Neither your father nor your uncle ever served the Tsar,' Dutlov was saying at the same time. 'Why, you don't even serve the mistress or the commune, but spend all your time carousing. Your sons have separated from you because it's impossible to live with you, so you go suggesting other people's sons for recruits! But I have done police duty for ten years, served as elder, been burnt out twice, and no one helped me, and now, because things are peaceful and decent in my home, am I to be ruined? Give me back my brother, then! He has died in service for sure. Judge justly according to God's law, as an Orthodox commune, and don't listen to a drunkard's drivel.'

And at the same time Geraska was saying to Dutlov:

'You keep mentioning your brother, though he was not sent by the commune, but by the master because of his evil ways, so he's no excuse for you.'

Geraska had not finished when the lank yellow-faced Fyodor Melnichny stepped forward and began gloomily:

'Yes, that's the way! The masters send whom they please, and then the commune has to get the muddle straight. The commune has fixed on your lad, and if you don't like it, go and ask the mistress. Perhaps she will order me, the one man of our family, to leave my children and go! There's law for you!' he said bitterly, and waving his hand he went back to his former place.

Red-haired Roman, whose son had been chosen as a recruit, raised his head and muttered: 'That's it, that's it!' and even sat down on the step in vexation.

But these were not the only ones who were speaking at once. Besides those at the back who were talking about their own affairs, the babblers did not forget to do their part.

'That's it precisely, Orthodox commune,' said little Zhidkov, repeating Dutlov's words. 'One must judge in a Christian way. Like Christians I mean, brothers, we must judge.'

'One must judge according to one's conscience, my dear friend,' said the good-hearted Khrapkov, repeating Garaska Kopylov's words and pulling Dutlov by his sheepskin coat. 'It was the master's will and not the commune's decision.'

'That's right! So it was!' said others.

'What drunkard is drivelling there?' Rezun retorted to Dutlov. 'Did you stand me any drinks? Or is your son, whom they pick up by the roadside, going to reproach me for drinking? Brothers, we must decide! If you want to spare the Dutlovs, choose not only from families with two sons, but even from those with one, and he will have the laugh of us!'

'A Dutlov will have to go! What's the good of talking?'

'Of course the three-men families must be the first to draw lots,' some voices began to say.

'We must first see what the mistress will say. Yegor Mikhaylovich was saying that she wished to send a house-serf,' put in a voice.

This remark checked the dispute for a while, but soon it flared up anew and again came to personalities.

Ignat, whom Rezun had accused of being picked up drunk by the roadside, began to point out that Rezun had stolen a saw from some travelling carpenters, and that he had almost beaten his wife to death when he was drunk.

Rezun replied that he beat his wife drunk or sober, and still it was not enough, and this set everybody laughing. But about the saw he became suddenly indignant, stepped closer to Ignat and asked:

'Who stole?'

'You did,' replied the sturdy Ignat, drawing still closer.

'Who stole? Wasn't it you?' shouted Rezun.

'No, it was you,' shouted Ignat.

From the saw they went on to the theft of a horse, a sack of oats, some strip of communal kitchen-garden, and to a certain dead body. The two peasants said such terrible things of one another that if a hundredth part of them had been true they would by law at the very least have deserved exile to Siberia.

In the meantime old Dutlov had chosen another way of defending himself. He did not like his son's shouting, and tried to stop him, saying: 'It's a sin. Leave off, I tell you!' At the same time he argued that not only those who had three young men at home were three-men families, but also those whose sons had separated from them, and he also pointed to Starostin.

Starostin smiled slightly, cleared his throat, and stroking his beard with the air of a well-to-do peasant, answered that it all depended on the mistress, and that evidently his son had served well, since the order was for him to be exempt.

Garaska smashed Dutlov's arguments about the families that had broken up with the remark that they ought not to have been allowed to break up, as was the rule during the lifetime of the late master, but that no one went raspberry-picking when summer was over, and that one could not now conscript the only man left in a household.

'Did they break up their households for fun? Why should they now be completely ruined?' came the voices of the men whose families had separated, and the babblers joined in too.

'You'd better buy a substitute if you're not satisfied. You can afford it!' said Rezun to Dutlov.

Dutlov wrapped his coat round him with a despairing gesture and stepped back behind the others.

'It seems you've counted my money!' he muttered angrily. 'We shall see what Yegor Mikhaylovich will say when he comes from the mistress.'

VI

At that very moment Yegor Mikhaylovich came out of the house. One cap after another was raised, and as the steward approached one head after another was revealed, grey, grizzled, red, brown, fair, or bald in front or on top, and little by little the voices began to die down till at last all were quiet. Yegor Mikhaylovich stepped onto the porch, evidently intending to speak. In his long coat, his hands awkwardly thrust into the front pockets, his town-made cap pulled over his forehead, standing firmly, with feet apart, in this elevated position, towering above all these heads, mostly old, bearded, and handsome, that were turned towards him, he looked quite different from what he had been when he stood before his mistress. He was majestic.

'Here is the mistress's decision, men! It is not her pleasure to give up any of the house-serfs, but from among you, the one you yourselves decide on shall go. Three are wanted this time. By rights only two and a half are wanted, but the half will be taken into account next time. It comes to the same thing: if not today it would have to be tomorrow.'

'Of course, that's quite right!' some voices said.

'In my opinion,' continued Yegor Mikhaylovich, 'Kharyushkin and Vaska Mityukhin must go, that is evidently God's will.'

'Yes, that's quite right!' said the voices.

'The third will have to be one of the Dutlovs, or one out of a two-men family. What do you say?'

'Dutlov!' cried the voices. 'There are three of them!'

And again, little by little, the shouting increased, and again somehow the question of the saw, the strip of kitchen-garden, and certain sacks stolen from the mistress's yard came up. Yegor Mikhaylovich had been managing the estate for the last twenty years and was a shrewd and experienced man. He stood and listened for about a quarter of an hour, then he ordered all to be silent and the three Dutlovs to draw lots to see which of them was to go. The lots were prepared, shaken up in a hat, and Khrapkov drew one out. It was Ilyushka's. All became silent.

'Is it mine? Let me see it!' said Ilya* in a faltering voice.

All remained silent. Yegor Mikhaylovich ordered that the next day everybody should bring the recruit money, a tax of seven kopeks from each household, and saying that all was over, dismissed the meeting. The crowd moved off, the men covered their heads as they turned the corner, and their voices and the sound of their footsteps mingled into a hum. The steward stood on the porch watching the departing crowd, and when the young Dutlovs were round the corner he beckoned old Dutlov, who had stopped of his own accord, and they went into the office.

'I am sorry for you, old man,' said Yegor Mikhaylovich, sitting down in an armchair before the table. 'It was your turn though. Will you buy a recruit to take your nephew's place, or not?'

The old man, without speaking, gave Yegor Mikhaylovich a significant look.

'There's no getting out of it,' said Yegor Mikhaylovich in answer to that look.

'We'd be glad enough to buy a substitute, Yegor Mikhaylovich, but we haven't the means. Two horses went to the knacker's this summer, and there was my nephew's wedding. Evidently it's our fate just for living honestly. It's very well for him to talk!' (He was thinking of Rezun.)

Yegor Mikhaylovich rubbed his face with his hand and yawned. He was evidently tired of the business and ready for his tea.

'Eh, old fellow, don't be mean!' he said. 'Have a look under your floor, I dare say you'll turn up some four hundred old rouble notes, and I'll get you a substitute, a regular wonder! The other day a fellow came offering himself.'

'In the *government*?' asked Dutlov, meaning the town.

'Well, will you buy him?'

'I'd be glad enough, God is my witness! But . . .'

Yegor Mikhaylovich interrupted him sternly.

'Well then, listen to me, old man! See that Ilyushka does himself no mischief,* and as soon as I send word, whether today or tomorrow, he is to be taken to town at once. You will take him and you will be responsible for him, but if anything should happen to him, God forbid, I'll send your eldest son instead! Do you hear?'

'But could not one be sent from a two-men family? Yegor Mikhaylovich, this is not fair!' he said. Then after a pause he went on, almost with tears: 'When my brother has died a soldier, now they are taking my son! How have I deserved such a blow?' and he was ready to fall on his knees.

'Now, now, go away!' said Yegor Mikhaylovich. 'Nothing can be done. It's the law. Keep an eye on Ilyushka, you are responsible for him!'

Dutlov went home, thoughtfully tapping the ruts with his linden stick as he walked.

VII

Early next morning a big-boned bay gelding (for some reason called Drum) harnessed to a small cart (in which the steward himself used to drive), stood at the porch of the house-serfs' quarters. Anyutka, Polikey's eldest daughter, barefoot in spite of the falling sleet and the cold wind, and evidently frightened, stood at the horse's head holding the bridle with one hand, while with her other she held a faded yellowy-green jacket that was thrown over her head, and which served the family as blanket, cloak, hood, carpet, overcoat for Polikey, and many other things besides. Polikey's *corner* was all in a bustle. It was still dark. The morning light of a rainy day was just peeping through the window, which was broken here and there and mended with paper. Having left her cooking in the oven and her children, of whom the younger were still in bed and shivering, because the jacket that served them as a blanket had been taken away to serve as a garment and replaced by their mother's shawl, Akulina was busy getting her husband ready for his journey. His shirt was clean. His boots, which as they say were 'begging for porridge', gave her much trouble. First of all, she took off her only pair of thick worsted stockings and gave them to her husband, secondly, she managed to cut out a pair of inner soles from a saddle-cloth, which had been carelessly left about in the stable and had been brought home by Ilyich two days before, in such a way as to stop up the holes in his boots and keep his feet dry. Ilyich sat, feet and all, on the bed, untwisting his sash, so that it should not look like a dirty cord. The cross, lisping little girl, wrapped in the sheepskin (which though it covered her head was trailing round her feet), had been dispatched to ask Nikita to lend them a cap. The bustle was increased by house-serfs coming in to ask Ilyich to get different things for them in town. One wanted needles, another tea, a third some tobacco, and another some olive oil. The carpenter's wife, who to conciliate Polikey had already found time to make her samovar* boil and bring him a mug full of liquid which she called tea, wanted some sugar. Though Nikita refused to lend a cap and they had to mend his own, that is, to push in the protruding bits of wadding and sew them up with a veterinary needle; though at first the boots with the saddle-cloth soles would not go on his feet; though Anyutka, chilled through, nearly let Drum get out of hand, and Mashka in the long sheepskin had to take her place, and then Mashka had to take off the sheepskin and Akulina had to hold the horse herself—it all ended with Ilyich successfully getting all the warm family garments on himself, leaving only the jacket and a pair of slippers behind. When ready, he got into the little cart, wrapped the sheepskin round him, shook up the bag of hay at the bottom of the cart, again wrapped himself up, took the reins, wrapped the coat still closer round him as very important people do, and started.

His little boy Mishka, running out onto the steps, begged to have a ride; the lisping Mashka also begged that she might 'have a lide', and was 'not cold even without the theepthkin'; so Polikey stopped Drum and smiled his weak smile while Akulina put the children into the cart and, bending towards him, begged him in a whisper to remember his oath and not drink anything on the way. Polikey took the children through the village as far as the smithy, put them down, wrapped himself up and put his cap straight again, and drove off at a slow, sedate trot, his cheeks quivering at every jolt and his feet knocking against the bark sides of the cart. Mashka and Mishka, barefoot, rushed down the slippery hill to the house at such a rate and yelling so loudly that a stray dog from the village looked up at them and scurried home with its tail between its legs, which made Polikey's heirs yell ten times louder.

It was abominable weather. The wind was cutting. Something between rain, snow, and fine hail beat on Polikey's face and on his bare hands, which held the reins and over which he kept drawing the sleeves of his coat, and on the leather of the horse-collar, and on the head of old Drum, who set back his ears and half closed his eyes.

Then suddenly the precipitation stopped and in a moment it brightened up. The bluish snowclouds could be seen clearly and the sun began to come out, but uncertainly and cheerlessly like Polikey's own smile. Notwithstanding all this, Ilyich was deep in pleasant thoughts. He whom they threatened to exile and conscript, whom only those who were too lazy did not scold and beat, who was always shoved into the worst places, *he* was driving now to fetch *a sum of money*, and a large sum too, and his mistress trusted him, and he was driving in the steward's cart behind Drum, with whom the lady herself sometimes drove out, just as if he were some proprietor with leather collar-strap and reins. And Polikey sat up straighter, pushed in the bits of wadding hanging out of his cap, and again wrapped his coat closer.

If Ilyich, however, imagined that he looked just like a wealthy peasant proprietor he deluded himself. It is true, as everyone knows, that tradesmen worth ten thousand roubles drive in carts with leather harness, only this was not quite the same thing. A bearded man in a blue or black coat drives past sitting alone in a cart, driving a well-fed horse, and you just glance to see if the horse is sleek and he himself well fed, and at the way he sits, at the horse's harness, and the tyres on the cartwheels, and at his belt, and you know at once whether the man does business in hundreds or in thousands of roubles. Every experienced person looking closely at Polikey, at his hands, his face, his newly grown beard, his sash, at the hay carelessly thrown into the cart, at the lean Drum, at the worn tyres, would know at once that it was only a serf driving past, and not a merchant or a cattle-dealer or even a peasant proprietor, and that he did not deal in thousands or hundreds, or even tens of roubles. But Ilyich did not think so: he deceived himself, and deceived himself agreeably. He is going to carry home fifteen hundred roubles in the bosom of his coat. If he liked, he might turn Drum's head towards Odessa instead of homewards, and drive off where God might take him. But he will not do such a thing; he will faithfully bring the mistress her money, and will talk about having had larger sums than that on him. When they came to a tavern Drum began pulling at the left rein, turning towards the tavern and stopping; but Polikey, though he had the money given him to do the shopping with, gave Drum the whip and drove on. The same thing happened at the next tavern. About noon he got out of the cart, and opening the gate of the innkeeper's house where all his mistress's people put up, he led the horse and cart into the yard, where he unharnessed, gave the horse some hay, dined with the innkeeper's men, not omitting to mention what important business he had come on, and then with the letter in his cap went out to see the market-gardener.

The market-gardener (who knew and evidently mistrusted Polikey) having read the letter questioned him as to whether he had really been sent for the money. Ilyich tried to seem offended, but could not manage it, and only smiled his peculiar smile. The market-gardener read the letter over once more and handed him the money. Having received the money, Polikey put it into his bosom and went back to the inn. Neither the beershop nor the bar nor anything tempted him. He felt a pleasant agitation through his whole being, and stopped more than once in front of shops that showed tempting wares: boots, coats, caps, chintz, and foodstuffs, and then continued on his way with that pleasant feeling: 'I could buy it all, but there now, I won't do it!' He went to the bazaar for the things he had been asked to buy, got them all, and started bargaining for a lined sheepskin coat, for which he was asked twenty-five roubles. For some reason the dealer, after looking at Polikey, seemed to doubt his ability to buy it. But Polikey pointed to his bosom, saying that he could buy the whole shop if he liked, and insisted on trying the coat on; felt it, patted it, blew into the wool till he became permeated with the smell of it, and then took it off with a sigh. 'The price does not suit me. If you'll let it go for fifteen roubles, now!' he said. The dealer angrily threw the coat across the table, and Polikey went out and cheerfully returned to his inn. After supper, having watered Drum and given him some oats, he climbed up on the stove, took out the envelope with the money and examined it for a long time, and then asked a porter who knew how to read to read him the address and the inscription: 'With enclosure of one thousand six hundred and seventeen assignation roubles.'* The envelope was made of common paper and sealed with brown sealing-wax with the impression of an anchor. There was one large seal in the middle, four at the corners, and there were some drops of sealing-wax near the edge. Ilyich examined all this, and studied it. He even felt the sharp edges of the notes. It gave him a kind of childish pleasure to know that he had such a sum in his hands. He thrust the envelope into a hole in the lining of his cap and lay down with the cap under his head, but even in the night he kept waking and feeling the envelope. And each time he found it in its place he experienced the pleasant feeling of awareness that here was he, the disgraced, the down-trodden Polikey, carrying such a sum and delivering it up more accurately than even the steward could have done.

VIII

About midnight the innkeeper's men and Polikey were awakened by a knocking at the gate and the shouting of peasants. It was the party of recruits from Pokrovskoe. There were about ten people: Khoryushkin, Mityukin, and Ilyushka (Dutlov's nephew), two substitutes in case of need, the village elder, old Dutlov, and the men who had driven them. A night-light was burning in the room, and the cook was sleeping on a bench under the icons. She jumped up and began lighting a candle. Polikey also awoke, and leaning over from the top of the stove looked at the peasants as they came in. They came in crossing themselves and sat down on the benches round the room. They all seemed perfectly calm, so that one could not tell which of them were the conscripts and which their escorts. They were greeting the people of the inn, talking loudly, and asking for food. It is true that some were silent and sad; but on the other hand others were unusually merry, evidently drunk. Among these was Ilya, who had never had too much to drink before.

'Well, lads, shall we go to sleep or have some supper?' asked the elder.

'Supper!' said Ilya, throwing open his coat and setting himself on a bench. 'Send for some vodka.'

'Enough of your vodka!' answered the elder shortly, and turning to the others he said: 'You just cut yourselves a bit of bread, lads! Why wake people up?'

'Give me vodka!' Ilya repeated, without looking at anybody, and in a voice that showed that he would not soon stop.

The peasants took the elder's advice, fetched some bread out of their carts, ate it, asked for a little *kvas*,* and lay down, some on the floor and some on the stove.

Ilya kept repeating at intervals: 'Let me have some vodka, I say, let me have some.' Then, suddenly noticing Polikey: 'Ilyich! Hi, Ilyich! You're here, dear friend? You know, I am going to be a soldier. Have said goodbye to my mum and my missus. How she howled! They've packed me off to the army. Get me some vodka!'

'I haven't got any money,' answered Polikey, and to comfort him added: 'Who knows? With God's aid you may still be rejected!'

'No, friend. I'm as sound as a young birch. I've never had an illness. There's no rejecting for me! What better soldier can the Tsar want?'

Polikey began telling him how a peasant gave a doctor a five-rouble note and got rejected.

Ilya drew nearer the oven, and they talked more freely.

'No, Ilyich, it's all up now! I don't want to stay now myself. Uncle has done me in. He'd have bought out his own, wouldn't he? No, he cares for* his son and he cares for his money. Me, he's giving away. Now I myself don't want to stay.' (He spoke gently, confidingly, under the influence of quiet sorrow.) 'One thing only, I am sorry for mum, how she grieved! And the missus, too! They've ruined the woman just for nothing; now she'll perish, in a word, she'll be a soldier's wife! Better not to have married. What did they marry me for? They're coming here tomorrow.'

'But why have they brought you so soon?' asked Polikey; 'nothing was heard about it, and then, all of a sudden . . .'

'Ya see, they're afraid I shall do myself some mischief,' answered Ilyushka, smiling. 'No fear! I'll do nothing of the kind. I shall not be lost even as a soldier; only I'm sorry for mum. Why did they get me married?' he said gently and sadly.

The door opened and shut with a loud slam as old Dutlov came in, shaking the wet off his cap, and as usual in bast shoes so big that they looked like boats.

'Afanasy,' he said to the porter, when he had crossed himself, 'isn't there a lantern to get some oats by?'

And without looking at Ilya Dutlov began slowly lighting a bit of candle. His mittens and whip were stuck into the sash tied neatly round his coat, and his toil-worn face appeared as usual, simple, quiet, and full of business cares, as if he had just arrived with a train of loaded carts.

Ilya became silent when he saw his uncle, and looked dejectedly down at the bench again. Then, addressing the elder, he muttered:

'Vodka, Yermil! I want some drink!' His voice sounded angry and dejected.

'Drink, at this time?' answered the elder, who was eating something out of a bowl. 'Don't you see the others have had a bite and lain down? Why are you making a row?'

The word 'row' evidently gave Ilya an idea.

'Elder, I'll do some mischief if you don't give me vodka!'

'Can't you bring him to reason?' the elder said, turning to Dutlov, who had lit the lantern, but had stopped, evidently to see what would happen, and was looking with condolence at his nephew out of the corner of his eyes, as if surprised at his childishness.

Ilya, looking down, again muttered:

'Gimme some vodka or I'll do some mischief!'

'Leave off, Ilya!' said the elder mildly. 'Really, now, leave off! You'd better!'

But before the words were out Ilya had jumped up and hit a window-pane with his fist, and shouting at the top of his voice: 'You would not listen to me, so there you have it!' he rushed to the other window to break that too.

Ilyich in the twinkling of an eye rolled over twice and hid in the furthest corner of the top of the stove, so quickly that he scared all the cockroaches there. The elder threw down his spoon and rushed toward Ilya. Dutlov slowly put down his lantern, untied his sash, and shaking his head and making a clicking noise with his tongue, went up to Ilya, who was already struggling with the elder and the inn-keeper's man, who were keeping him away from the window. They had caught his arms and seemed to be holding him fast; but the moment he saw his uncle with the sash his strength increased tenfold and he tore himself away, and with rolling eyes and clenched fists stepped up to Dutlov.

'I'll kill you! Keep away, you brute! You have ruined me, you and your brigands of sons, you've ruined me! Why did you get me married? Keep away! I'll kill you!'

Ilyushka was terrifying. His face was purple, his eyes rolled, the whole of his healthy young body trembled as in a fever. It seemed as though he wanted to and could kill all the three men who were facing him.

'You're drinking your brother's blood, you blood-sucker!'

Something flashed across Dutlov's ever-serene face. He took a step forward.

'You won't take it peacefully!' he said and suddenly, getting the energy from somewhere, with a quick motion he caught hold of his nephew, rolled to the ground with him, and with the aid of the elder began binding his hands with the sash. They struggled for about five minutes. At last with the help of the peasants Dutlov rose, pulling his coat out of Ilya's clutch. Then he raised Ilya, whose hands were tied behind his back, and made him sit down on a bench in a corner.

'I told you it would be the worse for you,' he said, still out of breath with the struggle, and pulling straight the narrow belt tied over his shirt. 'Why sin? We shall all have to die! Fold a coat for a pillow for him,' he said, turning to the innkeeper's men, 'or the blood will go to his head.' And he tied the cord round his waist over his sheepskin and, taking up the lantern, went to see after the horses.

Ilya, pale, dishevelled, his shirt pulled out of place, kept gazing round the room as though trying to remember where he was. The innkeeper's men picked up the broken bits of glass and stuffed a coat into the hole in the window to keep the draught out. The elder sat down again to his bowl.

'Ah, Ilyukha, Ilyukha! I'm sorry for you, really! What's to be done? There's Khoryushkin, he too is married. Seems it can't be helped!'

'It's all on account of that fiend, my uncle, that I'm being ruined!' Ilya repeated, dryly and bitterly. 'He took pity on his own son! My mum said the steward told him to buy me off. He won't, he says he can't afford it. As if what my brother and I have brought into his house were a trifle! He is a villain!'

Dutlov returned to the room, said a prayer in front of the icons, took off his outdoor things, and sat down beside the elder. The cook brought more *kvas* and another spoon. Ilya grew silent, and closing his eyes lay down on the folded coat. The elder pointed to him and shook his head silently. Dutlov waved his hand.

'As if I wasn't sorry! My own brother's son! And as if things were not bad enough it seems they also made me out a villain to him. Maybe it's his wife—she's a cunning little woman for all her youth—who's put it into his head that we could afford to buy a substitute! Anyhow, he's reproaching me. But how I do pity the lad!'

'Ah! he's a fine lad,' said the elder.

'But I'm at the end of my tether with him! Tomorrow I shall let Ignat come, and his wife wanted to come too.'

'All right, let them come,' said the elder, rising and climbing onto the stove. 'What is money? Money is dross!'

'If one had the money, who would begrudge it?' muttered one of the innkeeper's men, lifting his head.

'Ah, money, money! It causes much sin,' replied Dutlov. 'Nothing in the world causes so much sin, and the scriptures say so too.'

'Everything is said there,' the workman agreed. 'There was a man told me how a merchant had stored up a heap of money and did not want to give up any; he loved it so that he took it with him to the grave. As he was dying he asked to have a small pillow buried with him. No one suspected anything, and so it was done. Then his sons began looking for his money and nothing was to be found. At last one of them guessed that probably the notes were all in the pillow. The matter went to the Tsar, and he allowed the grave to be opened. And what do you think? They opened the coffin. There was nothing in the pillow, but the coffin was full of small snakes, and so it was buried again. You see what money does!'

'It's a fact, it brings much sin,' said Dutlov, and he got up and began saying his prayers.

When he had finished he looked at his nephew. The lad was asleep. Dutlov came up to him, untied the sash with which he was bound, and then lay down. Another peasant went out to sleep with the horses.

IX

As soon as all was quiet Polikey climbed down softly, like a guilty man, and began to get ready. For some reason he felt uneasy at the thought of spending the night there among the recruits. The cocks were already crowing to one another more often. Drum had eaten all his oats and was straining towards the drinking trough. Polikey harnessed him and led him out past the peasants' carts. His cap with its contents was safe, and the wheels of the cart were soon rattling along the frosty road to Pokrovskoe. Polikey felt more at ease only when he had left the town behind. Till then he kept imagining that at any moment he might hear himself being pursued, that he would be stopped, and they would tie up his hands instead of Ilya's, and he would be taken to the recruiting station next morning. It might have been the frost, or it might have been fear, but something made cold shivers run down his back, and again and again he gently urged

Drum with his whip. The first person he met was a priest in a tall fur cap, accompanied by a one-eyed labourer. Taking this for an evil omen Polikey grew still more alarmed, but outside the town this fear gradually passed. Drum went on at a walking pace and the road in front became more visible. Polikey took off his cap and felt the notes. 'Shall I hide it inside my coat?' he thought. 'No, I should have to undo my belt. Wait! When I get to the foot of the hill I'll get down and straighten myself out. The cap is sewn up tight at the top, and it can't fall through the lining. So I won't take the cap off till I get home.' When he had reached the foot of the incline Drum of his own accord galloped up the next hill and Polikey, who was as eager as Drum to get home, did not hold him back. All was well, at any rate so Polikey imagined, and he gave himself up to his mistress's grati-tude, of the five roubles she would give him, and of the joy of his family. He took off his cap, felt for the envelope, and, smiling, put the cap tighter on his head. The velveteen crown of the cap was very rotten, and just because Akulina had the day before carefully sewn up the holes in one place, it burst open in another; and that movement by which Polikey in the dusk had thought to push the envelope with the money deeper under the wadding, that very movement ripped the cap and pushed out a corner of the envelope through the velveteen crown.

The dawn was appearing, and Polikey, who had not slept all night, began to drowse. Pulling his cap lower down and thereby pushing the envelope still further out, Polikey in his drowsiness let his head knock against the front of the cart. He woke up near home. His first movement was to reach for his cap, but feeling that it sat firmly on his head he did not take it off, convinced that the envelope was inside. He gave Drum a touch, arranged the hay in the cart again, assumed once more the appearance of a well-to-do peasant, and proudly looking about him rattled homewards.

There was the kitchen, there were the house-serfs' quarters, there was the carpenter's wife carrying some linen, there was the office, and there was the mistress's house where in a few moments Polikey would show that he was a trustworthy and honest man, that 'one can say anything about anybody', and the mistress would say, 'Well, thank you, Polikey! Here are three, and maybe even five, and maybe even ten roubles, and she would tell them to give him some tea, and maybe even some vodka. It would not be so bad, after being out in the cold! 'With ten roubles we would have a treat for the holiday, and buy boots, and return Nikita his four and a half roubles, it can't be helped! He has begun pestering.' When he was about a hundred paces from the house, Polikey again wrapped his coat round him, fixed his belt and his collar, took off his cap, smoothed his hair, and without haste thrust his hand under the lining. The hand began to fumble faster and faster inside the lining, then the other hand went in too, while his face grew paler and paler. One hand went right through the cap. Polikey fell on his knees, stopped the horse, and began searching in the cart among the hay and the things he had bought, feeling inside his coat and in his trousers. The money was nowhere to be found.

'Heavens! What does it mean? What will happen?' He began to howl, clutching at his hair.

But recollecting that he might be seen, he turned the horse round, pulled the cap on, and drove the surprised and disgruntled Drum back along the road.

'I can't bear going out with Polikey,' Drum must have thought. 'For once in his life he has fed and watered me properly, and then only to deceive me so unpleasantly! How hard I tried, running home! I am tired, and hardly have we got within smell of our hay than he starts driving me back!'

'Now then, you devil's nag!' shouted Polikey through his tears, while standing up in the cart, pulling the reins on Drum's mouth, and beating him with the whip.

X

All that day no one saw Polikey in Pokrovskoe. The mistress asked for him several times after dinner, and Aksyutka flew down to Akulina, but Akulina said he had not yet returned, and that evidently the merchant had detained him or something had happened to the horse. 'If only it has not gone lame!' she said. 'Last time, when Maxim went, he was on the road a whole day, had to walk back all the way.' And Aksyutka turned her pendulums back to the house again, while Akulina, trying to calm her own fears, invented reasons to account for her husband's absence, but in vain! Her heart was heavy and she could not get herself to work at any of the preparations for the morrow's holiday. She suffered all the more because the carpenter's wife assured her that she herself had seen 'a man just like Ilyich drive up to the avenue and then turn back again'. The children, too, were anxiously and impatiently expecting Daddy, but for another reason. Anyutka and Mashka, being left without the sheepskin and the coat which made it possible to take turns out of doors, could only run out in their indoor dresses with increasing rapidity in a small circle round the house. This was not a little inconvenient to all the dwellers in the serfs' quarters who wanted to go in or out. Once Mashka ran against the legs of the carpenter's wife who was carrying water, and though she began to yell out beforehand, as soon as she bumped against the woman's knees she got her curls cuffed all the same and cried still louder. When she did not bump against anyone, she would fly through the door, and immediately climb up by means of a tub onto the top of the oven. Only the mistress and Akulina were really anxious about Polikey; the children were concerned only about what he had on. Yegor Mikhaylovich reporting to his mistress, in response to her questions, 'Hasn't Polikey come back yet?' and 'Where can he be?' smiled and answered: 'I can't say,' and seemed pleased that his expectations were being fulfilled. 'He ought to have been back by noon,' he added significantly.

All that day at Potrovskoe, no one heard anything of Polikey. Only later on it was learned that some neighbouring peasants had seen him running about on the road bareheaded, and asking everyone whether they hadn't found a letter. Another man had seen him asleep by the roadside beside a tied-up horse and cart. 'I thought he was tipsy,' the man said, 'and the horse looked as if it had not been watered or fed for two days, its sides were so fallen in.' Akulina did not sleep all night and kept listening, but Polikey did not return. Had she been alone and had a cook and a maid, she would have felt still more unhappy; but as soon as the cocks crowed and the carpenter's wife got up, Akulina was obliged to rise and light the fire. It was a holiday. The bread had to come out of the oven before daybreak, *kvas* had to be made, cakes baked, the cow milked, frocks and shirts ironed, the children washed, water fetched, and her neighbour prevented from taking up the whole oven. So Akulina, still listening, set to work. It had grown light and the church bells were ringing, the children were up, but still Polikey had not returned. There had been a first frost the day before, a little snow had fallen and lay in patches on the fields, on the road, and on the roofs; and now, as if in honour of the holiday, the day was fine, sunny, and frosty, so that one could see and hear a long way. But Akulina, standing by the brick oven, her head thrust into the opening, was so busy with her cakes that she did not hear Polikey drive up, and only knew from the children's cries that her husband had returned. Anyutka, as the eldest, had greased her hair and dressed herself without help. She wore a new but crumpled print dress, a present from the mistress, which stuck out as stiff as if it were made of bast and was an object of envy to the neighbours; her hair, on which she had smeared half an inch of tallow candle, glistened; her shoes, though not new, were dainty. Mashka was still wrapped in the old jacket and was covered with mud, and Anyutka would not let her come near her for fear of getting soiled. Mashka was outside when she saw her father drive up with a sack. 'Daddy has come!' she shrieked, and rushed headlong through the door past Anyutka, dirtying her. Anyutka, no longer fearing to be soiled, went for her at once and hit her. Akulina could not leave her work, and only shouted at the children: 'Hey you, I'll whip you all!' and looked round at the door. Ilyich came in with a sack, and at once made his way to his own corner. It seemed to Akulina that he was pale, and his face looked as if he were either smiling or crying, but she had no time to work out which it was.

'Well, Ilyich, is everything all right?' she called to him from the oven.

Ilyich muttered something that she did not understand.

'Eh?' she cried. 'Have you been to the mistress?'

Ilyich sat down on the bed in his corner looking wildly round him and smiling his guilty, intensely miserable smile. He did not answer for a long time.

'Eh, Ilyich? Why so long?' came Akulina's voice.

'Yes, Akulina, I have handed the lady her money. How she thanked me!' he said suddenly, and began looking round and smiling still more uneasily. Two things attracted his restless and feverishly staring eyes: the rope attached to the hanging cradle and the baby. He went up to where the cradle hung, and began hastily undoing the knot of the rope with his thin fingers. Then his eyes fixed themselves on the baby; but just then Akulina entered, carrying a board of cakes. Ilyich quickly hid the rope in his shirt and sat down on the bed.

'What is it, Ilyich? You are not like yourself,' said Akulina.

'Haven't slept,' he answered.

Suddenly something flitted past the window, and in a moment Aksyutka, the maid from 'up there', darted in like an arrow.

'The mistress has ordered Ilyich to come this minute,' she said— 'this minute, Avdotya Mikolavna has ordered . . . this minute!'

Polikey looked at Akulina, then at the girl.

'I'm coming. What can she want?' he said, so simply that Akulina grew quieter. 'Perhaps she wants to reward me. Tell her I'm coming.'

He rose and went out. Akulina took the washing trough, put it on a bench, filled it with water from the pails which stood by the door and from the cauldron in the oven, rolled up her sleeves, and tested the water.

'Come, Mashka, I'll wash you.'

The cross, lisping little girl began howling.

'Come, you brat! I'll give you a clean smock. Now then, don't make a fuss. Come along. I've still got your brother to wash.'

Meanwhile Polikey had not followed the maid from 'up there', but had gone to quite a different place. In the passage by the wall was a ladder leading to the loft. Polikey, when he got into the passage, looked round, and, seeing no one, bent down and almost at a run, nimbly and hurriedly climbed that ladder.

'What does it mean that Polikey hasn't come?' asked the mistress impatiently of Dunyasha, who was dressing her hair. 'Where is Polikey? Why hasn't he come?'

Aksyutka again flew to the serfs' quarters, and again rushed into the entry, calling Ilyich to her mistress.

'Why, he went long ago,' answered Akulina, who, having washed Mashka, had just put her baby boy into the wash trough and was moistening his thin, short hair, regardless of his cries. The boy screamed, puckered his face, and tried to clutch something with his helpless little hands. Akulina supported his soft, plump, dimpled little back with one large hand, while she washed him with the other.

'See if he has not fallen asleep somewhere,' she said, looking round anxiously.

Just then the carpenter's wife, unkempt and with her dress unfastened and holding up her skirts, went up into the loft to get some things she had hung there to dry. Suddenly a shriek of horror filled the loft, and the carpenter's wife, like one demented, with her eyes closed, came down the ladder on all fours, backwards, sliding rather than running.

'Ilyich!' she screamed.

Akulina let go the baby.

'He's hanged himself!' roared the carpenter's wife.

Akulina rushed out into the passage, paying no heed to the baby, who rolled over like a ball and fell backwards with his little legs in the air and his head under water.

'He's hanging on a rafter!' the carpenter's wife blurted out, but stopped when she saw Akulina.

Akulina darted up the ladder, and before anyone could stop her she was at the top, but from there with a terrible scream she fell back like a corpse, and would have been killed if the people who had come running from every corner had not been in time to catch her.

XI

For several minutes nothing could be made out amidst the general uproar. A crowd of people had collected, everyone was shouting and talking, the children and old women were crying. Akulina lay unconscious. At last the men, the carpenter and the steward who had run to the place, went up the ladder, and the carpenter's wife began telling for the twentieth time how she, 'suspecting nothing, went to fetch a dress, and just looked round like this and saw a man standing there, and I looked again, and a cap is lying inside out, close by. I look and his legs are dangling. I went cold all over! It's no trifle, a man hanging himself, and I should be the one to see him! How I came clattering down I myself don't remember. It's a miracle how God preserved me! Truly, the Lord has had mercy on me! It's no trifle, so steep and from such a height. Why, I might have been killed!'

The men who had gone up had the same tale to tell. Polikey, in his shirt and trousers, was hanging from a rafter by the rope he had taken from the cradle. His cap, turned inside out, lay beside him, his coat and sheepskin were neatly folded and lay close by. His feet touched the ground, but he no longer showed signs of life. Akulina regained consciousness, and again made for the ladder, but was held back.

'Mamma, Syomka is dwownded!' the lisping little girl suddenly cried from their *corner*. Akulina tore herself away and ran to the *corner*. The baby lay on his back in the trough and did not stir, and his little legs were not moving. Akulina snatched him out, but he did not breathe or move. She threw him on the bed, and with arms akimbo burst into such loud, piercing, terrifying laughter that Mashka, who at first laughed too, covered her ears with her hands, and ran out into the passage crying. The neighbours thronged into the *corner*, weeping and wailing. They carried out the little boy and began rubbing him, but in vain. Akulina tossed about on the bed and laughed, laughed so that all who heard her were horror-stricken. Only now, seeing this motley crowd of men and women, old people and children, did one realize what a number of people and what sort of people lived in the serfs' quarters. All were bustling and talking, many wept, but nobody did anything. The carpenter's wife still found people who had not heard her tale of how her sensitive feelings were shocked by the unexpected sight, and how God had preserved her from falling down the ladder. An old man who had been a foot-man, with a woman's jacket thrown over his shoulders, was telling how in the days of the old master a woman had drowned herself in the pond. The steward sent messengers to the priest and to the constable, and appointed men to keep guard. Aksyutka, the maid from 'up there', kept gazing with staring eyes at the opening that led to the loft, and though she could not see anything was unable to tear herself away and go back to her mistress. Agatha Mikhaylovna, who had been lady's-maid to the former mistress, was weeping and asking for some tea to soothe her nerves. Granny Anna the midwife was laying out the little body on the table, with her plump practised hands moistened with olive oil. Other women stood round Akulina, silently looking at her. The children, huddled together in the corner, peeped at their mother and burst into howls; and then subsiding for a moment, peeped again, and huddled still closer. Boys and men thronged round the porch, looking in at the door and the windows with frightened faces unable to see or understand anything, and asking one another what was the matter. One said the carpenter had chopped off his wife's foot with an axe. Another said that the laun-dress had given birth to triplets. A third that the cook's cat had gone mad and bitten several people. But the truth gradually spread, and at last it reached the ears of the mistress. And it seems no one knew

how to break it to her. That rough Yegor blurted the facts straight
out to her and so upset the lady's nerves that it was a long time
before she could recover. The crowd had already begun to quiet
down, the carpenter's wife set the samovar to boil and made tea, and
the outsiders, not being invited, thought it improper to stay longer.
Boys had begun fighting out on the porch. Everybody now knew
what had happened, and crossing themselves they began to disperse,
when suddenly the cry was raised: 'The mistress! The mistress!' and
everybody crowded and pressed together to make way for her, but at
the same time everybody wanted to see what she was going to do.
The mistress, with pale and tear-stained face, entered the passage,
crossed the threshold, and went into Akulina's *corner*. Dozens of
heads squeezed together and gazed in at the door. One pregnant
woman was squeezed so that she gave a squeal, but took advantage of
that very circumstance to secure a front place for herself. And how
could one help wishing to see the mistress in Akulina's *corner*? For
the house-serfs it was just what the coloured lights are at the end of a
show. It's sure to be great when they burn the coloured lights; and
it's sure to be great when the mistress in her silks and lace enters
Akulina's *corner*. The mistress went up and took Akulina's hand, but
Akulina snatched it away. The old house-serfs shook their heads
reprovingly.

'Akulina!' said the mistress. 'You have your children, so take care
of yourself!'

Akulina burst out laughing and got up.

'My children are all silver, all silver! I don't keep paper money,'
she muttered very rapidly. 'I told Ilyich, "Take no notes," and there
now, they've smeared him, smeared him with tar, tar and soap,
madam! Any scabbiness you may have it will get rid of at once.' And
again she laughed some more.

The mistress turned away, and gave orders that the doctor's assistant should come with mustard poultices. 'Bring some cold water!'
she said, and began looking for it herself; but seeing the dead baby
with Granny Anna beside it, the mistress turned away, and everybody saw how she hid her face in her handkerchief and burst into
tears; while Granny Anna (it was a pity the mistress did not see it,
she would have appreciated it, and it was all done for her benefit)
covered the baby with a piece of linen, straightened his arms with
her plump, deft hands, shook her head, pouted, drooped her eyelids,

and sighed with so much feeling that everybody could see how excellent a heart she had. But the mistress did not see it, she could not see anything. She burst out sobbing and went into hysterics. Holding her up under the arms they led her out into the porch and took her home. 'That's all there was to be seen of her!' thought many, and again began to disperse. Akulina went on laughing and talking nonsense. She was taken into another room, bled, plastered over with mustard poultices, and ice put on her head. Yet she did not come to her senses and did not weep, but laughed, and kept doing and saying such things that the kind people who were looking after her could not help laughing themselves.

XII

The holiday was not a cheerful one at Pokrovskoe. Though the day was beautiful the people did not go out to amuse themselves: no girls sang songs in the street, the factory hands who had come home from town for the day did not play on their concertinas and balalaikas and did not play with the girls. Everybody sat about in the *corners*, and if they spoke did so as softly as if an evil one were there who could hear them. It was not quite so bad in the daytime, but when the twilight fell and the dogs began to howl, and when, to make matters worse, a wind sprang up and whistled down the chimneys, such fear seized all the people of the place that those who had candles lit them before their icons. Anyone who happened to be alone in his *corner* went to ask the neighbours' permission to stay the night with them, to be less lonely, and anyone whose business should have taken him into one of the barns did not go, but pitilessly left the cattle without fodder that night. And the holy water, of which everyone kept a little bottle to charm away anything evil, was all used up during the night. Many even heard something walking about with heavy steps up in the loft, and the blacksmith saw a serpent fly straight towards it. In Polikey's *corner* there was no one; the children and the mad woman had been taken elsewhere. Only the little dead body lay there, and two old women sat and watched it, while a third, a pilgrim woman, was reading the psalms, actuated by her own zeal, not for the sake of the baby but in a vague way because of the whole calamity. The mistress had willed it so. The pilgrim woman and these old women

themselves heard how, as soon as they finished reading a passage of
the psalter, the rafters above would tremble and someone would
groan. Then they would read, 'Let God arise,' and all would be quiet
again. The carpenter's wife invited a friend and, not sleeping all
night, with her aid drank up all the tea she had laid in for the whole
week. They, too, heard how the rafters creaked overhead, and a noise
as if sacks were tumbling down. The presence of the peasant watchmen kept up the courage of the house-serfs somewhat, or they would
have died of fear that night. The peasants lay on some hay in the
passage, and afterwards declared that they too had heard wonderful
things up in the loft, though at the time they were conversing very
calmly together about the conscription, munching crusts of bread,
scratching themselves, and above all so filling the passage with the
peculiar odour characteristic of peasants that the carpenter's wife,
happening to pass by, spat and cursed them. However that might be,
the dead man was still dangling in the loft, and it seemed as if the evil
spirit himself had overshadowed the serfs' quarters with his huge
wings that night, showing his power and coming closer to these
people than he had ever done before. So at least they all felt. I do not
know if they were right; I even think they were quite mistaken. I
think that if some bold fellow had taken a candle or lantern that
terrible night, and crossing himself, or even without crossing himself, had gone up into the loft—slowly dispelling before him the
horror of the night with the candle, lighting up the rafters, the sand,
the cobweb-covered flue-pipe, and the dress left behind by the carpenter's wife—till he came to Ilyich, and, conquering his fears, had
raised the lantern to the level of the face, he would have beheld the
familiar thin body bending lifelessly to one side, with the feet
touching the ground (the cord had stretched), no cross visible under
the open shirt, the head drooping on the breast, the good-natured
face with open sightless eyes, and the meek, guilty smile, and a
solemn calmness and silence over all. Really the carpenter's wife,
crouching in a corner of her bed with dishevelled hair and frightened
eyes and telling how she heard the sacks falling, was far more terrible
and frightful than Ilyich, though his cross had been taken off and lay
on the rafter.

'Up there', that is, in the mistress's house, reigned the same horror as in the serfs' quarters. Her bedroom smelt of eau-de-cologne
and medicine. Dunyasha was melting yellow wax and making a

plaster. What the plaster was for I don't know, but it was always made when the mistress was unwell. And now she was so upset that she was quite ill. To keep Dunyasha's courage up her aunt had come to stay the night, so there were four of them, including the girl, sitting in the maid's room, and talking in low voices.

'Who will go to get some oil?' asked Dunyasha.

'Nothing will induce me to go, Avdotya Mikolavna!' the second maid said decidedly.

'Nonsense! You and Aksyutka go together.'

'I'll run across alone. I'm not afraid of anything!' said Aksyutka, and at once became frightened.

'Well then, go, dear; ask Granny Anna to give you some in a tumbler and bring it here; don't spill any,' said Dunyasha.

Aksyutka lifted her skirt with one hand, and being thereby prevented from swinging both arms, swung one of them twice as violently across the line of her progression, and darted away. She was afraid, and felt that if she should see or hear anything, even her own living mother, she would perish with fright. She flew, with her eyes shut, along the familiar pathway.

XIII

'Is the mistress asleep or not?' suddenly asked a deep peasant voice close to Aksyutka. She opened her eyes, which she had kept shut, and saw a figure that seemed to her taller than the house. She screeched, and flew back so fast that her skirts floated behind her. With one bound she was on the porch and with another in the maid's room, where she threw herself on her bed with a wild yell. Dunyasha, her aunt, and the second maid almost died of terror, and before they had time to recover they heard heavy, slow, hesitating steps in the passage and at their door. Dunyasha rushed to her mistress, spilling the melted wax. The second maid hid herself behind the skirts that hung on the wall; the aunt, a more determined character, was about to hold the door to the passage closed, but it opened and a peasant entered the room. It was Dutlov, with his boatlike shoes. Paying no heed to the maids' fears, he looked round for an icon, and not seeing the tiny one in the left-hand corner of the room, he crossed himself in front of a cupboard in which teacups were kept, laid his cap on the window-sill, and thrusting his arm deep into the bosom of his coat as if he were going to scratch himself under his other arm, he pulled out the letter stamped with the five brown anchor-shaped seals. Dunyasha's aunt held her hands to her heart and with difficulty brought out the words:

'Well, you did give me a fright, Naumych! I can scarcely speak! I thought my last moment had come!'

'Is that the way to behave?' said the second maid, appearing from under the skirts.

'The mistress herself is upset,' said Dunyasha, coming out of her mistress's door. 'What do you mean, shoving yourself in through the maids' entrance without permission? Just like a peasant!'

Dutlov, without excusing himself, explained that he wanted to see the mistress.

'She is not well,' said Dunyasha.

At this moment Aksyutka burst into such loud and unseemly laughter that she was obliged to hide her face in the pillow on the bed, from which for a whole hour, in spite of Dunyasha's and the aunt's threats, she could not for long lift it without going off again as if something were bursting in her pink bosom and rosy cheeks. It seemed to her so funny that everybody should have been so scared, that she again hid her head in the pillows and scraped the floor with her shoe and jerked her whole body as if in convulsions.

Dutlov stopped and looked at her attentively, as if to ascertain what was happening to her, but turned away again without having discovered what it was all about, and continued:

'You see, it's just this—it's a very important matter,' he said. 'You just go and say that a peasant has found the letter with the money.'

'What money?'

Dunyasha, before going to report, read the address and questioned Dutlov as to when and how he had found this money which Ilyich was to have brought back from town. Having heard all the details and pushed the little errand-girl, who was still convulsed with laughter, out into the vestibule, Dunyasha went to her mistress; but to Dutlov's surprise the mistress would not see him and did not say anything intelligible to Dunyasha.

'I know nothing about it and don't want to know anything!' the mistress said. 'What peasant? What money? I can't and won't see anyone! He must leave me in peace.'

'What am I to do?' said Dutlov, turning the envelope over; 'it's not a small sum. What is written on it?' he asked Dunyasha, who again read the address to him.

Dutlov seemed in doubt. He was still hoping that perhaps the money was not the mistress's and that the address had not been read to him right, but Dunyasha confirmed it, and he put the envelope back into his bosom with a sigh, and was about to go.

'I suppose I shall have to hand it over to the police constable,' he said.

'Wait a bit! I'll try again,' said Dunyasha, stopping him, after attentively following the disappearance of the envelope into the bosom of the peasant's coat. 'Let me have the letter.'

Dutlov took it out again, but did not at once put it into Dunyasha's outstretched hand.

'Say that Semyon Dutlov found it on the road.'

'Well, let me have it!'

'I did think it was nothing, just a letter, but a soldier read out to me that there was money inside.'

'Well then, let me have it.'

'I dared not even go home first,' Dutlov continued, still not parting with the precious envelope. 'Let her know that.'

Dunyasha took it from him and went again to her mistress.

'O my God, Dunyasha, don't speak to me of that money!' said the lady in a reproachful tone. 'Only to think of that little baby.'

'The peasant does not know to whom you wish it to be given, madam,' Dunyasha again said.

The mistress opened the envelope, shuddering at the sight of the money, and pondered.

'Dreadful money! How much evil it has done!' she said.

'It is Dutlov, madam. Do you order him to go, or do you wish to come out and see him; is all the money still there?' asked Dunyasha.

'I don't want this money. It is terrible money! What it has done! Tell him to take it himself if he likes,' said the mistress suddenly, feeling for Dunyasha's hand. 'Yes, yes, yes!' she repeated to the astonished Dunyasha; 'let him take it altogether and do what he likes with it.'

'Fifteen hundred roubles,' remarked Dunyasha, smiling as if at a child.

'Let him take it all!' the mistress repeated impatiently. 'How is it you don't understand me? It is unlucky money. Never speak of it to me again! Let the peasant who found it take it. Go, go along!'

Dunyasha went out into the maids' room.

'Is it all there?' asked Dutlov.

'You'd better count it yourself,' said Dunyasha, handing him the envelope. 'My orders are to give it to you.'

Dutlov put his cap under his arm, and, bending forward, began to count the money.

'Have you got an abacus?'*

Dutlov had an idea that the mistress was stupid and could not count, and that that was why she ordered him to do so.

'You can count it at home, the money is yours!' Dunyasha said crossly. ' "I don't want to see it," she said; "give it to the man who brought it." '

Dutlov, without unbending his back, stared at Dunyasha.

Dunyasha's aunt flung up her hands.

'O holy Mother! What luck the Lord has sent him! O holy Mother!'

The second maid would not believe it.

'You don't mean it, Avdotya Mikolavna; you're joking!'

'Joking, indeed! She told me to give it to the peasant. There, take your money and go!' said Dunyasha, without hiding her vexation. 'One man's sorrow is another man's good fortune!'

'It's no joke, fifteen hundred roubles!' said the aunt.

'It's even more,' stated Dunyasha. 'Well, you'll have to give a ten-kopek candle to St Nikolay,' she added sarcastically. 'Why don't you come to your senses? If it had come to a poor man, fine! But this man has plenty of his own.'

Dutlov at last grasped that it was not a joke, and began gathering together the notes he had spread out to count and putting them back into the envelope. But his hands trembled, and he kept glancing at the maids to assure himself that it was not a joke.

'See! He can't come to his senses he's so pleased,' said Dunyasha, implying that she despised both the peasant and the money. 'Come, I'll put it back for you.'

She was going to take the notes, but Dutlov would not let her. He crumpled them together, pushed them in deeper, and took his cap.

'Are you glad?'

'I hardly know what to say! It's really . . .'

He did not finish, but waved his hand, smiled, and went out almost crying.

The mistress rang.

'Well, have you given it to him?'

'I have.'

'Well, was he very glad?'

'He was just like a madman.'

'Ah! call him back. I want to ask him how he found it. Call him in here; I can't come out.'

Dunyasha ran out and found the peasant in the entry. He was still bareheaded, but had drawn out his purse and was stooping, untying its strings, while he held the money between his teeth. Perhaps he imagined that as long as the money was not in his purse it was not his. When Dunyasha called him he grew frightened.

'What is it, Avdotya . . . Avdotya Mikolavna? Does she want to take it back? Couldn't you say a word for me? Now really, and I'd bring you some nice honey.'

'Indeed! Much you ever brought!'

Again the door was opened, and the peasant was brought in to the mistress. He felt anything but cheerful. 'Oh dear, she'll want it back!' he thought on his way through the rooms, lifting his feet for some reason as if he were walking through high grass, and trying not to stamp with his bast shoes. He could make nothing of his surroundings. Passing by a mirror he saw flowers of some sort and a peasant in bast shoes lifting his feet high, a gentleman with an eyeglass painted on the wall, some kind of green tub, and something white. . . . There, now! The something white began to speak. It was his mistress. He did not understand anything but only stared. He did not know where he was, and everything appeared as in a fog.

'Is that you, Dutlov?'

'Yes, ma'am. Just as it was, so I left it,' he said. 'I am not glad so help me God! How I've tired out my horse! . . .'

'Well, it's your good fortune!' she remarked contemptuously, though with a kindly smile. 'Take it, take it for yourself.'

He just stared at her.

'I am glad that you got it. God grant that it may be of use. Well, are you glad?'

'How could I help being glad? I'm so glad, ma'am, so glad! I will

pray for you always! So glad that, thank Heaven, our mistress is alive!
It was not my fault.'

'How did you find it?'

'Well, I mean, we can always do our best for our mistress, quite
honourably, and not anyhow . . .'

'He is in a regular muddle, madam,' said Dunyasha.

'I had taken my nephew, the conscript, and as I was driving back
along the road I found it. Polikey must have dropped it.'

'Well, then, go, go, my good man! I am glad you found it!'

'I am so glad, ma'am!' said the peasant.

Then he remembered that he had not thanked her properly, and
did not know how to behave. The mistress and Dunyasha smiled,
and then he again began stepping as if he were walking in very high
grass, and could hardly refrain from running so afraid was he that he
might be stopped and the money taken from him.

XIV

When he got out into the fresh air Dutlov stepped aside from the
road to the lindens, even undoing his belt to get at his purse more
easily, and began putting away the money. His lips were twitching,
stretching and drawing together again, though he uttered no sound.
Having put away his money and fastened his belt, he crossed himself
and went staggering along the road as though he were drunk, so full
was he of the thoughts that came rushing to his mind. Suddenly he
saw the figure of a man coming towards him. He called out. It was
Yefimka, who with a cudgel in his hand was on watch at the serfs'
quarters.

'Ah, Daddy Semyon!' said Yefimka cheerfully, drawing nearer
(Yefimka felt it uncanny to be alone). 'Have you got the conscripts
off, daddy?'

'We have. What are you after?'

'Why, I've been put here to watch over Ilyich who's hanged
himself.'

'And where is he?'

'Up there, hanging in the loft, so they say,' answered Yefimka,
pointing with his cudgel through the darkness to the roof of the
serfs' quarters.

Dutlov looked in the direction of the arm, and though he could see nothing he puckered his brows, screwed up his eyes, and shook his head.

'The police constable has come,' said Yefimka, 'so the coachman said. He'll be taken down at once. Isn't it horrible at night, daddy? Nothing would make me go up at night even if they ordered me to. If Yegor Mikhaylovich were to kill me outright I wouldn't go.'

'What a sin, oh, what a sin!' Dutlov kept repeating, evidently for propriety's sake and not even thinking what he was saying. He was about to go on his way, but the voice of Yegor Mikhaylovich stopped him.

Hey! watchman! Come here!' shouted Yegor Mikhaylovich from the porch of the office.

Yefimka replied to him.

'Who was that other peasant standing with you?'

'Dutlov.'

'Ah! and you too, Semyon! Come here!'

Having drawn near, Dutlov, by the light of a lantern the coachman was carrying, recognized Yegor Mikhaylovich and a short man with a cockade on his cap, dressed in a long uniform overcoat. This was the police constable.

'Here, this old man will come with us too,' said Yegor Mikhaylovich on seeing him.

The old man felt a bit uncomfortable, but there was no getting out of it.

'And you, Yefimka, you're a bold lad! Run up into the loft where he's hanged himself, and set the ladder straight for his honour to mount.'

Yefimka, who had declared that he would not go near the loft for anything in the world, now ran towards it, clattering with his bast shoes as if they were logs.

The police officer struck a light and lit a pipe. He lived about a mile and a half off, and having just been severely reprimanded for drunkenness by his superior, was in a zealous mood. Having arrived at ten o'clock at night, he wished to view the corpse at once. Yegor Mikhaylovich asked Dutlov how he came to be there. On the way Dutlov told the steward about the money he had found and what the mistress had done, and said he was coming to ask Yegor Mikhaylovich's sanction. To Dutlov's horror the steward asked for the envelope and examined it. The police constable even took the envelope in his hand and briefly and drily asked the details.

'Oh dear, the money is gone!' thought Dutlov, and began justifying himself. But the police constable handed him back the money.

'What a piece of luck for the clodhopper!' he said.

'It comes handy for him,' said Yegor Mikhaylovich. 'He's just been taking his nephew to be conscripted, and now he'll buy him out.'

'Ah!' said the policeman, and went on in front.

'Will you buy him off, Ilyushka, I mean?' asked Yegor Mikhaylovich.

'How am I to buy him off? Will there be money enough? And perhaps it's too late.'

'Well, you know best,' said the steward, and they both followed the police constable.

They approached the serfs' house, where the ill-smelling watchmen stood waiting in the passage with a lantern. Dutlov followed them. The watchmen looked guilty, perhaps because of the smell they were spreading, for they had done nothing wrong. All were silent.

'Where is he?' asked the police constable.

'Here,' said Yegor Mikhaylovich in a whisper. 'Yefimka,' he added, 'you're a bold lad, go on in front with the lantern.'

Yefimka had already put a plank straight at the top of the ladder, and seemed to have lost all fear. Taking two or three steps at a time, he clambered up with a cheerful look, only turning round to light the way for the police constable. The constable was followed by Yegor Mikhaylovich. When they had disappeared above, Dutlov, with one foot on the bottom step, sighed and stopped. Two or three minutes passed. The footsteps in the loft were no longer heard; they had no doubt reached the body.

'Daddy, they want you,' Yefimka called down through the opening.

Dutlov began going up. The light of the lantern showed only the upper part of the bodies of the police constable and of Yegor Mikhaylovich beyond the rafters. Beyond them again someone else was standing with his back turned. It was Polikey. Dutlov climbed over a rafter and stopped, crossing himself.

'Turn him round, lads!' said the police constable.

No one stirred.

'Yefimka, you're a bold lad,' said Yegor Mikhaylovich.

The bold lad stepped across a rafter, turned Ilyich round, and stood beside him, looking with a most cheerful face now at Ilyich now at the constable, as a showman exhibiting an albino or Julia Pastrana* looks now at the public and now at what he is exhibiting, ready to do anything the spectators may wish.

'Turn him round again.'

Ilyich was turned round, his arms slightly swaying and his feet dragging in the sand on the floor.

'Catch hold, and take him down.'

'Shall we cut the rope through, your honour?' asked Yegor Mikhaylovich. 'Hand us an axe, lads!'

The watchmen and Dutlov had to be told twice before they set to, but the 'bold lad' handled Ilyich as he would have handled a sheep's carcass. At last the rope was cut through and the body taken down and covered up. The police constable said that the doctor would come next day and dismissed them all.

XV

Still moving his lips, Dutlov took off towards home. At first he had an uncanny feeling, but it passed as he drew nearer home, and a feeling of gladness gradually penetrated his heart. In the village he heard songs and drunken voices. Dutlov never drank, and this time too he went straight home. It was late when he entered his hut. His old wife was asleep. His eldest son and grandsons were asleep on the stove, and his second son in the storeroom. Ilyushka's wife alone was awake, and sat on the bench bareheaded, in a dirty, working-day smock, wailing. She did not come out to meet her uncle, but only sobbed louder, lamenting her fate, when he entered. According to the old woman, she 'lamented' very fluently and well, taking into consideration the fact that at her age she could not have had much practice.

The old woman rose and got supper for her husband. Dutlov turned Ilyushka's wife away from the table, saying: 'That's enough, that's enough!' Aksinya went away, and lying down on a bench continued to lament. The old woman put the supper on the table and afterwards silently cleared it away again. The old man did not speak either. When he had said grace he hiccuped, washed his hands, took the counting-frame from a nail in the wall, and went into the storeroom. There he and the old woman spoke in whispers for a little while, and then, after she had gone away, he began counting on the frame, making the beads click. Finally he banged the lid of the chest standing there, and clambered into the space under the floor. For a long time he went on bustling about in the room and in the space below. When he came back to the living room it was dark in the hut. The wooden splint that served for a candle had gone out. His old woman, quiet and silent in the daytime, had rolled herself up on the sleeping-bunk and filled the hut with her snoring. Ilyushka's noisy young wife was also asleep, breathing quietly. She lay on the bench dressed just as she had been, and with nothing under her head for a pillow. Dutlov began to pray, then looked at Ilyushka's wife, shook his head, put out the light, hiccuped again, and climbed up on the stove, where he lay down beside his little grandson. He threw down his plaited bast shoes from the stove in the dark and lay on his back, looking up at the rafter which was hardly discernible just over his head above the stove and listening to the sounds of the cockroaches swarming along the walls, and to the sighs, the snoring, the rubbing of one foot against another, and the noise made by the cattle outside. It was a long time before he could sleep. The moon rose. It grew lighter in the hut. He could see Aksinya in her corner and something he could not make out: was it a coat his son had forgotten, or a tub the women had put there, or a man standing there? Perhaps he was drowsing, perhaps not; anyhow he began to peer into the darkness. Evidently that evil spirit who had led Ilyich to commit his awful deed, and whose presence was felt that night by all the house-serfs, had stretched out his wing and reached across the village to the house in which lay the money that *he* had used to ruin Ilyich. At least, Dutlov felt *his* presence and was ill at ease. He could neither sleep nor get up. After noticing the something he could not make out, he remembered Ilya with his arms bound, and Aksinya's face and her eloquent lamentations; and he recalled Ilyich with his swaying hands. Suddenly it seemed to the old man that someone passed by the window. 'Who was that? Could it be the village elder coming so early with a notice?' he thought. 'How did he open the door?' thought the old man, hearing a step in the passage. 'Had the old woman not put up the bar when she went out into the passage?' The dog began to howl in the yard and *he* came stepping along the passage, so the old man related afterwards, as though he were trying to find the door, then passed on and began groping along the wall, stumbled over a tub and made it clatter, and again began groping as if feeling for the latch. Now *he* had hold of the latch. A shiver ran down the old man's body. Now *he* pulled the latch and entered in the shape of a man. Dutlov knew it was *he*. He wished to cross himself, but could not. *He* went up to the table which was covered with a cloth, and, pulling it off, threw it on the floor and began climbing onto the stove. The old man knew that *he* had taken the shape of Ilyich. *He* was showing his teeth and his hands were swinging about. *He* climbed up, fell on the old man's chest, and began to strangle him.

'The money's mine!' muttered Ilyich.

'Let me go! I won't do it!' Semyon tried to say, but could not.

Ilyich was pressing down on him with the weight of a mountain of stone. Dutlov knew that if he said a prayer *he* would let him go, and he knew which prayer he ought to recite, but could not utter it. His grandson sleeping beside him uttered a shrill scream and began to cry. His grandfather had pressed him against the wall. The child's cry loosened the old man's lips. 'Let God arise!' he said. *He* pressed less hard. 'And let his enemies be scattered,' spluttered Dutlov. *He* got off the stove. Dutlov heard his two feet strike the floor. Dutlov went on repeating in turn all the prayers he knew. *He* went towards the door, passed the table, and slammed the door so that the whole hut shook. Everybody but the grandfather and grandson continued to sleep however. The grandfather, trembling all over, muttered prayers, while the grandson was crying himself to sleep and pressing close to his grandfather. All became quiet once more. The old man lay still. A cock crowed behind the wall close to Dutlov's ear. He heard the hens stirring, and a cockerel unsuccessfully trying to crow in answer to the old cock. Something moved over the old man's legs. It was the cat; she jumped on her soft pads from the stove to the floor, and stood mewing by the door. The old man got up and opened the window. It was dark and muddy in the street. The front of the cart was standing there close to the window. Crossing himself he went out barefoot into the yard to the horses. One could see that *he* had been there too. The mare, standing under the lean-to beside a tub of chaff, had got her foot into the cord of her halter and had spilt the chaff, and now, lifting her foot, turned her head and waited for her master. Her foal had tumbled over a heap of manure. The old man raised him to his feet, disentangled the mare's foot and fed her, and went back to the hut. The old woman got up and lit the splint. 'Wake the lads, I'm going to town!' And taking a wax taper from before the icon Dutlov lit it and went down with it into the opening under the floor. When he came up again lights were burning not only in his hut but in all the neighbouring houses. The young fellows were up and preparing to start. The women were coming in and out with pails of milk. Ignat was harnessing the horse to one cart and the second son was greasing the wheels of another. The young wife was no longer wailing. She had made herself neat and had bound a shawl over her head, and now sat waiting till it would be time to go to town to say goodbye to her husband.

The old man seemed particularly stern. He did not say a word to anyone, put on his best coat, tied his belt round him, and with all Ilyich's money in the bosom of his coat, went to Yegor Mikhaylovich.

'Don't dawdle,' he called to his son, who was turning the wheels round on the raised and newly greased axle. 'I'll be back in a minute; see that everything is ready.'

The steward had only just got up and was drinking tea. He himself was preparing to go to town to deliver up the recruits.

'What is it?' he asked.

'Yegor Mikhaylovich, I want to buy the lad off. Do be so good! You said t'other day that you knew one in the town that was willing. Explain to me how to do it; we are ignorant people.'

'Why, have you reconsidered it?'

'I have, Yegor Mikhaylovich. I'm sorry for him. My brother's child after all, whatever he may be. I'm sorry for him! It's the cause of much sin, money is. Do be good enough to explain it to me!' he said, bowing to his waist.

Yegor Mikhaylovich, as was his wont on such occasions, stood for a long time thoughtfully smacking his lips. Then, having considered the matter, he wrote two notes and told him what to do in town and how to do it.

When Dutlov got home, the young wife had already set off with Ignat. The fat roan mare stood ready harnessed at the gate.

Dutlov broke a stick out of the hedge and, lapping his coat over, got into the cart and whipped up the horse. He made the mare run so fast that her fat sides quickly shrank, and Dutlov did not look at her so as not to feel sorry for her. He was tormented by the thought that he might come too late for the recruiting, that Ilyukha would go as a soldier and the devil's money would be left on his hands.

I will not describe all Dutlov's proceedings that morning. I will only say that he was specially fortunate. The man to whom Yegor Mikhaylovich had given him a note had a volunteer quite ready who was already twenty-three silver roubles in debt and had been passed by the recruiting board. His master wanted four hundred silver roubles for him and a buyer in the town had for the last three weeks been offering him three hundred. Dutlov settled the matter in a couple of words. 'Will you take three twenty-five?' he said, holding out his hand, but with a look that showed that he was prepared to give more. The master held back his hand and went on asking four hundred. 'You won't take three and a quarter?' Dutlov said, catching hold with his left hand of the man's right and preparing to slap his own right hand down on it. 'You won't take it? Well, God be with you!' he said suddenly, smacking the master's hand with the full swing of his other hand and turning away with his whole body. 'It seems it has to be so, take three and a half hundred! Get out the discharge and bring the fellow along. And now here are two ten-rouble notes on account. Is it enough?'

And Dutlov unfastened his girdle and got out the money.

The man, though he did not withdraw his hand, yet did not seem quite to agree and, not accepting the deposit money, went on stipulating that Dutlov should wet the bargain and stand treat to the volunteer.

'Don't commit a sin,' Dutlov kept repeating as he held out the money. 'We shall all have to die some day,' he went on, in such a mild, persuasive and assured tone that the master said:

'So be it, then!' and again clapped Dutlov's hand and began praying for God's blessing. 'God grant you luck,' he said.

They woke the volunteer, who was still sleeping after yesterday's carouse, examined him for some reason, and went with him to the offices of the administration. The recruit was merry. He demanded rum as a refresher, for which Dutlov gave him some money, and only when they came into the vestibule of the recruiting board did his courage fail him. For a long time they stood in the entrance hall, the old master in his full blue cloak and the recruit in a short sheepskin, his eyebrows raised and his eyes staring. For a long time they whispered, tried to get somewhere, looked for somebody, and for some reason took off their caps and bowed to every copying-clerk they met, and meditatively listened to the decision which a scribe whom the master knew brought out to them. All hope of getting the business done that day began to vanish, and the recruit was growing more cheerful and unconstrained again, when Dutlov saw Yegor Mikhaylovich, seized on him at once, and began to beg and bow to him. Yegor Mikhaylovich helped him so efficiently that by about three o'clock the recruit, to his great dissatisfaction and surprise, was taken into the hall and placed for examination, and amid general merriment (in which for some reason everybody joined, from the watchmen to the president), he was undressed, dressed again, shaved, and led out at the door; and five minutes later Dutlov counted out the money, received the discharge, and, having taken leave of the volunteer and his master, went to the lodging-house where the Pokrovskoe recruits were staying. Ilya and his young wife were sitting in a corner of the kitchen, and as soon as the old man came in they stopped talking and looked at him with a resigned expression, but not with goodwill. As was his wont the old man said a prayer, and he then unfastened his belt, got out a paper, and called into the room his eldest son Ignat and Ilyushka's mother, who were in the yard.

'Don't sin, Ilyukha,' he said, coming up to his nephew. 'Last night you spoke such words to me. Don't I pity you? I remember how my brother left you to me. If it had been in my power would I have let you go? God has sent me good fortune, and I am not begrudging it you. Here it is, the paper'; and he put the discharge on the table and carefully smoothed it out with his stiff, unbending fingers.

All the Pokrovskoe peasants, the innkeeper's men, and even some outsiders, came in from the yard. All guessed what was happening, but no one interrupted the old man's solemn discourse.

'Here it is, the paper! Four hundred silver roubles I've given for it. Don't reproach your uncle.'

Ilyukha rose, but remained silent not knowing what to say. His lips quivered with emotion. His old mother came up and would have thrown herself sobbing on his neck; but the old man motioned her away slowly and authoritatively and continued speaking.

'You spoke those words to me yesterday,' the old man again repeated. 'You stabbed me to the heart with those words as with a knife! Your dying father left you to me and you have been as my own son to me, and if I have wronged you in any way, well, we all live in sin! Is it not so, good Orthodox folk?' he said, turning to the peasants who were standing round. 'Here is your own mother and your young wife, and here is the discharge for you. I don't care about the money, but forgive me for Christ's sake!'

And, turning up the skirts of his coat, he deliberately sank to his knees and bowed down to the ground before Ilyushka and his wife. The young people tried in vain to restrain him, but not till his forehead had touched the floor did he get up. Then, after giving his skirts a shake, he sat down on a bench. Ilyushka's mother and wife howled with joy, and words of approval were heard among the crowd. 'That is just, that's the godly way,' said one. 'What's money? You can't buy a fellow for money,' said another. 'What happiness!' said a third; 'no two ways about it, he's a just man!' Only the peasants who were to go as recruits said nothing, and went quietly out into the yard.

Two hours later Dutlov's two carts were driving through the outskirts of the town. In the first, to which was harnessed the roan mare, her sides fallen in and her neck moist with sweat, sat the old man and Ignat. Behind them jerked strings of ring-shaped fancy-bread. In the second cart, in which nobody held the reins, the young wife and her mother-in-law, with shawls over their heads, were sitting, sedate and happy. The former held a bottle of vodka under her apron. Ilyushka, very red in the face, sat all in a heap with his back to the horse, jolting against the front of the cart, biting into a roll and talking incessantly. The voices, the rumbling of the cartwheels on the stony road, and the snorting of the horses, blent into one note of merriment. The horses, swishing their tails, increased their speed more and more, feeling themselves on the homeward road. The passers-by, whether driving or on foot, involuntarily turned round to look at the happy family party.

Just as they left the town the Dutlovs overtook a party of recruits. A group of them were standing in a ring outside a tavern. One of the recruits, with that unnatural expression on his face which comes of having the front of the head shaved,* his grey cap pushed back, was vigorously strumming a balalaika; another, bareheaded and with a bottle of vodka in his hand, was dancing in the middle of the ring. Ignat stopped his horse and got down to tighten the traces. All the Dutlovs looked with curiosity, approval, and amusement at the dancer. The recruit seemed not to see anyone, but felt that the public admiring him had grown larger, and this added to his strength and agility. He danced briskly. His brows were knitted, his flushed face was set, and his lips were fixed in a grin that had long since lost all meaning. It seemed as if all the strength of his soul was concentrated on placing one foot as quickly as possible after the other, now on the heel and now on the toe. Sometimes he stopped suddenly and winked to the balalaika-player, who began playing still more briskly, strumming on all the strings and even striking the case with his knuckles. The recruit would stop, but even when he stood still he still seemed to be dancing all over. Then he began slowly jerking his shoulders, and suddenly twirling round, leaped in the air with a wild cry, and descending, crouched down, throwing out first one leg and then the other. The little boys laughed, the women shook their heads, the men smiled approvingly. An old sergeant stood quietly by, with a look that seemed to say: 'You think it wonderful, but we have long been familiar with it.' The balalaika-player seemed tired; he looked lazily round, struck a false chord, and suddenly knocked on the case with his knuckles, and the dance came to an end.

'Eh, Alyokha,' he said to the dancer, pointing at Dutlov, 'there's your sponsor!'

'Where? You, my dearest friend!' shouted Alyokha, the very recruit whom Dutlov had bought; and staggering forward on his weary legs and holding the bottle of vodka above his head he moved towards the cart. 'Mishka, a glass!' he cried to the player. 'Master! My dearest friend! What a pleasure, really!' he shouted, drooping his tipsy head over the cart, and he began to treat the men and women to vodka. The men drank, but the women refused. 'My dear friends, what can I offer you?' exclaimed Alyokha, embracing the old women.

A woman selling eatables was standing among the crowd. Alyokha noticed her, seized her tray, and poured its contents into the cart.

'I'll pay, no fear, you devil!' he howled tearfully, pulling a purse from his pocket and throwing it to Mishka.

He stood leaning with his elbows on the cart and looking with moist eyes at those who sat in it.

'Which is the mother, you?' he asked. 'I must treat you too.'

He stood thinking for a moment, then he put his hand in his pocket and drew out a new folded handkerchief, hurriedly took off a sash which was tied round his waist under his coat, and also a red scarf he was wearing round his neck, and, crumpling them all together, thrust them into the old woman's lap.

'There! I'm sacrificing them for you,' he said in a voice that was growing more and more subdued.

'What for? Thank you, sonny! Just see what a simple lad it is!' said the old woman, addressing Dutlov, who had come up to their cart.

Alyokha was now quite quiet, quite stupefied, and looked as if he were falling asleep. He drooped his head lower and lower.

'It's for you I am going, for you I am perishing!' he muttered; 'that's why I am giving you gifts.'

'I dare say he, too, has a mother,' said someone in the crowd. 'What a simple fellow! What a pity!'

Alyokha lifted his head.

'I have a mother,' said he; 'I have a father too. All have given me up. Listen to me, old woman,' he went on, taking Ilyushka's mother by the hand. 'I have given you presents. Listen to me for Christ's sake! Go to Vodnoe village, ask for the old woman Nikonovna, she's my own mother, see? Tell this same old woman, Nikonovna, the third hut from the end, by the new well, tell her that Alyokha, her son, you see. Eh! musician! strike up!' he shouted.

And muttering something he immediately began dancing again, and hurled the bottle with the remaining vodka to the ground.

Ignat got into the cart and was about to start.

'Goodbye! May God bless you!' said the old woman, wrapping her cloak closer round her.

Alyokha suddenly stopped.

'Go to the Devil!' he shouted, clenching his fists threateningly. 'May your mother be . . .'

'O Lord!' exclaimed Ilyushka's mother, crossing herself.

Ignat touched the reins, and the carts rattled on again. Alyokha, the recruit, stood in the middle of the road with clenched fists and with a look of fury on his face, and abused the peasants with all his might.

'What are you stopping for? Go on, devils! cannibals!' he cried. 'You won't escape me! Devil's clodhoppers!'

At these words his voice broke, and he fell full length to the ground just where he stood.

Soon the Dutlovs reached the open fields, and looking back could no longer see the crowd of recruits. Having gone some four miles at a walking pace Ignat got down from his father's cart, in which the old man lay asleep, and walked beside Ilyushka's cart.

Between them they emptied the bottle they had brought from town. After a while Ilya began a song, the women joined in, and Ignat shouted merrily in time with the song. A post-chaise drove merrily towards them. The driver called lustily to his horses as he passed the two festive carts, and the post-boy turned round and winked at the red faces of the peasant men and women who sat being jolted around while singing their jovial song.

STRIDER: THE STORY OF A HORSE

I

Higher and higher rose the sky, wider spread the dawn, whiter grew the pallid silver of the dew, more lifeless the sickle of the moon, more sonorous the forest, while people began to arise, and in the owner's stable-yard the sounds of snorting, the rustling of litter, and even the shrill angry neighing of horses crowded together and squabbling about something, grew more and more frequent.

'Hold on! Plenty of time! Hungry?' said the old herdsman, quickly opening the creaking gate. 'Where are you going?' he shouted, threateningly raising his arm at a mare that was pushing through the gate.

The herdsman, Nester, wore a short Cossack coat with an ornamental leather belt, had a whip slung over his shoulder, and a hunk of bread wrapped in a cloth stuck in his belt. He carried a saddle and bridle in his arms.

The horses were not at all frightened or offended at the herdsman's sarcastic tone: they pretended that it was all the same to them and moved leisurely away from the gate; only one old brown mare, with a thick mane, laid back an ear and quickly turned her back on him. A small filly standing behind her and not at all concerned in the matter took this opportunity to whinny and kick out at a horse that happened to be near.

'Now then!' shouted the herdsman still louder and more sternly, and he went to the opposite corner of the yard.

Of all the horses in the enclosure (there were about a hundred of them) a piebald gelding, standing by himself in a corner under the overhang and licking an oak post with half-closed eyes, displayed the least impatience. It is impossible to say what flavour the piebald gelding found in the post, but his expression was serious and thoughtful while he licked.

'Stop that!' shouted the herdsman again in that same tone, drawing nearer to him and putting the saddle and a glossy saddle-cloth on the manure heap beside him.

The piebald gelding stopped licking, and without moving gave Nester a long look. The gelding did not laugh, nor grow angry, nor frown, but his whole belly heaved with a profound sigh and he turned away. The herdsman put his arm round the gelding's neck and placed the bridle on him.

'What are you sighing for?' said Nester.

The gelding switched his tail as if to say, 'Nothing in particular, Nester!' Nester put the saddle-cloth and saddle on him, and this caused the gelding to lay back his ears, probably to express dissatisfaction, but he was only called a 'good-for-nothing' for it and his saddle-girths were tightened. At this the gelding snorted, but a finger was thrust into his mouth and a knee hit him in the stomach, so that he had to let out his breath. In spite of this, when the saddle-cloth was being buckled on he again laid back his ears and even looked round. Though he knew it would do no good he considered it necessary to show that it was disagreeable to him and that he would always express his dissatisfaction with it. When he was saddled he thrust forward his swollen right foot and began champing his bit, this too for some reason of his own, for he ought to have known by that time that a bit cannot have any flavour at all.

Nester mounted the gelding by the short stirrup, unwound his long whip, straightened his coat out from under his knee, seated himself in the manner peculiar to coachmen, huntsmen, and herdsmen, and jerked the reins. The gelding lifted his head to show his readiness to go where ordered, but did not move. He knew that before starting there would be much shouting, and that Nester, from the seat on his back, would give many orders to Vaska, the other herdsman, and to the horses. And Nester did shout: 'Vaska! Hey, Vaska. Have you let out the brood mares? Where are you going, you devil? Now then! Are you asleep? Open the gate! Let the brood mares get out first!'—and so on.

The gate creaked. Vaska, cross and sleepy, stood at the gate-post holding his horse by the bridle and letting the other horses pass out. The horses followed one another and stepped carefully over the straw, smelling at it: fillies, yearling colts with their manes and tails cut, suckling foals, and mares in foal carrying their burden heedfully, passed one by one through the gateway. The fillies sometimes crowded together in twos and threes, throwing their heads across one another's backs and hitting their hoofs against the gate, for which they received a rebuke from the herdsman every time. The foals sometimes darted under the legs of the wrong mares and neighed loudly in response to the short whinny of their own mothers.

A playful filly, as soon as she had got out at the gate, bent her head sideways, kicked up her hind legs, and squealed, but all the same she did not dare to run ahead of old dappled Zhuldyba who at a slow and heavy pace, swinging her belly from side to side, marched as usual ahead of all the other horses.

In a few minutes the enclosure that had been so animated became deserted, the posts stood gloomily under the empty overhang, and only trampled straw mixed with manure was to be seen. Used as he was to that desolate sight it probably depressed the piebald gelding. As if making a bow he slowly lowered his head and raised it again, sighed as deeply as the tightly drawn girth would allow, and hobbling along on his stiff and crooked legs shambled after the herd, bearing old Nester on his bony back.

'I know that as soon as we get out on the road he will begin to strike a light and smoke his wooden pipe with its brass mountings and little chain,' thought the gelding. 'I am glad of it because early in the morning when it is dewy I like that smell, it reminds me of much that was pleasant; but it's annoying that when his pipe is between his teeth the old man always begins to swagger and thinks himself somebody and sits sideways, always sideways, and that side hurts. However, it can't be helped! Suffering for the pleasure of others is nothing new to me. I have even begun to find a certain horse pleasure in it. Let him swagger, poor fellow! Of course he can only do that when he is alone and no one sees him, let him sit sideways!' thought the gelding, and stepping carefully on his crooked legs he went along the middle of the road.

II

Having driven the horses to the riverside where they were to graze, Nester dismounted and unsaddled. Meanwhile the herd had begun gradually to spread over the untrampled meadow, covered with dew and by the mist that rose from it and the encircling river.

When he had taken the bridle off the piebald gelding, Nester scratched him under the neck, in response to which the gelding expressed his gratitude and satisfaction by closing his eyes. 'He likes it, the old dog!' muttered Nester. The gelding however did not really care for the scratching at all, and pretended that it was agreeable merely out of courtesy. He nodded his head in assent to Nester's words; but suddenly Nester quite unexpectedly and without any reason, perhaps imagining that too much familiarity might give the gelding a wrong idea of his importance, pushed the gelding's head away from himself without any warning and, swinging the bridle, struck him painfully with the buckle on his lean leg, and then without saying a word went up the hillock to a tree-stump beside which he generally seated himself.

Though this action grieved the piebald gelding he gave no indication of it, but leisurely switching his scanty tail, sniffed at something and, biting off some wisps of grass merely to divert his mind, walked to the river. He took no notice whatever of the antics of the young mares, colts, and foals around him, who were filled with the joy of the morning; and knowing that, especially at his age, it is healthier to have a good drink on an empty stomach and to eat afterwards, he chose a spot where the bank was widest and least steep, and wetting his hoofs and fetlocks, dipped his muzzle in the water and began to suck it up through his torn lips, to expand his sides as he filled up, and from pleasure to switch his scanty tail with its half bald stump.

An aggressive chestnut filly, who always teased the old fellow and did all kinds of unpleasant things to him, now came up to him in the water as if attending to some business of her own, but in reality merely to foul the water before his nose. But the piebald gelding, who had already had his fill, as though not noticing the filly's intention quietly drew one foot after the other out of the mud in which they had sunk, jerked his head, and stepping aside from the youthful crowd started grazing. Sprawling his feet apart in different ways and not trampling the grass needlessly, he went on eating without straightening himself up for exactly three hours. Having eaten till his belly hung down from his steep skinny ribs like a sack, he balanced himself equally on his four sore legs so as to have as little pain as possible, especially in his right foreleg which was the weakest, and fell asleep.

Old age is sometimes majestic, sometimes ugly, and sometimes pathetic. But old age can be both ugly and majestic together, and the gelding's old age was just of that kind.

He was tall, rather over fifteen hands high. His spots were black, or rather they had been black, but had now turned a dirty brown. He had three spots, one on his head, starting from a crooked bald patch on the side of his nose and reaching halfway down his neck. His long mane, filled with burrs, was white in some places and brownish in others. Another spot extended down his right side to the middle of his belly, the third, on his croup, touched part of his tail and went halfway down his quarters. The rest of the tail was whitish and speckled. The big bony head, with deep hollows over the eyes and a black sagging lip that had been torn at some time, hung low and heavily on his neck, which was so lean that it looked as though it were carved of wood. The sagging lip revealed a blackish, bitten tongue and the yellow stumps of the worn lower teeth. The ears, one of which was slit, hung low on either side, and only occasionally moved lazily to drive away the pestering flies. One tuft of the fore-lock, still long, hung back behind an ear, the uncovered forehead was dented and rough, and the skin hung down like bags on his broad jawbones. The veins of his neck had grown knotty and twitched and shuddered at every touch of a fly. The expression of his face was one of stern patience, thoughtfulness, and suffering.

His forelegs were bent like a bow at the knees, there were swellings over both hoofs, and on one leg, on which the piebald spot reached halfway down, there was a swelling at the knee as big as a fist. The hind legs were in better condition, but apparently long ago his haunches had been so rubbed that in places the hair would not grow again. The leanness of his body made all four legs look disproportionately long. The ribs, though straight, were so exposed and close together that it seemed the skin had adhered to the spaces between. His back and withers were covered with marks of old lashings, and there was a fresh sore behind, still swollen and festering; the black dock of his tail, which showed the vertebrae, hung down long and almost bare. Near the tail on his dark-brown croup there was a scar, as though of a bite, the size of a man's hand and covered with white hair. Another scarred sore was visible on one of his shoulders. His tail and hocks were dirty because of chronic bowel troubles. The hair on the whole body, though short, stood out straight. Yet in spite of the hideous old age of this horse one involuntarily paused to reflect when one saw him, and an expert would have said at once that he had been a remarkably fine horse in his day.

The expert would even have said that there was only one breed in Russia that could furnish such breadth of bone, such immense knees, such hoofs, such slender cannons, such a well-shaped neck, and above all such a skull, such eyes—large, black, and clear—and such a thoroughbred network of veins on head and neck, and such delicate skin and hair. There was really something majestic in that horse's figure and in the terrible union in him of repulsive signs of decrepitude, emphasized by the motley colour of his hair, and his manner which expressed the self-confidence and calm assurance that go with beauty and strength.

Like a living ruin he stood alone in the midst of the dewy meadow, while not far from him could be heard the tramping, snorting and youthful neighing and whinnying of the scattered herd.

III

The sun had risen above the forest and now shone brightly on the grass and the winding river. The dew was drying up and condensing into drops, the last of the morning mist was dispersing like tiny smoke-clouds. The cloudlets were becoming curly but there was as yet no wind. Beyond the river the green rye stood bristling, its ears curling into little horns, and there was an odour of fresh greenery and flowers. A cuckoo called rather hoarsely from the forest, and Nester, lying on his back in the grass, was counting the calls to ascertain how many years he still had to live. The larks were rising over the rye and the meadow. A belated hare, finding himself among the horses, leaped into the open, sat down by a bush, and pricked his ears to listen. Vaska fell asleep with his head in the grass, the fillies, making a still wider circle about him, scattered over the field below. The old mares went about snorting, and made a shining track across the dewy grass, always choosing a place where no one would disturb them. They no longer grazed, but only nibbled at choice tufts of grass. The whole herd was moving imperceptibly in one direction.

And again it was old Zhuldyba who, stepping sedately in front of the others, showed the possibility of going further. Black Mushka, a young mare who had foaled for the first time, with uplifted tail kept whinnying and snorting at her bluish foal; the young filly Satin, sleek and brilliant, bending her head till her black silky forelock hid her forehead and eyes, played with the grass, nipping off a little and tossing it and stamping her leg with its shaggy fetlock all wet with dew. One of the older foals, probably imagining he was playing some kind of game, with his curly tail raised like a plume, ran for the twenty-sixth time round his mother, who quietly went on grazing, having grown accustomed to her son's ways, and only occasionally glanced askance at him with one of her large black eyes. One of the very youngest foals, black, with a big head, a tuft sticking up in astonishment between his ears, and a little tail still twisted to one side as it had been in his mother's womb, stood motionless, his ears pricked and his dull eyes fixed, gazing at the frisking and prancing foal, whether admiring or condemning him it is unclear. Some of the foals were sucking and butting with their noses, some—it is unclear why—despite their mothers' call were running at an awkward little trot in quite the opposite direction as if searching for something, and then, for no apparent reason, stopping and neighing with desperate shrillness. Some lay on their sides in a row, some were learning to eat grass, some again were scratching themselves behind their ears with their hind legs. Two mares still in foal were walking apart from the rest, and while slowly moving their legs continued to graze. The others evidently respected their condition, and none of the young ones ventured to come near to disturb them. If any saucy youngsters thought of approaching them, the mere movement of an ear or tail sufficed to show them all how improper such behaviour was.

The colts and yearling fillies, pretending to be grown up and sedate, rarely jumped or joined the merry company. They grazed in a dignified manner, curving their close-cropped swanlike necks, and flourished their little broom-like tails as if they also had long ones. Just like the grown-ups they lay down, rolled over, or rubbed one another. The merriest group was composed of the two- and three-year-old fillies and mares not yet in foal. They walked about almost all together in a separate merry girlish crowd. Among them you could hear sounds of tramping, whinnying, neighing, and snorting. They drew close together, put their heads over one another's necks, sniffed at one another, jumped, and sometimes at a semi-trot semi-amble, with tails lifted like an oriflamme, raced proudly and coquettishly past their companions. The most beautiful and spirited of them was the mischievous chestnut filly. What she devised the others did; wherever she went the whole crowd of beauties followed. That morning the naughty one was in a specially playful mood. She was seized with a joyous fit, just as human beings sometimes are. Already at the riverside she had played a trick on the old gelding, and after that she ran along through the water pretending to be frightened by something, gave a hoarse squeal, and raced full speed into the field so that Vaska had to gallop after her and the others who followed her. Then after grazing a little she began rolling, then teasing the old mares by dashing in front of them, then she drove away a small foal from its dam and chased it as if meaning to bite it. Its mother was frightened and stopped grazing, while the little foal cried in a piteous tone, but the mischievous one did not touch him at all, she only wanted to frighten him and give a performance for the benefit of her companions, who watched her escapade approvingly. Then she set out to turn the head of a little roan horse with which a peasant was ploughing in a rye-field far beyond the river. She stopped, proudly lifted her head somewhat to one side, shook herself, and neighed in a sweet, tender, long-drawn voice. Mischief, and feeling, and a certain sadness were expressed in that call. In it there was both the desire for and the promise of love, and a pining for it.

There in the thick reeds is a corncrake running backwards and forwards and calling passionately to his mate; over there both the cuckoo and the quails are singing of love, and the flowers are sending their fragrant dust to each other by the wind.

'And I too am young and beautiful and strong,' the mischievous one's voice said, 'but it has not yet been allowed me to experience the sweetness of that feeling, and not only to experience it, but no lover, not a single one, has ever seen me!'

And this neighing, sad and youthful and fraught with feeling, was borne over the lowland and the field to the roan horse far away. He pricked up his ears and stopped. The peasant kicked him with his bast shoe, but the little horse was so enchanted by the silvery sound of the distant neighing that he neighed too. The peasant grew angry, pulled at the reins, and kicked the little roan so painfully in the stomach with his bast shoes that he could not finish his neigh and walked on. But the little roan felt a sense of sweetness and sadness, and for a long time the sounds of unfinished and passionate neighing, and of the peasant's angry voice, were carried from the distant rye-field over to the herd.

If the sound of her voice alone so overpowered the little roan that he forgot his duty, what would have happened had he seen the naughty beauty as she stood pricking her ears, breathing in the air with dilated nostrils, ready to run, trembling with her whole beautiful body, and calling to him?

But the mischievous one did not brood long over her impressions. When the neighing of the roan died away she gave another scornful neigh, lowered her head and began pawing the ground, and then she went to wake and to tease the piebald gelding. The piebald gelding was the constant martyr and butt of those happy youngsters. He suffered more from them than at the hands of men. He did no harm to either. People needed him, but why should these young horses torment him?

IV

He was old, they were young; he was lean, they were sleek; he was miserable, they were gay; and so he was quite alien to them, an outsider, an utterly different creature whom it was impossible for them to pity. Horses only have pity for themselves, and very occasionally for those in whose skins they can easily imagine themselves to be. But was it the old gelding's fault that he was old, poor, and ugly? One might think not, but in horse ethics it was, and only those were right who were strong, young, and happy, those who had life still before them, whose every muscle quivered with superfluous energy, and whose tails stood erect. Maybe the piebald gelding himself understood this and in his quiet moments was ready to agree that it was his fault that he had already lived his life, and that he had to pay for that life; but after all he was a horse and often could not suppress a sense of resentment, sadness, and indignation, when he looked at those youngsters who tormented him for what would befall them all at the end of their lives. Another cause of the horses' lack of pity was their aristocratic pride. Every one of them traced back its pedigree, through father or mother, to the famous Creamy, while the piebald was of unknown parentage. He was an alien resident, purchased three years before at a fair for eighty assignation roubles.*

The chestnut filly, as if taking a stroll, passed close by the piebald gelding's nose and pushed him. He knew at once what it was, and without opening his eyes laid back his ears and showed his teeth.

The filly wheeled round as if to kick him. The gelding opened his eyes and stepped aside. He did not want to sleep any more and began to graze. The mischief-maker, followed by her companions, again approached the gelding. A very stupid two-year-old white-spotted filly who always imitated the chestnut in everything, went up with her and, as imitators always do, went to greater lengths than the instigator. The chestnut always went up as if intent on business of her own, and passed by the gelding's nose without looking at him, so that he really did not know whether to be angry or not, and that was really funny. She did the same now, but the white-spotted one, who followed her and had grown particularly lively, bumped right against the gelding with her chest. He again showed his teeth, whinnied, and with an agility one could not have expected of him, rushed after her and bit her flank. The white-spotted one kicked out with all her strength and dealt the old horse a heavy blow on his thin bare ribs. He snorted heavily and was going to rush at her again, but bethought himself and drawing a deep sigh stepped aside. The whole crowd of young ones must have taken as a personal affront the impertinence the piebald gelding had permitted himself to offer to the white-spotted one, and for the rest of the day did not let him graze in peace for a moment, so that the herdsman had to quieten them several times and could not understand what had come over them. The gelding felt so offended that he went up himself to Nester when the old man was getting ready to drive the horses home, and felt happier and quieter when he was saddled and the old man had mounted him.

God knows what the gelding was thinking as he carried old Nester on his back: whether he thought bitterly of the pertinacious and merciless youngsters, or forgave his tormenters with the contemptuous and silent pride suited to old age. At all events he did not betray his thoughts till he reached home.

That evening, as Nester drove the horses past the huts of the domestic serfs, he noticed a peasant horse and cart tethered to his porch: some friends had come to see him. When driving the horses in he was in such a hurry that he let the gelding in without unsaddling him and, shouting to Vaska to do it, shut the gate and went to his friends. Whether because of the affront to the white-spotted filly—Creamy's great-granddaughter—by that 'mangy trash' bought at the horse fair, who did not know his father or mother, and the consequent outrage to the aristocratic sentiment of the whole herd, or because the gelding with his high saddle and without a rider presented a strangely fantastic spectacle to the horses, at any rate something quite unusual occurred that night in the paddock. All the horses, young and old, ran after the gelding, showing their teeth and driving him all round the yard; one heard the sound of hoofs striking against his bare ribs, and his deep groaning. He could no longer endure this, nor could he avoid the blows. He stopped in the middle of the paddock, his face expressing first the repulsive weak malevolence of helpless old age, and then despair: he dropped his ears, and then something happened that caused all the horses to quiet down. The oldest of the mares, Vyazapurikha, went up to the gelding, sniffed at him and sighed. The gelding sighed too . . .

V

In the middle of the moonlit paddock stood the tall gaunt figure of the gelding, still wearing the high saddle with its prominent peak at the bow. The horses stood motionless and in deep silence around him as if they were learning something new and unexpected from him. And they did learn something new and unexpected from him. This is what they learnt from him.

First Night

'Yes, I am the son of Affable I and of Baba. My pedigree name is Muzhik I. I am Muzhik I by pedegree and I was nicknamed Strider by the crowd because of my long and sweeping strides, the like of which was nowhere to be found in all Russia. There is no more thoroughbred horse in the world. I should never have told you this. What good would it have done? You would never have recognized me: even Vyazapurikha, who was with me in Khrenovo, did not recognize me till now. You would not have believed me if Vyazapurikha were not here to be my witness, and I should never have told you this. I don't need horse sympathy. But you wished it. Yes, I am that Strider whom connoisseurs are looking for and cannot find, that Strider whom the count himself knew and got rid of from his stud because I outran Swan, his favourite.

'When I was born I did not know what *piebald* meant. I thought I was just a horse. I remember that the first remark we heard about my colour struck my mother and me deeply. I suppose I was born in the night; by the morning, having been licked over by my mother, I already stood on my feet. I remember I kept wanting something and that everything seemed very surprising and yet very simple. Our stalls opened into a long warm passage and had latticed doors through which everything could be seen. My mother offered me her teats but I was still so innocent that I poked my nose now between her forelegs and now under her udder. Suddenly she glanced at the latticed door and lifting her leg over me stepped aside. The groom on duty was looking into our stall through the lattice.

' "Why, Baba has foaled!" he said, and began to draw the bolt. He came in over the fresh bedding and put his arms round me. "Just look, Taras!" he shouted, "what a piebald he is—a regular magpie!"

'I darted away from him and fell on my knees.

' "Look at him—the little devil!"

'My mother became disquieted, but did not take my part, she only stepped a little to one side with a very deep sigh. Other grooms came to look at me, and one of them ran to tell the stud groom. Everybody laughed when they looked at my spots, and they gave me all kinds of strange names, but neither I nor my mother understood those words. Till then there had been no piebalds among all my relatives. We did not think there was anything bad in it. Everybody even then praised my strength and my form.

' "See what a frisky fellow!" said the groom. "There's no holding him."

'Before long the stud groom came and began to express astonishment at my colour; he even seemed aggrieved.

' "And who does the little monster take after?" he said. "The general won't keep him in the stud. Oh, Baba, you have played a trick on me!" he addressed my mother. "You might at least have dropped one with just a star, but this one is all piebald!"

'My mother did not reply, but as usual on such occasions drew a sigh.

' "And what devil does he take after, he's just like a peasant horse!" he continued. "He can't be left in the stud, he'd shame us. But he's well built, very well!" he said, and so did everyone who saw me. A few days later the general himself came and looked at me, and again everyone seemed horrified at something, and abused me and my mother for the colour of my hair. "But he's well built, very well!" said all who saw me.

'Until spring we all lived separately in the brood mares' stable, each with our mother, and only occasionally when the snow on the stable roofs began to melt in the sun were we let out with our mothers into the large paddock strewn with fresh straw. There I first came to know all my near and my distant relations. Here I saw all the famous mares of the day coming out from different doors with their little foals. There was the old mare Dutch, Fly (Creamy's daughter), Ruddy the riding-horse, Wellwisher—all celebrities at that time. They all gathered together with their foals, walking about in the sunshine, rolling on the fresh straw and sniffing at one another like ordinary horses. I have never forgotten the sight of that paddock full of the beauties of that day. It seems strange to you to think, and hard to believe, that I was ever young and frisky, but it was so. This same Vyazapurikha was then a yearling filly whose mane had just been cut; a dear, merry, lively little thing, but—and I do not say it to offend her—although among you she is now considered a remarkable thoroughbred she was then among the poorest horses in the stud. She will herself confirm this.

'My mottled appearance, which men so disliked, was very attractive to all the horses; they all came round me, admired me, and frisked about with me. I began to forget what men said about my mottled appearance and felt happy. But I soon experienced the first sorrow of my life and the cause of it was my mother. When the thaw had set in, the sparrows twittered under the eaves, spring was felt more strongly in the air, and my mother began to treat me differently. Her whole disposition changed: she would frisk about without any reason and run round the yard, which did not at all accord with her dignified age; then she would consider and begin to neigh, and would bite and kick her sister mares, and then begin to sniff at me and snort discontentedly; then on going out into the sun she would lay her head across the shoulder of her cousin, Lady Merchant, dreamily rub her back, and push me away from her teats.

'One day the stud groom came and had a halter put on her and she was led out of the stall. She neighed and I answered and rushed after her, but she did not even look back at me. The groom, Taras, seized me in his arms while they were closing the door after my mother had been led out. I bolted and upset the groom on the straw, but the door was shut and I could only hear the receding sound of my mother's neighing; and that neigh did not sound like a call to me but had another expression. Her voice was answered from afar by a powerful voice—that of Kindly I, as I learned later, who was being led by two grooms, one on each side, to meet my mother. I don't remember how Taras got out of my stall: I felt too sad, for I knew that I had lost my mother's love for ever. "And it's all because I am piebald!" I thought, remembering what people said about my colour, and such passionate anger overcame me that I began to beat my head and knees against the walls of the stall and continued till I was sweating all over and quite exhausted.

'After a while my mother came back to me. I heard her run up the passage at a trot and with an unusual gait. They opened the door for her and I hardly knew her, for she had grown so much younger and more beautiful. She sniffed at me, snorted, and began to whinny. Her whole demeanour showed that she no longer loved me. She told me of Kindly's beauty and her love of him. Those meetings continued and the relations between my mother and me grew colder and colder.

'Soon after that we were let out to pasture. I now discovered new joys which made up to me for the loss of my mother's love. I had friends and companions. Together we learnt to eat grass, to neigh like the grown-ups, and to gallop round our mothers with lifted tails. That was a happy time. Everything was forgiven me, everybody loved me, admired me, and looked indulgently at anything I did. But that did not last long.

'Soon afterwards something dreadful happened to me.' (The gelding heaved a deep sigh and walked away from the other horses.)

The dawn had broken long before. The gates creaked. Nester came in, and the horses separated. The herdsman straightened the saddle on the gelding's back and drove the herd out.

VI

Second Night

As soon as the horses had been driven in they again gathered round the piebald.

'In August they separated me from my mother and I did not feel particularly grieved. I saw that she was again heavy (with my brother, the famous Usan) and that I could no longer be to her what I had been. I was not jealous, but felt that I had become colder towards her. Besides I knew that having left my mother I should be put in the general division of foals, where we were kept two or three together and were every day let out in a crowd into the open. I was in the same stall with Darling. Darling was a saddle-horse, who was subsequently ridden by the Emperor and portrayed in pictures and sculpture. At that time he was a mere foal, with soft glossy coat, a swanlike neck, and straight slender legs taut as the strings of an instrument. He was always lively, good-tempered, and amiable, always ready to gambol, exchange licks, and play tricks on horse or man. Living together as we did we involuntarily made friends, and our friendship lasted the whole of our youth. He was merry and giddy. Even then he began to make love, courted the fillies, and laughed at my innocence. To my misfortune vanity led me to imitate him, and I was soon infatuated and fell in love. And this early tendency of mine was the cause of the greatest change in my fate. It happened because I was infatuated.

'Vyazapurikha was a year older than I, and we were special friends, but towards the autumn I noticed that she began to shun me. But I will not speak of that unfortunate period of my first love; she herself remembers my mad infatuation, which ended for me in the most important change of my life. The herdsmen rushed to drive her away and to beat me. That evening I was shut up in a special stall where I neighed all night as if foreseeing what was to happen the next day.

'In the morning the general, the stud groom, the grooms, and the herdsmen came into the passage where my stall was, and there was a terrible hubbub. The general shouted at the stud groom, who tried to justify himself by saying that he had not told them to let me out but that the grooms had done it of their own accord. The general said that he would have everybody flogged, and that it would not do to keep young stallions. The stud groom promised that he would have everything attended to. They grew quiet and went away. I did not understand anything, but could see that they were planning something concerning me.

'The day after that I ceased neighing for ever. I became what I am now. The whole world was changed in my eyes. Nothing mattered any more; I became self-absorbed and began to brood. At first everything seemed repulsive to me. I even ceased to eat, drink, or walk, and there was no idea of playing. Now and then it occurred to me to give a kick, to gallop, or to start neighing, but immediately there arose the terrifying question: Why? What for? and all my energy died away.

'One evening I was being exercised just when the horses were driven back from pasture. I saw in the distance a cloud of dust enveloping the indistinct but familiar outlines of all our brood mares. I heard their cheerful snorting and the trampling of their feet. I stopped, though the cord of the halter by which the groom was leading me cut the nape of my neck, and I gazed at the approaching herd as one gazes at a happiness that is lost for ever and cannot return. They approached, and I could distinguish one after another all the familiar, beautiful, stately, healthy, sleek figures. Some of them also turned to look at me. I was unconscious of the pain the groom's jerking at my halter inflicted. I forgot myself and from old habit involuntarily neighed and began to trot, but my neighing sounded sad, ridiculous, and meaningless. No one in the herd made fun of me, but I noticed that out of decorum many of them turned away from me. To look at me evidently made them feel repelled and sorry and ashamed, and above all ridiculous. They felt ridiculous looking at my thin expressionless neck, my large head (I had grown lean in the meantime), my long, awkward legs, and the silly awkward gait with which by force of habit I trotted round the groom. No one answered my neighing, they all looked away. Suddenly I understood it all, understood how far I was for ever removed from them, and I do not remember how I got home with the groom.

'Already before that I had shown a tendency towards seriousness and deep thought, but now a crucial change came over me. My being piebald, which aroused such curious contempt in men, my terrible and unexpected misfortune, and also my peculiar position in the stud farm which I felt but was unable to explain, made me retire into myself. I pondered over the injustice of men, who blamed me for being piebald; I pondered over the inconstancy of maternal love and feminine love in general and on its dependence on physical conditions; and above all I pondered over the characteristics of that strange race of animals with whom we are so closely connected, and whom we call men, those characteristics which were the source of my own peculiar position in the stud farm, which I felt but could not understand. The meaning of this peculiarity in people and the characteristic on which it is based was shown me by the following occurrence.

'It was in winter at holiday time. I had not been fed or watered all day. As I learnt later this happened because the groom was drunk. That day the stud groom came in, saw that I had no food, began to use bad language about the missing groom, and then went away. Next day the groom came into our stable with another groom to give us hay. I noticed that he was particularly pale and sad and that in the expression of his long back especially there was something significant which evoked compassion. He threw the hay angrily over the grating. I made a move to put my head over his shoulder, but he struck me such a painful blow on the nose with his fist that I started back. Then he kicked me in the belly with his boot.

' "If it hadn't been for this scurvy beast," he said, "nothing would have happened!"

' "How's that?" inquired the other groom.

' "You see, he doesn't go to look after the count's horses, but visits his own twice a day."

' "What, have they given him the piebald?" asked the other.

' "Given it, or sold it—the devil only knows! The count's horses might all starve, he wouldn't care, but just dare to leave *his* colt without food! 'Lie down!' he says, and they begin walloping me! No Christianity in it. He has more pity on a beast than on a man. He must be an infidel, he counted the strokes himself, the barbarian! The general never flogged like that! My whole back is covered with weals. There's no Christian soul in him!"

'What they said about flogging and Christianity I understood well enough, but I was quite in the dark as to what they meant by the words "*his* colt", from which I perceived that people considered that there was some connection between me and the stud groom. What that connection was I could not at all understand then. Only much later when they separated me from the other horses did I learn what it meant. At that time I could not at all understand what they meant by speaking of *me* as being a man's property. The words "*my* horse" applied to me, a live horse, seemed to me as strange as to say "my land", "my air", or "my water".

'But those words had an enormous effect on me. I thought of them constantly and only after long and varied relations with men did I at last understand the meaning they attach to these strange words, which indicate that men are guided in life not by deeds but by words. They like not so much the ability to do or not do something, as the ability to speak of various objects in conventionally agreed upon words. Such words, considered very important among them, are *my* and *mine*, which they apply to various things, creatures, or objects: even to land, people, and horses. They have agreed that of any given thing only one person may use the word *mine*, and he who in this game of theirs may use that conventional word about the greatest number of things is considered the happiest. Why this is so I do not know, but it is so. For a long time I tried to explain it by some direct advantage they derive from it, but this proved wrong.

'For instance many of those who called me their horse did not ride me, quite other people rode me; nor did they feed me, quite other people did that. Again it was not those who called me *their* horse who treated me kindly, but coachmen, veterinaries, and in general quite other people. Later on, having widened my field of observation, I became convinced that not only as applied to us horses, but in regard to other things, the idea of *mine* has no other foundation than a base, animal instinct in men, which they call the feeling or right of property. A man says "my house" and never lives in it, but only concerns himself with its building and maintenance. A merchant talks of "my cloth store", but has none of his clothes made of the best cloth that is in his store. There are people who call land theirs, though they have never seen that land and never walked on it. There are people who call other people theirs, but have never seen those others, and the whole relationship of the owners to the owned is that they do them harm. There are men who call women their women or their wives; yet these women live with other men. And men strive in life not to do what they think right, but to call as many things as possible *their own*. I am now convinced that in this lies the essential difference between men and us. Therefore, not to speak of other things in which we are superior to men, on this ground alone we may boldly say that in the scale of living creatures we stand higher than man. The activity of men, at any rate of those I have had to do with, is guided by words, while ours is guided by deeds. It was this right to speak of me as *my horse* that the stud groom had obtained, and that was why he had the groom flogged. This discovery much astonished me and, together with the thoughts and opinions aroused in men by my piebald colour, and the pensiveness produced in me by my mother's betrayal, caused me to become the serious and deep-thinking gelding that I am.

'I was thrice unfortunate: I was piebald, I was a gelding, and people considered that I did not belong to God and to myself, as is natural to all living creatures, but that I belonged to the stud groom.

'Their thinking this about me had many consequences. The first was that I was kept apart from the other horses, better fed, taken out on the line more often, and broken in at an earlier age. I was first harnessed in my third year. I remember how the stud groom, who imagined I was his, himself began to harness me with a crowd of other grooms, expecting me to prove unruly or to resist. They put ropes round me to lead me into the shafts; put a cross of broad straps on my back and fastened it to the shafts so that I could not kick, while I was only awaiting an opportunity to show my readiness and love of work.

'They were surprised that I started out like an old horse. They began to break me in but I began to practise trotting. Every day I made greater and greater progress, so that after three months the general himself and many others approved of my pace. But strange to say, just because they considered me not as their own, but as belonging to the head groom, they regarded my paces quite differently.

'The stallions who were my brothers were raced, their records were kept, people went to look at them, drove them in gilt sulkies, and expensive horse-cloths were thrown over them. I was driven in a common sulky to Chesmenka and other farms on the head groom's business. All this was the result of my being piebald, and especially of my being in their opinion not the count's, but the head groom's property.

'Tomorrow, if we are alive, I will tell you the chief consequence for me of this right of property the head groom considered himself to have.'

All that day the horses treated Strider respectfully, but Nester's treatment of him was as rough as ever. The peasant's little roan horse neighed again on coming up to the herd, and the chestnut filly again coquettishly replied to him.

VII

Third Night

The new moon had risen and its narrow crescent lit up Strider's figure as he once again stood in the middle of the stable-yard. The other horses crowded round him.

'For me the most surprising consequence of my not being the count's, nor God's, but the stud groom's, was that the very thing that constitutes our chief merit, a fast pace, was the cause of my banishment. They were driving Swan round the track, and the stud groom, returning from Chesmenka, drove me up and stopped there. Swan went past. He went well, but all the same he was showing off and had not the exactitude I had developed in myself, so that no sooner did one foot touch the ground than another instantaneously lifted and not the slightest effort was lost but every bit of exertion carried me forward. Swan went by us. I pulled towards the ring and the stud groom did not check me. "Here, shall I try my piebald?" he shouted, and when next Swan came abreast of us he let me go. Swan was already going fast, and so I was left behind during the first round, but in the second I began to gain on him, drew near to his sulky, drew level, and passed him. They tried us again—it was the same thing. I was the faster. And this dismayed everybody. The general asked that I should be sold at once to some distant place, so that nothing more should be heard of me: "Or else the count will get to know of it and there will be trouble!" So they sold me to a horse-dealer as a shaft-horse. I did not remain with him long. A hussar who came to buy remounts bought me. All this was so unfair, so cruel, that I was glad when they took me away from Khrenovo and parted me for ever from all that had been familiar and dear to me. It was too painful for me among them. They had love, honour, freedom, before them; I had labour, humiliation; humiliation, labour, to the end of my life. And why? Because I was piebald, and because of that had to become somebody's horse.'

Strider could not continue that evening. An event occurred in the enclosure that upset all the horses. Kupchikha, a mare big with foal, who had stood listening to the story, suddenly turned away and walked slowly into the shed, and there began to groan so that it drew the attention of all the horses. Then she lay down, then got up again, and again lay down. The old mares understood what was happening to her, but the young ones became excited and, leaving the gelding, surrounded the invalid. Towards morning there was a new foal standing unsteadily on its little legs. Nester shouted to the groom, and the mare and foal were taken into a stall and the other horses driven to the pasture without them.

VIII

Fourth Night

In the evening when the gate was closed and all had quieted down, the piebald continued:

'I have had opportunity to make many observations both of men and horses during the time I passed from hand to hand. I stayed longest of all with two masters, with a prince who was a hussar officer and later with an old lady who lived near the church of St Nicholas the Wonder Worker.

'The happiest years of my life I spent with the hussar officer.

'Though he was the cause of my ruin, and though he never loved anything or anyone, I loved and still love him for that very reason. What I liked about him was that he was handsome, happy, rich, and therefore never loved anybody. You understand that lofty horse feeling of ours. His coldness, his cruelty, and my dependence on him gave special strength to my love for him. Kill me, drive me till my wind is broken! I used to think in our good days, and I shall be all the happier.

'He bought me from an agent to whom the stud groom had sold me for eight hundred roubles, and he did so just because no one else had piebald horses. That was my best time. He had a mistress. I knew this because I took him to her every day and sometimes took them both out. His mistress was a handsome woman, and he was handsome, and his coachman was handsome, and I loved them all because they were. Life was worth living then. This was how my time was spent: in the morning the groom came to rub me down, not the coachman himself but the groom. The groom was a lad from among the peasants. He would open the door, let out the steam from the horses, toss out the manure, take off our rugs, and begin to fidget over our bodies with a brush and lay whitish streaks of dandruff from a curry-comb on the boards of the floor that was dented by our rough horseshoes. I would playfully nip his sleeve and paw the ground. Then we were led out one after another to the trough filled with cold water, and the lad would admire the smoothness of my spotted coat which he had polished, my foot with its broad hoof, my legs straight as an arrow, my glossy quarters, and my back wide enough to sleep on. Hay was piled onto the high racks, and the oak cribs were filled with oats. Then Feofan, the head coachman, would come in.

'The master and the coachman resembled one another. Neither of them was afraid of anything or cared for anyone but himself, and for that reason everybody liked them. Feofan wore a red shirt, black velveteen knickerbockers, and a sleeveless coat. I liked it on a holiday when he would come into the stable, his hair pomaded, and wearing his sleeveless coat, and would shout, "Now then, beastie, have you forgotten?" and push me with the handle of the stable fork, never so as to hurt me but just as a joke. I immediately knew that it was a joke, and laid back an ear, making my teeth click.

'We had a black stallion, who drove in a pair. At night they used to put me in harness with him. This Polkan, as he was called, did not understand a joke but was simply vicious as the devil. I was in the stall next to his and sometimes we bit one another seriously. Feofan was not afraid of him. He would come up and give a shout, it looked as if Polkan would kill him, but no, he'd miss, and Feofan would put the harness on him. Once he and I bolted down Smiths Bridge Street. Neither the master nor the coachman was frightened; they laughed, shouted at the people, checked us, and turned so that no one was run over.

'In their service I lost my best qualities and half my life. They ruined me by watering me wrongly, and they ruined my legs. Still for all that it was the best time of my life. At twelve o'clock they would come to harness me, black my hoofs, moisten my forelock and mane, and put me in the shafts.

'The sledge was of plaited cane upholstered with velvet; the reins were of silk, the harness had silver buckles, sometimes there was a cover of silken fly-net, and altogether it was such that when all the traces and straps were fastened it was difficult to say where the harness ended and the horse began. We were harnessed at ease in the stable. Feofan would come, broader at his hips than at the shoulders, his red belt up under his arms. He would examine the harness, take his seat, wrap his coat round him, put his foot into the sledge stirrup, let off some joke, and for appearance' sake always hang a whip over his arm though he hardly ever hit me, and would say, "Let go!", and playfully stepping from foot to foot I would move out of the gate, and the cook who had come out to empty the slops would stop on the threshold and the peasant who had brought wood into the yard would open his eyes wide. We would come out, go a little way, and stop. Footmen would come out and other coachmen, and the talk would begin. Everybody would wait, sometimes we had to stand for three hours at the entrance, moving a little way, turning back, and standing again.

'At last there would be a stir in the hall, old Tikhon with his paunch would rush out in his dress-coat and cry, "Drive up!" In those days there was not that stupid way of saying, "Forward!" as if one did not know that we moved forward and not back. Feofan would smack his lips, drive up, and the prince would hurry out carelessly, as though there were nothing remarkable about the sledge, or the horse, or Feofan, who bent his back and stretched out his arms so that it seemed it would be impossible for him to keep them long in that position. The prince would have a shako on his head and wear a fur coat with a grey beaver collar hiding his rosy, black-browed, handsome face that should never have been concealed. He would come out clattering his sabre, his spurs, and the brass backs of the heels of his overshoes, stepping over the carpet as if in a hurry and taking no notice of me or Feofan whom everybody but he looked at and admired. Feofan would smack his lips, I would tug at the reins, and respectably, at a slow pace, we would draw up to the entrance and stop. I would turn my eyes on the prince and jerk my thoroughbred head with its delicate forelock. The prince would be in good spirits and would sometimes jest with Feofan. Feofan would reply, half turning his handsome head, and without lowering his arms would make a scarcely perceptible movement with the reins which I understand and then one, two, three, with ever wider and wider strides, every muscle quivering, and sending the muddy snow against the front of the sledge, I would take off. In those days, too, there was none of the present-day stupid habit of crying, "Oh!" as if the coachman were in pain, instead of the incomprehensible, "Be off! Take care!" Feofan would shout "Be off! Take care!" and the people would step aside and stand craning their necks to see the handsome gelding, the handsome coachman, and the handsome gentleman.

'I was particularly fond of passing a trotter. When Feofan and I saw at a distance a turnout worthy of the effort, we would fly like a whirlwind and gradually gain on it. Now, throwing the dirt right to the back of the sledge, I would draw level with the occupant of the vehicle and snort above his head, then I would reach the horse's harness and the arch of his troika,* and then would no longer see it but only hear its sounds in the distance behind. And the prince, Feofan, and I, would all be silent, and pretend to be merely going on our own business and not even to notice those with slow horses whom we happened to meet on our way. I liked to pass another horse, but I also liked to meet a good trotter. An instant, a sound, a glance, and we had passed each other and were flying in opposite directions.'

The gate creaked and the voices of Nester and Vaska were heard.

Fifth Night

The weather began to break up. It had been overcast since morning and there was no dew, but it was warm and the mosquitoes were troublesome. As soon as the horses were driven in they collected round the piebald, and he finished his story as follows:

'The happy period of my life was soon over. I lived in that way only two years. Towards the end of the second winter the happiest event of my life occurred, and following it came my greatest misfortune. It was during carnival week. I took the prince to the races. Glossy and Bull were running. I don't know what people were doing in the pavilion, but I know the prince came out and ordered Feofan to drive onto the track. I remember how they took me in and placed me beside Glossy. He was harnessed to a racing sulky and I, just as I was, to a town sledge. I outstripped him at the turn. Roars of laughter and howls of delight greeted me.

When I was led in, a crowd followed me and five or six people offered the prince thousands for me. He just laughed, showing his white teeth.

' "No," he said, "this isn't a horse, but a friend. I wouldn't sell him for mountains of gold. *Au revoir*,[1] gentlemen!"

---

[1] 'Goodbye.'

'He unfastened the sledge apron and got in. "To Ostozhenka Street!" That was where his mistress lived, and off we flew. That was our last happy day.

'We reached her home. He spoke of her as *his*, but she loved someone else and had run away with him. The prince learnt this at her lodgings. It was five o'clock, and without unharnessing me he started in pursuit of her. He did what had never been done to me before, struck me with the whip and made me gallop. For the first time I fell out of step and felt ashamed and wished to correct it, but suddenly I heard the prince shout in an unnatural voice: "Get on!" The whip whistled through the air and cut me, and I galloped, striking my foot against the iron front of the sledge. We overtook her after going sixteen miles. I got him there, but trembled all night long and could not eat anything. In the morning I was given some water. I drank it and after that was never again the horse that I had been. I was ill, and they tormented and maimed me, doctoring me, as people call it. My hoofs came off, I had swellings, and my legs grew bent; my chest sank in and I became altogether limp and weak. I was sold to a horse-dealer who fed me on carrots and something else and made something of me quite unlike myself, though good enough to deceive one who did not know. My strength and my pace were gone. Moreover, when purchasers came the horse-dealer would torment me by coming into my stall and beating me with a heavy whip to frighten and madden me. Then he would rub down the stripes on my coat and lead me out. An old woman bought me from him. She always drove to the Church of St Nicholas the Wonder Worker and flogged her coachman. He used to weep in my stall and I learnt that tears have a pleasant, salty taste. Then the old woman died. Her steward took me to the country and sold me to a hawker. Then I overate myself with wheat and grew still worse. They sold me to a peasant. There I ploughed, had hardly anything to eat, my foot got cut by a ploughshare, and I again became ill. Then a gypsy took me in exchange for something. He tormented me terribly and finally sold me to the steward here. And here I am.'

All were silent. A sprinkling of rain began to fall.

IX

The Evening After

As the herd returned home the following evening they encountered their master with a visitor. Zhuldyba when nearing the house looked askance at the two male figures: one was the young master in his straw hat, the other a tall, stout, bloated military man. The old mare gave the man a side-glance and, swerving, went near him; the others, the young ones, were flustered and hesitated, especially when the master and his visitor purposely stepped among them, pointing something out to one another and talking.

'That one, the dapple grey, I bought from Voekov,' said the master.

'And where did you get that young black mare with the white legs? She's a fine one!' said the visitor. They looked over many of the horses, going forward and stopping them. They noticed the chestnut filly too.

'That is one I kept from Khrenov's saddle-horse breed,' said the master.

They could not see all the horses as they walked past, and the master called to Nester, and the old man, tapping the sides of the piebald with his heels, trotted forward. The piebald limped on one leg but moved in a way that showed that as long as his strength lasted he would not murmur on any account, even if they wanted him to run in that way to the end of the world. He was even ready to gallop and tried to do so with his right leg.

'There, I can say for certain that there is no better horse in Russia than this one,' said the master, pointing to one of the mares. The visitor admired it. The master walked about excitedly, ran forward, and showed his visitor all the horses, mentioning the origin and pedigree of each. The visitor evidently found the master's talk dull, but devised some questions to show interest.

'Yes, yes,' he said absent-mindedly.

'Just look,' said the master, not answering a question. 'Look at her legs. She cost me a lot but has a third foal already in harness.'

'And trots well?' asked the guest.

So they went past all the horses till there were no more to show. Then they were silent.

'Well, shall we go now?'

'Yes, let's go.'

They went through the gate. The visitor was glad the exhibition was over and that he could now go to the house where they could eat and drink and smoke, and he grew perceptibly brighter. As he went past Nester, who sat on the piebald waiting for orders, the visitor slapped the piebald's crupper with his big fat hand.

'What an ornamented one!' he said. 'I once had a piebald like him; do you remember my telling you of him?'

The master, finding that it was not his horse that was being spoken about, paid no attention but kept looking round at his own herd.

Suddenly above his ear he heard a dull, weak, senile neigh. It was the piebald that had begun to neigh and had broken off as if embarrassed. Neither the visitor nor the master paid any attention to this neighing, but went into the house. In the flabby old man Strider had recognized his beloved master, the once brilliant, handsome, and wealthy Serpukhovskoy.

X

It kept on drizzling. In the stable yard it was gloomy, but in the master's house it was very different. The table was laid in a luxurious drawing room for a luxurious evening tea, and at it sat the host, the hostess,* and their guest.

The hostess, her pregnancy made very noticeable by her figure, her strained convex pose, her plumpness, and especially by her large eyes with their mild inward look, sat by the samovar.*

The host held in his hand a box of special, ten-year-old cigars, such as he said no one else had, and he was preparing to boast about them to his guest. The host was a handsome man of about twenty-five, fresh-looking, well cared for, and well groomed. In the house he was wearing a new loose, thick suit made in London. Large expensive pendants hung from his watch-chain. His gold-mounted turquoise shirt studs were also large and massive. He had a beard *à la* Napoléon III,* and the tips of his moustache stuck out in a way that could only have been learned in Paris. The hostess wore a dress of fine muslin with a large floral pattern of many colours, and large gold hairpins of a peculiar pattern held up her thick, light-brown hair, beautiful though not all her own. On her arms and hands she wore many bracelets and rings, all of them expensive. The tea-service was of delicate china and the samovar of silver. A footman, resplendent in dress-coat, white waistcoat, and necktie, stood like a statue by the door awaiting orders. The furniture was elegantly carved and upholstered in bright colours, the wallpaper dark with a large flowered pattern. Beside the table, tinkling the silver bells on its collar, was a particularly fine whippet, whose difficult English name its owners, neither of whom knew English, pronounced badly. In the corner, surrounded by plants, stood a piano *incrusté*.* Everything gave an impression of newness, luxury, and rarity. Everything was good, but it all bore an imprint of superfluity, wealth, and the absence of intellectual interests.

The master, a lover of trotting races, was sturdy and full-blooded, one of that never-dying race which drives about in sable coats, throws expensive bouquets to actresses, drinks the most expensive wines with the most fashionable labels at the most expensive restaurants, offers prizes engraved with the donor's name, and keeps the most expensive mistress.

Nikita Serpukhovskoy, their guest, was a man of over forty, tall, stout, bald-headed, with heavy moustaches and whiskers. He must once have been very handsome, but had now evidently sunk physically, morally, and financially.

He had such debts that he had been obliged to enter the government service to avoid imprisonment for debt, and was now on his way to a provincial town to become the head of a stud farm, a post some important relatives had obtained for him. He wore a military coat and blue trousers of a kind only a rich man would have had made for himself. His shirt was of similar quality and so was his English watch. His boots had wonderful soles as thick as a man's finger.

Nikita Serpukhovskoy had during his life run through a fortune of two million roubles and was now a hundred and twenty thousand in debt. In cases of that kind there always remains a certain momentum of life enabling a man to obtain credit and continue living almost luxuriously for another ten years. These ten years were however coming to an end, the momentum was exhausted, and life was growing hard for Nikita. He was already beginning to drink, that is, to get tipsy on wine, a thing that used not to happen, though strictly speaking he had never begun or left off drinking. His decline was most noticeable in the restlessness of his glance (his eyes had grown shifty) and in the uncertainty of his voice and movements. This restlessness struck one the more as it had evidently got hold of him only recently, for one could see that he had all his life been accustomed not to be afraid of anything or anybody, and had only recently, through heavy suffering, reached this state of fear so unnatural to him. His host and hostess noticed this, and exchanged glances which showed that they understood one another and were only postponing till bedtime a detailed discussion of the subject, putting up meanwhile with poor Nikita and even paying him particular attention. The sight of the young master's good fortune humiliated Serpukhovskoy, awakening a painful envy in him as he recalled his own irrecoverable past.

'Do you mind my smoking a cigar, Marie?' he asked, addressing the lady in that peculiar tone acquired only by experience, the tone, polite and friendly but not quite respectful, in which men who know the world speak to kept women in contradistinction to wives. Not that he wished to offend her, on the contrary he now wished rather to curry favour with her and her master, though he would on no account have acknowledged the fact to himself. But he was accustomed to speak in that way to such women. He knew she would herself be surprised and even offended were he to treat her as a lady. Besides he had to retain a certain shade of a respectful tone for the real wife of one of his equals. He always treated such ladies with respect, not because he shared the so-called convictions promulgated in periodicals (he never read trash of that kind) about the respect due to the personality of every human being, about the meaninglessness of marriage, and so forth, but because all decent men do so and he was a decent, though fallen, man.

He took a cigar. But his host awkwardly picked up a whole handful and offered them to him.

'Just see how good these are. Take them!'

Serpukhovskoy pushed aside the hand with the cigars, and a gleam of offence and shame showed itself in his eyes.

'Thank you!' He took out his cigar-case. 'Try mine!'

The hostess was sensitive. She noticed his embarrassment and hastened to talk to him.

'I am very fond of cigars. I should smoke myself if everyone about me did not smoke.'

And she smiled her pretty, kindly smile. He smiled in return, but irresolutely. Two of his teeth were missing.

'No, take this!' the tactless host continued. 'The others are weaker. Fritz, *bringen Sie noch einen Kasten*,' he said, '*dort zwei*.'[1]

The German footman brought another box.

'Do you prefer big ones? Strong ones? These are very good. Take them all!' he continued, forcing them on his guest. He was evidently glad to have someone to boast to of the rare things he possessed, and he noticed nothing amiss. Serpukhovskoy lit his cigar and hastened to resume the conversation they had begun.

'So, how much did you pay for Velvet?' he asked.

'He cost me a great deal, not less than five thousand, but at any rate I am already safe on him. What colts he gets, I tell you!'

'Do they race?' asked Serpukhovskoy.

'They race well! His colt took three prizes this year: in Tula, in Moscow, and in Petersburg he ran with Voekov's Raven. The driver, that rascal, let him make four false steps or he'd have left him behind the flag.'

'He's a bit green. Too much Dutch blood in him, that's what I say,' remarked Serpukhovskoy.

'Well, but what about the mares? I'll show Goody to you to-morrow. I gave three thousand for her. For Amiable I gave two thousand.'

And the host again began to enumerate his possessions. The hostess saw that this hurt Serpukhovskoy and that he was only pretending to listen.

'Will you have some more tea?' she asked.

'I won't,' replied the host and went on talking. She rose, the host stopped her, embraced her, and kissed her.

As he looked at them Serpukhovskoy for their sakes tried to force a smile, but after the host had got up, embraced her, and led her to the portière, Serpukhovskoy's face suddenly changed. He sighed heavily, and a look of despair showed itself on his flabby face. Even malevolence appeared on it.

---

[1] 'Bring another box. There are two there.'

The host returned and smilingly sat down opposite him. They were silent awhile.

XI

'Yes, you were saying you bought her from Voekov,' remarked Serpukhovskoy with assumed carelessness.

'Oh yes, that was Velvet's, you know. I always meant to buy some mares from Dubovitzki, but he had nothing but rubbish left.'

'He's gone bankrupt,' said Serpukhovskoy, and suddenly stopped and glanced round. He remembered that he owed that bankrupt twenty thousand roubles, and if it came to talking of going bankrupt it could certainly be said of him. He laughed.

Both again sat silent for a long time. The host considered what he could brag about to his guest. Serpukhovskoy was thinking what he could say to show that he did not consider himself bankrupt. But the minds of both worked with difficulty, in spite of efforts to brace themselves up with cigars. 'When are we going to have a drink?' thought Serpukhovskoy. 'I must certainly have a drink or I shall die of boredom with this fellow,' thought the host.

'Will you be remaining here long?' Serpukhovskoy asked.

'Another month. Well, shall we have supper, eh? Fritz, is it ready?'

They went into the dining room. There under a hanging lamp stood a table on which were candles and all sorts of extraordinary things: siphons, and little dolls fastened to corks, rare wine in decanters, unusual hors d'œuvres and vodka. They drank, ate, drank again, ate again, and their conversation got into swing. Serpukhovskoy was flushed and began to speak without timidity.

They spoke of women and of who kept this one or that, a gypsy, a ballet-dancer, or a Frenchwoman.

'And have you given up Mathieu?' asked the host. That was the kept woman who had ruined Serpukhovskoy.

'No, she left me. Ah, my dear fellow, when I recall what I have got through in my life! Now I am really glad when I have a thousand roubles, and am glad to get away from everybody. I can't stand it in Moscow. But what's the good of talking!'

The host found it tiresome to listen to Serpukhovskoy. He wanted to speak about himself, to brag. But Serpukhovskoy also wished to talk about himself, about his brilliant past. His host filled his glass for him and waited for him to stop, so that he might tell him about himself and how his stud was now arranged as no one had ever had a stud arranged before. And that his Marie loved him with her heart and not merely for his wealth.

'I wanted to tell you that in my stud . . .' he began, but Serpukhovskoy interrupted him.

'I may say that there was a time,' Serpukhovskoy began, 'when I liked to live well and knew how to do it. Now you talk about racing, tell me which is your fastest horse.'

The host, glad of an opportunity to tell more about his stud, was beginning, when Serpukhovskoy again interrupted him.

'Yes, yes,' he said, 'but you breeders do it just out of vanity and not for pleasure, not for the joy of life. It was different with me. You know I told you I had a driving-horse, a piebald with just the same kind of spots as the one your keeper was riding. Oh, what a horse that was! You can't possibly know: it was in 1842, when I had just come to Moscow; I went to a horse-dealer and there I saw a well-bred piebald gelding. I liked him. The price? One thousand roubles. I liked him, so I took him and began to drive with him. I never had, and you have not and never will have, such a horse. I never knew one like him for speed and for strength. You were a boy then and couldn't have known, but you may have heard of him. All Moscow was talking about him.'

'Yes, I heard of him,' the host unwillingly replied. 'But what I wished to say about mine . . .'

'Ah, then you did hear! I bought him just as he was, without his pedigree and without a certificate; it was only afterwards that I got to know Voekov and found out. He was a colt by Affable I. Strider—because of his long strides. On account of his piebald spots he was removed from the Khrenov stud and given to the head keeper, who had him castrated and sold him to a horse-dealer. There are no such horses now, my dear chap. Ah, those were days! Ah, vanished youth!'—and he sang the words of the gypsy song. He was getting tipsy. 'Ah, those were good times. I was twenty-five and had eighty thousand roubles a year, not a single grey hair, and all my teeth like pearls. Whatever I touched succeeded, and now it is all ended.'

'But there was not the same spiritedness then,' said the host, availing himself of the pause. 'Let me tell you that my first horses began to race without . . .'

'Your horses! But they used to be more spirited.'

'How—more spirited?'

'Yes, more spirited! I remember as if it were today how I drove him once to the trotting races in Moscow. No horse of mine was running. I did not care for trotters, mine were thoroughbreds: General Chaulet, Mahomet. I drove up with my piebald. My driver was a fine fellow, I was fond of him, but he also took to drink. Well, so I got there.

' "Serpukhovskoy," I was asked, "When are you going to keep trotters?" "The devil take your lubbers!" I replied. "I have a piebald hack that can outpace all your trotters!" "Oh no, he won't!" "I'll bet a thousand roubles!" Agreed, and they started. He came in five seconds ahead and I won the thousand roubles. But what of it? I did a hundred versts* in three hours with a troika of thoroughbreds. All Moscow knows it.'

And Serpukhovskoy began to brag so glibly and continuously that his host could not get a single word in and sat opposite him with a dejected countenance, filling up his own and his guest's glass every now and then by way of distraction.

The dawn was breaking and still they sat there. It became intolerably boring for the host. He got up.

'If we are to go to bed, let's go!' said Serpukhovskoy rising, and reeling and puffing he went to the room prepared for him.

The host was lying beside his mistress.

'No, he is unendurable,' he said. 'He gets drunk and swaggers incessantly.'

'And plays up to me.'

'I'm afraid he'll be asking for money.'

Serpukhovskoy was lying on the bed in his clothes, breathing heavily.

'I must have been lying a lot,' he thought. 'Well, no matter! The wine was good, but he is an awful swine. There's something cheap about him. And I'm an awful swine,' he said to himself and laughed aloud. 'First I used to keep women, and now I'm kept. Yes, Winkler's wife will support me. I take money from her. Serves him right, serves him right. Still, I must undress. Can't get my boots off.

Hey! Hey!' he called out, but the man who had been told to wait on him had long since gone to bed.

He sat down, took off his coat and waistcoat and somehow managed to kick off his trousers, but for a long time could not get his boots off, his soft stomach being in the way. He got one off at last, and struggled for a long time with the other, panting and becoming exhausted. And so with his foot in the boot-top he rolled over and began to snore, filling the room with the smell of tobacco, wine, and slovenly old age.

XII

If Strider recalled anything that night, he was distracted by Vaska, who threw a rug over him, galloped off on him, and kept him standing till morning at the door of a tavern, near a peasant horse. They licked one another. In the morning when Strider returned to the herd he kept rubbing himself.

'Something itches dreadfully,' he thought.

Five days passed. They called in a veterinary, who said cheerfully: 'It's the itch, let me sell him to the gypsies.'

'What's the use? Cut his throat, and get it done today.'

The morning was calm and clear. The herd went to pasture, but Strider was left behind. A strange man came, thin, dark, and dirty, in a coat splashed with something black. It was the knacker. Without looking at Strider he took him by the halter they had put on him and led him away. Strider went quietly without looking round, dragging along as usual and catching his hind feet in the straw.

When they were out of the gate he strained towards the well, but the knacker jerked his halter, saying: 'Not worth while.'

The knacker and Vaska, who followed behind, went to a hollow behind the brick barn and stopped as if there were something peculiar about this very ordinary place. The knacker, handing the halter to Vaska, took off his coat, rolled up his sleeves, and produced a knife and a whetstone from his boot-leg. The gelding stretched towards the halter meaning to chew it a little from dullness, but he could not reach it. He sighed and closed his eyes. His lower lip hung down, disclosing his worn yellow teeth, and he began to drowse to the sound of the sharpening of the knife. Only his swollen, aching, outstretched leg kept jerking. Suddenly he felt himself being taken by the lower jaw and his head lifted. He opened his eyes. There were two dogs in front of him; one was sniffing at the knacker, the other was sitting and watching the gelding as if expecting something from him. The gelding looked at them and began to rub his jaw against the arm that was holding him.

'Want to doctor me probably—well, let them!' he thought.

And in fact he felt that something had been done to his throat. It hurt, and he shuddered and gave a kick with one foot, but restrained himself and waited for what would follow. Then he felt something liquid streaming down his neck and chest. He heaved a profound sigh and felt much better. The whole burden of his life was eased. He closed his eyes and began to droop his head. No one was holding it. Then his legs quivered and his whole body swayed. He was not so much frightened as surprised. Everything was so new to him. He was surprised, and started forward and upward, but instead of this, in moving from the spot his legs got entangled, he began to fall sideways, and trying to take a step fell forward and down on his left side. The knacker waited till the convulsions had ceased; drove away the dogs that had crept nearer, took the gelding by the legs, turned him on his back, told Vaska to hold a leg, and began to skin the horse.

'It too was a horse,' remarked Vaska.

'If he had been better fed the skin would have been fine,' said the knacker.

The herd returned down hill in the evening, and those on the left saw down below something red, round which dogs were busy and above which hawks and crows were flying. One of the dogs, pressing its paws against the carcass and swinging his head, with a crackling sound tore off what it had seized hold of. The chestnut filly stopped, stretched out her head and neck, and sniffed the air for a long time. They could hardly drive her away.

At dawn, in a ravine of the old forest, down in an overgrown glade, big-headed wolf cubs were howling joyfully. There were five of them: four almost alike and one little one with a head bigger than his body. A lean old wolf who was shedding her coat, dragging her full belly with its hanging dugs along the ground, came out of the bushes and sat down in front of the cubs. The cubs came and stood round her in a semicircle. She went up to the smallest, and bending her

knee and holding her muzzle down, made some convulsive movements, and opening her large sharp-toothed jaws disgorged a large
piece of horseflesh. The bigger cubs rushed towards her, but she
moved threateningly at them and let the little one have it all. The
little one, growling as if in anger, pulled the horseflesh under him
and began to gorge. In the same way the mother wolf coughed up a
piece for the second, the third, and all five of them, and then lay
down in front of them to rest.

A week later only a large skull and two shoulder-blades lay behind
the barn, the rest had all been taken away. In summer a peasant,
collecting bones, carried away these shoulder blades and skull and
put them to use.

The dead body of Serpukhovskoy, which had walked about the earth
eating and drinking, was put under ground much later. Neither his
skin, nor his flesh, nor his bones, were of any use. Just as for the last
twenty years his body that had walked the earth had been a great
burden to everybody, so the putting away of that body was again an
additional trouble to people. He had not been wanted by anybody for
a long time and had only been a burden, yet the dead who bury their
dead found it necessary to clothe that swollen body, which at once
began to decompose, in a good uniform and good boots and put it
into a new and expensive coffin with new tassels at its four corners,
and then to place that new coffin in another lead one, to take it to
Moscow and there dig up some long-buried human bones and right
in that spot hide this decomposing maggoty body in its new uniform
and polished boots and cover it all up with earth.

GOD SEES THE TRUTH, BUT WAITS

In the town of Vladimir lived a young merchant named Ivan Dmitrich Aksyonov. He had two shops and a house of his own.

Aksyonov was a handsome, fair-haired, curly-headed fellow, full of fun and very fond of singing. When quite a young man he had been given to drink and was riotous when he had had too much; but after he married he gave up drinking except now and then.

One summer Aksyonov was going to the Nizhny Fair, and as he bade goodbye to his family his wife said to him, 'Ivan Dmitrich, do not start today; I have had a bad dream about you.'

Aksyonov laughed, and said, 'You are afraid that when I get to the fair I shall go on a spree.'

His wife replied: 'I do not know what I am afraid of; all I know is that I had a bad dream. I dreamt you returned from the town, and when you took off your cap I saw that your hair was quite grey.'

Aksyonov laughed. 'That's a lucky sign,' said he. 'See if I don't sell out all my goods and bring you some expensive presents from the fair.'

So he said goodbye to his family and drove away.

When he had travelled halfway, he met a merchant whom he knew, and they put up at the same inn for the night. They had some tea together, and then went to bed in adjoining rooms.

It was not Aksyonov's habit to sleep late, and, wishing to travel while it was still cool, he aroused his driver before dawn and told him to harness the horses. Then he made his way across to the innkeeper's black cottage, paid his bill, and left.

When he had gone about forty versts* he stopped for the horses to be fed, rested awhile in the passage of the inn, then stepped out onto the porch and, ordering a samovar* to be heated, got out his guitar and began to play. Suddenly a troika* drove up with tinkling bells, and an official alighted, followed by two soldiers. He went up to Aksyonov and began to question him, asking him who he was and where he came from. Aksyonov answered him fully, and said, 'Won't you have some tea with me?' But the official went on cross-questioning him and asking him, 'Where did you spend last night?

Were you alone, or with a fellow-merchant? Did you see the other merchant this morning? Why did you leave the inn so early?' Aksyonov wondered why he was asked all these questions, but he described all that had happened, and then added, 'Why are you cross-questioning me as if I were a thief or a robber? I am travelling on business of my own, and there is no need to question me.'

Then the official called over the soldiers and said, 'I am the police officer of this district, and I question you because the merchant with whom you spent last night has been found with his throat cut. Show me your things, and you men search him.'

They entered the cottage, took Aksyonov's suitcase and sack, and started to open them and search them. Suddenly the officer drew a knife out of the sack and shouted, 'Whose knife is this?'

Aksyonov looked, saw a bloodstained knife taken from his sack, and became frightened.

'How is it there is blood on this knife?'

Aksyonov tried to answer, but could not utter a word. 'I . . . I don't know . . . I . . . the knife . . . I . . . not mine.'

Then the police officer said, 'This morning the merchant was found in bed with his throat cut. You are the only person who could have done it. The cottage was locked from inside, and no one else was there. Here is this bloodstained knife in your sack, and your face and manner betray you! Tell me how you killed him and how much money you stole?'

Aksyonov swore he had not done it, that he had not seen the merchant after they had had tea together, that he had no money except the eight thousand of his own, and that the knife was not his. But his voice was broken, his face pale, and he trembled with fear as though he were guilty.

The police officer ordered the soldiers to bind Aksyonov and to put him in the cart. As they tied his feet together and flung him into the cart, Aksyonov crossed himself and began to weep. His money and goods were taken from him, and he was sent to the nearest town and imprisoned there. Enquiries as to his character were made in Vladimir. The merchants and other inhabitants of that town said that in former days he used to drink and waste his time, but that he was a good man. Then they tried him. He was charged with murdering a merchant from Ryazan and robbing him of twenty thousand roubles.

His wife grieved for him and did not know what to think. Her children were all quite small; one was a baby at the breast. Taking them all with her, she went to the town where her husband was in jail. At first she was not allowed to see him, but after much begging she obtained permission from the officials and was taken to him. When she saw her husband in prison garb in chains, together with thieves, she threw herself on the ground and did not come to her senses for a long time. Then she drew her children to her and sat down near him. She told him of things at home and asked about what had happened to him. He told her all, and she said, 'What can we do now?'

He said, 'We must petition the Tsar. They should not let an innocent man perish.'

His wife told him that she had sent a petition to the Tsar, but that it had not been accepted.

Aksyonov did not reply, but only looked downcast.

Then his wife said, 'It was not for nothing I dreamt your hair had turned grey. You remember? You should not have started that day.' And passing her fingers through his hair she said: 'Vanya dearest, tell your wife the truth; was it not you who did it?'

'So you, too, suspect me!' said Aksyonov, and, hiding his face in his hands, he began to weep. Then a soldier came to say that the wife and children must go away, and Aksyonov said goodbye to his family for the last time.

When they were gone, Aksyonov recalled what had been said, and when he remembered that his wife also had suspected him, he said to himself, 'It seems that only God can know the truth; it is to him alone we must appeal and from him alone expect mercy.'

And Aksyonov wrote no more petitions, gave up all hope, and only prayed to God.

Aksyonov was condemned to be flogged and sent to the mines. So he was flogged with a knout, and when the wounds caused by the knout were healed, he was driven with other convicts to Siberia.

For twenty-six years Aksyonov lived as a convict in Siberia. His hair turned white as snow, and his beard grew long, thin, and grey. All his mirth vanished. He became stooped over, started to walk slowly, spoke little, never laughed, and often prayed to God.

In prison Aksyonov learnt to make boots, and earned a little money, with which he bought *Cheti-Minei** and read it when it was light enough in the prison; and on Sundays in the prison church he read the epistle and sang in the choir, for his voice was still good. The prison authorities liked Aksyonov for his meekness, and his fellow-prisoners respected him: they called him 'Granddad' and a 'man of God'.* When they wanted to petition the prison authorities about anything, they always made Aksyonov their spokesman, and when there were quarrels among the prisoners they came to him to put things right, and to judge the matter.

No news reached Aksyonov from his home, and he did not even know if his wife and children were still alive.

One day a fresh gang of convicts came to the prison. In the evening the old prisoners gathered round the new ones and asked them what towns or villages they came from and what they were sentenced for. Among the rest Aksyonov sat down near the newcomers and listened with downcast air to who said what. One of the new convicts, a tall, strong man of sixty, with a closely cropped grey beard, was telling the others what he had been arrested for.

'Well, friends,' he said, 'I only took a horse that was tied to a sledge, and I was arrested and accused of stealing. I said I had only taken it to get home quicker, and had then let it go; besides, the driver was a personal friend of mine. So I said, "It's all right." "No," said they, "you stole it." But how or where I stole it they could not say. I once really did something wrong, and ought by rights to have come here long ago, but that time I was not found out. Now I have been sent here illegally. Eh, but it's lies I'm telling you; I've been to Siberia before, but I did not stay long.'

'Where are you from?' asked one of the convicts.

'From Vladimir. My family are tradesmen there. My name is Makar Semyonovich.'

Aksyonov raised his head and said: 'Tell me, Semyonich, do you know anything of the Aksyonov merchants of Vladimir? Are they still alive?'

'Know them? Of course I do. The Aksyonovs are rich, though their father is in Siberia; a sinner like ourselves, it seems! As for you, Granddad, how did you come here?'

Aksyonov did not like to speak of his misfortune. He only sighed, and said, 'For my sins I have been in prison these twenty-six years.'

'What sins?' asked Makar Semyonov.

But Aksyonov only said, 'Well, well, I must have deserved it!' He would have said no more, but his companions told the newcomer how Aksyonov came to be in Siberia: how someone had killed a merchant and had put a knife among Aksyonov's things, and he had been unjustly condemned.

When Makar Semyonov heard this he looked at Aksyonov, slapped his own knee, and exclaimed, 'Well, this is a miracle! Really a miracle! But how old you've grown, Granddad!'

The others asked him why he was so surprised, and where he had seen Aksyonov before; but Makar Semyonov did not reply. He only said: 'It's miraculous that we should meet here, lads!'

These words made Aksyonov wonder whether this man knew who had killed the merchant; so he said, 'Perhaps, Semyonich, you have heard of that affair, or maybe you've seen me before?'

'How could I help hearing? The world's full of rumours. But it's long ago, and I've forgotten what I heard.'

'Perhaps you heard who killed the merchant?' asked Aksyonov.

Makar Semyonov laughed, and replied, 'It must have been him in whose sack the knife was found! If someone else hid the knife there, well "He's not a thief till he's caught," as the saying goes. How could anyone put a knife into your sack while it was under your head? It would surely have woken you up?'

When Aksyonov heard these words he felt sure this was the man who had killed the merchant. He rose and went away. All that night Aksyonov lay awake. He felt a terrible longing, and all sorts of images rose in his mind. There was the image of his wife as she was when he parted from her to go to the fair. He saw her as if she were present; her face and her eyes rose before him, he heard her speak and laugh. Then he saw his children, quite little, as they were at that time: one with a little cloak on, another at his mother's breast. And then he remembered himself as he used to be, young and merry. He remembered how he sat playing the guitar in the porch of the inn where he was arrested, and how merry he had been. And he recalled the place where he was flogged, and the executioner, and the people standing around, and the chains, and the convicts, and all the twenty-six years of his prison life, and his premature old age. The thought of it all made him so wretched that he was ready to kill himself.

'And it's all that villain's doing!' thought Aksyonov. And his anger was so great against Makar Semyonov that he longed for vengeance, even if he himself should perish for it. He kept saying prayers all night, but could get no peace. During the day he did not go near Makar Semyonov, nor even look at him.

A fortnight passed in this way. Aksyonov could not sleep at nights and was so miserable that he did not know what to do.

One night as he was walking about the prison he noticed some earth that came rolling out from under one of the shelves on which the prisoners slept. He stopped to see what it was. Suddenly Makar Semyonov crept out from under the shelf, and looked up at Aksyonov with a frightened face. Aksyonov tried to pass without looking at him, but Makar seized his hand and told him that he had dug a hole under the wall, getting rid of the earth by putting it into his high boots and emptying it out every day on the road when the prisoners were driven to their work.

'Just you keep quiet, old man, and you shall get out too. If you blab they'll flog the life out of me, but I will kill you first.'

Aksyonov trembled with anger as he looked at his enemy. He drew his hand away, saying, 'I have no wish to escape, and you have no need to kill me; you killed me long ago! As to telling on you, I may do so or not, as God shall guide me.'

Next day, when the convicts were led out to work, the convoy soldiers noticed that Makar Semyonov was emptying some earth out of his boots. The prison was searched and the tunnel found. The director came and questioned all the prisoners to find out who had dug the hole. They all denied any knowledge of it. Those who knew would not betray Makar Semyonov, knowing he would be flogged almost to death. At last the director turned to Aksyonov, whom he knew to be a just man, and said:

'You are a truthful old man; tell me, before God, who dug the hole?'

Makar Semyonov stood as if he were quite unconcerned, looking at the director and not so much as glancing at Aksyonov. Aksyonov's lips and hands trembled, and for a long time he could not utter a word. He thought, 'If I do cover for him, still why should I forgive him, when he ruined my life? Let him pay for what I have suffered. But if I tell on him, they will probably flog the life out of him, and what if I suspect him wrongly? And, after all, what good would it be to me?'

'Well, old man,' repeated the director, 'tell us the truth: who has been digging under the wall?'

Aksyonov glanced at Makar Semyonov and said, 'I didn't see and don't know.'

So they did not learn who was digging the hole.

That night, when Aksyonov was lying on his bed and just beginning to doze, someone came quietly and sat down on his bed. He peered through the darkness and recognized Makar.

'What more do you want of me?' asked Aksyonov. 'Why have you come here?'

Makar Semyonov was silent. So Aksyonov sat up and said, 'What do you want? Go away or I will call the guard!'

Makar Semyonov bent close over Aksyonov, and whispered, 'Ivan Dmitrich, forgive me!'

'What for?' asked Aksyonov.

'It was I who killed the merchant and hid the knife among your things. I meant to kill you too, but I heard a noise outside, so I hid the knife in your sack and escaped through the window.'

Aksyonov was silent and did not know what to say. Makar Semyonov slid off the bed-shelf and knelt upon the ground. 'Ivan Dmitrich,' he said, 'forgive me! For the love of God, forgive me! I will confess that it was I who killed the merchant, and you will be forgiven and can go to your home.'

'It is easy for you to talk,' said Aksyonov, 'but how I have suffered. Where could I go to now? My wife is dead, and my children have forgotten me. I have nowhere to go.'

Makar Semyonov did not rise, but beat his head on the floor. 'Ivan Dmitrich, forgive me!' he cried. 'When they flogged me with the knout it was not so hard to bear as it is to see you now, yet you had pity on me and did not tell. For Christ's sake forgive me, wretch that I am, forgive me!' And he began to sob.

When Aksyonov heard him sobbing he too began to weep.

'God will forgive you!' he said. 'Maybe I am a hundred times worse than you.' And at these words his heart suddenly grew light and the longing for home left him. He no longer had any desire to leave the prison, but only hoped for his last hour to come.

In spite of what Aksyonov had said, Makar Semyonov confessed his guilt. But when the order for his release came, Aksyonov was already dead.

THE NOTES OF A MADMAN

20th October 1883.

Today I was taken to the Provincial Government Board to be certified. Opinions differed. They disputed, and finally decided that I was not insane, but they arrived at this decision only because during the examination I did my utmost to restrain myself and not give myself away. I did not speak out, because I am afraid of the mad-house, where they would prevent me from doing my mad work. So they came to the conclusion that I am subject to hallucinations and something else, but am of sound mind.

They came to that conclusion, but I myself know that I am mad. A doctor prescribed a treatment for me, and assured me that if I would follow his instructions exactly all would be right, all that troubled me would pass. Ah, what would I not give that it might pass! The torment is too great. I will tell in due order how and from what this medical certification came about, how I went mad and how I betrayed myself.

Up to the age of thirty-five I lived just as everybody else does and nothing strange was noticed about me. Perhaps in early childhood, before the age of ten, there was at times something resembling my present condition, but only by fits, and not continually as now. Moreover in childhood it used to affect me rather differently. For instance I remember that once when going to bed, at the age of five or six, my nurse Evpraksia, a tall thin woman who wore a brown dress and a cap and had flabby skin under her chin, was undressing me and lifting me up to put me into my bed. 'I will get into bed by myself, myself!' I said, and stepped over the side of the bed.

'Well, lie down then. Lie down, Fedya! Look at Mitya. He's a good boy and is lying down already,' she said, indicating my brother with a jerk of her head.

I jumped into the bed still holding her hand, and then let it go, kicked about under my blanket, and wrapped myself up. And I had such a pleasant feeling. I grew quiet and thought: 'I love Nurse; Nurse loves me and Mitenka; and I love Mitenka, and Mitenka loves me and Nurse. Nurse loves Taras, and I love Taras, and Mitenka loves him. And Taras loves me and Nurse. And Mamma loves me and Nurse, and Nurse loves Mamma and me and Papa—and everybody loves everybody and everybody is happy!' Then suddenly I heard the housekeeper run in and angrily shout something about a sugar-basin, and nurse answering indignantly that she had not taken it. And I felt pained, frightened, and bewildered, and horror, cold horror, seized me, and I hid my head under the blanket but felt no better in the dark. I also remembered how a serf-boy was once beaten in my presence, how he screamed, and how dreadful Foka's face looked when he was beating the boy. 'Then you won't do it any more, you won't?' he kept repeating as he went on beating. The boy cried, 'I won't!' but Foka still repeated, 'You won't!' and went on beating him. And then I was overcome by it! I began to sob and sob, and for a long time they could not quiet me. Those sobs, that despair, were the first attacks of my present madness.

I remember another time when I was overcome by it when my aunt told us about Christ. She told the story and was about to go away, but we said: 'Tell us some more about Jesus Christ!'

'No, I have no time now,' she said.

'No, tell us now!'

Mitenka also asked her to, and my aunt began to repeat what she had told us. She told us how they crucified, beat, and tortured him, and how he went on praying and did not reproach them.

'Why did they torment him, Auntie?'

'They were cruel people.'

'But why, when he was good?'

'There, that's enough. It's past eight! Do you hear?'

'Why did they beat him? He forgave them, then why did they hit him? Did it hurt him, Auntie? Did it hurt?'

'That will do! I'm going to have tea now.'

'But perhaps it isn't true and they didn't beat him?'

'Now, now, that will do!'

'No, no! Don't go away!'

And again I was overcome by it. I sobbed and sobbed, and began knocking my head against the wall.

That was how it would overcome me in my childhood. But by the time I was fourteen, and from the time the instincts of sex were aroused and I yielded to vice, all that passed away and I became a boy like other boys, like all the rest of us reared on rich, overabundant food, pampered, doing no physical work, surrounded by all possible temptations that inflamed sensuality, and among other equally spoilt children. Boys of my own age taught me vice, and I indulged in it. Later on that vice was replaced by another, and I began to know women. And so, seeking enjoyments and finding them, I lived till the age of thirty-five. I was perfectly well and there were no signs of my madness.

Those twenty years of my healthy life passed for me so that I can hardly remember anything of them, and now recall them with difficulty and disgust. Like all mentally healthy boys of our circle I entered high school and afterwards the university, where I completed the course of law studies. Then I was in the civil service for a short time, and then I met my present wife, married, lived in the country and, as it is called, 'brought up' our children, managed the estates, and was a justice of the peace. In the tenth year of my married life I again had an attack, the first since my childhood.

My wife and I had accumulated some money, some inherited by her and some from my buy-out bonds,* and we decided to buy an estate. I was much interested, as was proper, in the growth of our property and in increasing it in the shrewdest way, better than other people. At that time I enquired everywhere where there were estates for sale and read all the advertisements in the papers. I wanted to buy an estate so that the income from it, or the timber on it, should cover the whole purchase price and I should get it for nothing. I looked out for some fool who did not understand business, and thought I had found such a man. An estate with large forests was being sold in Penza province. From all I could learn about it, it seemed that its owner was just such a fool as I wanted and the timber would cover the whole cost of the estate. So I got ready and set out.

We (my servant and I) travelled at first by rail and then by road in a post-chaise. The journey was a very pleasant one for me. My servant, a young good-natured fellow, was in just as good spirits as I. We saw new places and met new people and enjoyed ourselves. To reach our destination we had to go about two hundred and some versts,* and decided to go without stopping except to change horses. Night came and we still went on. We grew drowsy. I fell asleep, but suddenly awoke feeling that there was something terrifying. As often happens, I woke up thoroughly alert and feeling as if sleep had gone for ever. 'Why am I going? Where am I going?' I suddenly asked myself. It was not that I did not like the idea of buying an estate cheaply, but it suddenly occurred to me that there was no need for me to travel all that distance, that I should die here in this strange place, and I was filled with dread. Sergey, my servant, woke up, and I availed myself of the opportunity to talk to him. I spoke about that part of the country, he replied and joked, but I felt depressed. I spoke about our folks at home, and of the business before us, and I was surprised that his answers were so cheerful. Everything seemed pleasant and amusing to him while it repelled me. But for all that while we were talking I felt easier. But besides being bored and filled with dread, I began to feel tired and wished to stop. It seemed to me that I should feel better if I could enter a house, see people, drink tea, and above all have some sleep. We were nearing the town of Arzamas.

'Shall we put up here and rest a bit?'

'Why not? Splendid!'

'Are we still far from the town?'

'About seven versts.'

The driver was a respectable man, careful and taciturn, and he drove rather slowly and wearily. We drove on. I remained silent and felt better because I was looking forward to a rest and hoped that everything would pass there. We went on and on in the darkness for a terribly long time as it seemed to me. We reached the town. Everybody was already asleep. Mean little houses showed up through the darkness, and the sound of our jingling bells and the clatter of the horses' feet reverberated, especially near the houses, and all this was far from cheerful. Here and there we passed some houses, large and white. I was impatient to get to the post-station and a samovar,* and to lie down and rest. At last we came up to a small house with a post beside it. The house was white, but appeared terribly melancholy to me, so much so that I was even filled with dread. I got out of the carriage slowly.

Sergey briskly took out all that would be wanted, running clattering up the porch, and the sound of his steps depressed me. I entered a little corridor. A sleepy man with a spot on his cheek, which seemed to me terrifying, showed us into a room. It was gloomy. I entered, and again I was filled with dread.

'Do you have a bedroom? I should like to rest.'

'Yes, we have. This is it.'

It was a small square room, with freshly whitewashed walls. I remember that it particularly tormented me that this room was square. It had one window with a red curtain, a birchwood table, and a sofa with bent-wood arms. We went in. Sergey prepared the samovar and made tea, while I took a pillow and lay down on the sofa. I was not asleep and heard how Sergey was busy with the tea and called me to have some. But I was terrified of getting up and arousing myself completely, and I thought how terrifying it would be to sit up in that room. I did not get up but began to doze. I must have fallen asleep, for when I awoke I found myself alone in the room and it was dark. I was again as wide awake as I had been in the chaise. I felt that to sleep would be quite impossible. Why have I come here? Where am I betaking myself? From what and to where am I running away? I am running away from something terrifying and cannot run away from it. I am always with myself, and it is I who am tormenting to myself. Here I am, the whole of me. Neither the Penza nor any other property will add anything to or take anything from me. And it is myself I am weary of and find intolerable and tormenting. I want to fall asleep and forget myself and cannot. I cannot get away from myself! I went out into the passage. Sergey was sleeping on a narrow bench with one arm hanging down, but he was sleeping peacefully and the watchman with the spot was also asleep. I had gone out into the corridor thinking to escape from what tormented me. But it had come out with me and cast a gloom over everything. I felt just as filled with terror or even more so.

'But what folly this is!' I said to myself. 'Why am I depressed? What am I afraid of?'

'Me!' answered the voice of death, inaudibly. 'I am here!'

A cold shudder ran down my back. Yes! Death! It will come, here it is, but it ought not to be. Had I been actually facing death I could not have experienced what I did then. I would have been frightened. But now I was not frightened. I saw and felt the approach of death, and at the same time I felt that it ought not to exist. My whole being was conscious of the necessity and the right to live, and yet I felt that death was being accomplished. And this inward conflict was horrible. I tried to throw off the horror. I found a brass candlestick with a bit of a candle left and lighted it. The red glow of the candle and its size, little less than the candlestick itself, told me the same thing.

There is nothing in life, but there's death, and death ought not to exist.

I tried to turn my thoughts to things that had interested me, to the estate I was to buy and to my wife, but found nothing to cheer me. It had all become nothing. Everything was hidden by the terrible consciousness that my life was ebbing away. I needed sleep. I lay down, but the next instant I jumped up again in horror. A fit of depression seized me, a depression such as one feels before being sick, only it was a spiritual depression. It was dreadful and terrifying. It seems that death is terrifying, but when remembering and thinking of life it is one's dying life that is terrifying. Life and death somehow merged into one another. Something was tearing my soul apart and could not complete the severance. Again I went to look at the sleepers, and again I tried to go to sleep. Always the same horror: red, white, and square. Something was tearing that could not be torn apart. A tormenting, tormentingly dry and spiteful feeling, not a touch of kindness, but just a dull and steady spitefulness towards myself and towards that which had made me. What made me? God, they say. God. I should pray, I remembered. For some twenty years I had not prayed, and I did not believe in anything, though as a matter of propriety I fasted and went to communion every year. Now I began to pray. 'Lord have mercy!' 'Our Father.' 'Mother of God.' I began to compose new prayers, crossing myself, bowing down to the ground and glancing around me for fear that I might be seen. This seemed to divert me, the fear of being seen distracted my terror, and I lay down. But I had only to lie down and close my eyes for the same feeling of horror to jog and rouse me. I could bear it no longer. I woke the watchman and Sergey, gave orders to harness, and we drove off again. The fresh air and the drive made me feel better. But I realized that something new had come into my soul and poisoned all my former life.

By nightfall we reached our destination. The whole day I had been fighting my depression and had mastered it, but it had left its terrible dregs in my soul as if some misfortune had befallen me, and I could forget it only for a time. There it remained at the bottom of my soul and had me in its power.

The old steward of the estate received me well, though without any pleasure. He was sorry the estate was to be sold. Clean little rooms with upholstered furniture. A new, brightly polished samovar.

A large-sized tea-service, and honey for tea. Everything was fine. But I questioned him about the estate unwillingly, as if it were some old forgotten lesson. It was all without cheer. However, I fell asleep without any depression, and this I attributed to my having prayed again before going to bed.

After that I went on living as before, but the fear of that depression always hung over me. I had to live without stopping to think, and above all to live in my accustomed surroundings. As a schoolboy repeats a lesson learnt by heart without thinking, so I had to live to avoid falling prey to that awful depression I had first experienced at Arzamas. I returned home safely. I did not buy the estate, I had not enough money, and I continued to live as before, only with this difference, that I began to pray and went to church. As before it seemed to me, but I now remember that it was not as before. I lived on what had been begun before. I continued to go along the rails laid before by my former strength, but I did not undertake anything new. And I took less part in those things I had begun before. Everything seemed dull to me. I became pious. My wife noticed this, and scolded and nagged me on account of it. But my depression did not recur at home.

But once I had unexpectedly to go to Moscow. I got ready in the afternoon and left in the evening. It was in connection with a lawsuit. I arrived in Moscow cheerful. On the way I had talked with a landowner from Kharkov about estate-management and banks, and about where to stay, and about the theatre. We both decided to stay at the Moscow Hotel on the Myasnitsky Street, and to go to see *Faust* that same evening. When we arrived I was shown into a small room. The oppressive air of the corridor filled my nostrils. A porter brought in my portmanteau and a chambermaid lighted a candle. The wick was lighted and then as usual the flame went down. In the next room someone coughed, probably an old man. The maid went out, but the porter remained and asked if he should untie my luggage. The flame of the candle flared up, revealing the blue wallpaper with yellow stripes on the partition, a shabby table, a small sofa, a looking-glass, a window, and the narrow dimensions of the room. And suddenly I was seized with an attack of the same horror as in Arzamas. 'My God! How can I stay here all night?' I thought.

'Yes, untie it, my good fellow,' I told the porter to keep him longer in the room. 'I'll dress quickly and go to the theatre.' When the porter had untied it, I said: 'Please go to Number Eight and tell the gentleman who came here with me that I shall be ready immediately and will come to him.'

The porter went out and I dressed hurriedly, afraid to look at the walls. 'What nonsense!' I thought. 'What am I afraid of? Just like a child! I am not afraid of ghosts. Ghosts! Ghosts would be better than what I am afraid of. Why, what is it? Nothing. Myself. What nonsense!' However, I put on a hard, cold, starched shirt, inserted the studs, donned my evening coat and new boots, and went to find the Kharkov landowner, who was ready. We started for the opera. He stopped on the way at a hairdresser's to have his hair curled, and I had mine cut by a French assistant and had a chat with him, and bought a pair of gloves. All was well, and I quite forgot my oblong room with its partition. In the theatre, too, it was pleasant. After the opera the Kharkov landowner suggested that we should have supper. That was contrary to my habit, but just then I again remembered the partition in my room and accepted his suggestion.

We got back after one. I had had two glasses of wine, to which I was unaccustomed, but in spite of that I felt cheerful. But no sooner had we entered the corridor in which the lamp was turned low and I was surrounded by the hotel smell, than a shiver of horror ran down my spine. There was nothing to be done however, and I pressed my companion's hand and went into my room.

I spent a terrible night, worse than at Arzamas. Not till dawn, when the old man at the other side of the door was coughing again, did I fall asleep, and then not in the bed, in which I had lain down several times during the night, but on the sofa. I had suffered all night unbearably. Again my soul and body were being tormentingly torn asunder. 'I am living, have lived, and ought to live, and suddenly here is death, the destruction of everything. Then what is life for? To die? To kill myself at once? No, I am afraid. To wait for death till it comes? I fear that even more. Then I must live. But what for? In order to die?' And I could not escape from that circle. I took up a book, read, and forgot myself for a moment, but then again the same question and the same horror. I lay down in bed and closed my eyes. It was worse still! God has so arranged it. Why? They say: 'Don't ask, but pray!' Very well. I prayed and prayed now as I had done at Arzamas. Then and afterwards I prayed simply, like a child. But now my prayers had a meaning. 'If thou dost exist, reveal to me why and what I am!' I bowed down, repeated all the prayers I knew, composed my own, and added: 'Then reveal it!' and became silent, awaiting an answer. But no answer came, just as if there were no one who could give an answer. And I remained alone with myself. And in place of him who would not reply I answered my own questions. 'Why? In order to live in a future life,' I said to myself. 'Then why this obscurity, this torment? I cannot believe in a future life. I believed when I did not ask with my whole soul, but now I cannot, I cannot. If thou didst exist thou wouldst speak to me and to all men. And if thou dost not exist there is nothing but despair. And I do not want that, I do not want that!' I became indignant. I asked him to reveal the truth to me, to reveal himself to me. I did all that everybody does, but he did not reveal himself. 'Ask and it shall be given you' I remembered, and I had asked and in that asking had found not consolation but relaxation. Perhaps I did not pray to him but repudiated him. 'You recede an inch and he recedes a mile' as the proverb has it. I did not believe in him but I asked, and he still did not reveal anything to me. I was balancing accounts with him and blaming him. I simply did not believe.

The next day I did all in my power to get through my ordinary affairs so as to avoid another night in the hotel. Although I did not finish everything, I left for home that evening. I did not feel depressed. That night in Moscow still further changed my life which had begun to change from the time I was at Arzamas. I now attended still less to my affairs and became apathetic. I also grew weaker in health. My wife insisted that I should undergo treatment. She said that my talks about faith and God arose from ill health. But I knew that my weakness and ill health were the effect of the unresolved question within me. I tried not to let that question dominate me and tried to fill my life amid my customary surroundings. I went to church on Sundays and feast days, prepared to receive communion, and even fasted, as I had begun to do since my visit to Penza, and I prayed, though more as a custom. I did not expect any result from this, but as it were kept the demand-note and presented it at the due date, though I knew it was impossible to secure payment. I only did it on the chance. I did not fill my life by estate management, it repelled me by the struggle it involved (I had no energy), but by reading magazines, newspapers, and novels, and playing cards for small stakes. I only showed energy by hunting, which I did from habit. I had been fond of hunting all my life.

One winter day a neighbouring huntsman came with his wolf-hounds. I rode out with him. When we reached the place we put on snowshoes and went to the spot where a wolf might be found. The hunt was unsuccessful, the wolves broke through the ring of beaters. I became aware of this from a distance and went through the forest following the fresh tracks of a hare. These led me far into a glade, where I spied the hare, but it jumped out so that I lost it. I turned back through the thick forest. The snow was deep, my snowshoes sank in, and branches of the trees entangled me. The trees grew ever more and more dense. I began to ask myself: 'Where am I?' The snow had altered the look of everything.

Suddenly I realized that I had lost my way. I was far from the house and from the hunters too, and could hear nothing. I was tired and bathed in perspiration. If I stopped I should freeze. If I went on my strength would fail me. I shouted. All was still. No one answered. I turned back, but again it was not right. I looked around, nothing but trees, impossible to tell which was east or west. Again I turned back. My legs were tired. I grew frightened, stopped, and was seized with the same horror as in Arzamas and Moscow, but a hundred times worse. My heart palpitated, my arms and legs trembled. 'Is this death? I don't want it! Why death? What is death?' Once again I wanted to question and reproach God, but here I suddenly felt that I dare not and must not do so, that it is impossible to present one's account to God, that he had said what is needful and I alone was guilty. I began to implore his forgiveness and felt disgusted with myself.

The horror did not last long. I stood there for awhile, came to myself, went on in one direction and soon emerged from the forest. I had not been far from its edge, and came out on to the road. My arms and legs still trembled and my heart was beating, but I felt happy. I found the hunting party and we returned home. I was cheerful, but I knew there was something joyful which I would make out when alone. And so it was. I remained by myself in my study and began to pray, asking forgiveness and remembering my sins. There seemed to me to be but few, but when I recalled them they became hateful to me.

After that I began to read the scriptures. The Old Testament I found unintelligible though enchanting, but the Gospels moved me pro-foundly. But most of all I read the lives of the saints, and that reading consoled me, presenting examples that it seemed more and more possible to follow. From that time forth farming and family matters occupied me less and less. They even repelled me. They all seemed to me not right. What it was that was right I did not know, but what had formerly constituted my life had now ceased to do so. This became plain to me when I was going to buy another estate.

Not far from us an estate was for sale on very advantageous terms. I went to see it. Everything was excellent and advantageous; especially so was the fact that the peasants there had no land of their own except their kitchen-gardens. I saw that they would have to work on the landlord's land merely for permission to use his pastures. And so it was. I grasped all this, and by old habit felt pleased about it. But on my way home I met an old woman who asked her way. I had a talk with her, during which she told me about her poverty. I got home, and when telling my wife of the advantages that estate offered, I suddenly felt ashamed and disgusted. I told her I could not buy it because the advantages we should get would be based on the peasants' destitution and sorrow. As I said this I suddenly realized the truth of what I was saying, the chief truth, that the peasants, like ourselves, want to live, that they are human beings, our brothers, and sons of the Father as the Gospels say. Suddenly something that had long troubled me seemed to have broken away, as though it had come to birth. My wife was vexed and scolded me, but I felt glad.

That was the beginning of my madness. But my utter madness began later, about a month after that. It began by my going to church. I stood there through the liturgy and prayed well, and listened and was touched. Then suddenly they brought me some consecrated bread: after that we went up to the cross, and people began pushing one another. Then at the exit there were beggars. And it suddenly became clear to me that this ought not to be, and not only ought not to be but in reality was not. And if this was not, then neither was there either death or terror, and there was no longer the former tearing asunder within me and I no longer feared anything. Then the light fully illumined me and I became what I now am. If there is nothing of all that, then it certainly does not exist within me. And there at the church door I gave away to the beggars all I had with me, some thirty-five roubles, and went home on foot talking with the peasants.

WHERE LOVE IS, GOD IS

In a certain town there lived a cobbler, Martyn Avdeich by name. He had a tiny room in a basement, the one window of which looked out on to the street. Through it one could only see the feet of those who passed by, but Martyn Avdeich recognized the people by their boots. Martyn Avdeich had lived long in the place and had many acquaintances. There was hardly a pair of boots in the neighbourhood that had not been once or twice through his hands, so he often saw his own handiwork through the window. Some he had resoled, some patched, some stitched up, and to some he had even put fresh uppers. He had plenty to do, for Avdeich worked well, used good material, did not charge too much, and could be relied on. If he could do a job by the day required, he undertook it; if not, he told the truth and gave no false promises. So Avdeich was well known and never short of work. Avdeich had always been a good man, but in his old age he began to think more about his soul and to draw nearer to God. While Martyn still lived with and worked for a master, his wife had died, leaving him with a three-year-old son. None of his elder children had lived, they had all died in infancy. At first Martyn thought of sending his little son to his sister's in the country, but then he felt sorry to part with the boy, thinking: 'It would be hard for my Kapitoshka to have to grow up in a strange family, I will keep him with me.' And Avdeich left his master and started living in an apartment with his little son. But he had no luck with his children. No sooner had the boy reached an age when he could help his father and be a support as well as a joy to him, than he fell ill and, after being laid up for a week with a burning fever, died. Martyn buried his son, and gave way to despair so great and overwhelming that he murmured against God. In his sorrow he prayed again and again that he too might die, reproaching God for having taken the son he loved, his only son, while he, old as he was, remained alive. After that Avdeich stopped going to church. One day an old man from Avdeich's native village, who had been a wanderer* for the last eight years, stopped by on his way from the Troitsa Monastery.* Avdeich opened his heart to him and began to complain to him of his sorrow.

'Oh man of God,* I no longer even wish to live,' he said. 'All I ask of God is that I soon may die. I am now quite without hope in the world.'

The old man replied: 'You have no right to say such things, Martyn. We cannot judge God's ways. Not by our reasoning, but by God's judgement.* If God willed that your son should die and you should live, it must be best so. As to your despair, that comes because you wish to live for your own happiness.'

'What else should one live for?' asked Martyn.

'For God, Martyn,' said the old man. 'He gives you life, and you must live for him. When you have learnt to live for him, you will grieve no more, and all will seem easy to you.'

Martyn was silent awhile, and then asked: 'But how is one to live for God?'

The old man answered: 'How one may live for God has been shown us by Christ. Can you read? Then buy the Gospels and read them: there you will see how God would have you live. It's all there.'

These words sank deep into Avdeich's heart, and that same day he went and bought himself a New Testament in large print, and began to read.

At first he meant only to read on holidays, but having once begun he found it made his heart so light that he read every day. Sometimes he was so absorbed in his reading that the oil in his lamp burnt out before he could tear himself away from the book. He continued to read every night, and the more he read the more clearly he understood what God required of him, and how he might live for God. And his heart grew lighter and lighter. Before, when he went to bed he used to lie with a heavy heart, moaning as he thought of his Kapitoshka, but now he only repeated again and again: 'Glory to thee, glory to thee, O Lord! Thy will be done!' From that time Avdeich's whole life changed. Formerly, on holidays he used to go and have tea at the public house and did not even refuse a glass or two of vodka. Sometimes, after having had a drop with a friend, he left the public house not drunk, but rather merry, and would say foolish things: shout at a man, or abuse him. Now all that sort of thing passed away from him. His life became peaceful and joyful. He sat down to his work in the morning, and when he had finished his day's work he took the lamp down from the wall, stood it on the table, fetched his book from the shelf, opened it, and sat down to read. The more he read the better he understood and the clearer and happier he felt in his heart.

It happened once that Martyn sat up late, absorbed in his book. He was reading Luke's Gospel, and in the sixth chapter he read the verses, 'Unto him that smiteth thee on the one cheek offer also the other; and him that taketh away thy cloak forbid not to take thy coat also. Give to every man that asketh thee; and of him that taketh away thy goods ask them not again. And as ye would that men should do to you, do ye also to them likewise.'*

He also read the verses where our Lord says:

'And why call ye me, Lord, Lord, and do not the things which I say? Whosoever cometh to me, and heareth my sayings, and doeth them, I will shew you to whom he is like: He is like a man which built an house, and digged deep, and laid the foundation on a rock: and when the flood arose, the stream beat vehemently upon that house, and could not shake it: for it was founded upon a rock. But he that heareth, and doeth not, is like a man that without a foundation built an house upon the earth, against which the stream did beat vehemently, and immediately it fell; and the ruin of that house was great.'*

When Avdeich read these words his soul was glad within him. He took off his spectacles and laid them on the book, and leaning his elbows on the table pondered over what he had read. He began to measure his own life by the standard of those words, asking himself:

'Is my house built on a rock, or on sand? It's fine, if it stands on a rock. It seems easy enough while you sit here alone, and think you have done all that God commands; but as soon as you cease to be on your guard, you sin again. Still I will persevere. It brings such joy. Help me, O Lord!'

He thought all this, and was about to go to bed, but was loath to leave his book. So he went on reading the seventh chapter. He read about the centurion, the widow's son, and the answer to John's disciples, and he came to the part where a rich Pharisee invited the Lord to his house, and he read how the woman who was a sinner anointed his feet and washed them with her tears, and how he justified her. Coming to the forty-fourth verse, he read:

'And turning to the woman, he said unto Simon, Seest thou this woman? I entered into thine house, thou gavest me no water for my feet: but she hath washed my feet with tears, and wiped them with the hairs of her head. Thou gavest me no kiss: but she, since the time I came in, hath not ceased to kiss my feet. My head with oil thou didst not anoint: but she hath anointed my feet with ointment.'* He read these verses and thought: '*Water for his feet he did not give, a kiss he did not give, his head with oil he did not anoint.*'

And Avdeich took off his spectacles once more, laid them on his book, and pondered. 'He must have been like me, that Pharisee. He too thought only of himself, how to get a cup of tea, how to keep warm and comfortable, never a thought of his guest. He took care of himself, but for his guest he cared not a bit. Yet who was the guest? The Lord himself! If he came to me, should I behave like that?'

Then Avdeich laid his head upon both his arms and, before he was aware of it, he fell asleep.

'Martyn!' as if suddenly something started to breathe above his ear.

He roused himself from his sleep. 'Who's there?' he asked.

He turned round and looked at the door; no one was there. He called again. Then he heard quite distinctly: 'Martyn, Martyn! Look out into the street tomorrow, for I shall come.'

Martyn woke up, rose from his chair and rubbed his eyes, but did not know whether he had heard these words in a dream or awake. He put out the lamp and lay down to sleep.

Next morning Avdeich rose before daylight and after saying his prayers he lit the fire and prepared his cabbage soup and buckwheat porridge. Then he lit the samovar,* put on his apron, and sat down by the window to his work. As he sat working Avdeich thought over what had happened the night before. At times it seemed to him like a dream, and at times he thought that he had really heard the voice. 'Such things have happened before now,' he thought.

So Martyn sat by the window, looking out into the street more than he worked, and whenever anyone passed in unfamiliar boots he would stoop and look up, so as to see not the feet only but the face of the passer-by as well. A house-porter passed in new felt boots, then a water-carrier, then an old soldier of Nicholas's reign came near the window with a shovel in his hand. Avdeich knew him by his boots, which were shabby old felt ones. The old man was called Stepanych: a neighbouring tradesman kept him in his house for charity. His duty was to help the house-porter. He began to clear away the snow before

Martyn's window. Avdeich glanced at him and then went on with his work.

'I must be growing crazy with age,' said Martyn, laughing at his fancy. 'Stepanych comes to clear away the snow, and I have to imagine it's Christ coming to visit me. Old dotard that I am!'

Yet after he had made a dozen stitches he felt drawn to look out of the window again. He saw that Stepanych had leaned his shovel against the wall and was either resting himself or trying to get warm. The man was old and broken down, and had evidently not enough strength even to clear away the snow.

'What if I called him in and gave him some tea?' thought Avdeich. 'The samovar is just starting to boil.'

Avdeich stuck his awl in its place, and got up, placed the samovar on the table, made tea, and tapped the window with his fingers. Stepanych turned and came to the window. Avdeich beckoned to him to come in and went himself to open the door.

'Come in,' he said, 'and warm yourself a bit. I'm sure you must be cold.'

'May Christ save you,' Stepanych said. 'My bones do ache for sure.' He came in, first shaking off the snow, and lest he should leave marks on the floor he began wiping his feet, but as he did so he tottered and nearly fell.

'Don't trouble to wipe your feet,' said Avdeich; 'I'll wipe up the floor, it's all in the day's work. Come, friend, sit down and have some tea.'

Filling two tumblers, he passed one to his visitor, and pouring his own out into the saucer, began to blow on it.

Stepanych emptied his glass, and, turning it upside down,* put the remains of his piece of sugar on the top. He began to express his thanks, but it was plain that he would be glad to have some more.

'Have another glass,' said Avdeich, refilling the visitor's tumbler and his own. But while he drank his tea Avdeich kept looking out into the street.

'Are you expecting someone?' asked the visitor.

'Am I expecting someone? Well now, I'm ashamed to tell you. It isn't that I really expect anyone; but I heard something last night which I can't get out of my mind. Whether it was a vision, or only a fancy, I can't tell. You see, friend, last night I was reading the Gospel, about Christ the Lord, how he suffered and how he walked on earth. You have heard of it, I suppose.'

'As for hearing, I've heard,' answered Stepanych; 'but I'm an ignorant man and not able to read.'

'Well, you see, I was reading of how he walked on earth. I came to that part, you know, where he went to a Pharisee who did not receive him well. Well, friend, as I read about it, I thought how that man did not receive Christ the Lord with proper honour. Suppose such a thing could happen to such a man as myself, I thought, what would I not do to receive him! But that man gave him no reception at all. Well, friend, as I was thinking of this I began to doze, and as I dozed I heard someone call me by name. I got up, and thought I heard someone whispering, "Expect me; I will come tomorrow." This happened twice over. And to tell you the truth, it sank so into my mind that, though I am ashamed of it myself, I keep on expecting him, the dear Lord!'

Stepanych shook his head in silence, finished his tumbler and laid it on its side, but Avdeich stood it up again and refilled it for him.

'Here, drink another glass, for your health! And I was thinking, too, how he walked on earth and despised no one, but went mostly among common folk. He went with plain people and chose his disciples from among the likes of us, from workmen like us, sinners that we are. He who exalts himself, he says, shall be humbled; and he who humbles himself shall be exalted. You call me Lord, he says, but I will wash your feet. He who would be first, he says, let him be the servant of all; because, he says, blessed are the poor, the humble, the meek, and the merciful.'

Stepanych forgot his tea. He was an old man, easily moved to tears, and as he sat and listened the tears ran down his cheeks.

'Come, drink some more,' said Avdeich. But Stepanych crossed himself, thanked him, moved away his tumbler, and rose.

'Thank you, Martyn Avdeich,' he said, 'you have given me food and comfort both for soul and body.'

'You're very welcome. Come again another time. I am glad to have a guest,' said Avdeich.

Stepanych went away; and Martyn poured out the last of the tea and drank it up. Then he put away the tea things and sat down to his work, stitching the back seam of a boot. And as he stitched he kept looking out of the window, waiting for Christ and thinking about him and his doings. And his head was full of Christ's sayings.

Two soldiers went by, one in government boots, the other in boots of his own, then the master of a neighbouring house, in shining goloshes, then a baker carrying a basket. All these passed on. Then a woman came up in worsted stockings and peasant-made shoes. She passed the window, but stopped by the wall. Avdeich glanced up at her through the window and saw that she was a stranger, poorly dressed and with a baby in her arms. She stopped by the wall with her back to the wind, trying to wrap the baby up though she had hardly anything to wrap it in. The woman had only summer clothes on, and even they were shabby and worn. Through the window Avdeich heard the baby crying, and the woman trying to soothe it but unable to do so. Avdeich rose, and going out of the door and up the steps he called to her.

'My dear, I say, my dear!'

The woman heard and turned round.

'Why do you stand out there with the baby in the cold? Come inside. You can wrap him up better in a warm place. Come this way!'

The woman was surprised to see an old man in an apron, with spectacles on his nose, calling to her, but she followed him in.

They went down the steps, entered the little room, and the old man led her to the bed.

'There, sit down, my dear, near the stove. Warm yourself and feed the baby.'

'Haven't any milk. I have eaten nothing myself since early morning,' said the woman, but still she took the baby to her breast.

Avdeich shook his head, went to the table, got some bread and a cup, opened the oven door, poured some cabbage soup into the cup, took out the porridge pot, but the porridge was not yet ready, so he spread a cloth on the table and served only the soup. He got the bread, took a hand towel from a hook, and placed them on the table.

'Sit down and eat, my dear, and I'll mind the baby. Why, I've had children of my own, I know how to manage them.'

The woman crossed herself, and sitting down at the table began to eat, while Avdeich put the baby on the bed and sat down by it. He kept on smacking his lips, but having no teeth he could not do it well and the baby continued to cry. Then Avdeich tried poking at him with his finger; he drove his finger straight at the baby's mouth and then quickly drew it back, and did this again and again. He did not let the baby take his finger in its mouth, because it was all black with cobbler's wax. But the baby first grew quiet watching the finger, and then began to laugh. And Avdeich felt quite pleased. The woman sat eating and talking, and told him who she was, and where she had been.

'I'm a soldier's wife,' she said. 'They sent my husband some-where, far away, eight months ago, and I have heard nothing of him since. I had a place as a cook till my baby was born, but then they would not keep me with a child. For three months now I have been struggling, unable to find a place, and I've had to sell all I had for food. I tried to go as a wet-nurse, but no one would have me, they said I was too starved-looking and thin. Now I have just been to see a tradesman's wife (a woman from our village is in service with her) and she has promised to take me. I thought it was all settled at last, but she tells me not to come till next week. It is far to her place, and I am tired out, and my baby is quite starved, poor mite. Fortunately our landlady has pity on us, and lets us lodge free, else I don't know what we should do.'

Avdeich sighed. 'Haven't you any warmer clothing?' he asked.

'How could I get warm clothing?' she said. 'Why, I pawned my last shawl for twenty kopeks yesterday.'

Then the woman came and took the child, and Avdeich got up. He went and looked among some things that were hanging on the wall, and brought back an old cloak.

'Here,' he said, 'though it's a worn-out old thing, it will do to wrap him up in.'

The woman looked at the cloak, then at the old man, and taking it, burst into tears. Avdeich turned away, and groping under the bed brought out a small trunk. He fumbled about in it and again sat down opposite the woman. And the woman said:

'May Christ save you, Granddad. Surely Christ must have sent me to your window, else the child would have frozen. It was mild when I started, but now see how cold it has turned. Surely it must have been Christ who made you look out of your window and take pity on me, poor wretch!'

Avdeich smiled and said, 'It is quite true; it was he made me do it. It was no mere chance made me look out.'

And he told the woman his dream, and how he had heard the Lord's voice promising to visit him that day.

'All things are possible,' said the woman. And she got up and threw the cloak over her shoulders, wrapping it round herself and round the baby. Then she bowed, and thanked Avdeich once more.

'Take this for Christ's sake,' said Avdeich, and gave her twenty kopeks to get her shawl out of pawn. The woman crossed herself, and Avdeich did the same, and then he saw her out.

After the woman had gone, Avdeich ate some cabbage soup, cleared the things away, and sat down to work again. He sat and worked, but did not forget the window, and every time a shadow fell on it he looked up at once to see who was passing. People he knew and strangers passed by, but no one remarkable.

After a while Avdeich saw an old woman stop just in front of his window. She was a street vendor and had a large apple basket, but there did not seem to be many apples left in it; she had evidently sold most of her stock. On her shoulder she had a sack full of wood chips, which she was taking home. No doubt she had gathered them at some place where building was going on. The sack evidently hurt her and she wanted to shift it from one shoulder to the other, so she put it down on the footpath and, placing her basket on a post, began to shake down the chips in the sack. While she was doing this a boy in a tattered cap ran up, snatched an apple out of the basket and tried to slip away; but the old woman noticed it, and turning, caught the boy by his sleeve. He began to struggle, trying to free himself, but the old woman held on with both hands, knocked his cap off his head, and seized hold of his hair. The boy screamed and the old woman scolded. Avdeich dropped his awl, not waiting to stick it in its place, and rushed out of the door. Stumbling up the steps and dropping his spectacles in his hurry, he ran out into the street. The old woman was pulling the boy's hair and scolding him, and threatening to take him to the police. The lad was struggling and protesting, saying, 'I did not take it. What are you beating me for? Let me go!'

Avdeich separated them. He took the boy by the hand and said, 'Let him go, Granny. Forgive him for Christ's sake.'

'I'll forgive him, so that he won't forget it for a year! I'll take the rascal to the police!'

Avdeich began entreating the old woman.

'Let him go, Granny. He won't do it again. Let him go for Christ's sake!'

The old woman let go, and the boy was about to run away, but Avdeich stopped him.

'Ask the Granny's forgiveness!' he said. 'And don't do it another time. I saw you take the apple.'

The boy began to cry and to beg forgiveness.

'That's right. And now here's an apple for you,' and Avdeich took an apple from the basket and gave it to the boy, saying, 'I will pay you, Granny.'

'You will spoil them that way, the young rascals,' said the old woman. 'He ought to be whipped so that he should remember it for a week.'

'Oh, Granny, Granny,' said Avdeich, 'that's our way, but it's not God's way. If he should be whipped for stealing an apple, what should be done to us for our sins?'

The old woman was silent.

And Avdeich told her the parable of the lord who forgave his servant a large debt, and how the servant went out and seized his debtor by the throat. The old woman listened to it all, and the boy, too, stood by and listened.

'God bids us forgive,' said Avdeich, 'or else we shall not be forgiven. Forgive everyone, and a thoughtless youngster most of all.'

The old woman wagged her head and sighed.

'It's true enough,' said she, 'but they are getting terribly spoilt.'

'Then we old ones must show them better ways,' Avdeich replied.

'That's just what I say,' said the old woman. 'I have had seven of them myself, and only one daughter is left.' And the old woman began to tell how and where she was living with her daughter, and how many grandchildren she had. 'There now,' she said, 'I have but little strength left, yet I work hard for the sake of my grandchildren, and nice children they are, too. No one comes out to meet me but the children. Little Annushka, now, won't leave me for anyone. "It's grandmother, dear grandmother, darling grandmother."' And the old woman completely softened at the thought.

'Of course it was only his childishness, God help him,' said she, referring to the boy.

As the old woman was about to hoist her sack on her shoulder, the lad sprang forward to her, saying, 'Let me carry it for you, Granny. I'm going that way.'

The old woman nodded her head, and put the sack on the boy's back, and they went down the street together, the old woman quite forgetting to ask Avdeich to pay for the apple. Avdeich stood and watched them as they went along talking to each other.

When they were out of sight Avdeich went back to the house. Having found his spectacles unbroken on the steps, he picked up his awl and sat down again to work. He worked a little, but could soon not see to pass the bristle through the holes in the leather; and presently he noticed the lamplighter passing on his way to light the street lamps.

'Seems it's time to light up,' he thought. So he trimmed his lamp, hung it up, and sat down again to work. He finished off one boot and, turning it about, examined it. It was all right. Then he gathered his tools together, swept up the cuttings, put away the bristles and the thread and the awls, and, taking down the lamp placed it on the table. Then he took the Gospels from the shelf. He meant to open them at the place he had marked the day before with a bit of morocco, but the book opened at another place. As Martyn opened it, his yesterday's dream came back to his mind, and no sooner had he thought of it than he seemed to hear footsteps, as though someone were moving behind him. Martyn turned round, and it seemed to him as if people were standing in the dark corner, but he could not make out who they were. And a voice whispered in his ear: 'Martyn, Martyn, don't you know me?'

'Who is it?' muttered Avdeich.

'It is I,' said the voice. And out of the dark corner stepped Stepanych, who smiled and vanishing like a cloud was seen no more.

'It is I,' said the voice again. And out of the darkness stepped the woman with the baby in her arms, and the woman smiled and the baby laughed, and they too vanished.

'It is I,' said the voice once more. And the old woman and the boy with the apple stepped out and both smiled, and then they too vanished.

And Avdeich's soul grew glad. He crossed himself, put on his spectacles, and began reading the Gospel just where it had opened; and at the top of the page he read:

'I was an hungred, and ye gave me meat: I was thirsty, and ye gave me drink: I was a stranger, and ye took me in.'*

And at the bottom of the page he read:

'Inasmuch as ye did it unto one of the least of these my brethren, ye have done it unto me.'*

And Avdeich understood that his dream had not deceived him, and that the Saviour had really come to him that day, and he had taken him in.

THE DEVIL

*But I say unto you, that whosoever looketh on a woman to lust after her
hath committed adultery with her already in his heart.*

*And if thy right eye offend thee, pluck it out, and cast it from thee: for
it is profitable for thee that one of thy members should perish, and not
that thy whole body should be cast into hell.*

*And if thy right hand offend thee, cut it off, and cast it from thee: for it
is profitable for thee that one of thy members should perish, and not that
thy whole body should be cast into hell.* Matthew v. 28, 29, 30.

I

A brilliant career lay before Yevgeny Irtenev. He had everything
necessary to attain it: an admirable education at home, high honours
when he graduated in law at Petersburg University, connections in
the highest society through his recently deceased father, even his
beginning service in one of the ministries under the protection of the
minister. Moreover he had a fortune, even a large one, though
insecure. His father had lived abroad and in Petersburg, allowing his
sons, Yevgeny and Andrey (who was older than Yevgeny and in the
horse guards), six thousand roubles a year each, while he himself and
his wife spent a great deal. He only used to visit his estate for a
couple of months in summer and did not concern himself with its
direction, entrusting it all to an unscrupulous manager who also
failed to attend to it, but in whom he had complete confidence.

After the father's death, when the brothers began to divide the
property, so many debts were discovered that their lawyer even
advised them to refuse the inheritance and retain only an estate left
them by their grandmother, which was valued at a hundred thousand
roubles. But a neighbouring landed proprietor who had done business with the old man Irtenev, that is to say, who had promissory
notes from him and had come to Petersburg on that account, said
that in spite of the debts they could straighten out affairs so as to
retain a large fortune (it would only be necessary to sell the forest

and some outlying land, retaining the rich Semyonov estate with four thousand *desyatins** of black earth, the sugar factory, and two hundred *desyatins* of water-meadows) if one devoted oneself to the management of the estate, settled there, and farmed it wisely and economically.

And so, having visited the estate in spring (his father had died in Lent), Yevgeny looked into everything, resolved to retire from the civil service, settle in the country with his mother, and undertake the management with the object of preserving the main estate. He arranged with his brother, with whom he was very friendly, that he would pay him either four thousand roubles a year, or a lump sum of eighty thousand, for which Andrey would hand over to him his share of the inheritance.

So he arranged matters and, having settled down with his mother in the big house, began managing the estate eagerly, yet cautiously.

It is generally supposed that conservatives are usually old people, and that those in favour of change are the young. That is not quite correct. Usually conservatives are young people, those who want to live but who do not think about how to live, and have not time to think, and therefore take as a model for themselves a way of life that has already existed.

Thus it was with Yevgeny. Having settled in the village, his aim and ideal was to restore the form of life that had existed, not in his father's time, his father had been a bad manager, but in his grandfather's. And now in the house, and in the garden, and in the estate management he tried to resurrect, of course with changes suited to the times, the general spirit of his grandfather's life, everything on a large scale, good order, method, and everybody satisfied. But to do this entailed much work. It was necessary to meet the demands of the creditors and the banks, and for that purpose to sell some land and arrange renewals of credit. It was necessary to get money to carry on (partly by farming out land, and partly by hiring labour) the immense operations on the Semyonov estate, with its four hundred *desyatins* of ploughland and its sugar factory. It was necessary to care for the house and garden so that they should not seem to be neglected or in decay.

There was much work to do, but Yevgeny had plenty of strength, physical and spiritual. He was twenty-six, of medium height, strongly built, with muscles developed by gymnastics, full-blooded with glowing red cheeks, bright teeth and lips, and fine, soft, curly hair. His only physical defect was short-sightedness, which he had himself developed by using spectacles, so that he could not now do without a pince-nez, which had already formed a line on the bridge of his nose.

Such he was physically. For his spiritual portrait it might be said that the better people knew him the better they liked him. His mother had always loved him more than anyone else, and now after her husband's death she concentrated on him not only her whole affection but her whole life. Nor was it only his mother who so loved him. All his comrades at the high school and the university not merely liked him very much, but respected him. He had this effect on all who met him. It was impossible not to believe what he said, impossible to suspect any deception or falseness in one who had such an open, honest face and in particular such eyes.

In general his personality helped him much in his affairs. A creditor who would have refused another trusted him. The clerk, the village elder, or a peasant, who would have played a dirty trick and cheated someone else, forgot to deceive under the pleasant impression of this kindly, agreeable, and above all candid man.

It was the end of May. Yevgeny had somehow managed in town to get the vacant land freed from the mortgage, so as to sell it to a merchant, and had borrowed money from that same merchant to replenish his stock, that is to say, to procure horses, bulls, and carts, and in particular to begin to build a necessary farmhouse. The matter had been arranged. The timber was being carted, the carpenters were already at work, and eighty carts of manure were being brought in, but everything still hung by a thread.

II

Amid these cares something came about which though unimportant tormented Yevgeny at the time. As a young man he had lived as all healthy, young, unmarried men live, that is, he had had relations with women of various kinds. He was not a libertine but neither, as he himself said, was he a monk. He only turned to this, however, in so far as was necessary for physical health and mental freedom, as he used to say. This had begun when he was sixteen and had gone on satisfactorily, in the sense that he had never given himself up to debauchery, never once been infatuated, and had never contracted a disease. At first he had had a seamstress in Petersburg, then she got spoilt and he made other arrangements, and that side of his affairs was so well secured that it did not trouble him.

But now he was living in the country for the second month and did not at all know what he was to do. Compulsory self-restraint was beginning to have a bad effect on him. Must he really go to town for that purpose? And where? How? That was the only thing that disturbed Yevgeny Ivanovich, but as he was convinced that it was necessary and that he needed it, it really became a necessity, and he felt that he was not free and that against his will his eyes followed every young woman.

He did not approve of having relations with a married woman or a girl in his own village. He knew by report that both his father and grandfather had been quite different in this matter from other landowners of that time. At home they had never had any entanglements with peasant women, and he had decided that he would not do so either; but afterwards, feeling himself ever more and more under compulsion and imagining with horror what might happen to him in the neighbouring country town, and reflecting on the fact that the days of serfdom were now over, he decided that it might be done on the spot. Only it must be done so that no one should know of it, and not for the sake of debauchery but merely for health's sake, as he said to himself. And when he had decided this he became still more restless. When talking to the village elder, the peasants, or the carpenters, he involuntarily brought the conversation round to women, and when it turned to women he kept it on that theme. He noticed women more and more.

III

To settle the matter in his own mind was one thing but to carry it out was another. To approach a woman himself was impossible. Which one? Where? It must be done through someone else, but to whom should he speak about it?

He once happened to go into a watchman's hut in the forest to get a drink of water. The watchman had been his father's huntsman, and

Yevgeny Ivanovich chatted with him, and the man began telling some strange tales of hunting sprees. It occurred to Yevgeny Ivanovich that it would be convenient to arrange matters here, in this hut or in the wood, only he did not know how to manage it and whether old Danila would undertake the arrangement. 'Perhaps he will be horrified at such a proposal and I shall have disgraced myself, but perhaps he will agree to it quite simply.' So he thought while listening to Danila's stories. Danila was telling how once when they had been stopping at the hut of the sexton's wife in an outlying field, He had brought a woman for Fyodor Zakharich Pryanichnikov.

'I can,' thought Yevgeny.

'Your father, may the kingdom of heaven be his, did not go in for nonsense of that kind.'

'I can't,' thought Yevgeny. But to test the matter he said: 'How was it you got involved in such bad things?'

'But what was there bad in it? She was glad, and Fyodor Zakharich was satisfied, very satisfied. I got a rouble. Why, what was he to do? He too is a lively sort, and drinks wine.'

'Yes, I may speak,' thought Yevgeny, and at once proceeded to do so.

'And do you know, Danila, I don't know how to endure it.' He felt himself turning scarlet. Danila smiled. 'After all I am not a monk and am accustomed to it.'

He felt that what he was saying was stupid, but was glad to see that Danila approved.

'Why of course, you should have told me long ago. It can all be arranged,' he said: 'only tell me which one you want.'

'Oh, it is really all the same to me. Of course not an ugly one, and she must be healthy.'

'I understand!' said Danila briefly. He reflected.

'Ah! There is a tasty morsel,' he began. Again Yevgeny went red. 'A tasty morsel. See here, she was married last autumn,' Danila whispered, 'and he hasn't been able to do anything. Think what that is worth to one who wants it!'

Yevgeny even frowned with shame.

'No, no,' he said. 'I don't want that at all. I want, on the contrary (what could the contrary be?), on the contrary I only want that she should be healthy and that there should be as little fuss as possible—

a woman whose husband is away in the army or something of that kind.'

'I understand. That means I must bring you Stepanida. Her husband is away in town, just the same as a soldier. And she is a fine woman, and clean. You will be satisfied. As it is I was saying to her the other day, you should go, but she . . .'

'Well then, when is it to be?'

'Tomorrow if you like. I shall be going to get some tobacco and I will go and see her, and at the dinner-hour come here, or to the bathhouse behind the kitchen-garden. There will be nobody about. Besides after dinner everybody takes a nap.'

'All right then.'

A terrible excitement seized Yevgeny as he rode home. 'What will happen? What is a peasant woman like? Suppose it turns out that she is hideous, horrible? No, they are beautiful,' he told himself, remembering some he had been noticing. 'But what shall I say? What shall I do?'

He was not himself all that day. Next day at noon he went to the forester's hut. Danila stood at the door and silently and significantly nodded towards the woods. The blood rushed to Yevgeny's heart, he was conscious of it and went to the kitchen-garden. No one was there. He went to the bath-house, there was no one about, he looked in, came out, and suddenly heard the crackling of a breaking twig. He looked round, and she was standing in the thicket beyond the little ravine. He rushed there across the ravine. There were nettles in it which he had not noticed. They stung him and, losing the pince-nez from his nose, he ran up the slope on the farther side. She stood there, in a white embroidered apron, a red-brown skirt, and a bright red kerchief, barefoot, fresh, firm, and beautiful, smiling shyly.

'There is a path leading round, you should have gone round,' she said. 'I came long ago, ever so long.'

He went up to her and, looking her over, touched her.

A quarter of an hour later they separated; he found his pince-nez, stopped by to see Danila, and in reply to his question: 'Are you satisfied, master?' gave him a rouble and went home.

He was satisfied. Only at first did he feel ashamed. Then it went away. And everything went well. The best thing was that he now felt at ease, tranquil and vigorous. As for her, he had not even seen her thoroughly. He remembered that she was clean, fresh, not bad-looking, and simple, without any pretence. 'Whose wife is she?' said he to himself. 'Pechnikov's, Danila said. What Pechnikov is that? There are two households of that name. Probably she is old Mikhayla's daughter-in-law. Yes, that must be it. His son does live in Moscow. I'll ask Danila about it some time.'

From then onward that previously important drawback to country life, enforced self-restraint, was eliminated. Yevgeny's freedom of mind was no longer disturbed and he was able to attend freely to his affairs.

And the matter Yevgeny had undertaken was far from easy: it sometimes seemed to him that he would not be able to go through with it and that it would end in his having to sell the estate after all, which would mean that all his efforts would be wasted and that he had failed to accomplish what he had undertaken. That prospect disturbed him most of all. Before he had time somehow to stop up one hole a new one would unexpectedly show itself.

All this time more and more of his father's debts unexpectedly came to light. It was evident that towards the end of his life his father had borrowed right and left. At the time of the settlement in May, Yevgeny had thought he at last knew everything, but in the middle of the summer he suddenly received a letter from which it appeared that there was still a debt of twelve thousand roubles to the widow Yesipova. There was no promissory note, but only an ordinary receipt which his lawyer told him could be disputed. But it did not enter Yevgeny's head to refuse to pay his father's debt merely because the document could be challenged. He only wanted to know for certain whether there had been such a debt.

'Mamma! Who is Kaleriya Vladimirovna Yesipova?' he asked his mother when they met as usual for dinner.

'Yesipova? She was your grandfather's ward. Why?'

Yevgeny told his mother about the letter.

'I wonder she is not ashamed to ask for it. Your father gave her so much!'

'But do we owe her this?'

'Well now, how shall I put it? It is not a debt. Papa, out of his unbounded kindness . . .'

'Yes, but did papa consider it a debt?'

'I cannot say. I don't know. I only know it is hard enough for you without that.'

Yevgeny saw that Marya Pavlovna did not know what to say, and was as it were sounding him out.

'I see from what you say that it must be paid,' he said. 'I will go to see her tomorrow and have a chat, and see if it cannot be deferred.'

'Ah, how sorry I am for you, but you know that will be best. Tell her she must wait,' said Marya Pavlovna, evidently reassured and proud of her son's decision.

Yevgeny's position was particularly hard because his mother, who was living with him, did not at all understand his position. She had been so accustomed all her life long to live extravagantly that she could not even imagine to herself the position her son was in, that is to say, that today or tomorrow matters might shape themselves so that they would have nothing left and he would have to sell everything and live and support his mother on what salary he could earn, which at the very most would be two thousand roubles. She did not understand that they could only save themselves from that position by cutting down expenses in everything, and so she could not understand why Yevgeny was so careful about trifles, in expenditure on gardeners, coachmen, servants, even on food. Also, like most widows, she nourished feelings of devotion to the memory of her departed spouse quite different from those she had felt for him while he lived, and she did not admit the thought that anything the departed had done or arranged could be wrong or could be altered.

Yevgeny by great efforts managed to keep up the garden and the greenhouse with two gardeners, and the stables with two coachmen. And Marya Pavlovna naively thought that she was sacrificing herself for her son and doing all a mother could do, by not complaining of the food which the old cook prepared, of the fact that the paths in the park were not all swept clean, and that instead of footmen they had only a boy.

So, too, concerning this new debt, in which Yevgeny saw an almost crushing blow to all his undertakings, Marya Pavlovna only saw an incident displaying Yevgeny's noble nature. Moreover she did not feel much anxiety about Yevgeny's position, because she was confident that he would make a brilliant marriage which would put everything right. And he could make a very brilliant marriage. She knew a dozen families who would be glad to give their daughters to him. And she wished to arrange the matter as soon as possible.

IV

Yevgeny himself dreamt of marriage, but not in the same way as his mother. The idea of using marriage as a means of putting his affairs in order was repulsive to him. He wished to marry honourably, for love. He observed the girls whom he met and those he knew, and compared himself with them, but no decision had yet been taken. Meanwhile, contrary to his expectations, his relations with Stepanida continued, and even acquired the character of a settled affair. Yevgeny was so far from debauchery, it was so hard for him secretly to do this thing which he felt to be bad, that he could not arrange these meetings himself and even after the first one hoped not to see Stepanida again; but it turned out that after some time the same restlessness which he believed due to that cause again overcame him. And his restlessness this time was no longer impersonal, but suggested just those same bright, black eyes and that deep voice, saying, 'ever so long', that same scent of something fresh and strong, and that same full breast lifting the bib of her apron, and all this in that hazel and maple thicket, bathed in bright sunlight.

Though he felt ashamed he again approached Danila. And again a rendezvous was fixed for midday in the wood. This time Yevgeny looked her over more carefully and everything about her seemed attractive. He tried talking to her and asked about her husband. He really was Mikhayla's son and lived as a coachman in Moscow.

'Well, then, how is it you . . .' Yevgeny wanted to ask how it was she was untrue to him.

'What about "how is it"?' she asked. Evidently she was clever and quick-witted.

'Well, how is it you come to me?'

'Well now,' she said merrily. 'I bet he goes on a spree there. Why shouldn't I?'

Evidently she was putting on an air of sauciness and assurance, and this seemed charming to Yevgeny. But all the same he did not himself fix a rendezvous with her. Even when she proposed that they should meet without the aid of Danila, to whom she seemed not very well disposed, he did not consent. He hoped that this meeting would be the last. He liked her. He thought such contact was necessary for him and that there was nothing bad about it, but in the depth of his soul there was a stricter judge who did not approve of it and hoped that this would be the last time, or if he did not hope that, at any rate did not wish to participate in arrangements to repeat it another time.

So the whole summer passed, during which they met a dozen times and always through Danila. It happened once that she could not be there because her husband had come home, and Danila proposed another woman, but Yevgeny refused with disgust. Then the husband went away and the meetings continued as before, at first through Danila, but afterwards he simply fixed the time and she came with another woman, Prokhorova, as it would not do for a peasant woman to go about alone.

Once at the very time fixed for a rendezvous a family came to call on Marya Pavlovna, with the very girl she wished Yevgeny to marry, and it was impossible for Yevgeny to get away. As soon as he could do so, he went out as though to the threshing-floor, and round by the path to their meeting place in the wood. She was not there, but at the accustomed spot everything within reach had been broken, the black alder, the hazel-twigs, and even a young maple the thickness of a stake. She had waited, had become excited and angry, and had skittishly left him a remembrance. He waited and waited, and then went to Danila to ask him to call her for tomorrow. She came and was just as usual.

So the summer passed. The meetings were always arranged in the wood, and only once, when it grew towards autumn, in the shed that stood in her backyard. It did not enter Yevgeny's head that these relations of his had any importance for him. About her he did not even think. He gave her money and nothing more. At first he did not know and did not think that the affair was known and that she was envied throughout the village, or that her relations took money from her and encouraged her, and that her conception of any sin in the matter had been quite obliterated by the influence of the money and her family's approval. It seemed to her that if people envied her, then what she was doing was good.

'It is simply necessary for my health,' thought Yevgeny. 'I grant it is not right, and though no one says anything, everybody, or many people, know of it. The woman who comes with her knows. And once she knows she is sure to have told others. But what's to be done? I am acting badly,' thought Yevgeny, 'but what's one to do? Anyhow it is not for long.'

What chiefly disturbed Yevgeny was the thought of the husband. At first for some reason it seemed to him that the husband must be a poor sort, and this as it were partly justified his conduct. But he saw the husband and was struck by his appearance: he was a fine fellow and smartly dressed, in no way a worse man than himself, but surely better. At their next meeting he told her he had seen her husband and had been surprised to see that he was such a fine fellow.

'There's not another man like him in the village,' she said proudly.

This surprised Yevgeny, and the thought of the husband tormented him still more after that. He happened to be at Danila's one day and Danila, having begun chatting, said to him quite openly:

'And Mikhayla asked me the other day: "Is it true that the master is living with my son's wife?" I said I did not know. Anyway, I said, better with the master than with a peasant.'

'Well, and what did he say?'

'He said: "Wait a bit. I'll find out and I'll give it her all the same."'

'Yes, if the husband returned to live here I would give her up,' thought Yevgeny. But the husband lived in town and for the present their relations continued. 'When necessary I will break it off, and there will be nothing left of it,' he thought.

And this seemed to him certain, especially as during the whole summer many different things occupied him very fully: the arrangement of the new farmhouse, and the harvest, and the building, and above all paying off the debts and selling the waste land. All these were affairs that completely absorbed him and on which he spent his thoughts when he lay down and when he got up. All that was real life. His relations, he did not even call it a relationship, with Stepanida he paid no attention to. It is true that when the wish to see her arose it came with such strength that he could think of nothing else. But this did not last long. A meeting was arranged, and he again forgot her for a week or even for a month.

In autumn Yevgeny often rode to town, and there became friendly with the Annenskys. They had a daughter who had just finished the Institute.* And then, to Marya Pavlovna's great grief, it happened that Yevgeny 'cheapened himself', as she expressed it, by falling in love with Liza Annenskaya and proposing to her.

From that time his relations with Stepanida ceased.

V

It is impossible to explain why Yevgeny chose Liza Annenskaya, as it is always impossible to explain why a man chooses this and not that woman. There were many reasons, positive and negative. One reason was that she was not a very rich heiress such as his mother sought for him, another that she was naive and to be pitied in her relations with her mother, another that she was not a beauty who attracted general attention to herself, and yet she was not bad-looking. But the chief reason was that his acquaintance with her began at the time when he was ripe for marriage. He fell in love because he knew that he would marry.

Liza Annenskaya was at first merely pleasing to Yevgeny, but when he decided to make her his wife his feelings for her became much stronger. He felt that he was in love.

Liza was tall, slender, and long. Everything about her was long; her face and her nose, not prominent but longish, and her fingers, and her gait. The colour of her face was very delicate, creamy white and delicately pink; she had long, soft, and curly, light-brown hair, and beautiful eyes, clear, meek, and trusting. Those eyes especially struck Yevgeny, and when he thought of Liza he always saw those clear, meek, trusting eyes.

Such was she physically; he knew nothing of her spiritually, but only saw those eyes. And those eyes seemed to tell him all he needed to know. The meaning of their expression was this:

While still in the Institute, when she was fifteen, Liza used continually to fall in love with all the attractive men she met and was animated and happy only when she was in love. After leaving the Institute she continued to fall in love in just the same way with all the young men she met, and of course fell in love with Yevgeny as soon as she made his acquaintance. It was this being in love which gave her eyes that particular expression which so captivated Yevgeny. Already that winter she had been in love with two young men at one and the same time, and blushed and became excited not only when they entered the room but whenever their names were mentioned. But afterwards, when her mother hinted to her that Irtenev seemed to have serious intentions, her love for him increased so that she became almost indifferent to the two previous attractions, and when

Irtenev began to come to their balls and parties and danced with her more than with others and evidently only wished to know whether she loved him, her love for him became painful. She dreamed of him in her sleep and seemed to see him when she was awake in a dark room, and everyone else vanished from her mind. But when he proposed and they were formally engaged, and when they had kissed one another and were a betrothed couple, then she had no thoughts but of him, no desire but to be with him, to love him, and to be loved by him. She was also proud of him and felt emotional about him and herself and her love, and quite melted and felt faint from love of him.

The more he got to know her the more he too loved her. He had not at all expected to find such love, and it strengthened his own feeling still more.

VI

Towards spring he went to his estate at Semyonovskoe to have a look at it and to give directions about the management, and especially about the house which was being done up for his wedding.

Marya Pavlovna was dissatisfied with her son's choice, not only because the match was not as brilliant as it might have been, but also because she did not like Varvara Alexeevna, his future mother-in-law. Whether she was good-natured or not she did not know and could not decide, but that she was not well-bred, not *comme il faut*,[1] 'not a lady' as Marya Pavlovna said to herself, she saw from their first acquaintance, and this distressed her. It distressed her because she was accustomed to value breeding and knew that Yevgeny was sensitive to it, and she foresaw that he would suffer much annoyance on this account. But she liked the girl. Liked her chiefly because Yevgeny did. One could not help loving her, and Marya Pavlovna was quite sincerely ready to do so.

Yevgeny found his mother contented and in good spirits. She was getting everything straight in the house and preparing to go away herself as soon as he brought his young wife. Yevgeny tried to persuade her to stay for the time being, but the question remained unresolved. In the evening after tea Marya Pavlovna played patience

---

[1] 'Fashionable', lit. 'as it ought to be'.

as usual. Yevgeny sat by, helping her. This was the hour of their most intimate talks. Having finished one game and while preparing to begin another, she looked up at him and, with a little hesitation, began thus:

'I wanted to tell you, Zhenya, of course I do not know, but in general I wanted to suggest to you, that before your wedding it is absolutely necessary to have finished with all your bachelor affairs so that nothing may disturb either you or, God forbid, your wife. You understand me?'

And indeed Yevgeny at once understood that Marya Pavlovna was hinting at his relations with Stepanida which had ended in the previous autumn, and that she attributed much more importance to those relations than they deserved, as solitary women always do. Yevgeny blushed, not from shame so much as from vexation that goodnatured Marya Pavlovna was bothering, out of affection no doubt, but still was bothering, about matters that were not her business and that she did not and could not understand. He answered that there was nothing that needed concealment, and that he had always conducted himself so that there should be nothing to hinder his marrying.

'Well, dear, that is excellent. Only, Zhenya, don't be vexed with me,' said Marya Pavlovna, and broke off in embarrassment.

Yevgeny saw that she had not finished and had not said what she wanted to. And this was confirmed when a little later she began to tell him how, in his absence, she had been asked to stand godmother at the Pechnikovs.

Yevgeny flushed again, not with vexation or shame this time, but with some strange awareness of the importance of what was about to be told him, an involuntary awareness quite at variance with his conscious thoughts. And what he expected happened. Marya Pavlovna, as if merely by way of conversation, mentioned that this year only boys were being born, evidently a sign of a coming war. Both at the Vasins and the Pechnikovs the young wife had a first child, at each house a boy. Marya Pavlovna wanted to say this casually, but she herself felt ashamed when she saw the colour mount to her son's face and saw him nervously removing, tapping, and replacing his pincenez and hurriedly lighting a cigarette. She became silent. He too was silent and could not think how to break that silence. So they both understood that they had understood one another.

'Yes, the chief thing is that there should be justice and no favouritism in the village, as with your grandfather.'

'Mamma,' said Yevgeny suddenly, 'I know why you are saying this. You have no need to be disturbed. My future family life is so sacred to me that I should not violate it in any case. And as to what occurred in my bachelor days, that is quite ended. I never formed any union and no one has any claims on me.'

'Well, I am glad,' said his mother. 'I know how noble your feelings are.'

Yevgeny accepted his mother's words as a tribute due to him and did not reply.

Next day he drove to town thinking of his fiancée and of anything in the world except of Stepanida. But, as if purposely to remind him, on approaching the church he met people walking and driving back from it. He met old Matvey and Simyon, some lads and girls, and then two women, one elderly, the other, who seemed familiar, smartly dressed and wearing a bright-red kerchief. This woman was walking lightly and boldly, carrying a child in her arms. He came up to them, and the elder woman bowed, stopping in the old-fashioned way, but the young woman with the child only bent her head, and from under the kerchief gleamed familiar, merry, smiling eyes.

'Yes, that's her, but all that is over and it's no use looking at her. But the child may be mine,' flashed through his mind. 'No, what nonsense! There was her husband, she used to see him.' He did not even consider the matter further, so settled in his mind was it that it had been necessary for his health, he had paid her money and there was nothing more; there was, there had been, and there could be, no question of any union between them. It was not that he stifled the voice of conscience, no, his conscience simply said nothing to him. And he thought no more about her after the conversation with his mother and this meeting. Nor did he meet her again.

Yevgeny was married in town the week after Easter, and left at once with his young wife for his country estate. The house had been arranged as usual for a young couple. Marya Pavlovna wished to leave, but Yevgeny and especially Liza begged her to remain. She just moved into a detached wing of the house.

And so a new life began for Yevgeny.

VII

The first year of his marriage was a hard one for Yevgeny. It was hard because affairs he had managed to put off during the time of his courtship now, after his marriage, all came upon him at once.

To escape from debts was impossible. An outlying part of the estate was sold and the most pressing debts paid, but others remained, and he had no money. The estate yielded a good revenue, but he had had to send payments to his brother and pay for his own wedding, so that there was no ready money and the factory could not carry on and would have to be closed down. The only way of escape was to use his wife's money. Liza, having realized her husband's position, insisted on this herself. Yevgeny agreed, but only on condition that he should give her a mortgage on half his estate, which he did. Of course this was done not for his wife's sake, who felt offended at it, but to appease his mother-in-law.

These affairs with various fluctuations of success and failure helped to poison Yevgeny's life that first year. Another thing was his wife's ill health. That same first year in autumn, seven months after their marriage, a misfortune befell Liza. She was driving out in an open carriage to meet her husband on his return from town, when the submissive horse became rather playful and she got frightened and jumped out. Her jump was comparatively fortunate, she might have been caught by the wheel, but she was pregnant, and that same night the pains began and she had a miscarriage from which she was long in recovering. The loss of the expected child and his wife's illness, together with the disorder in his affairs, and above all the presence of his mother-in-law, who arrived as soon as Liza fell ill, all this together made the year still harder for Yevgeny.

But notwithstanding these difficult circumstances, towards the end of the first year Yevgeny felt very well. First of all his cherished hope of restoring his fallen fortune and renewing his grandfather's way of life in a new form was approaching accomplishment, though slowly and with difficulty. There was no longer any question of having to sell the whole estate to meet the debts. The chief estate, though transferred to his wife's name, was saved, and if only the beet crop succeeded and the price kept up, by next year his position of want and stress might be replaced by one of complete prosperity. That was one thing.

Another was that however much he had expected from his wife, he had never expected to find in her what he actually found. He found not what he had expected, but something much better. Raptures of love, though he tried to produce them, did not take place or were very slight, but he discovered something quite different, namely, that he was not merely more cheerful and happier but that it had become easier to live. He did not know why this should be so, but it was.

And it was so because immediately after marriage his wife decided that Yevgeny Irtenev was superior to anyone else in the world, wiser, purer, and nobler than they, and that therefore it was right for everyone to serve him and please him. But since it was impossible to make everyone do this, she had to do it herself to the limit of her strength. And she did, directing all her strength of mind towards learning and guessing what he liked, and then doing just that thing, whatever it was and however difficult it might be.

She had the gift which furnishes the chief delight of a relationship with a loving woman, thanks to her love of her husband she penetrated into his soul. She knew every state of his soul and every shade of his feelings, better it seemed to him than he himself, and she behaved correspondingly and therefore never hurt his feelings, but always lessened his distresses and strengthened his joys. And she understood not only his feelings but also his joys. Things quite foreign to her, concerning the farming, the factory, or the appraisement of others, she immediately understood so that she could not merely converse with him, but could often, as he himself said, be a useful and irreplaceable counsellor. She regarded affairs and people and everything in the world only through his eyes. She loved her mother, but having seen that Yevgeny disliked his mother-in-law's interference in their life she immediately took her husband's side, and did so with such decision that he had to restrain her.

Besides all this she had very good taste, much tact, and above all she had repose. All that she did, she did unnoticed; only the results of what she did were observable, namely, that always and in everything there was cleanliness, order, and elegance. Liza had at once understood in what her husband's ideal of life consisted, and she tried to attain, and in the arrangement and order of the house did attain, what he wanted. Children it is true were lacking, but there was hope of that also. In winter she went to Petersburg to see a specialist and he assured them that she was quite well and could have children.

And this desire was accomplished. By the end of the year she was again pregnant.

The one thing that threatened, not to say poisoned, their happiness was her jealousy, a jealousy she restrained and did not exhibit, but from which she often suffered. Not only might Yevgeny not love any other woman, because there was not a woman on earth worthy of him (as to whether she herself was worthy or not she never asked herself), but not a single woman might therefore dare to love him.

VIII

This was how they lived. He rose early, as he always had done, and went to see to the farm or the factory where work was going on, or sometimes to the fields. Towards ten o'clock he would come back for his coffee, which they had on the veranda, Marya Pavlovna, an uncle who lived with them, and Liza. After a conversation which was often very animated while they drank their coffee, they dispersed till dinner-time. At two o'clock they dined and then went for a walk or a drive. In the evening when he returned from his office they drank their evening tea and sometimes he read aloud while she worked, or when there were guests they had music or conversation. When he went away on business he wrote to his wife and received letters from her every day. Sometimes she accompanied him, and then they were particularly merry. On his name-day and on hers guests assembled, and it pleased him to see how well she managed to arrange things so that everybody enjoyed coming. He saw and heard that they all admired her, the young, agreeable hostess, and he loved her still more for this.

All went excellently. She bore her pregnancy easily and, though they were afraid, they both began making plans as to how they would bring the child up. The system of education and the arrangements were all decided by Yevgeny, and her only wish was to carry out his desires obediently. Yevgeny on his part studied medical works and intended to bring the child up according to all the precepts of science. She of course agreed to everything and made preparations, making warm and cool 'envelopes',* and preparing a cradle. Thus the second year of their marriage arrived and the second spring.

IX

It was just before Trinity Sunday. Liza was in her fifth month, and though careful she was still brisk and active. Both his mother and hers were living in the house, but under pretext of watching and safeguarding her only upset her by their tiffs. Yevgeny was specially engrossed in a new experiment for the cultivation of sugar-beet on a large scale.

Just before Trinity Liza decided that it was necessary to have a thorough house-cleaning as it had not been done since Easter, and she hired two women by the day to help the servants wash the floors and windows, beat the furniture and the carpets, and put covers on them. These women came early in the morning, heated the coppers, and set to work. One of the two was Stepanida, who had just weaned her baby boy and had begged for the job of washing the floors through the office-clerk, whom she was now carrying on with. She wanted to have a good look at the new mistress. Stepanida was living by herself as formerly, her husband being away, and she was fooling around as she had formerly been first with old Danila (who had once caught her taking some logs of firewood), then with the master, and now with the young clerk. She was not concerning herself any longer about her master. 'He has a wife now,' she thought. 'But it would be good to have a look at the lady and at her establishment: they say it is well arranged.'

Yevgeny had not seen her since he had met her with the child. Having a baby to attend to she had not been going out to work, and he seldom walked through the village. That morning, on the eve of Trinity Sunday, he got up at five o'clock and rode to the fallow land which was to be sprinkled with phosphates, and had left the house before the women were about, and while they were still engaged lighting the copper fires.

He returned to breakfast merry, contented, and hungry. Dismounting from his mare at the gate and handing her over to the gardener, he walked towards the house, flicking the high grass with his whip and repeating a phrase he had just uttered, as one often does. The phrase was: 'phosphates justify', what or to whom, he neither knew nor reflected.

They were beating a carpet on the grass. The furniture had been brought out.

'There now! What a house-cleaning Liza has undertaken! Phosphates justify. What a manager she is! A manager! Yes, a real manager,' he said to himself, vividly imagining her in her white housecoat and with her smiling joyful face, as it nearly always was when he looked at her. 'Yes, I must change my boots, or else phosphates justify, that is, smell of manure, and the manager is in a family way. Why in a family way? Because a new little Irtenev is growing there inside her,' he thought. 'Yes, phosphates justify,' and smiling at his thoughts he put his hand to the door of his room.

But he had not time to push the door before it opened of itself and he came face to face with a woman coming towards him carrying a pail, barefoot and with sleeves turned up high. He stepped aside to let her pass and she too stepped aside, adjusting her kerchief with a wet hand.

'Go on, go on, I won't go in, if you . . .' Yevgeny began and suddenly stopped, recognizing her.

She glanced merrily at him with smiling eyes, and rearranging her skirt went out of the door.

'What nonsense! . . . It is impossible,' said Yevgeny to himself, frowning and waving his hand as though to get rid of a fly, displeased at having noticed her. He was vexed that he had noticed her and yet he could not take his eyes from her strong body, swayed by her agile strides, from her bare feet, or from her arms and shoulders, and the pleasing folds of her shirt and the handsome skirt tucked up high above her white calves.

'But why am I looking?' he said to himself, lowering his eyes so as not to see her. 'And anyhow I must go in to get some other boots.' And he turned back to go into his own room, but had not gone five steps before he again glanced round to have another look at her without knowing why or what for. She was just going round the corner and also glanced at him.

'Ah, what am I doing!' he said to himself. 'She may get ideas. It is even certain that she already has.'

He entered his damp room. Another woman, an old and skinny one, was there, and was still washing it. Yevgeny passed on tiptoe across the floor, wet with dirty water, to the wall where his boots stood, and he was about to leave the room when the woman herself went out.

'This one has gone and the other, Stepanida, will come here alone,' someone within him began to reflect.

'My God, what am I thinking of and what am I doing!' He seized his boots and ran out with them into the hall, put them on there, brushed himself, and went out onto the veranda where both the mammas were already drinking coffee. Liza had evidently been expecting him and came onto the veranda through another door at the same time.

'My God! If she, who considers me so honourable, pure, and innocent, if she only knew!' he thought.

Liza as usual met him with a shining face. But today somehow she seemed to him particularly pale, yellow, long, and weak.

X

During coffee, as often happened, a peculiarly feminine kind of conversation went on which had no logical sequence but which evidently was connected in some way for it went on uninterruptedly.

The two old ladies were needling one another, and Liza was skilfully manoeuvring between them.

'I am so vexed that we had not finished washing your room before you got back,' she said to her husband. 'But I do so want to get everything arranged.'

'Well, did you sleep well after I got up?'

'Yes, I slept well and I feel fine.'

'How can a woman be well in her condition during this intolerable heat, when her windows face the sun,' said Varvara Alexeevna, her mother. 'And they have no venetian blinds or awnings. I always had awnings.'

'But you know we are in the shade after ten o'clock,' said Marya Pavlovna.

'That's what causes fever, it comes of dampness,' said Varvara Alexeevna, not noticing that what she was saying did not agree with what she had just said. 'My doctor always says that it is impossible to diagnose an illness unless one knows the patient. And he certainly knows, for he is the leading physician and we pay him a hundred roubles a visit. My late husband did not believe in doctors, but he did not begrudge me anything.'

'How can a man begrudge anything to a woman when perhaps her life and the child's depend . . .'

'Yes, when she has means a wife need not depend on her husband. A good wife submits to her husband,' said Varvara Alexeevna, 'only Liza is too weak after her illness.'

'Oh no, mamma, I feel quite well. But why have they not brought you any boiled cream?'

'I don't want any. I can do with raw cream.'

'I offered some to Varvara Alexeevna, but she declined,' said Marya Pavlovna, as if justifying herself.

'No, I don't want any today.' And as if to terminate an unpleasant conversation and yield magnanimously, Varvara Alexeevna turned to Yevgeny and said: 'Well, and have you sprinkled the phosphates?'

Liza ran to fetch the cream.

'But I don't want it. I don't want it.'

'Liza, Liza, walk gently,' said Marya Pavlovna. 'Such rapid movements do her harm.'

'Nothing does harm if one's mind is at peace,' said Varvara Alexeevna as if referring to something, though she knew that there was nothing her words could refer to.

Liza returned with the cream and Yevgeny drank his coffee and listened morosely. He was accustomed to such conversation, but today he was particularly annoyed by its lack of sense. He wanted to think over what had happened to him but this chatter disturbed him. Having finished her coffee Varvara Alexeevna went away in a bad humour. Liza, Yevgeny, and Marya Pavlovna stayed behind, and their conversation was simple and pleasant. But Liza, being sensitive, at once noticed that something was tormenting Yevgeny, and she asked him whether anything unpleasant had happened. He was not prepared for this question and hesitated a little before replying that there had been nothing. This reply made Liza think all the more. That something was tormenting him, and greatly tormenting, was as evident to her as that a fly had fallen into the milk, yet he would not speak of it. What could it be?

XI

After breakfast they all dispersed. Yevgeny as usual went to his study, but instead of beginning to read or write his letters, he sat smoking one cigarette after another and thinking. He was terribly surprised and disturbed by the unexpected recrudescence within him of the nasty feeling from which he had thought himself free since his marriage. Since then he had not once experienced that feeling, either for her, the woman he had known, or for any other woman except his wife. He had often rejoiced in his heart over this freedom, and now suddenly a chance meeting, seemingly so unimportant, revealed to him the fact that he was not free. What now tormented him was not that he was yielding to that feeling and desired her, he did not dream of so doing, but that the feeling was awake within him and he had to be on his guard against it. He had no doubt but that he would suppress it.

He had a letter to answer and a paper to write, and sat down at his writing table and began to work. Having finished it and quite forgotten what had disturbed him, he went out to go to the stables. And again as ill luck would have it, either by unfortunate chance or intentionally, as soon as he stepped from the porch a red skirt and red kerchief appeared from round the corner, and she went past him swinging her arms and swaying her body. She not only went past him, but on passing him ran, as if playfully, to overtake her fellow-servant.

Again the bright midday, the nettles, the back of Danila's hut, and her smiling face biting some leaves in the shade of the plane trees rose in his imagination.

'No, it is impossible to let matters continue so,' he said to himself, and waiting till the women had passed out of sight he went to the office.

It was dinner-time and he hoped to find the steward still there, and so it happened. The steward had just awakened. He was standing in the office, stretching himself and yawning, looking at the herdsman who was telling him something.

'Vasily Nikolaevich!' said Yevgeny to the steward.

'What is your pleasure?'

'I want to speak to you.'

'What is your pleasure?'

'Just finish what you are saying.'

'Aren't you going to bring it in?' said Vasily Nikolaevich to the herdsman.

'It's heavy, Vasily Nikolaevich.'

'What is it?' asked Yevgeny.

'Why, a cow has calved in the meadow. Well, all right, I'll order them to harness a horse at once. Tell Nikolay Lysukh to get out the dray cart.'

The herdsman went out.

'Do you know,' began Yevgeny, flushing and conscious that he was doing so, 'do you know, Vasily Nikolaevich, while I was a bachelor I went off the track a bit. You may have heard.'

Vasily Nikolaevich, evidently sorry for his master, said with smiling eyes, 'Is it about Stepanida?'

'Why, yes. Look here. Please, please do not engage her to help in the house. You understand, it is very awkward for me.'

'Yes, it must have been Vanya the clerk who arranged it.'

'Yes, please, and hadn't the rest of the phosphates better be strewn?' said Yevgeny, to hide his embarrassment.

'Yes, I am just going to see to it.'

So the matter ended, and Yevgeny calmed down, hoping that as he had lived for a year without seeing her, so things would go on now. 'Besides, Vasily Nikolaevich will speak to Ivan the clerk; Ivan will speak to her, and she will understand that I don't want it,' said Yevgeny to himself, and he was glad that he had forced himself to speak to Vasily Nikolaevich, hard as it had been to do so.

'Yes, it is better, much better, than that feeling of doubt, that feeling of shame.' He shuddered at the mere remembrance of his transgression in thought.

XII

The moral effort he had made to overcome his shame and speak to Vasily Nikolaevich calmed Yevgeny. It seemed to him that the matter was all over now. Liza at once noticed that he was quite peaceful, and even happier than usual. 'No doubt he was upset by our mothers needling one another. It really is disagreeable, especially for him who is so sensitive and noble, always to hear such unfriendly and ill-mannered insinuations,' she thought.

The next day was Trinity Sunday. It was a beautiful day, and the peasant women, on their way into the woods to plait wreaths, came, according to custom, to the landowner's home and began to sing and dance. Marya Pavlovna and Varvara Alexeevna went out onto the porch in smart clothes, carrying parasols, and went up to the circle of singing dancers. With them, in a jacket of Chinese silk, came the uncle, a flabby libertine and drunkard, who was living that summer with Yevgeny.

As usual there was a bright, many-coloured circle of young women and girls, the centre of everything, and around these from different sides, like attendant planets that had detached themselves and were circling round, went girls hand in hand, rustling in their new print gowns; young lads giggling and running backwards and forwards after one another; full-grown lads in dark blue or black coats and caps and with red shirts, who unceasingly spat out sun-flower-seed shells; and the domestic servants or other outsiders watching the dance circle from the sidelines. Both the old ladies went close up to the circle, and Liza accompanied them in a light blue dress, with light blue ribbons on her head, and with wide sleeves under which her long white arms and angular elbows were visible.

Yevgeny did not wish to come out, but it was ridiculous to hide, and he too came out onto the porch smoking a cigarette, bowed to the men and lads, and talked with one of them. The women mean-while shouted a dance-song with all their might, snapping their fingers, clapping their hands, and dancing.

'They are calling for the master,' said a youngster coming up to Yevgeny's wife, who had not noticed the call. Liza called Yevgeny to look at the dance and at one of the women dancers who particularly pleased her. This was Stepanida. She wore a yellow skirt, a velveteen sleeveless jacket and a silk kerchief, and was broad, energetic, ruddy, and merry. No doubt she danced well. He saw nothing.

'Yes, yes,' he said, removing and replacing his pince-nez. 'Yes, yes,' he repeated. 'So it seems I cannot be rid of her,' he thought.

He did not look at her, fearing her attraction, and just on that account what his passing glance caught of her seemed to him espe-cially attractive. Besides this he saw by her sparkling look that she saw him and saw that he admired her. He stood there as long as propriety demanded, and seeing that Varvara Alexeevna had called her 'my dear' senselessly and insincerely and was talking to her, he turned aside and went away. He went into the house in order not to see her, but on reaching the upper storey he approached the window, without knowing how or why, and as long as the women remained at the porch he stood there and looked and looked at her, feasting his eyes on her.

He ran, while there was no one to see him, and then went with quiet steps onto the veranda, and from there, smoking a cigarette, he passed through the garden as if going for a stroll, and followed the direction she had taken. He had not gone two steps along the alley before he noticed behind the trees a velveteen sleeveless jacket, with a pink and yellow skirt and a red kerchief. She was going somewhere with another woman. 'Where are they going?'

And suddenly a passionate lust scorched him as though a hand were seizing his heart. As if by someone else's will he looked round and went towards her.

'Yevgeny Ivanich, Yevgeny Ivanich! I have come to see your honour,' said a voice behind him, and Yevgeny seeing old Samokhin who was digging a well for him, roused himself and turning quickly round went to meet Samokhin. While speaking with him he turned sideways and saw that she and the woman who was with her went down the slope, evidently to the well or making of the well an excuse, and having stopped there a little while ran back to the dance circle.

XIII

After talking to Samokhin, Yevgeny returned to the house as depressed as if he had committed a crime. In the first place she had understood him, believed that he wanted to see her, and desired it herself. Secondly that other woman, Anna Prokhorova, evidently knew of it.

Above all he felt that he was conquered, that he did not have his own will but that there was another power moving him, that he had been saved only by good fortune, and that if not today then tomorrow or a day later, he would perish all the same.

'Yes, perish,' he did not understand it otherwise: to be unfaithful to his young and loving wife with a peasant woman in the village, in the sight of everyone what was it but to perish, perish utterly, so that it would be impossible to live? No, something must be done.

'My God, my God! What am I to do? Can it be that I shall perish like this?' he said to himself. 'Is it not possible to do anything? Yet something must be done. Do not think about her,' he ordered himself. 'Do not think!' and immediately he began thinking and seeing her before him, and seeing also the shade of the plane tree.

He remembered having read of a hermit who, to avoid the temptation he felt for a woman on whom he had to lay his hand to heal her, thrust his other hand into a brazier and burnt his fingers. He called that to mind. 'Yes, I am ready to burn my fingers rather than to perish.' He looked round to make sure that there was no one in the room, lit a candle, and put a finger into the flame. 'There, now think about her,' he said to himself ironically. It hurt him and he withdrew his smoke-stained finger, threw away the match, and laughed at himself. What nonsense! That was not what had to be done. But it was necessary to do something, to avoid seeing her, either to go away himself or to send her away. Yes, send her away. Offer her husband money to move to town or to another village. People would hear of it and would talk about it. Well, what of that? At any rate it was better than this danger. 'Yes, that must be done,' he said to himself, and at that very moment he was looking at her without moving his eyes. 'Where is she going?' he suddenly asked himself. She, it seemed to him, had seen him at the window and now, having glanced at him and taken another woman by the hand, was going towards the garden swinging her arm briskly. Without knowing why or what for, merely in accord with what he had been thinking, he went to the office.

Vasily Nikolaevich in holiday costume and with oiled hair was sitting at tea with his wife and a guest who was wearing an oriental kerchief.

'I want a word with you, Vasily Nikolaevich!'

'Please say what you want to. We have finished tea.'

'No. I'd rather you came out with me.'

'Right away, only let me get my cap. Tanya, put out the samovar,'* said Vasily Nikolaevich, stepping outside cheerfully.

It seemed to Yevgeny that Vasily had been drinking, but what was to be done? It might be all the better, he would sympathize with him in his difficulties the more readily.

'I have come again to speak about that same matter, Vasily Nikolaevich,' said Yevgeny, 'about that woman.'

'Well, what of her? I told them not to take her again on any account.'

'No, I have been thinking in general, and this is what I wanted to get your advice about. Isn't it possible to get them away, to send the whole family away?'

'Where can they be sent?' said Vasily, disapprovingly and ironically as it seemed to Yevgeny.

'Well, I thought of giving them money, or even some land in Koltovsky, so that she should not be here.'

'But how can they be sent away? Where is he to go, torn up from his roots? And why should you do it? What harm can she do you?'

'Ah, Vasily Nikolaevich, you must understand that it would be dreadful for my wife to hear of it.'

'But who will tell her?'

'How can I live with this dread? The whole thing is very painful for me.'

'But really, why should you distress yourself? Whoever stirs up the past—out with his eye! Who is not a sinner before God and to blame before the Tsar?'

'All the same it would be better to get rid of them. Can't you speak to the husband?'

'But it is no use speaking! Eh, Yevgeny Ivanovich, what is the matter with you? It is all past and forgotten. All sorts of things happen. Who is there that would now say anything bad of you? Everybody sees you.'

'But all the same go and have a talk with him.'

'All right, I will speak to him.'

Though he knew that nothing would come of it, this talk somewhat calmed Yevgeny. Above all, it made him feel that through excitement he had been exaggerating the danger.

Had he gone to meet her by appointment? That was impossible. He had simply gone to stroll in the garden and she had happened to run out at the same time.

XIV

After dinner that very Trinity Sunday Liza while walking from the garden to the meadow, where her husband wanted to show her the clover, took a false step and fell when crossing a little ditch. She fell gently, on her side, but she gave an exclamation, and her husband saw an expression in her face not only of fear but of pain. He was about to help her up, but she motioned him away with her hand.

'No, wait a bit, Yevgeny,' she said, with a weak smile, and looked up guiltily as it seemed to him. 'My foot only gave way under me.'

'There, I always say,' remarked Varvara Alexeevna, 'can anyone in her condition possibly jump over ditches?'

'But it is all right, mamma. I shall get up right away.' With her husband's help she did get up, but she immediately turned pale and looked frightened.

'Yes, I am not well!' and she whispered something to her mother.

'Oh, my God, what have you done! I said you shouldn't come,' cried Varvara Alexeevna. 'Wait, I will get the servants. She must not walk. She must be carried!'

'Don't be afraid, Liza, I will carry you,' said Yevgeny, putting his left arm round her. 'Hold me by the neck. Like that.' And stooping down he put his right arm under her knees and lifted her. He could never afterwards forget the suffering and yet beatific expression on her face.

'I am too heavy for you, dear,' she said with a smile. 'Look, mamma is running, tell her!' And she bent towards him and kissed him. She evidently wanted her mother to see how he was carrying her.

Yevgeny shouted to Varvara Alexeevna not to hurry, and that he would carry Liza home. Varvara Alexeevna stopped and began to shout still louder.

'You will drop her, you'll be sure to drop her. You want to destroy her. You have no conscience!'

'But I am carrying her excellently.'

'I do not want to watch you killing my daughter, and I can't.' And she ran round the bend in the alley.

'Never mind, it will pass,' said Liza, smiling.

'Yes. If only it does not have consequences like last time.'

'No. I am not speaking of that. That was nothing. I mean mamma. You are tired. Rest a bit.'

But though he found it heavy, Yevgeny carried his burden proudly and gladly to the house and did not hand her over to the housemaid and the cook whom Varvara Alexeevna had found and sent to meet them. He carried her to the bedroom and put her on the bed.

'Now go away,' she said, and drawing his hand to her she kissed it. 'Annushka and I will manage all right.'

Marya Pavlovna also ran in from her rooms in the wing. They undressed Liza and laid her on the bed. Yevgeny sat in the drawing room with a book in his hand, waiting. Varvara Alexeevna went past him with such a reproachfully gloomy air that he felt alarmed.

'Well, how is it?' he asked.

'How is it? What's the good of asking? It is probably what you wanted when you made your wife jump over the ditch.'

'Varvara Alexeevna!' he cried. 'This is impossible. If you want to torment people and to poison their life' (he wanted to say, 'then go elsewhere to do it,' but restrained himself). 'How is it that it does not hurt you?'

'It is too late now.' And shaking her cap in a triumphant manner she went out by the door.

The fall had really been a bad one. Liza's foot had twisted awkwardly and there was danger of her having another miscarriage. Everyone knew that there was nothing to be done but that she must just lie quietly, yet all the same they decided to send for a doctor.

'Dear Nikolay Semyonich,' wrote Yevgeny to the doctor, 'you have always been so kind to us that I hope you will not refuse to come to my wife's assistance. She . . .' and so on. Having written the letter he went to the stables to arrange about the horses and the carriage. Horses had to be got ready to bring the doctor and others to take him back. When an estate is not run on a large scale, such things cannot be quickly decided but have to be considered. Having arranged it all and dispatched the coachman, it was past nine before he got back to the house. His wife was lying down, and said that she felt perfectly well and had no pain. But Varvara Alexeevna was sitting near a lamp screened from Liza by some sheets of music and knitting a large red coverlet, with a look that said that after what had happened peace was impossible, but that she at any rate would do her duty no matter what anyone else did.

Yevgeny noticed this, but, to appear as if he had not done so, tried to assume a cheerful and tranquil air and told how he had chosen the horses and how well the mare, Kabushka, had galloped as left trace-horse in the troika.*

'Yes, of course, it is just the time to exercise the horses when help is needed. Probably the doctor will also be thrown into the ditch,' remarked Varvara Alexeevna, examining her knitting from under her pince-nez and moving it close up to the lamp.

'But you know we had to send one of them, and I did the best I could.'

'Yes, I remember very well how your horses galloped with me under the arch of the gateway.' This was a long-standing fancy of hers, and Yevgeny now was injudicious enough to remark that that was not quite what had happened.

'It is not for nothing that I have always said, and have often remarked to the prince, that it is hardest of all to live with people who are untruthful and insincere. I can endure anything except that.'

'Well, if anyone has to suffer more than another, it is certainly I,' said Yevgeny.

'Yes, it is evident.'

'What?'

'Nothing, I am only counting my stitches.'

Yevgeny was standing at the time by the bed and Liza was looking at him, and one of her moist hands outside the coverlet caught his hand and pressed it. 'Bear with her for my sake. You know she cannot prevent our loving one another,' was what her look said.

'I won't do so again. It's nothing,' he whispered, and he kissed her moist, long hand and then her affectionate eyes, which closed while he kissed them.

'Can it be the same thing over again?' he asked. 'How are you feeling?'

'I am afraid to say for fear of being mistaken, but I feel that he is alive and will live,' she said, glancing at her stomach.

'Ah, it is dreadful, dreadful to think of.'

Notwithstanding Liza's insistence that he should go away, Yevgeny spent the night with her, hardly closing an eye and ready to tend to her needs.

But she passed the night well, and had they not sent for the doctor she would perhaps have got up.

By dinner-time the doctor arrived and of course said that though if the symptoms recurred there might be cause for apprehension, yet actually there were no positive symptoms, but as there were also no contrary indications one might suppose on the one hand that, and on the other hand that ... And therefore she must lie still, and that though I do not like prescribing, yet all the same she should take this mixture and should lie quiet. Besides this, the doctor gave Varvara Alexeevna a lecture on woman's anatomy, during which Varvara Alexeevna nodded her head significantly. Having received his fee, as usual into the backmost part of his palm, the doctor drove away and the patient was left to lie in bed for a week.

XV

Yevgeny spent most of his time by his wife's bedside, talking to her, reading to her, and, what was hardest of all, enduring without murmur Varvara Alexeevna's attacks, and even contriving to turn these into jokes.

But he could not stay at home all the time. In the first place his wife sent him away, saying that he would fall ill if he always remained with her, and secondly the farming was progressing in a way that demanded his presence at every step. He could not stay at home, but had to be in the fields, in the wood, in the garden, at the threshing-floor, and everywhere he was pursued not merely by the thought but by the vivid image of Stepanida, and he only occasionally forgot her. But that would not have mattered, he could perhaps have mastered his feeling, but what was worst of all was that, whereas he had previously lived for months without seeing her, he now continually came across her. She evidently understood that he wished to renew relations with her and tried to come in his way. Nothing was said either by him or by her, and therefore neither he nor she went directly to a rendezvous, but only sought opportunities of meeting.

The most possible place for them to meet was in the forest, where peasant women went with sacks to collect grass for their cows. Yevgeny knew this and therefore went there every day. Every day he told himself that he would not go, and every day it ended by his making his way to the forest and, on hearing the sound of voices, standing behind the bushes with sinking heart looking to see if she was there.

Why he wanted to know whether it was she who was there, he did not know. If it had been she and she had been alone, he would not have gone to her, so he thought, he would have run away, but he wanted to see her.

Once he met her. As he was entering the forest she came out of it with two other women, carrying a heavy sack full of grass on her back. A little earlier he would perhaps have met her in the forest. Now, with the other women there, she could not go back to him. But though he realized this impossibility, he stood for a long time behind a hazelbush, at the risk of attracting the other women's attention. Of course she did not return, but he stayed there a long time. And, my God, how delightful his imagination made her appear to him! And this not only once, but five or six times, and each time more intensely. Never had she seemed so attractive, and never had he been so completely in her control.

He felt that he had lost his willpower and had become almost insane. His strictness with himself had not weakened a bit; on the contrary he saw all the abomination of his desires and even of his actions, for his going to the wood was an action. He knew that he only need come near her anywhere in the dark, and if possible touch her, and he would yield to his feelings. He knew that it was only shame before people, before her, and no doubt before himself also, that restrained him. And he knew too that he had sought conditions in which that shame would not be apparent, darkness or such proximity that the shame would be stifled by animal passion. And therefore he knew that he was a wretched criminal, and despised and hated himself with all his soul. He hated himself because he still had not yielded. Every day he prayed God to strengthen him, to save him from perishing; every day he determined that from today onward he would not take a step to see her, and would forget her. Every day he devised means of delivering himself from this enticement, and he made use of those means.

But it was all in vain.

One of the means was continual occupation, another was intense physical work and fasting, a third was imagining clearly to himself the shame that would fall upon him when everybody knew of it, his wife, his mother-in-law, the servants. He did all this and it seemed to him that he was conquering, but midday came, the hour of their former meetings and the hour when he had met her carrying the grass, and he went to the forest. Thus five days of torment passed. He only saw her from a distance, and did not once get together with her.

XVI

Liza was gradually recovering, she could move about and was only uneasy at the change that had taken place in her husband, which she did not understand.

Varvara Alexeevna had gone away for a while, and the only visitor was Yevgeny's uncle. Marya Pavlovna was as usual at home.

Yevgeny was in his semi-insane condition when there came two days of pouring rain, as often happens after thunderstorms in June. The rain stopped all work. They even ceased carting manure on account of the dampness and dirt. The peasants remained at home. The herdsmen wore themselves out with the cattle, but eventually drove them home. The cows and sheep wandered about in the pasture-land and ran loose on the grounds. The peasant women, barefoot and wrapped in shawls, splashing through the mud, rushed about to seek the runaway cows. Streams flowed everywhere along the paths, all the leaves and all the grass were saturated with water, and streams flowed unceasingly from the gutters into bubbling puddles. Yevgeny sat at home with his wife, who was particularly wearisome that day. She questioned Yevgeny several times as to the cause of his discontent, and he replied with vexation that nothing was the matter. She ceased questioning him but was still distressed.

They were sitting after breakfast in the drawing room. His uncle for the hundredth time was recounting fabrications about his society acquaintances. Liza was knitting a jacket and sighed, complaining of the weather and of a pain in the small of her back. The uncle advised her to lie down, and asked for vodka for himself. Yevgeny was dreadfully bored in the house. Everything was slack and stultifying. He read a book and a magazine, but understood nothing of them.

'I must go out and look at the rasping-machine they brought yesterday,' he said, and got up and went out.

'Take an umbrella with you.'

'Oh, no, I have a leather coat. And I am only going as far as the smelting-room.'

He put on his boots and his leather coat and went to the factory; and he had not gone twenty steps before he met her coming towards him, with her skirts tucked up high above her white calves. She was walking, holding down the shawl in which her head and shoulders were wrapped.

'Where are you going?' he said, not recognizing her the first instant. When he recognized her it was already too late. She stopped and, smiling, looked at him for a long time.

'I am looking for a calf. Where are you off to in such weather?' she said, as if she were seeing him every day.

'Come to the shed,' he said suddenly, without knowing how he said it. It was as if someone else had uttered the words.

She bit her shawl, winked, and ran in the direction which led from the garden to the shed, and he continued his path, intending to turn off beyond the lilac bush and go there too.

'Master,' he heard a voice behind him. 'The mistress is calling you and wants you to come back for a minute.'

This was Misha, his manservant.

'My God! This is the second time you have saved me,' thought Yevgeny, and immediately turned back. His wife reminded him that he had promised to take some medicine at the dinner-hour to a sick woman, and he had better take it with him.

While they were getting the medicine some five minutes elapsed, and then, going away with the medicine, he hesitated to go direct to the shed lest he should be seen from the house, but as soon as he was out of sight he promptly turned and made his way to it. He already saw her in his imagination inside the shed smiling gaily. But she was not there, and there was nothing in the shed to show that she had been there.

He was already thinking that she had not come, had not heard or understood his words. He had muttered them through his nose as if afraid of her hearing them. 'Or perhaps she had not wanted to come. And why did I imagine that she would rush to me? She has her own husband; it is only I who am such a wretch as to have a wife, and a good one, and to run after another.' Thus he thought sitting in the shed, the thatch of which had a leak and dripped from its straw. 'But how delightful it would be if she did come, alone here in this rain. If only I could embrace her once again, then let happen what may. 'Oh, of course,' he recalled, 'if she were here I can tell by her footprints.' He looked at the trodden ground near the shed and at the path overgrown by grass, and the fresh print of bare feet, and even of one that had slipped, was visible. 'Yes, she has been here. Well, now it is settled. Wherever I see her I shall go straight to her. I will go to her at night.' He sat for a long time in the shed and left it exhausted and crushed. He delivered the medicine, returned home, and lay down in his room to wait for dinner.

XVII

Before dinner Liza came to him and, still wondering what could be the cause of his discontent, began to say that she was afraid he did not like the idea of her going to Moscow for her confinement, and that she had decided that she would remain at home and on no account go to Moscow. He knew how she feared both her confinement itself and the risk of not having a healthy child, and therefore he could not help being touched at seeing how ready she was to sacrifice everything for his sake. All was so nice, so pleasant, so clean, in the house; and in his soul it was dirty, despicable, and horrible. The whole evening Yevgeny was tormented by knowing that notwithstanding his sincere repulsion at his own weakness, notwithstanding his firm intention to break off, the same thing would happen again tomorrow.

'No, this is impossible,' he said to himself, walking up and down in his room. 'There must be some remedy for it. My God! What am I to do?'

Someone knocked at the door as foreigners do. He knew this must be his uncle. 'Come in,' he said.

The uncle had come as a self-appointed ambassador from Liza.

'Do you know, I really do notice that there is a change in you,' he said, 'and Liza, I understand how it troubles her. I understand that it must be hard for you to leave all the business you have so excellently started, but *que veux-tu?*[1] I should advise you to go away. It will be more satisfactory both for you and for her. And do you know, I should advise you to go to the Crimea. The climate is beautiful and

---

[1] 'What would you have?'

there is an excellent midwife there, and you would be just in time for the best of the grape season.'

'Uncle,' Yevgeny suddenly exclaimed. 'Can you keep a secret? A secret that is horrible to me, a shameful secret.'

'Oh, come, do you really feel any doubt of me?'

'Uncle, you can help me. Not only help, but save me!' said Yevgeny. And the thought of disclosing his secret to his uncle whom he did not respect, the thought that he would show himself in the worst light and humiliate himself before him, was pleasant. He felt himself to be despicable and guilty, and wished to punish himself.

'Speak, my dear fellow, you know how fond I am of you,' said the uncle, evidently well content that there was a secret and that it was a shameful one, and that it would be communicated to him, and that he could be of use.

'First of all I must tell you that I am a wretch, a good-for-nothing, a scoundrel, a real scoundrel.'

'Now what are you saying,' his uncle began, as if he were offended.

'What! Not a wretch when I, Liza's husband, Liza's! One has only to know her purity, her love, and that I, her husband, want to be untrue to her with a peasant woman!'

'What is this? Why do you want, you have not been unfaithful to her?'

'Yes, at least just the same as being unfaithful, for it did not depend on me. I was ready to do so. I was hindered, or else I would now . . . would now. I do not know what I would have done.'

'But please, explain to me.'

'Well, it is like this. When I was a bachelor I was stupid enough to have relations with a woman here in our village. That is to say, I used to have meetings with her in the forest, in the field.'

'Was she pretty?' asked his uncle.

Yevgeny frowned at this question, but he was in such need of external help that he made as if he did not hear it, and continued:

'Well, I thought this was just casual and that I should break it off and have done with it. And I did break it off before my marriage. For nearly a year I did not see her or think about her.' It seemed strange to Yevgeny himself to hear the description of his own condition. 'Then suddenly, I don't myself know why—really one sometimes believes in witchcraft—I saw her, and a worm crept into my heart and is gnawing at me. I reproach myself, I understand the full horror of my action, that is to say, of the act I may commit any moment, and yet I myself turn to it, and if I have not committed it, it is only because God preserved me. Yesterday I was on my way to see her when Liza sent for me.'

'What, in the rain?'

'Yes. I am worn out, Uncle, and have decided to confess to you and to ask your help.'

'Yes, of course, it's a bad thing on your own estate. People will get to know. I understand that Liza is weak and that it is necessary to spare her, but why on your own estate?'

Again Yevgeny tried not to hear what his uncle was saying and hurried on to the core of the matter.

'Yes, save me from myself. That is what I ask of you. Today I was hindered by chance. But tomorrow or next time no one will hinder me. And she knows now. Don't leave me alone.'

'Yes, all right,' said his uncle, 'but are you really so much in love?'

'Oh, it is not that at all. It is not that, it is some kind of power that has seized me and holds me. I do not know what to do. Perhaps I shall gain strength, and then . . .'

'Well, it turns out as I suggested,' said his uncle. 'Let us be off to the Crimea.'

'Yes, yes, let us go, and meanwhile I will be with you and will talk to you.'

XVIII

The fact that Yevgeny had confided his secret to his uncle, and still more the sufferings of his conscience and the feeling of shame he experienced after that rainy day, sobered him. It was settled that they would start for Yalta in a week's time. During that week Yevgeny drove to town to get money for the journey, gave instructions from the house and from the office concerning the management of the estate, again became gay and close with his wife, and began to awaken morally.

So without having once seen Stepanida after that rainy day he left with his wife for the Crimea. There he spent an excellent two months. He received so many new impressions that it seemed to him that the past was obliterated from his memory. In the Crimea they met former acquaintances and became particularly friendly with them, and they also made new acquaintances. Life in the Crimea was a continual holiday for Yevgeny, besides being instructive and beneficial. They became friendly there with the former marshal of the nobility of their province, a clever and liberal-minded man who became fond of Yevgeny and coached him and attracted him to his party. At the end of August Liza gave birth to a beautiful, healthy daughter, and her confinement was unexpectedly easy.

In September they returned home, the four of them, including the baby and its wet-nurse, as Liza was unable to nurse it herself. Yevgeny returned home entirely free from the former horrors and quite a new and happy man. Having gone through all that a husband goes through when his wife bears a child, he loved her more than ever. His feeling for the child when he took it in his arms was a funny, new, very pleasant, and, as it were, a tickling feeling. Another new thing in his life now was that, besides his occupation with the estate, thanks to his acquaintance with Dumchin (the ex-marshal) a new interest occupied his mind, that of the *zemstvo*,* partly an ambitious interest, partly a feeling of duty. In October there was to be a special assembly, at which he was to be elected. After arriving home he drove once to town and another time to Dumchin.

Of the torments of his temptation and struggle he had forgotten even to think, and could with difficulty recall them to mind. It seemed to him something like an attack of insanity he had undergone.

To such an extent did he now feel free from it that he was not even afraid to make enquiries on the first occasion when he remained alone with the steward. As he had previously spoken to him about the matter he was not ashamed to ask.

'Well, and is Sidor Pechnikov still away from home?' he inquired.

'Yes, he is still in town.'

'And his wife?'

'Oh, she is a worthless woman. She is now carrying on with Zinovey. She has gone quite on the loose.'

'Well, that's just fine,' thought Yevgeny. 'How wonderfully indifferent to it I am! How I have changed.'

XIX

All that Yevgeny had wished had been realized. He had obtained the property, the factory was working successfully, the beet crops were excellent, and he expected a large income; his wife had borne a child satisfactorily, his mother-in-law had left, and he had been unanimously elected to the *zemstvo*.

He was returning home from town after the election. He had been congratulated and had had to return thanks. He had had dinner and had drunk some five glasses of champagne. Quite new plans of life now presented themselves to him, and he was thinking about these as he drove home. It was Indian summer, an excellent road and a hot sun. As he approached his home Yevgeny was thinking of how, as a result of this election, he would occupy among the people the position he had always dreamed of, that is to say, one in which he would be able to serve them not only by production, which gave employment, but also by direct influence. He imagined what his own and the other peasants would think of him in three years' time. 'For instance this one,' he thought, driving just then through the village and glancing at a peasant and a peasant woman who were crossing the street in front of him carrying a full water tub. They stopped to let his carriage pass. The peasant was old Pechnikov, and the woman was Stepanida. Yevgeny looked at her, recognized her, and was glad to feel that he remained quite tranquil. She was still as good-looking as ever, but this did not touch him at all. He drove home. His wife met him on the porch. It was a wonderful evening.

'Well, may we congratulate you?' said his uncle.

'Yes, I was elected.'

'Excellent! We must drink to it!'

Next day Yevgeny drove about to see to the farming which he had been neglecting. At the outlying farmstead a new threshing-machine was at work. While watching it Yevgeny stepped among the women, trying not to take notice of them, but try as he would he once or twice noticed the black eyes and red kerchief of Stepanida, who was carrying away the straw. Once or twice he glanced sideways at her and felt that something was happening, but could not account for it to himself. Only the next day, when he again drove to the threshing-floor and spent two hours there quite unnecessarily, without ceasing to caress with his eyes the familiar, handsome figure of the young woman, did he feel that he was lost, irremediably lost. Again those torments! Again all that horror and terror. And there was no salvation.

What he expected happened to him. The evening of the next day, without knowing how, he found himself at her backyard, by her hay-shed, where in autumn they had once had a meeting. As though having a stroll, he stopped there to light a cigarette. A neighbouring peasant woman saw him, and as he turned back he heard her say to someone: 'Go, he is waiting for you, on my dying word he is standing there. Go, you fool!'

He saw a woman, it was her, run to the hay-shed; but as a peasant had met him it was no longer possible for him to turn back, and so he went home.

XX

When he entered the drawing room everything seemed strange and unnatural to him. He had risen that morning vigorous, determined to fling it all aside, to forget it and not allow himself to think about it. But without noticing how it occurred he had all the morning not merely not interested himself in the work, but tried to avoid it. What had formerly cheered him and been important was now insignificant. Unconsciously he tried to free himself from business. It seemed to him that he had to do so in order to think and to plan. And he freed himself and remained alone. But as soon as he was alone he began to wander about in the garden and the forest. And all those spots were besmirched in his recollection by memories that gripped him. He felt that he was walking in the garden and pretending to himself that he was thinking out something, but that really he was not thinking out anything, but insanely and unreasonably expecting her, expecting that by some miracle she would be aware that he was expecting her, and would come here at once and go somewhere where no one would see them, or would come on a night when there was no moon, and no one, not even she herself, would see, on such a night she would come and he would touch her body. . . .

'There now, talking of breaking off when I wish to,' he said to himself. 'Yes, and that is having a clean healthy woman for one's health's sake! No, it seems one can't play with her like that. I thought I had taken her, but it was she who took me, took me and has not let me go. Why, I thought I was free, but I was not free and was deceiving myself when I married. It was all nonsense, deception. From the time I had her I experienced a new feeling, the real feeling of a husband. Yes, I ought to have lived with her.

'One of two lives is possible for me: the one which I began with Liza, service, estate management, the child, and people's respect. If that is life, it is necessary that she, Stepanida, should not be here. She must be sent away, as I said, or destroyed so that she shall not exist. And the other life is this: take her away from her husband, pay him money, disregard the shame and disgrace, and live with her. But in that case it is necessary that Liza should not exist, nor Mimi (the baby). No, that is not so, the baby does not matter, but it is necessary that there should be no Liza, that she should go away, that she should know, curse me, and go away. That she should know that I have exchanged her for a peasant woman, that I am a deceiver and a scoundrel! No, that is too terrible! It is impossible. But it might happen,' he went on thinking, 'it might happen that Liza might fall ill and die. Die, and then everything would be wonderful.

'Wonderful! Oh, scoundrel! No, if someone must die it should be Stepanida. If she were to die, how good it would be.

'Yes, that is how men come to poison or kill their wives or lovers. Take a revolver and go and call on her, and instead of embracing her, shoot her in the breast and have done with it.

'Really she is a devil. Simply a devil. She has taken possession of me against my own will. Kill? Yes. There are only two ways out, to kill my wife or her. For it is impossible to live like this.* Impossible! I must consider the matter and look ahead. If things remain as they are, what will happen?

What will happen is that I shall again be saying to myself that I do not wish it and that I will throw her off, but it will be merely words and in the evening I shall be at her backyard, and she will know it and will come out. And if people know of it and tell my wife, or if I tell her myself, for I can't even lie, I shall not be able to live so. I cannot! People will know. They will all know, Parasha, and the blacksmith. Well, is it possible even to live so?

'Impossible! There are only two ways out: to kill my wife, or to kill her. Yes, or else . . . Ah, yes, there is a third way: to kill myself,' he said softly, and suddenly a shudder ran over his skin. 'Yes, kill myself, then I shall not need to kill them.' He became frightened, for he felt that that was the only way possible. He had a revolver. 'Shall I really kill myself? It is something I never thought of. How strange it will be.'

He returned to his study and at once opened the cupboard where the revolver lay, but before he had taken it out of its case his wife entered the room.

XXI

He threw a newspaper over the revolver.

'Again the same!' she said aghast when she had looked at him.

'What is the same?'

'The same horrible expression that you had before and would not explain to me. Zhenya, dear one, tell me about it. I see that you are suffering. Tell me and you will feel easier. Whatever it may be, it will be better than for you to suffer so. I know that it is nothing bad.'

'You know? Later.'

'Tell me, tell me, tell me. I won't let you go.'

He smiled a piteous smile.

'Shall I? No, it is impossible. And there is nothing to tell.'

Perhaps he might have told her, but at that moment the wet-nurse entered to ask if she should go for a walk. Liza went out to dress the baby.

'Then you will tell me? I will be right back.'

'Yes, perhaps . . .'

She never could forget the piteous smile with which he said this. She went out.

Hurriedly, stealthily like a robber, he seized the revolver and took it out of its case. It was loaded, yes, but long ago, and one cartridge was missing.

'Well, how will it be?' He put it to his temple and hesitated a little, but as soon as he remembered Stepanida, his decision not to see her, his struggle, temptation, fall, and renewed struggle, he shuddered with horror. 'No, this is better,' and he pulled the trigger.

When Liza ran into the room, she had only had time to step down from the balcony, he was lying face downwards on the floor, black, warm blood was gushing from the wound, and his corpse was twitching.

There was an inquest. No one could understand or explain the suicide. It never even entered his uncle's head that its cause could have anything to do with the confession Yevgeny had made to him two months previously.

Varvara Alexeevna assured them that she had always foreseen it. It had been evident from his way of disputing. Neither Liza nor Marya Pavlovna could at all understand why it had happened, but still they did not believe what the doctors said, namely, that he was mentally deranged, a psychopath. They were quite unable to accept this, for they knew he was saner than hundreds of their acquaintances.

And indeed if Yevgeny Irtenev was mentally deranged, then everyone is just as mentally deranged. The most mentally deranged people are certainly those who see in others indications of insanity they do not notice in themselves.

Variation of the Conclusion of 'The Devil'

... he said to himself, and going up to the table he took from it a revolver and, having examined it, one cartridge was wanting, he put it in his trouser pocket.

'My God! What am I doing?' he suddenly exclaimed, and folding his hands he began to pray.

'O God, help me and deliver me! Thou knowest that I do not desire evil, but by myself am powerless. Help me,' he said, making the sign of the cross on his breast before the icon.

'Yes, I can control myself. I will go out, walk about and think things over.'

He went to the entrance hall, put on his overcoat and went out onto the porch. Unconsciously his steps took him past the garden along the field path to the outlying farmstead. There the threshing-machine was still droning and the cries of the driver lads were heard. He entered the barn. She was there. He saw her at once. She was raking up the corn, and on seeing him she ran briskly and merrily about, with laughing eyes, raking up the scattered corn with agility. Yevgeny could not help watching her though he did not wish to do so. He only recollected himself when she was no longer in sight. The clerk informed him that they were now finishing threshing the corn that had been beaten down, that was why it was going slower and the output was less. Yevgeny went up to the drum, which occasionally gave a knock as sheaves not evenly fed in passed under it, and he asked the clerk if there were many such sheaves of beaten-down corn.

'There will be five cartloads of it.'

'Then look here . . .' Yevgeny began, but he did not finish the sentence. She had gone close up to the drum and was raking the corn from under it, and she scorched him with her laughing eyes. That look spoke of a merry, careless love between them, of the fact that she knew he wanted her and had come to her shed, and that she as always was ready to live and be merry with him regardless of all conditions or consequences. Yevgeny felt himself to be in her control but did not wish to yield.

He remembered his prayer and tried to repeat it. He began saying it to himself, but at once felt that it was useless. A single thought now engrossed him entirely, how to arrange a meeting with her so that the others should not notice it.

'If we finish this lot today, are we to start on a fresh stack or leave it till tomorrow?' asked the clerk.

'Yes, yes,' replied Yevgeny, involuntarily following her to the heap to which with the other women she was raking the corn.

'But can I really not master myself?' he said to himself. 'Have I really perished? O God! But there is no God. There is only the devil. And it is her. She has possessed me. But I won't, I won't! The devil, yes, the devil.'

Again he went up to her, drew the revolver from his pocket and shot her, once, twice, thrice, in the back. She ran a few steps and fell on the heap of corn.

'My God, my God! What is that?' cried the women.

'No, it was not an accident. I killed her on purpose,' cried Yevgeny. 'Send for the police officer.'

He went home and went to his study and locked himself in, without speaking to his wife.

'Do not come to me,' he cried to her through the door. 'You will know all about it.'

An hour later he rang and bade the manservant who answered the bell: 'Go and find out whether Stepanida is alive.'

The servant already knew all about it and told him she had died an hour ago.

'Well, all right. Now leave me alone. When the police officer or the magistrate comes, let me know.'

The police officer and magistrate arrived next morning, and Yevgeny, having bidden his wife and baby farewell, was taken to prison.

He was tried. It was during the early days of trial by jury* and the verdict was one of temporary insanity, and he was sentenced only to perform church penance.

He had been kept in prison for nine months and was then confined in a monastery for one month.

He had begun to drink while still in prison, continued to do so in the monastery, and returned home an enfeebled, irresponsible drunkard.

Varvara Alexeevna assured them that she had always predicted this. It was, she said, evident from the way he disputed. Neither Liza nor Marya Pavlovna could understand how the affair had happened, but for all that, they did not believe what the doctors said, namely, that he was mentally deranged, a psychopath. They could not accept that, for they knew that he was saner than hundreds of their acquaintances.

And indeed, if Yevgeny Irtenev was mentally deranged when he committed this crime, then everyone is just as mentally deranged. The most mentally deranged people are certainly those who see in others indications of insanity they do not notice in themselves.

FATHER SERGY

I

In Petersburg in the eighteen-forties a surprising event occurred. An officer of the cuirassier guards, a handsome prince who everyone predicted would become aide-de-camp to the Emperor Nikolay I and have a brilliant career, left the service, broke off his engagement to a beautiful maid of honour, a favourite of the Empress's, gave his small estate to his sister, and retired to a monastery to become a monk. This event appeared extraordinary and inexplicable to those who did not know his inner motives, but for Prince Stepan Kasatsky himself it all occurred so naturally that he could not imagine how he could have acted otherwise.

His father, a retired colonel of the guards, had died when Stepan was twelve, and sorry as his mother was to part from her son, she entered him at the military academy as her deceased husband had intended. The widow herself, with her daughter Varvara, moved to Petersburg to be near her son and have him with her for the holidays.

The boy was distinguished both by his brilliant ability and by his immense self-esteem, the result of which was that he was first both in his studies, especially in mathematics, of which he was particularly fond, and also in drill and riding. Though of more than average height, he was handsome and agile, and he would have been an altogether exemplary cadet had it not been for his quick temper. He was remarkably truthful, and was neither dissipated nor addicted to drink. The only faults that marred his conduct were fits of fury to which he was subject and during which he lost control of himself and became like a wild animal. He once nearly threw out of the window another cadet who had begun to tease him about his collection of minerals. On another occasion he came almost completely to grief by flinging a whole dish of cutlets at an officer who was acting as steward, attacking him and, it was said, striking him for having broken his word and told a barefaced lie. He would certainly have been reduced to the ranks had not the director of the academy hushed up the whole matter and dismissed the steward.

By the time he was eighteen he had received a commission as lieutenant in an aristocratic regiment of the guards.

The Emperor Nikolay Pavlovich (Nikolay I) had noticed him while he was still at the academy, and continued to take notice of him in the regiment, and it was on this account that people predicted for him an appointment as aide-de-camp to the Emperor. Kasatsky himself strongly desired this, not from ambition only but chiefly because since his cadet days he had been passionately devoted to Nikolay Pavlovich. The Emperor had often visited the military academy and every time Kasatsky saw that tall erect figure, with breast expanded in its military overcoat, entering with brisk step, every time he saw the cropped side-whiskers, the moustache, the aquiline nose and heard the sonorous voice exchanging greetings with the cadets, he was seized by the same rapture that he experienced later on when he met the woman he loved. Indeed, his passionate adoration of the Emperor was even stronger: he wished to sacrifice something, everything, even himself, to prove his complete devotion. And the Emperor Nikolay was conscious of evoking this rapture and deliberately aroused it. He played with the cadets, surrounded himself with them, treating them sometimes with childish simplicity, sometimes as a friend, and then again with majestic solemnity. After that affair with the officer, Nikolay Pavlovich said nothing to Kasatsky, but when the latter approached he waved him away theatrically, frowned, shook his finger at him, and afterwards when leaving, said: 'Remember that I know everything. There are some things I would rather not know, but they remain here,' and he pointed to his heart.

When the cadets were received by the Emperor on leaving the academy, he did not again refer to Kasatsky's offence, but told them all, as was his custom, that when necessary they might approach him directly, that they should serve him and the fatherland loyally, and that he would always be their best friend. All the cadets were as usual greatly moved, and Kasatsky even shed tears, remembering the past, and vowed that he would serve his beloved Tsar with all his soul.

When Kasatsky took up his commission his mother moved with her daughter first to Moscow and then to their country estate. Kasatsky gave half his property to his sister and kept only enough to maintain himself in the luxurious regiment he had joined.

To all appearance he was just an ordinary, brilliant young officer of the guards making a career for himself, but intense and complex strivings went on within him. From early childhood his efforts had seemed to be very varied, but essentially they were all one and the same. He tried in everything he took up to attain such success and perfection as would evoke people's praise and astonishment. Whether it was his studies or his military exercises, he took them up and worked at them till he was praised and held up as an example to others. Having mastered one thing he took up another. Thus he obtained first place in his studies, thus he achieved top honours in all his subjects, thus while still at the academy he noticed in himself an awkwardness in French conversation and contrived to master French till he spoke it as well as Russian, and thus when he later took up chess, also while still at the academy, he became an excellent player.

Apart from his main vocation in life, which was his service of the Tsar and fatherland, he always set himself some particular goal, and however unimportant it was, devoted himself completely to it and lived for it until it was accomplished. And as soon as it was attained another goal would immediately present itself, replacing its predecessor. This passion for distinguishing himself, or for accomplishing something in order to distinguish himself, filled his life. On taking up his commission he set himself to acquire the utmost perfection in knowledge of the service, and very soon became a model officer, though still with the same fault of ungovernable irascibility, which here in the service again led him to commit actions harmful to his success. Later, having once in conversation in society felt himself deficient in general education, he took to reading and again achieved his purpose. Later, wishing to secure a brilliant position in high society, he learnt to dance excellently and very soon was invited to all the balls in the best circles and to some of their evening gatherings. But this did not satisfy him. He was accustomed to being first, and in this society he was far from being so.

The highest society then consisted, and I think always and everywhere does consist, of four sorts of people: (1) rich people who are received at court, (2) people not wealthy but born and brought up in court circles, (3) rich people who ingratiate themselves into the court set, and (4) people neither rich nor belonging to the court but who ingratiate themselves into the first and second sets. Kasatsky did not belong to the first two sets, but was readily welcomed in the others. Even on entering society he set for himself the goal of having a relationship with some society lady and to his own surprise quickly accomplished this purpose. He soon realized, however, that the circles in which he moved were not the highest, and that though he was received in the highest spheres he did not belong to them. They were polite to him, but showed by their whole manner that they had their own set and that he was not of it. And Kasatsky wished to belong to that inner circle. To attain that end it would be necessary to be an aide-de-camp to the Emperor, which he expected to become, or to marry into that exclusive set, which he resolved to do. And his choice fell on a beauty belonging to the court, who not merely belonged to the circle into which he wished to be accepted, but whose friendship was coveted by the very highest people and those most firmly established in that highest circle. This was Countess Korotkova. Kasatsky began to pay court to her, and not merely for the sake of his career. She was extremely attractive and he soon fell in love with her. At first she was noticeably cool towards him, but then suddenly changed and became gracious, and her mother gave him pressing invitations to visit them. Kasatsky proposed and was accepted. He was surprised at the facility with which he attained such happiness. But though he noticed something strange and unusual in the behaviour towards him of both mother and daughter, he was blinded by being so deeply in love and did not realize what almost the whole town knew, namely, that his fiancée had been Nikolay Pavlovich's mistress the previous year.

II

Two weeks before the day arranged for the wedding, Kasatsky was at Tsarskoe Selo* at his fiancée's country place. It was a hot day in May. He and his betrothed had walked about the garden and were sitting on a bench in a shady linden alley. Mary's* white muslin dress suited her particularly well. She seemed the personification of innocence and love. She sat, now bending her head, now gazing up at the very tall and handsome man who was speaking to her with particular tenderness and self-restraint, as if he feared by his every word or gesture to offend or sully her angelic purity. Kasatsky belonged to those men of the eighteen-forties, now no longer to be found, who while deliberately and without any conscientious scruples condoning impurity in themselves, required ideal and angelic purity in their women, regarded all unmarried women of their circle as possessed of such purity, and treated them accordingly. There was much that was false and harmful in this outlook, as concerning the laxity the men permitted themselves, but in regard to the women that old-fashioned view, which sharply differed from that held by young people today who see in every girl merely a female seeking a mate, was, I think, of value. The girls, perceiving such adoration, endeavoured with more or less success to be goddesses. Such was the view Kasatsky held of women, and that was how he regarded his fiancée. He was particularly in love that day, but did not experience any sensual desire for her. On the contrary he regarded her with tender adoration as something unattainable.

He rose to his full height, standing before her with both hands on his sabre.

'I have only now realized what happiness a man can experience! And it is you, my darling, who have given me this happiness,' he said with a timid smile.

Endearments had not yet become usual between them, and morally looking up to her from below he felt terrified at this stage to use them to such an angel.

'It is thanks to you that I have come to know myself. I have learnt that I am better than I thought.'

'I have known that for a long time. That was why I began to love you.'

Nightingales trilled near by and the fresh leafage rustled, moved by a passing breeze.

He took her hand and kissed it, and tears came into his eyes. She understood that he was thanking her for having said she loved him. He took a few steps, remained silent for a moment, then approached her and sat down.

'You know, my darling, I have to tell you. I was not disinterested when I began to court you. I wanted to get into society, but then how unimportant that became in comparison with you, when I got to know you. You are not angry with me for that?'

She did not reply but merely touched his hand. He understood that this meant: 'No, I am not angry.'

'You said . . .' He hesitated, for it seemed too bold to say. 'You said that you began to love me yet forgive me, I believe you, but there is something that troubles you and checks your feeling. What is it?'

'Yes—now or never!' she thought. 'He is bound to know of it anyway. But now he will not forsake me. Ah, if he should, it would be terrible!' And she threw a loving glance at his tall, noble, powerful figure. She loved him now more than she had loved Nikolay, and if it were not for the imperial dignity would not have preferred the Emperor to him.

'Listen! I cannot deceive you. I have to tell you. You ask what it is? It is that I have loved before.'

She again laid her hand on his with an imploring gesture. He was silent.

'You want to know who it was? It was him, the Emperor.'

'We all love him. I can imagine you, a schoolgirl at the Institute . . .'*

'No, it was later. I was infatuated, but it passed. But I must tell you . . .'

'Well, what then?'

'No, I was not simply,' She covered her face with her hands.

'What? You gave yourself to him?'

She was silent.

'His mistress?'

She was silent.

He sprang up and stood before her with trembling jaws, pale as death. He now remembered how Nikolay Pavlovich, meeting him on the Nevsky,* had amiably congratulated him.

'O God, what have I done! Stiva!'

'Don't touch me! Don't touch me! Oh, how painful it is!'

He turned away and went to the house. There he met her mother.

'What is the matter, Prince? I . . .' She became silent on seeing his face. The blood had suddenly rushed to his head.

'You knew it and used me to shield them! If you weren't a woman,' he cried, lifting his enormous fist, and turning aside he ran away.

Had his fiancée's lover been a private person he would have killed him, but it was his beloved Tsar.

The next day he applied both for furlough and his discharge, and professing to be ill, so as to see no one, he went away to the country.

He spent the summer at his village arranging his affairs. When summer was over he did not return to Petersburg, but entered a monastery and there became a monk.

His mother wrote to try to dissuade him from this decisive step, but he replied that he felt God's call which transcended all other considerations. Only his sister, who was as proud and ambitious as he, understood him.

She understood that he had become a monk in order to be above those who considered themselves to be above him. And she understood him correctly. By becoming a monk he showed contempt for all that seemed most important to others and had seemed so to him while he was in the service, and he now ascended a height from which he could look down from above on those he had formerly envied. But it was not this alone, as his sister Varvara supposed, that guided him. There was also in him something else that guided him, a sincere religious feeling that Varvara did not know, which intertwined itself with the feeling of pride and the desire to be first. His disillusionment with his fiancée Mary, whom he had considered such an angel, and his sense of injury were so strong that they brought him to despair, and the despair led him—to what? To God, to his childhood faith which had never been destroyed in him.

III

Kasatsky entered the monastery on the feast of Pokrov.* The abbot of that monastery was a gentleman by birth, a learned writer, and a *starets*, that is, he belonged to that succession of monks originating in Walachia who each choose a director and teacher whom they implicitly obey. The abbot had been a disciple of the renowned *starets* Amvrosy, who was a disciple of Makary, who was a disciple of the *starets* Leonid, who was a disciple of Paissy Velichkovsky.* Kasatsky submitted himself to this abbot as his *starets*.

Besides the feeling of superiority over others that such a life gave him, in the monastery, just as in everything that he did, even in the monastery, Kasatsky found joy in attaining the greatest possible perfection outwardly as well as inwardly. As in the regiment he had been not merely an irreproachable officer but had even exceeded his duties and widened the borders of perfection, so also as a monk he tried to be perfect, always industrious, abstemious, submissive, meek, pure not only in deed but in thought, and obedient. This last quality in particular made life far easier for him. If many of the demands of life in the monastery, which was near the capital and much frequented, did not please him and were temptations to him, they were all nullified by obedience: It is not for me to reason; my business is to do the task set me, whether it be standing beside the relics, singing in the choir, or making up accounts in the monastery guesthouse. All possibility of doubt about anything was silenced by obedience to the *starets*. Had it not been for this, he would have been oppressed by the length and monotony of the church services, the bustle of the many visitors, and the bad qualities of the other monks. As it was, he not only bore it all joyfully but found in it solace and support. 'I don't know why it is necessary to hear the same prayers several times a day, but I know that it is necessary, and knowing this I find joy in them.' The *starets* told him that as material food is necessary for the maintenance of the life of the body, so spiritual food, the church prayers, is necessary for the maintenance of the spiritual life. He believed this, and though the church services, for which he had to get up early in the morning, were a difficulty, they certainly calmed him and gave him joy. This was the result of his consciousness of humility and the certainty that whatever he had to do, being fixed by the *starets*, was right. The interest of his life consisted not only in an ever greater and greater subjugation of his will, in ever greater and greater humility, but in the attainment of all the Christian virtues, which at first seemed to him easily attainable. He had given his whole estate to his sister and did not regret it. He had no sloth. Humility towards his inferiors was not merely easy for him but afforded him joy. Even victory over the sins of the flesh, greed and lust, was easily attained. His *starets* had specially warned him against the latter sin, but Kasatsky rejoiced in his freedom from it.

One thing only tormented him, the remembrance of his fiancée. And not just the remembrance but the vivid image of what might have been. Involuntarily he imagined the Emperor's favourite, who had afterwards married and become an admirable wife and mother. The husband had a high position, influence and honour, and a good and penitent wife.

In his better moments Kasatsky was not disturbed by such thoughts, and when he recalled them at such times he was merely glad to feel that the temptation was past. But there were moments when all that made up his present life suddenly grew dim before him, moments when, if he did not cease to believe in the aims he had set himself, he ceased to see them and could evoke no confidence in them but was seized by a remembrance of and—terrible to say—a regret for the change of life he had made.

The only thing that saved him in that state of mind was obedience, work, and the whole day occupied by prayer. He went through the usual forms of prayer, he bowed in prayer, he even prayed more than usual, but it was lip-service only and his soul was not in it. This condition would continue for a day, or sometimes for two days, and would then pass of itself. But those days were dreadful. Kasatsky felt that he was neither in his own hands nor in God's, but in someone else's, someone alien. All he could do then was to obey the *starets*, to restrain himself, to undertake nothing, and simply to wait. In general all this time he lived not by his own will but by that of the *starets*, and in this obedience he found a special tranquillity.

Thus he lived in his first monastery for seven years. At the end of the third year he received the tonsure and was ordained to the priesthood with the name of Sergy. The profession was an important event in his inner life. He had previously experienced a great consolation and spiritual exaltation when receiving communion, and now when he himself officiated, the performance of the preparation filled him with ecstatic and deep emotion. But subsequently that feeling became more and more deadened, and once when he was officiating in a depressed state of mind he felt that the influence produced on him by the service would not endure. And it did in fact weaken till only the habit remained.

In general in the seventh year of his life in the monastery Sergy grew bored. He had learnt all there was to learn and had attained all there was to attain, there was nothing more to do. His spiritual drowsiness increased. During this time he heard of his mother's death and Mary's marriage, but both events were matters of indifference to him. His whole attention and his whole interest were concentrated on his inner life.

In the fourth year of his priesthood, during which the bishop had been particularly kind to him, the *starets* told him that he ought not to decline it if he were offered an appointment to higher duties. Then monastic ambition, the very thing he had found so repulsive in other monks, arose within him. He was assigned to a monastery near the capital. He wished to refuse but the *starets* ordered him to accept the appointment. He did so, and took leave of the *starets* and moved to the other monastery.

The move to the metropolitan monastery was an important event in Sergy's life. There he encountered many temptations, and his whole willpower was concentrated on meeting them.

In the former monastery women had not been a temptation to him, but here that temptation arose with terrible strength and even took definite shape. There was a lady known for her frivolous behaviour who began to seek his favour. She talked to him and asked him to visit her. Sergy sternly declined, but was horrified by the definiteness of his desire. He was so alarmed that he wrote about it to the *starets*. And in addition, to keep himself in hand, he spoke to a young novice and, conquering his sense of shame, confessed his weakness to him, asking him to keep watch on him and not let him go anywhere except to service and to fulfil his duties.

Besides this, a great temptation for Sergy lay in the fact of his extreme antipathy to the abbot of this monastery, a cunning, worldly man who was making a career for himself in the Church. Struggle with himself as he might, Sergy could not master that antipathy. He was submissive, but in the depths of his soul he never ceased to condemn him. And that ill feeling burst forth. It was the second year of his residence in the new monastery. And it happened like this. The vigil service was being performed in the large church on the eve of the feast of Pokrov. There were many visitors. The abbot himself was conducting the service. Father Sergy was standing in his usual place and praying, that is, he was in that condition of struggle which always occupied him during the service, especially in the large church when he was not himself conducting the service. This conflict was occasioned by his irritation at the presence of the visitors, the gentlemen and especially the ladies. He tried not to see them or to notice all that went on: how a soldier accompanied them shooing the common people out of their way, how the ladies pointed out the monks to one another, especially himself and a monk noted for his good looks. He tried as it were to keep his mind in blinkers, to see nothing but the light of the candles on the iconostasis,* the icons, and those conducting the service. He tried to hear nothing but the prayers that were being chanted or read, to feel nothing but self-oblivion in consciousness of the fulfilment of duty, a feeling he always experienced when hearing or reciting in advance the prayers he had so often heard.

So he stood, crossing and prostrating himself when necessary, and struggled with himself, now giving way to cold condemnation and now to a consciously evoked obliteration of thought and feeling. Then the sacristan, Father Nicodim, also a great temptation for Sergy who involuntarily reproached him for flattering and fawning on the abbot, approached him and, bowing low, requested his presence in the sanctuary. Father Sergy straightened his mantle, put on his *klobuk*,* and went circumspectly through the crowd.

'*Lise, regarde à droite, c'est lui!*'[1] he heard a woman's voice say.

'*Où, où? Il n'est pas tellement beau.*'[2]

He knew that they were speaking of him. He heard them and, as always at moments of temptation, he repeated the words, 'Lead us not into temptation', and bowing his head and lowering his eyes went past the *amvon** and in by the north door,* avoiding the canons in their cassocks who were just then passing the iconostasis. On entering the sanctuary he bowed, crossing himself as usual and bending double before the icon, then raising his head but without turning, he glanced out of the corner of his eye at the abbot, whom he saw standing beside another figure glittering with something.

The abbot was standing by the wall in his vestments. Having freed his short plump hands from beneath his chasuble he had folded them over his fat body and protruding stomach, and fingering the cords of his vestments was smilingly saying something to a military man in the uniform of a general of the imperial suite, with its insignia and shoulder-knots which Father Sergy's experienced eye at once recognized. This general had been the commander of the regiment in which Sergy had served. He now evidently occupied an important position, and Father Sergy at once noticed that the abbot was aware of this and that his red face and bald head beamed with satisfaction and pleasure. This vexed and disgusted Father Sergy, the more so when he heard that the abbot had only sent for him to satisfy the general's curiosity to see a man who had formerly served with him, as he expressed it.

'Very pleased to see you in the angelic image,'* said the general, holding out his hand. 'I hope you have not forgotten an old comrade.'

The abbot's red, smiling face amid its fringe of grey, the general's words, his well-cared-for face with its self-satisfied smile, and the

---

[1] 'Lise, look to the right. That is he.'

[2] 'Where? Where? He is not so very handsome.'

smell of wine from his breath and of cigars from his whiskers, all of this revolted Father Sergy. He bowed again to the abbot and said:

'Your reverence deigned to send for me?' He stopped, but the whole expression of his face and eyes was asking why.

'Yes, to meet the general,' replied the abbot.

'Your reverence, I left the world to save myself from temptation,' said Father Sergy, turning pale and with quivering lips. 'Why do you expose me to it during prayers and in the house of God?'

'You may go! Go!' said the abbot, flaring up and frowning.

Next day Father Sergy asked pardon of the abbot and of the brethren for his pride, but at the same time, after a night spent in prayer, he decided that he must leave this monastery, and he wrote to the *starets* begging permission to return to him. He wrote that he felt his weakness and incapacity to struggle against temptation without his help and penitently confessed his sin of pride. By return post came a letter from the *starets*, who wrote that Sergy's pride was the cause of all that had happened. The old man pointed out that his fits of anger were due to the fact that in refusing all clerical honours he humiliated himself not for the sake of God but for the sake of his pride. 'There now, am I not a splendid man not to want anything?' That was why he could not tolerate the abbot's action. 'I have renounced everything for the glory of God, and here I am exhibited like a wild beast!' 'Had you renounced vanity for God's sake you would have borne it. Worldly pride is not yet dead in you. I have thought about you, Sergy my son, and prayed also, and this is what God has suggested to me. At the Tambov hermitage the anchorite Illarion, a man of saintly life, has died. He had lived there eighteen years. The Tambov abbot is asking whether there is not a brother who would take his place. And here comes your letter. Go to Father Paisy of the Tambov Monastery. I will write to him about you, and you must ask for Illarion's cell. Not that you can replace Illarion, but you need solitude to quell your pride. May God bless you!'

Sergy obeyed the *starets*, showed his letter to the abbot, and, having obtained his permission, gave up his cell, handed all his possessions over to the monastery, and set out for the Tambov hermitage.

There the abbot, an excellent manager of merchant origin, received Sergy simply and quietly and placed him in Illarion's cell, at first assigning to him a lay brother but afterwards leaving him alone, at Sergy's own request. The cell was a dual cave, dug into the hillside, and in it Illarion had been buried. In the back part was Illarion's grave, while in the front was a niche for sleeping, with a straw mattress, a small table, and a shelf with icons and books. Outside the outer door, which fastened with a hook, was another shelf on which, once a day, a monk placed food from the monastery.

And so Sergy became a hermit.

IV

In Butter Week,* in the sixth year of Sergy's life at the hermitage, a merry company of rich people, men and women from a neighbouring town, made up a troika-party,* after a meal of *bliny** and wine. The company consisted of two lawyers, a wealthy landowner, an officer, and four ladies. One lady was the officer's wife, another the wife of the landowner, the third his sister, a young girl, and the fourth a divorcée, beautiful, rich, and eccentric, who amazed and shocked the town by her escapades.

The weather was excellent and the snow-covered road smooth as a floor. They drove some seven miles out of town, and then stopped and consulted as to whether they should turn back or drive further.

'But where does this road lead to?' asked Makovkina, the beautiful divorcée.

'To Tambov, eight miles from here,' replied one of the lawyers, who was courting her.

'And then where?'

'Then on to L——, past the monastery.'

'Where that Father Sergy lives?'

'Yes.'

'Kasatsky, the handsome hermit?'

'Yes.'

'Mesdames! Gentlemen! Let us drive on and see Kasatsky! We can stop at Tambov and have something to eat.'

'But we won't be able to get home tonight!'

'Never mind, we will stay at Kasatsky's.'

'Well, there is a very good hostelry at the monastery. I stayed there when I was defending Makhin.'

'No, I shall spend the night at Kasatsky's!'

'Impossible! Even your omnipotence could not accomplish that!'

'Impossible? Will you bet?'

'All right! If you spend the night with him, the stake shall be whatever you like.'

'*A discrétion!*'[1]

'And on your side too!'

'Yes, of course. Let us drive on.'

Vodka was handed to the drivers, and the party got out a box of *pirozhki,** wine, and sweets for themselves. The ladies wrapped themselves up in their white dog-fur coats. The drivers disputed as to whose troika should go ahead, and the youngest, seating himself sideways with a dashing air, swung his long knout and shouted to the horses. The troika bells tinkled and the sledge-runners squeaked over the snow.

The sledges swayed hardly at all, the shaft-horse, with his tightly bound tail under his decorated breechband, galloped smoothly and merrily, the smooth road seemed to run rapidly backwards, while the driver dashingly shook the reins, the lawyer and the officer sitting opposite talked nonsense to Makovkina's neighbour. Makovkina herself sat motionless and in thought, tightly wrapped in her fur. 'Always the same and always nasty! The same red shiny faces smelling of wine and cigars! The same talk, the same thoughts, and always about the same vileness! And they are all satisfied and confident that it should be so, and will go on living like that till they die. But I can't. It bores me. I want something that would upset it all and turn it upside down. Suppose it happened to us as to those people, at Saratov I think, who kept on driving and froze to death. What would our people do? How would they behave? Basely, for certain. Each for himself. And I too should act basely. But I at any rate have beauty. They all know it. And how about that monk? Is it possible that he no longer understands that? Not so! That is the one thing they all understand, like that cadet last autumn. What a fool he was!'

'Ivan Nikolaich!' she said.

'What are your commands?'

'How old is he?'

'Who?'

'Kasatsky.'

'Over forty, I should think.'

---

[1] 'As much as you like.'

'And does he receive everybody?'

'Yes, everybody, but not always.'

'Cover up my feet. Not like that, how clumsy you are! No! More, more, like that! But you need not squeeze them!'

So they came to the forest where the cell was.

Makovkina got out of the sledge and told them to drive on. They tried to dissuade her, but she grew irritable and ordered them to go on. When the sledges had gone she went up the path in her white dog-fur coat. The lawyer got out and stopped to watch her.

V

It was Father Sergy's sixth year as a hermit, and he was now forty-nine. His life in solitude was hard, not on account of the fasts and the prayers (they were no hardship to him) but on account of an inner conflict he had not at all anticipated. The sources of that conflict were two: doubt and the lust of the flesh. And both these foes always appeared together. It seemed to him that they were two different foes, but in reality they were one and the same. As soon as doubt was gone so was the lustful desire. But thinking them to be two different devils he fought them separately.

'O my God, my God!' he thought. 'Why dost thou not grant me faith? There is lust, of course, even the saints had to fight that, Saint Anthony and others. But they had faith, while I have moments, hours, and days, when it is absent. Why does the whole world, with all its delights, exist if it is sinful and must be renounced? Why hast thou created this temptation? Temptation? Is it not rather a temptation that I wish to abandon all the joys of the world and prepare something for myself there where perhaps there is nothing?' And he became horrified and filled with disgust at himself. 'Vile creature! And it is you who wish to be a saint!' he upbraided himself, and he began to pray. But as soon as he started to pray he saw himself vividly as he had been at the monastery, majestic in his *klobuk* and cope. He shook his head. 'No, that is not right. It is deception. I may deceive others, but not myself or God. I am not a majestic man, but a pitiable and ridiculous one!' And he threw back the folds of his cassock and smiled as he looked at his thin legs in their underclothing.

Then he dropped the folds of the cassock again and began reading the prayers, making the sign of the cross and prostrating himself. 'Can it be that this bed will be my bier?' he read. And it seemed as if the devil whispered to him: 'A solitary bed is itself a bier. It's a lie!' And in his imagination he saw the shoulders of a widow with whom he had lived. He shook himself and went on reading. Having read the precepts he took up the Gospels, opened the book, and happened on a passage he often repeated and knew by heart: 'Lord, I believe. Help my unbelief!' He put away all the doubts that had arisen. As one repositions an object of insecure equilibrium, so he carefully repositioned his belief on its shaky pedestal and carefully stepped back from it so as not to shake or upset it. The blinkers were adjusted again and he felt calm. He repeated his childhood prayer, 'Lord, take me, take me!' and he felt not merely at ease, but joyful and moved. He crossed himself and lay down on the bedding on his narrow bench, tucking his summer cassock under his head. He fell asleep at once, and in his light slumber he seemed to hear the tinkling of sledge bells. He did not know whether he was dreaming or awake, but a knock at the door aroused him. He sat up in disbelief, but the knock was repeated. Yes, it was a knock close at hand, at his door, and with it the sound of a woman's voice.

'My God! Can it be true, as I have read in the *Lives of the Saints*, that the devil takes on the form of a woman? Yes, it is a woman's voice, a tender, timid, pleasant voice. Phui!' And he spat. 'No, it was only my imagination,' he assured himself, and he went to the corner where his *analoychik** stood, falling on his knees in the regular and habitual manner which of itself gave him consolation and satisfaction. He sank down, his hair hanging over his face, and pressed his head, already going bald in front, to the cold damp piece of rug on the draughty floor. He read the psalm old Father Pimon had told him warded off temptation. He easily raised his light and emaciated body on his strong sinewy legs and tried to continue saying his prayers, but instead of doing so he involuntarily strained his hearing. He wished to hear more. All was quiet. From the corner of the roof regular drops continued to fall into the tub below. Outside was a mist and fog eating into the snow that lay on the ground. It was still, very still. And suddenly there was a rustling at the window and a voice, that same tender, timid voice which could only belong to an attractive woman, said:

'Let me in, for Christ's sake!'

It seemed as though his blood had all rushed to his heart and settled there. He could hardly breathe. 'Let God arise and let his enemies be scattered . . .'

'But I am not the devil!' It was obvious that the lips that uttered this were smiling. 'I am not the devil, but only a sinful woman who has lost her way, not figuratively but literally!' She laughed. 'I am frozen and beg for shelter.'

He pressed his face to the window, but the little icon-lamp was reflected by it and shone on the whole pane. He put his hands to both sides of his face and peered between them. Fog, mist, a tree, and just there to the right, she herself. Yes, there, a few inches from him, was the sweet, kindly frightened face of a woman in a cap and a coat of long white fur, leaning towards him. Their eyes met with instant recognition. Not that they had ever known one another, they had never met before, but by the look they exchanged they, and he particularly, felt that they knew and understood one another. After that glance to imagine her to be the devil, and not a simple, kindly, sweet, timid woman, was impossible.

'Who are you? Why have you come?' he asked.

'Do please open the door!' she replied, with capricious authority. 'I am frozen. I tell you I have lost my way.'

'But I am a monk, a hermit.'

'Oh, do please open the door, or do you wish me to freeze under your window while you say your prayers?'

'But how have you . . .'

'I won't eat you. For God's sake let me in! I am quite frozen.'

She really did feel afraid, and said this in an almost tearful voice.

He stepped back from the window and looked at the icon of the Saviour in his crown of thorns. 'Lord, help me! Lord, help me!' he exclaimed, crossing himself and bowing low. Then he went to the door, and opening it into the passageway, felt for the hook that fastened the outer door and began to lift it. He heard steps outside. She was coming from the window to the door. 'Ah!' she suddenly exclaimed, and he understood that she had stepped into the puddle that the dripping from the roof had formed at the threshold. His hands trembled, and he could not raise the hook of the tightly closed door.

'Oh, what are you doing? Let me in! I am all wet. I am frozen! You are thinking about saving your soul and are letting me freeze to death.'

He jerked the door towards him, raised the hook, and without considering what he was doing, pushed it open with such force that it struck her.

'Oh, I beg your pardon!' he suddenly exclaimed, reverting completely to his old manner with ladies.

She smiled on hearing that 'I beg your pardon'. 'He is not quite so terrible, after all,' she thought. 'It's all right. It is you who must forgive me,' she said, stepping past him. 'I should never have ventured, but for such an extraordinary circumstance.'

'Please come in,' he uttered, and stood aside to let her pass him. A strong smell of fine scent, which he had long not encountered, struck him. She went through the passageway into the cell where he lived. He closed the outer door without fastening the hook and stepped in after her.

'Lord Jesus Christ, Son of God, have mercy on me a sinner! Lord, have mercy on me a sinner!'* he prayed unceasingly, not merely to himself but involuntarily moving his lips. 'Please come in,' he said to her again. She stood in the middle of the room, moisture dripping from her to the floor as she looked him over. Her eyes were laughing.

'Forgive me for having disturbed your solitude. But you see what a position I am in. It all came about from our starting from town for a sledge drive, and my making a bet that I would walk back by myself from the Vorobyovka to the town. But then I lost my way, and if I had not happened to come upon your cell,' she began lying, but his face confused her so that she could not continue and became silent. She had not expected him to be at all such as he was. He was not as handsome as she had imagined, but was nevertheless beautiful in her eyes. His greyish hair and beard, slightly curling, his fine, regular nose, and his eyes like glowing coal when he looked at her, made a strong impression on her.

He saw that she was lying.

'Yes, so,' he said, looking at her and again lowering his eyes. 'I will go in there, and this place is at your disposal.'

And taking down the little lamp, he lit a candle, and bowing low to her went into the small cell beyond the partition, and she heard him begin to move something about there. 'Probably he is barricading himself in from me!' she thought with a smile, and throwing off her white dog-fur coat she tried to take off her cap, which had become entangled in her hair and in the woven kerchief she was wearing under it. She had not got at all wet when standing under the window and had said so only as a pretext to get him to let her in. But she really had stepped into the puddle at the door, and her left foot was wet up to the ankle and her overshoe full of water. She sat down on his bed, a bench only covered by a bit of carpet, and began to take off her boots. The little cell seemed to her charming. The narrow little room, some three *arshins** wide by four long, was as clean as glass. There was nothing in it but the bench on which she was sitting, the book-shelf above it, and an *analoychik* in the corner. A sheepskin coat and a cassock hung on nails by the door. Above the *analoychik* was a vigil light and an icon of Christ in his crown of thorns. The room smelt strangely of perspiration and of earth. It all pleased her, even that smell. Her wet feet, especially one of them, were uncomfortable, and she quickly began to take off her boots and stockings without ceasing to smile, pleased not so much at having achieved her object as because she perceived that she had abashed that charming, strange, striking, and attractive man. 'He did not respond, but what of that?' she said to herself.

'Father Sergy! Father Sergy! Or how does one call you?'

'What do you want?' replied a quiet voice.

'Please forgive me for disturbing your solitude, but really I could not help it. I should simply have fallen ill. And I don't know that I won't now. I am all wet and my feet are like ice.'

'Forgive me,' replied the quiet voice. 'I cannot be of any assistance to you.'

'I would not have disturbed you if I could have helped it. I am only here till daybreak.'

He did not reply and she heard him muttering something, probably his prayers.

'You will not be coming in here?' she asked, smiling. 'For I must undress to dry myself.'

He did not reply, but continued to read his prayers.

'Yes, that is a man!' she thought, getting her dripping boot off with difficulty. She tugged at it, but could not get it off. The absurdity of it struck her and she began to laugh almost inaudibly. But knowing that he would hear her laughter and would be moved by it just as she wished him to be, she laughed louder, and her laughter, gay, natural, and kindly, really acted on him just in the way she wished.

'Yes, I could love a man like that, such eyes and such a simple noble face, and passionate too despite all the prayers he mutters!' she thought. 'You can't deceive a woman in these things. As soon as he put his face to the window and saw me, he understood and knew. The glimmer of it was in his eyes and remained there. He began to love me and desired me. Yes, desired!' she said, getting her overshoe and her boot off at last and starting to take off her stockings. To remove those long stockings fastened with elastic it was necessary to raise her skirts. She felt embarrassed and said:

'Don't come in!'

But there was no reply from the other side of the wall. The steady muttering continued and also a sound of moving.

'He is prostrating himself to the ground, no doubt,' she thought. 'But he won't bow himself out of it. He is thinking of me just as I am thinking of him. He is thinking of these feet of mine with the same feeling that I have!' And she pulled off her wet stockings and put her feet up on the bench, pressing them under her. She sat a while like that with her arms round her knees and looking pensively before her. 'But it is a desert, here in this silence. No one would ever know . . .'

She rose, took her stockings over to the stove and hung them on the damper. It was an unusual damper, and she turned it about, and then, stepping lightly on her bare feet, returned to the bench and sat down there again with her feet up. There was complete silence on the other side of the partition. She looked at the tiny watch that hung round her neck. It was two o'clock. 'Our party should return about three!' She had not more than an hour before her. 'Well, am I to sit like this all alone? What nonsense! I don't want to. I will call him at once.'

'Father Sergy, Father Sergy! Sergy Dmitrich! Prince Kasatsky!'

Beyond the partition all was silent.

'Listen! This is cruel. I would not call you if it were not necessary. I am ill. I don't know what is the matter with me!' she exclaimed in a tone of suffering. 'Oh! Oh!' she groaned, falling back on the bench. And strange to say she really felt that her strength was failing, that she was becoming faint, that everything in her ached, and that she was shivering with fever.

'Listen! Help me! I don't know what is the matter with me. Oh!

Oh!' She unfastened her dress, exposing her breast, and lifted her arms, bare to the elbow. 'Oh! Oh!'

All this time he stood on the other side of the partition and prayed. Having finished all the evening prayers, he now stood motionless, his eyes looking at the end of his nose, and mentally repeated with all his soul: 'Lord Jesus Christ, Son of God, have mercy upon me!'

But he had heard everything. He had heard how the silk rustled when she took off her dress, how she stepped with bare feet on the floor, how she rubbed her feet with her hand. He felt his own weakness, and that he might be lost at any moment. That was why he prayed unceasingly. He felt rather as the hero in the fairy tale must have felt when he had to go on and on without looking round. So Sergy heard and felt that danger and destruction were there, hovering above and around him, and that he could only save himself by not looking in that direction for an instant. But suddenly the desire to look seized him. At the same instant she said:

'This is inhuman. I may die.'

'Yes, I will go to her, but like the Saint who laid one hand on the adulteress and thrust his other into the brazier. But there is no brazier here.' He looked round. The lamp! He put his finger over the flame and frowned, preparing himself to suffer. And for a rather long time, as it seemed to him, there was no sensation, but suddenly, he had not yet decided whether it was painful enough, he writhed all over, jerked his hand away, and waved it in the air. 'No, I can't stand that!'

'For God's sake come to me! I am dying! Oh!'

'Well, shall I perish? No, not in this way!'

'I will come to you right away,' he said, and having opened his door, he went without looking at her through the cell into the passageway where he used to chop wood. There he felt for the block and for an axe which leant against the wall.

'Right away,' he said, and taking up the axe with his right hand he laid the forefinger of his left hand on the block, swung the axe, and struck with it below the second joint. The finger flew off more lightly than a stick of similar thickness, and bounding up, turned over on the edge of the block and then fell to the floor.

He heard it fall before he felt any pain, but before he had time to be surprised he felt a burning pain and the warmth of flowing blood.

He hastily wrapped the stump in the skirt of his cassock, and pressing it to his hip went back into the room, and standing in front of the woman, lowered his eyes and asked in a low voice: 'What do you want?'

She looked at his pale face and his quivering left cheek, and suddenly felt ashamed. She jumped up, seized her fur coat, and throwing it round her shoulders, wrapped herself up in it.

'I was in pain . . . I have caught cold . . . I . . . Father Sergy . . . I . . .'

He let his eyes, shining with a quiet light of joy, rest upon her and said:

'Dear sister, why did you wish to ruin your immortal soul? Temptations must come into the world, but woe to him by whom temptation comes. Pray that God may forgive us!'

She listened and looked at him. Suddenly she heard the sound of something dripping. She looked down and saw that blood was flowing from his hand and down his cassock.

'What have you done to your hand? She remembered the sound she had heard, and seizing the vigil light ran out into the passageway. There on the floor she saw the bloody finger. She returned with her face paler than his and was about to speak to him, but he silently passed into the back cell and fastened the door.

'Forgive me!' she said. 'How can I atone for my sin?'

'Go away.'

'Let me tie up your hand.'

'Go away from here.'

She dressed hurriedly and silently, and when ready sat waiting in her furs. The sledge bells were heard outside.

'Father Sergy, forgive me!'

'Go away. God will forgive.'

'Father Sergy! I will change my life. Do not forsake me!'

'Go away.'

'Forgive me, and give me your blessing!'

'In the name of the Father and of the Son and of the Holy Ghost!', she heard his voice from behind the partition. 'Go!'

She burst into sobs and left the cell. The lawyer came forward to meet her.

'Well, I see I have lost the bet. It can't be helped. Where will you sit?'

'It is all the same to me.'

She took a seat in the sledge and did not utter a word all the way home.

A year later she entered a convent as a novice and lived a strict life under the direction of the hermit Arseny, who wrote letters to her at long intervals.

VI

Father Sergy lived as a recluse for another seven years.

At first he accepted much of what people brought him—tea, sugar, white bread, milk, clothing, and firewood. But as time went on he led a more and more austere life, refusing everything superfluous, and finally he accepted nothing but rye-bread once a week. Everything else that was brought him he gave to the poor who came to him. He spent his entire time in his cell, in prayer or in conversation with callers, who became more and more numerous as time went on. Only three times a year did he go out to church, and when necessary he went out to fetch water and wood.

The episode with Makovkina had occurred after five years of his hermit life. That occurrence soon became generally known, her nocturnal visit, the change she underwent, and her entry into a convent. From that time Father Sergy's fame increased. More and more visitors came to see him, other monks settled down near his cell, and a church and guesthouse was erected there. His fame, as usual exaggerating his feats, spread ever more and more widely. People began to come to him from a distance and began bringing invalids to him whom they declared he cured.

His first cure occurred in the eighth year of his life as a hermit. It was the healing of a fourteen-year-old boy, whose mother brought him to Father Sergy insisting that he should lay his hands on the child's head. It had never occurred to Father Sergy that he could cure the sick. He would have regarded such a thought as a great sin of pride, but the mother who brought the boy implored him insistently, falling at his feet and saying, 'Why do you, who heal others, refuse to help my son?' She besought him in Christ's name. When Father Sergy assured her that only God could heal the sick, she replied that she only wanted him to lay his hands on the boy and pray for him. Father Sergy refused and returned to his cell. But on going out for water the next day (it was in autumn and the nights were already cold), he saw the same mother with her son, a pale boy of fourteen, and was met by the same petition. Father Sergy remembered the parable of the unjust judge,* and though he had previously felt sure that he ought to refuse, he now began to feel doubt and, having felt doubt, he took to prayer and prayed until a decision formed itself in his soul. This decision was, that he ought to accede to the woman's request and that her faith might save her son. As for himself, Father Sergy would in this case be but an insignificant instrument chosen by God.

And going out to the mother he did what she asked, laid his hands on the boy's head and prayed.

The mother left with her son, and a month later the boy recovered, and the fame of the holy healing power of the *starets* Sergy (as they now called him) spread throughout the whole district. After that, not a week passed without sick people coming, riding or on foot, to Father Sergy; and having acceded to one petition he could not refuse others, and he laid his hands on many and prayed. Many recovered, and his fame spread more and more.

So seven years passed in the monastery and thirteen in his hermit's cell. He now had the appearance of a *starets*: his beard was long and grey, but his hair, though thin, was still black and curly.

VII

For some weeks Father Sergy had been living with one persistent thought, whether he was right in accepting the position in which he had not so much placed himself as been placed by the archimandrite and the abbot. That position had begun after the recovery of the fourteen-year-old boy. From that time, with each month, week, and day that passed, Sergy felt his own inner life was wasting away and being replaced by external life. It was as if he had been turned inside out.

Sergy saw that he was a means of attracting visitors and contributions to the monastery, and that therefore the authorities arranged matters in such a way as to make as much use of him as possible. For instance, they rendered it impossible for him to do any manual work. He was supplied with everything he could want, and they only demanded of him that he should not refuse his blessing to those who came to seek it. For his convenience they appointed days when he would receive. They arranged a reception room for men, and a place was railed in so that he would not be pushed over by the crowds of women visitors and so that he could conveniently bless those who came.

They told him that people needed him, and that fulfilling Christ's law of love he could not refuse their demand to see him, and that to avoid them would be cruel. He could not but agree with this, but the more he gave himself up to such a life the more he felt that what was internal became external, and that the fount of living water within him dried up, and that what he did now was done more and more for men and less and less for God. Whether he admonished people, or simply blessed them, or prayed for the sick, or advised people about their lives, or listened to expressions of gratitude from those he had helped by precepts, or alms, or healing (as they assured him), he could not help being pleased at it and could not be indifferent to the results of his activity and to the influence he exerted. He thought of himself as a shining light, and the more he felt this the more was he conscious of a weakening, a dying down of the divine light of truth that shone within him. 'How much is what I do for God and how much for men?' That was the question that insistently tormented him and to which he was not so much unable to give himself an answer as unable to face the answer. In the depth of his soul he felt that the devil had substituted activity for men in place of all his former activity for God. He felt this because, just as it had formerly been hard for him to be torn from his solitude, so now that solitude itself was hard for him. He was oppressed and wearied by visitors, but at the bottom of his heart he was glad of their presence and glad of the praise they heaped upon him.

There was a time when he decided to go away and hide. He even planned all that was necessary for that purpose. He prepared for himself a peasant's shirt, trousers, coat, and cap. He explained that he wanted these to give to those who asked. And he kept these clothes in his cell, planning how he would put them on, cut his hair short, and go away. First he would go some three hundred versts* by train, then he would leave the train and walk from village to village.

He asked an old man who had been a soldier how he tramped, what people gave him and what shelter they allowed him. The soldier told him where people were most charitable and where they would take a wanderer in for the night, and Father Sergy intended to avail himself of this information. He even put on those clothes one night in his desire to go, but he could not decide what was best, to remain or to escape. At first he was undecided, but afterwards this indecision passed. He was used to it and yielded to the devil, and the peasant garb just served as a reminder of his thoughts and feelings.

Every day more and more people flocked to him and less and less time was left him for prayer and for renewing his spiritual strength. Sometimes in lucid moments he thought he had become like a place where there had once been a spring. 'There used to be a feeble spring of living water which flowed quietly from me and through me. That was true life, the time when "she" (He always thought with ecstasy of that night and of her. She was now Mother Agniya.) tempted him!' She had tasted of that pure water. But since then there had not been time for the water to collect before thirsty people came crowding in and pushing one another aside. And they had trampled everything down and nothing was left but mud. So he thought in rare moments of lucidity, but his usual state of mind was one of weariness and a tender pity for himself because of that weariness.

It was in spring, on the eve of the mid-Pentecostal feast. Father Sergy was officiating at the vigil service in his hermitage church, where the congregation was as large as the little church could hold, about twenty people. They were all well-to-do proprietors or merchants. Father Sergy admitted everyone, but a selection was made by the monk in attendance and by an assistant who was sent to the hermitage every day from the monastery. A crowd of some eighty people, wanderers,* mostly peasant women, stood outside waiting for Father Sergy to come out and bless them. Meanwhile he conducted the service, but at the point at which he went out to the tomb of his predecessor, he staggered and would have fallen had he not been caught by a merchant standing behind him and by the monk acting as deacon.

'What is the matter, Father Sergy? Dear man! O Lord!' exclaimed the women. 'He is as white as a sheet!'

But Father Sergy recovered immediately, and though very pale, he waved the merchant and the deacon aside and continued to chant the service. Father Serapion, the deacon, the acolytes, and Sofya Ivanovna, a lady who always lived near the hermitage and tended Father Sergy, begged him to bring the service to an end.

'No, there's nothing the matter,' said Father Sergy, slightly smiling from beneath his moustache and continuing the service. 'Yes, that is the way the saints behaved!' he thought.

'A saint, an angel of God!' he heard just then the voice of Sofya Ivanovna behind him, and also of the merchant who had supported him. He did not heed their entreaties, but went on with the service. Again crowding together they all made their way by the narrow passages back into the little church, and there, though abbreviating it slightly, Father Sergy completed vespers.

Immediately after the service Father Sergy, having pronounced the benediction on those present, went over to the bench under the elm tree at the entrance to the cave. He wished to rest and breathe the fresh air which he felt in need of, but as soon as he left the church the crowd of people rushed to him soliciting his blessing, his advice, and his help. There were women wanderers who constantly tramped from one holy place to another and from one *starets* to another, and were always entranced by every shrine and every *starets*. Father Sergy knew this common, cold, conventional, and most irreligious type. There were men wanderers, for the most part discharged soldiers, unaccustomed to a settled life, poverty-stricken, and many of them old and drunken, who tramped from monastery to monastery merely to be fed. There were rough peasants and peasant women who had come with their selfish requirements, seeking cures or to have doubts about quite practical affairs solved for them, about marrying off a daughter, or hiring a shop, or buying a bit of land, or how to atone for smothering a child or having an illegitimate one.

All this was an old story and not in the least interesting to him. He knew he would hear nothing new from these folk, that they would arouse no religious emotion in him, but he liked to see the crowd to which his blessing and advice was necessary and precious, so while that crowd oppressed him it also pleased him. Father Serapion began to drive them away, saying that Father Sergy was tired. But Father Sergy, remembering the words of the Gospel: 'Forbid them' (children) 'not to come unto me',* and feeling tenderly towards himself at this recollection, said they should be allowed to approach.

He rose, went to the railing beyond which the crowd had gathered, and began blessing them and answering their questions, but in a voice so weak that he was touched with pity for himself. Yet despite his wish to receive them all he could not do it. Things again grew dark before his eyes, and he staggered and grasped the railings. He felt a rush of blood to his head and first went pale and then suddenly flushed.

'I must leave the rest till tomorrow. I cannot do more today,' and, pronouncing a general benediction, he returned to the bench. The merchant again supported him, and leading him by the arm helped him to be seated.

'Father!' came voices from the crowd. 'Dear Father! Do not forsake us. Without you we are lost!'

The merchant, having seated Father Sergy on the bench under the elm, took on himself police duties and drove the people off very resolutely. It is true that he spoke in a low voice so that Father Sergy might not hear him, but his words were incisive and angry.

'Be off, be off! He has blessed you, and what more do you want? Get along with you, or I'll wring your necks! Move on there! Get along, you old woman with your dirty leg-bands! Go, go! Where are you trying to get to? You've been told, that's enough. Tomorrow will be as God wills, but for today he has finished!'

'Father! Only let my eyes have a glimpse of his dear face!' said an old woman.

'I'll glimpse you! Where are you trying to get to?'

Father Sergy noticed that the merchant seemed to be acting roughly, and in a feeble voice told the attendant that the people should not be driven away. He knew that they would be driven away all the same, and he much desired to be left alone and to rest, but he sent the attendant with that message to produce an impression.

'All right, all right! I am not driving them away. I am only remonstrating with them,' replied the merchant. 'You know they wouldn't hesitate to drive a man to death. They have no pity, they only consider themselves. You've been told you cannot see him. Go away! Tomorrow!' And he got rid of them all.

He took all these pains because he liked order and liked to domineer and drive the people away, but chiefly because he wanted to have Father Sergy to himself. He was a widower with an only daughter who was an invalid and unmarried, and whom he had brought fourteen hundred versts to Father Sergy to be healed. For two years past he had been taking her to different places to be cured, first to the university clinic in the chief town of the province, but that did no good, then to a peasant in the province of Samara, where she got a little better, then to a doctor in Moscow to whom he paid much money, but this did no good at all. Now he had been told that Father Sergy wrought cures, and had brought her to him. So when all the people had been driven away he approached Father Sergy, and suddenly falling on his knees exclaimed loudly:

'Holy Father! Bless my afflicted offspring that she may be healed of her malady. I venture to prostrate myself at your holy feet.' And he folded his hands in supplication. He said and did all this as if he were doing something clearly and firmly appointed by law and custom, as if one must and should ask for a daughter to be cured in just this way and no other. He did it with such conviction that it seemed even to Father Sergy that it should be said and done in just that way. But nevertheless he bade him rise and tell him what the trouble was. The merchant said that his daughter, a girl of twenty-two, had fallen ill two years ago, after her mother's sudden death, that she had moaned (as he expressed it) and since then had grown worse. And now he has brought her fourteen hundred versts and she is waiting in the guesthouse till Father Sergy should give orders to bring her. She did not go out during the day, being afraid of the light, and could only come after sunset.

'Is she very weak?' asked Father Sergy.

'No, she has no particular weakness. She is quite plump and is only "nerastenic", as the doctor says. If you will only let me bring her this evening, Father Sergy, I'll fly like a spirit to fetch her. Holy Father! Revive a parent's heart, restore his line, save his afflicted daughter by your prayers!' And the merchant again threw himself on his knees and bending his head sideways over his folded hands, he remained stock still. Father Sergy again told him to get up, and thinking how heavy his activities were and how he went through with them patiently notwithstanding, he sighed heavily and after a few seconds of silence, said:

'Well, bring her this evening. I will pray for her, but now I am tired.' And he closed his eyes. 'I will send for you.'

The merchant went away, stepping on tiptoe, which only made his boots creak the louder, and Father Sergy remained alone.

Father Sergy's whole life was filled by church services and by people who came to see him, but today had been a particularly difficult one. In the morning an important official had arrived and had had a long conversation with him, and after that a lady had come with her son. This son was a young professor, a non-believer, whom the mother, an ardent believer and devoted to Father Sergy, had brought that he might talk to him. The conversation had been very trying. The young man, evidently not wishing to have a controversy with a monk, had agreed with him in everything as with someone who was mentally inferior. Father Sergy saw that the young man did not believe but yet was satisfied, tranquil, and at ease, and the memory of that conversation now disquieted him.

'Have something to eat, Father,' said the attendant.

'All right, bring me something.'

The attendant went to a hut that had been arranged some ten paces from the cave, and Father Sergy remained alone.

The time was long past when he had lived alone doing everything for himself and eating only rye-bread, or rolls prepared for the Church. He had been advised long since that he had no right to neglect his health, and he was given wholesome, though Lenten, food. He ate sparingly, though much more than he had done, and often he ate with much pleasure and not as formerly with aversion and a sense of guilt. So it was now. He had some gruel, drank a cup of tea, and ate half a white roll.

The attendant went away, and Father Sergy remained alone under the elm tree.

It was a wonderful May evening, when the birches, aspens, elms, wild cherries, and oaks had just burst into foliage. The bush of wild cherries behind the elm tree was in full bloom and had not yet begun to shed its blossoms. The nightingales, one quite near at hand and two or three others in the bushes down by the river, began to trill and then burst into full song. From the river came the far-off singing of peasants returning, no doubt, from their work. The sun was setting behind the forest, its last rays glowing through the leaves. All that side was brilliant green, the other side with the elm tree was dark. The cockchafers flew clumsily about, falling to the ground when they collided with anything.

After supper Father Sergy began to repeat a silent prayer: 'O Lord Jesus Christ, Son of God, have mercy upon us!' and then later he read a psalm, and suddenly in the middle of the psalm a sparrow flew out from the bush, alighted on the ground, and hopped towards him chirping as it came, but then it took fright at something and flew away. He said a prayer which referred to his renunciation of the world and hastened to finish it in order to send for the merchant with the sick daughter. She interested him because she was a distraction, a new face, and because both she and her father considered him a saint whose prayers were efficacious. Outwardly he disavowed that idea, but in the depths of his soul he considered it to be true.

He was often amazed that this had happened, that he, Stepan Kasatsky, had come to be such an extraordinary saintly type and even a worker of miracles, but of the fact that he was such there could not be the least doubt. He could not fail to believe in the miracles he himself witnessed, beginning with the sick boy and ending with the old woman who had recovered her sight when he had prayed for her.

Strange as it might be, it was so. Accordingly the merchant's daughter interested him as a new individual who had faith in him and also as a fresh opportunity to confirm his healing powers and enhance his fame. 'They bring people a thousand versts and write about it in the papers. The Emperor knows of it, and they know of it in Europe, in unbelieving Europe,' he thought. And suddenly he felt ashamed of his vanity and again began to pray. 'Lord, King of Heaven, Comforter, Soul of Truth! Come and enter into us and cleanse us from all sin and save and bless our souls. Cleanse me from the sin of worldly vanity that troubles me!* he repeated, and he remembered how often he had prayed about this and how vain till now his prayers had been in that respect. His prayers worked miracles for others, but in his own case God had not granted him liberation from this petty passion.

He remembered his prayers at the commencement of his life at the hermitage, when he prayed for purity, humility, and love, and how it seemed to him then that God heard his prayers. He had retained his purity and had chopped off his finger. And he lifted the shrivelled stump of that finger to his lips and kissed it. It seemed to him now that he had been humble then when he had always seemed loathsome to himself on account of his sinfulness. And when he remembered the tender feelings with which he had then met an old man who was bringing a drunken soldier to him to ask alms and how he had received *her*, it seemed to him that he had then possessed love also. But now? And he asked himself whether he loved anyone, whether he loved Sofya Ivanovna, or Father Serapion, whether he had any feeling of love for all who had come to him that day, for that learned young man with whom he had had that instructive discussion in which he was concerned only to show off his own intelligence and that he had not lagged behind the times in knowledge. He wanted and needed their love, but felt none towards them. He now had neither love nor humility nor purity.

He was pleased to know that the merchant's daughter was twenty-two, and he wondered whether she was good-looking. When he inquired whether she was weak, he really wanted to know if she had feminine charm.

'Can I have fallen so low?' he thought. 'Lord, help me! Restore me, my Lord and God!' And he clasped his hands and began to pray.

The nightingales burst into song, a cockchafer knocked against him and crept up the back of his neck. He brushed it off. 'But does he exist? What if I am knocking at a door fastened from outside? The bar is on the door for all to see. Nature, the nightingales and the cockchafers, is that bar. Perhaps the young man was right.' And he began to pray aloud. He prayed for a long time till these thoughts vanished and he again felt calm and confident. He rang the bell and told the attendant to say that the merchant might bring his daughter to him now.

The merchant came, leading his daughter by the arm. He led her into the cell and immediately left.

She was a very fair girl, plump and very short, with a pale, frightened, childish face and a much developed feminine figure. Father Sergy remained seated on the bench at the entrance and when she was passing and stopped beside him for his blessing he was aghast at himself for the way he looked at her body. As she passed by him he felt he'd been stung. He saw by her face that she was sensual and feeble-minded. He rose and went into the cell. She was sitting on a stool waiting for him, and when he entered she rose.

'I want to go back to my papa,' she said.

'Don't be afraid,' he replied. 'What are you suffering from?'

'I am in pain all over,' she said, and suddenly her face lit up with a smile.

'You will be well,' said he. 'Pray!'

'What is the use of praying? I have prayed and it does no good.'

And she continued to smile. 'I want you to pray for me and lay your hands on me. I saw you in a dream.'

'How did you see me?'

'I saw you put your hands on my breast like this.' She took his hand and pressed it to her breast. 'Right here.'

He yielded his right hand to her.

'What is your name?' he asked, trembling all over and feeling that he was overcome and that his desire had already passed beyond control.

'Marya. Why?'

She took his hand and kissed it, and then put her arm round his waist and pressed him to herself.

'What are you doing?' he said. 'Marya, you are the devil!'

'Oh, perhaps. What does it matter?'

And embracing him she sat down with him on the bed.

At dawn he went out onto the porch.

'Can this all have happened? Her father will come and she will tell him everything. She is the devil! What am I to do? Here is the axe with which I chopped off my finger.' He snatched up the axe and moved back towards the cell.

The attendant came up.

'Do you want some wood chopped? Let me have the axe.'

He yielded up the axe and entered the cell. She was lying there asleep. He looked at her with horror and passed on beyond the partition, where he took down the peasant clothes and put them on. Then he seized a pair of scissors, cut off his long hair, and went out along the path down the hill to the river, where he had not been for more than three years.

A road ran beside the river and he went along it and walked till noon. Then he went into a field of rye and lay down there. Towards evening he approached a village on a river. He did not enter the village, but went towards the river, towards a cliff.

It was early morning, half an hour before sunrise. All was damp and gloomy and a cold early wind was blowing from the west. 'Yes, I must end it all. There is no God. But how am I to end it? Throw myself into the river? I can swim, and wouldn't drown. Hang myself? Yes, just throw this sash over a branch.' This seemed so feasible and so easy that he was horrified. As usual at moments of despair he felt the need of prayer. But there was no one to pray to. There was no God. He lay down resting on his arm, and suddenly such a longing for sleep overcame him that he could no longer support his head on his hand, but stretched out his arm, laid his head upon it, and fell asleep. But that sleep lasted only for a moment. He woke up immediately and began either to daydream or remember.

He saw himself as a child in his mother's home in the country. A carriage drives up, and out of it steps Uncle Nikolay Sergeevich, with his long, spade-shaped, black beard, and with him Pashenka, a thin little girl with large meek eyes and a timid pathetic face. And into their company of boys Pashenka is brought and they have to play with her, but it is boring. She is stupid, and it ends by their making fun of her and forcing her to show how she can swim. She lies down on the floor and shows them, and they all laugh and make a fool of her. She sees this and blushes red in patches and becomes more pitiable than before, so pitiable that he feels ashamed and can never forget that crooked, kindly, submissive smile. And Sergy remembered having seen her since then. Long after, just before he became a monk, she had married a landowner who squandered all her fortune and was in the habit of beating her. She had had two children, a son and a daughter, but the son had died while still young. And Sergy remembered having seen her very wretched. Then again he had seen her in the monastery when she was a widow. She had been still the same, not exactly stupid, but insipid, insignificant, and pitiable. She had come with her daughter and her daughter's fiancé. They were already poor at that time and later on he had heard that she was living in a small provincial town and was very poor.

'Why am I thinking about her?' he asked himself, but he could not cease doing so. 'Where is she? How is she getting on? Is she still as unhappy as she was then when she had to show us how to swim on the floor? But why should I think about her? What am I doing? I must put an end to myself.'

And again he was terrified, and again, to escape from that thought, he went on thinking about Pashenka.

So he lay for a long time, thinking now of his unavoidable end and now of Pashenka. She presented herself to him as a means of salvation. At last he fell asleep, and in his sleep he saw an angel who came to him and said: 'Go to Pashenka and learn from her what you have to do, what your sin is, and wherein lies your salvation.'

He awoke, and having decided that this was a vision sent by God, he rejoiced and resolved to do what had been told him in the vision. He knew the town where she lived. It was some three hundred versts away, and he set out to walk there.

VIII

Pashenka had already long ceased to be Pashenka and had become old, withered, wrinkled Praskovya Mikhaylovna, mother-in-law of that failure, the drunken official Mavrikyev. She was living in the country town where he had had his last appointment, and there she was supporting the family, her daughter, her ailing neurasthenic son-in-law, and her five grandchildren. She did this by giving music lessons to tradesmen's daughters, giving four and sometimes five lessons a day of an hour each, and earning in this way some sixty roubles a month. So they lived for the present, in expectation of another appointment. She had sent letters to all her relations and acquaintances asking them to obtain a post for her son-in-law, including even a letter to Sergy, but that letter had not reached him.

It was a Saturday, and Praskovya Mikhaylovna was herself mixing dough for currant bread such as the serf-cook on her papa's estate used to make so well. She wished to give her grandchildren a treat on Sunday.

Masha, her daughter, was nursing her youngest child, the eldest boy and girl were at school, and her son-in-law was asleep, not having slept during the night. Praskovya Mikhaylovna had remained awake too for a great part of the night, trying to soften her daughter's anger against her husband.

She saw that it was impossible for her son-in-law, a weak creature, to be other than he was and realized that his wife's reproaches could do no good, so she used all her efforts to soften those reproaches and to avoid recrimination and anger. Unkindly relations between people caused her actual physical suffering. It was so clear to her that bitter feelings do not make anything better, but only make everything worse. She did not in fact think about this, she simply suffered at the sight of anger as she would from a bad smell, a harsh noise, or from blows on her body.

With a feeling of self-satisfaction she had just taught Lukerya how to mix the dough, when her six-year-old grandson Misha, wearing an apron and with darned stockings on his crooked little legs, ran into the kitchen with a frightened face.

'Grandma, a dreadful old man wants to see you.'

Lukerya looked out at the door.

'There is a wanderer of some kind, ma'am.'

Praskovya Mikhaylovna rubbed her thin arms against one another, wiped her hands on her apron and went upstairs to get a five-kopek piece out of her purse for him, but remembering that she had nothing less than a ten-kopek piece she decided to give him some bread instead. She returned to the cupboard, but suddenly blushed at the thought of having begrudged the ten-kopek piece, and telling Lukerya to cut a slice of bread, went upstairs again to fetch it. 'It serves you right,' she said to herself. 'You must now give twice over.'

She gave both the bread and the money to the wanderer, and when doing so, far from being proud of her generosity, she excused herself for giving so little. The man had such an imposing appearance.

Though he had tramped two hundred versts as a beggar, though he was tattered and had grown thin and weather-beaten, though he had cropped his long hair and was wearing a peasant's cap and boots, and though he bowed very humbly, Sergy still had the impressive appearance that made him so attractive. But Praskovya Mikhaylovna did not recognize him. She could hardly do so, not having seen him for almost twenty years.

'Don't think ill of me, father. Perhaps you want something to eat?'

He took the bread and the money, and Praskovya Mikhaylovna was surprised that he did not go, but stood looking at her.

'Pashenka, I have come to you! Take me in.'

His beautiful black eyes, shining with the tears that started in them, were fixed on her with imploring insistence. And under his greyish moustache his lips quivered piteously.

Praskovya Mikhaylovna pressed her hands to her withered breast, opened her mouth, and stood petrified, staring at the wanderer with dilated eyes.

'It can't be! Stepa! Sergy! Father Sergy!'

'Yes, it is I,' said Sergy in a low voice. 'Only not Sergy or Father Sergy, but a great sinner, Stepan Kasatsky, a great and lost sinner. Take me in and help me!'

'It's impossible! How have you so humbled yourself? But come in.'

She reached out her hand, but he did not take it and only followed her in.

But where was she to take him? The lodging was a small one. Formerly she had had a tiny room, almost a closet, for herself, but later she had given it up to her daughter, and Masha was now sitting there rocking the baby.

'Sit here for the present,' she said to Sergy, pointing to a bench in the kitchen.

He sat down at once, and with an evidently accustomed movement slipped the straps of his knapsack first off one shoulder and then off the other.

'My God, my God! How you have humbled yourself, Father! Such great fame, and now like this.'

Sergy did not reply, but only smiled meekly, placing his knapsack under the bench on which he sat.

'Masha, do you know who this is?' And in a whisper Praskovya Mikhaylovna told her daughter who he was, and together they then carried the bed and the cradle out of the tiny room and cleared it for Sergy.

Praskovya Mikhaylovna led him into it.

'Here you can rest. Don't take offence, but I must go out.'

'Where to?'

'I have to go to a lesson. I am ashamed to tell you, but I teach music!'

'Music? But that is good. Only just one thing, Praskovya Mikhaylovna, I have come to you with a definite object. When can I have a talk with you?'

'I shall be very glad. Will this evening do?'

'Yes. But one thing more. Don't speak about me, or say who I am. I have revealed myself only to you. No one knows where I have gone to. It must be so.'

'Oh, but I have told my daughter.'

'Well, ask her not to mention it.'

And Sergy took off his boots, lay down, and at once fell asleep after a sleepless night and a walk of nearly forty versts.

When Praskovya Mikhaylovna returned, Sergy was sitting in the little room waiting for her. He did not come out for dinner, but had some soup and gruel which Lukerya brought him.

'How is it that you have come back earlier than you said?' asked Sergy. 'Can I speak to you now?'

'How is it that I have the happiness to receive such a guest? I have skipped one of my lessons. That can wait. I had always been planning to go to see you. I wrote to you, and now this good fortune has come.'

'Pashenka, please listen to what I am going to tell you as to a confession made to God at my last hour. Pashenka, I am not a holy man, I am not even as good as a simple ordinary man, I am a loathsome, vile, and proud sinner who has gone astray, and who, if not worse than everyone else, is at least worse than most very bad people.'

Pashenka looked at him at first with staring eyes. But she believed what he said, and when she had quite grasped it she touched his hand, smiled pityingly, and said:

'Perhaps you exaggerate, Stiva?'

'No, Pashenka. I am an adulterer, a murderer, a blasphemer, and a deceiver.'

'My God! How is that?' exclaimed Praskovya Mikhaylovna.

'But I must go on living. And I, who thought I knew everything, who taught others how to live, I know nothing and ask you to teach me.'

'What are you saying, Stiva? You are laughing at me. Why do you always make fun of me?'

'Well, fine, if you think so. But tell me all the same how you live and how you have lived your life.'

'I? I have lived a very vile, horrible life, and now God is punishing me as I deserve. I live so wretchedly, so wretchedly.'

'How was it with your marriage? How did you live with your husband?'

'It was all bad. I married because I fell in love in the vilest way. Papa did not approve. But I would not listen to anything and just got married. Then instead of helping my husband I tormented him by my jealousy, which I could not restrain.'

'I heard that he drank.'

'Yes, but I did not give him any peace. I always reproached him, though you know it is a disease! He could not refrain from it. I now remember how I tried to prevent his having it, and the frightful scenes we had!'

And she looked at Kasatsky with beautiful eyes, suffering from the remembrance.

Kasatsky remembered how he had been told that Pashenka's husband used to beat her, and now, looking at her thin withered neck with prominent veins behind her ears, and her scanty coil of hair, half grey half auburn, he seemed to see just how it had occurred.

'Then I was left with two children and no means at all.'

'But you had an estate!'

'Oh, we sold that while Vasya was still alive, and the money was all spent. We had to live, and like all our young ladies I did not know how to earn anything. I was particularly useless and helpless. So we spent all we had. I taught the children and improved my own education a little. And then Mitya fell ill when he was already in the fourth form, and God took him. Masha fell in love with Vanya, my son-in-law. And well, he is well meaning but unfortunate. He is ill.'

'Mamma!' her daughter's voice interrupted her. 'Take Mitya! I can't be in two places at once.'

Praskovya Mikhaylovna shuddered, but rose and went out of the room, stepping quickly in her patched shoes. She soon came back with a boy of two in her arms, who threw himself backwards and grabbed at her shawl with his little hands.

'Where was I? Oh yes, he had a good appointment here, and his chief was a kind man too. But Vanya could not go on and had to give up his position.'

'What is the matter with him?'

'Neurasthenia, it is a dreadful illness. We consulted a doctor, who told us he ought to go away, but we had no means. I always hope it will pass of itself. He has no particular pain, but . . .'

'Lukerya!' cried an angry and feeble voice. 'She is always sent somewhere when I need her. Mamma!'

'I'm coming!' Praskovya Mikhaylovna again interrupted herself. 'He has not had his dinner yet. He can't eat with us.'

She went out and arranged something and came back wiping her thin dark hands.

'So that is how I live. I always complain and am always dissatisfied, but thank God the grandchildren are all nice and healthy, and we can still live. But why talk about me?'

'But what do you live on?'

'Well, I earn a little. How I used to dislike music, but how useful it is to me now!' Her small hand lay on the chest of drawers beside which she was sitting, and she drummed an exercise with her thin fingers.

'How much do you get for a lesson?'

'Sometimes a rouble, sometimes fifty kopeks, or sometimes thirty. They are all so kind to me.'

'And do your pupils get on well?' asked Kasatsky with a slight smile.

Praskovya Mikhaylovna did not at first believe that he was asking seriously and looked enquiringly into his eyes.

'Some of them do. One of them is a splendid girl, the butcher's daughter, such a good kind girl! With the connections papa had if I were a clever woman I should have been able, of course, to get an appointment for my son-in-law. But as it is I have not been able to do anything, and have brought them all to this, as you see.'

'Yes, yes,' said Kasatsky, lowering his head. 'And how is it, Pashenka, do you take part in church life?'

'Oh, don't speak of it. I am so bad that way, and have neglected it so! I keep the fasts with the children and sometimes go to church, and then again sometimes I don't go for months. I only send the children.'

'But why don't you go yourself?'

'To tell the truth,' she blushed, 'I am ashamed, for my daughter's sake and the children's, to go there in tattered clothes, and I haven't anything else. Besides, I am just lazy.'

'And do you pray at home?'

'I do. But what sort of prayer is it? Only mechanical. I know it should not be like that, but I lack real religious feeling. The only thing is that I know how vile I am.'

'Yes, yes, that's right!' said Kasatsky, as if approvingly.

'I'm coming! I'm coming!' she replied to a call from her son-in-law, and tidying her scanty plait she left the room.

But this time it was long before she returned. When she came back, Kasatsky was sitting in the same position, his elbows resting on his knees and his head bowed. But his knapsack was strapped on his back.

When she came in, carrying a small tin lamp without a shade, he raised his fine weary eyes and sighed very deeply.

'I did not tell them who you are,' she began timidly. 'I only said that you are a wanderer, a nobleman, and that I used to know you. Come into the dining room for tea.'

'No.'

'Well then, I'll bring some to you here.'

'No, I don't want anything. God bless you, Pashenka! I am going now. If you pity me, don't tell anyone that you have seen me. For the love of God don't tell anyone. Thank you. I would bow to your feet but I know it would make you feel awkward. Thank you, and forgive me for Christ's sake!'

'Give me your blessing.'

'God bless you! Forgive me for Christ's sake!'

He rose, but she would not let him go until she had given him bread and butter and rusks. He took it all and went away.

It was dark, and before he had passed the second house he was lost to sight. She only knew he was there because the dog at the priest's house was barking.

'So that is what my dream meant! Pashenka is what I ought to have been but failed to be. I lived for men on the pretext of living for God, while she lives for God imagining that she lives for men. Yes, one good deed, a cup of water given without thought of reward, is worth more than any benefit I imagined I was bestowing on people. But after all was there not some share of sincere desire to serve God?' he asked himself, and the answer was, 'Yes, there was, but it was all soiled and overgrown by desire for human fame. Yes, there is no God for the man who lives, as I did, for human fame. I will now seek him!'

And he walked from village to village as he had done on his way to Pashenka, meeting and parting from other wanderers, men and women, and asking for bread and a night's rest in Christ's name. Occasionally some angry housewife scolded him, or a drunken peasant reviled him, but for the most part he was given food and drink and even something to take with him. His noble bearing disposed some people in his favour, while others on the contrary seemed pleased at the sight of a gentleman who had come to beggary.

But his gentleness prevailed with everyone.

Often, finding a copy of the Gospels in a hut he would read it aloud, and when they heard him the people were always touched and surprised, as at something new yet familiar.

When he succeeded in helping people, either by advice, or by his knowledge of reading and writing, or by settling some quarrel, he did not wait to see their gratitude but went away directly afterwards. And little by little God began to reveal himself within him.

Once he was walking along with two old women and a soldier. They were stopped by a party consisting of a lady and gentleman in a gig and another lady and gentleman on horseback. The husband was on horseback with his daughter, while in the gig his wife was driving with a Frenchman, evidently a traveller.

The party stopped to let the Frenchman see the wanderers who, in accord with a popular Russian superstition, tramped about from place to place instead of working.

They spoke French, thinking that the others would not understand them.

'*Demandez-leur*,' said the Frenchman, '*s'ils sont bien sûr de ce que leur pèlerinage est agréable à Dieu.*'[1]

The question was asked, and one old woman replied: 'As God takes it. Our feet have reached the holy places, but our hearts may not have done so.'

They asked the soldier. He said that he was alone in the world and had nowhere else to go.

They asked Kasatsky who he was.

'A servant of God.'*

'*Qu'est-ce qu'il dit? Il ne répond pas.*'[2]

'*Il dit qu'il est un serviteur de Dieu. Cela doit être un fils de prêtre. Il a de la race. Avez-vous de la petite monnaie?*'[3]

The Frenchman found some small change and gave twenty kopeks to each of the wanderers.

'*Mais dites-leur que ce n'est pas pour les cierges que je leur donne, mais pour qu'ils se régalent de thé. Chay, chay pour vous, mon vieux!*'[4] he said with a smile. And he patted Kasatsky on the shoulder with his gloved hand.

'May Christ bless you,' replied Kasatsky without replacing his cap and bowing his bald head.

---

[1] 'Ask them whether they are quite sure that their pilgrimage pleases God.'

[2] 'What does he say? He does not answer.'

[3] 'He says that he is a servant of God. That one is probably a priest's son. He is not a common man. Have you any small change?'

[4] 'But tell them that I give it them not to spend on church candles, but that they should have some tea. Tea, tea for you, old fellow.'

He rejoiced particularly at this meeting, because he had disregarded the opinion of men and had done the simplest, easiest thing, humbly accepted twenty kopeks and given them to his comrade, a blind beggar. The less importance he attached to the opinion of men the more did he feel the presence of God within him.

For eight months Kasatsky tramped on in this manner, and in the ninth month he was arrested for not having a passport. This happened at a night-refuge in a provincial town where he had passed the night with some wanderers. He was taken to the police station, and when asked who he was and where was his passport, he replied that he had no passport and that he was a servant of God. He was classed as a vagrant, sentenced, and sent to live in Siberia.

In Siberia he settled down as the hired man of a well-to-do peasant and he is living there now. He works in the kitchen-garden, teaches the children, and attends to the sick.

AFTER THE BALL

A Tale

'So you're saying that on his own a person cannot understand what is good and what is evil, that it's all a matter of the environment, that a person is a victim of his environment. But I think that it's all a matter of chance. Let me tell you about myself.'

Thus Ivan Vasilyevich, whom we all respected, began to speak, after a conversation we had had about the attempt to attain personal perfection and the consequent prior necessity of changing the conditions in which people live. No one actually had said that on his own one could not understand what is good and what is evil, but Ivan Vasilyevich had the habit of responding to the thoughts that occurred to him during a conversation and then using those thoughts as the pretext for telling episodes from his life. Often, absorbed by his tale, he would completely forget why he was telling it, especially since he was telling it very sincerely and truthfully.

This is what he was doing now.

'I'll tell you about myself. My whole life turned out as it did and not otherwise, not because of the environment but from something completely different.'

'From what?' we asked.

'Now that's a long story. For you to understand I'll have to tell a lot.'

'So go on and tell us.'

Ivan Vasilyevich began to think and then shook his head.

'Yes,' he said, 'my whole life was changed because of one night, or rather one morning.'

'So what happened?'

'What happened was that I was deeply in love. I have been in love many times, but this was the deepest love of my life. It's long ago now; she already has daughters who are married. Her name was B . . ., yes Varenka B . . .' (Ivan Vasilyevich mentioned her last name.) 'Even at fifty she was a remarkably beautiful woman. But in her youth, at the age of eighteen, she was enchanting: tall, shapely, graceful, and stately, truly stately. She always held herself unusually erect, as if she could not do otherwise, with her head tossed just a bit back, and this together with her beauty and her height gave her a certain regal appearance which, despite her being thin, even bony, would have scared people off had it not been for the caressing and always merry smile of her mouth and of her enchanting, glistening eyes, and of her whole dear, young being.'

'Oh how Ivan Vasilyevich does paint a picture.'

'Well, however it's painted, it's impossible to paint it so that you could understand what she was like. But that's beside the point: what I want to tell you is that it was in the forties. At the time I was a student in a provincial university. Whether it was good or bad I don't know, but at that time in our university we did not have any circles or any theories,* and we were just young and lived as youth does—we studied and we made merry. I was a very merry and lively young man, and rich as well. I had a great horse, went tobogganing with the young ladies (skating had not yet come into fashion), caroused with my comrades (at that time we drank nothing but champagne; if we had no money, we drank nothing at all, not even vodka as they do now). My greatest pleasure came from the soirées and balls. I danced well and was not quite ugly.'

'Well, there's no reason to be modest,' one of the young ladies interrupted him. 'After all we have already seen your daguerreotype. It's not that you were just not ugly, you were handsome.'

'Handsome or not, that's beside the point. The point is that at the time of my deepest love for her, I was at a ball on the last day of Butter Week* at the provincial marshal's, a good-natured old man, rich and hospitable, and a court chamberlain. His wife, as good-natured as he, was receiving the guests in her puce velvet gown, a diamond diadem on her head, and with her old, puffy, white shoulders and breast exposed, as in the portraits of Yelizaveta Petrovna.* The ball was wonderful: the room was beautiful, with choirs, an orchestra composed of serfs who were renowned at the time and owned by an amateur musician, a magnificent buffet, and an ever-flowing ocean of champagne. Although I was very fond of champagne, I didn't drink because without it I was already drunk with love, but to make up for it I danced till I dropped, the quadrilles and the waltzes and the polkas, all of course as much as possible with Varenka. She was wearing a white dress with a pink sash, white kid gloves that didn't quite reach her thin, pointed elbows, and white satin shoes. I was robbed of the mazurka: a most offensive engineer named Anisimov—to this day I cannot fogive him for it—had asked her for this dance just as she arrived, while I was late because I went to the barber's and stopped off to get some gloves. As a result I didn't dance the mazurka with her, but with a certain young German girl I had previously pursued a bit. But I'm afraid that I was not very polite towards her that evening, I didn't speak with her or look at her, for I saw only that tall, shapely figure in a white dress with a pink sash, that flushed, radiant face with dimples, and those dear, caressing eyes. Not just me, but everyone was looking at her and admiring her, both the men and the women, even though she outshone them all. One couldn't help but admire her.

'Officially, so to say, I did not dance the mazurka with her, but in reality I danced it almost all the time with her. Without any embarrassment she crossed the whole room and came right up to me, and I jumped up without waiting for an invitation, and she thanked me with a smile for figuring it out. When we were led up to her and she failed to guess my quality,* she shrugged her thin shoulders as she extended her hand not to me and, as a sign of regret and consolation, she smiled at me. When the mazurka figures were replaced by a waltz, I waltzed for a long time with her and she, while breathing rapidly, smiled and said to me, "Encore." And I kept on waltzing and waltzing and did not even feel my body.'

'Now how could you not have felt your body; I think you felt it a good deal when you had your arms around her waist, and not only your own body, but hers as well,' said one of the guests.

Ivan Vasilyevich suddenly blushed and angrily began almost to shout. 'Now that's just how you are, today's youth. Except for the body you don't see a thing. In our time it was different. The more deeply I was in love, the less she seemed to me just a body. But nowadays you see the legs, ankles, and even something more, you undress the women with whom you are in love, while for me, as Alphonse Karr* would have said—a fine writer he was—the object of my love was always dressed in bronze clothing. We didn't just not undress them, but we tried to cover their nakedness, like the good son of Noah.* But then you wouldn't understand . . .'

'Don't listen to him. And so what else do you have to say?' said one of us.

'Yes, there I was and I danced more with her and didn't notice how the time passed. Already with a certain desperate exhaustion, as it happens you know at the end of a ball, the musicians kept on repeating the same mazurka tune, the mummies and daddies had already got up from their card tables and left the parlour in expectation of supper, the servants started rushing around more often, carrying something or other. It was three o'clock. I had to make use of the last few minutes. I chose her again and for the hundredth time we danced around the room.

' "May I have the quadrille after supper?" I asked her as I led her to her seat.

' "Of course, if they don't take me away," she said smiling.

' "I won't let them," I said.

' "Give me my fan," she said.

' "I'm sorry to have to give it back," I said as I handed her the inexpensive, white fan.

' "Then this is for you, so you won't have to feel sorry," she said, as she tore a feather from the fan and gave it to me.

'I took the feather and could express only with a glance all my rapture and gratitude. I was not only merry and satisfied, I was happy, blessed, I was good, I was not me, but some unearthly being that knew no evil and was capable only of the good. I hid the feather in my glove and stood, not having the strength to depart from her.

' "Look, they're asking papa to dance," she said to me, as she pointed out the tall, stately figure of her father, a colonel with silver epaulettes who was standing at the door with the hostess and some other ladies.

' "Varenka, come here," we heard the loud voice of the hostess with her diamond diadem and shoulders like the Empress Yelizaveta Petrovna. Varenka went up to the door, and I followed her. "*Ma chère*, persuade your father to dance with you. Now, please, Pyotr Vladislavich," the hostess turned to the colonel.

'Varenka's father was a very handsome, stately, tall, and well-preserved old man. He had a very ruddy face with temples covered with combed-down hair and a white moustache curled in the style of Nikolay I,* which met his equally white side-whiskers, and as with his daughter that same caressing, joyful smile was in his glistening eyes and on his lips. He was beautifully built, with strong shoulders, and long shapely legs, and a broad chest adorned with just a few medals and thrust forward in military fashion. He was a military

commander of a certain type, an old veteran of the discipline of the
era of Nikolay I.

'When we approached the door, the colonel was refusing to dance,
saying that he had forgotten how, but then, smiling, he swung his
arm to the left, drew his sword from its sheath, gave it over to an
obliging young man, and after having smoothed the suede glove on
his right hand, he said with a smile, "Everything according to the
rules," took his daughter's hand, and stood in the one-quarter-
turned position, waiting for the beat.

'As soon as the mazurka began, he smartly stamped with one foot,
thrust the other forward, and his tall, stout figure began, now softly
and smoothly, now loudly and quickly, to move through the room
with the thumping of boot soles and of foot against foot. Varenka
graciously floated beside him, rhythmically, yet imperceptibly short-
ening or lengthening the steps of her little white satin feet. The
whole room followed the couple's every movement. I not only
admired them, but I was moved to rapture as I looked at them. What
particularly moved me were his boots which were fastened with
straps—fine, calfskin boots, but not the fashionable kind with
pointed toes, but the old-styled ones with squared toes and without
heels. Obviously the boots were made by a regimental cobbler. "In
order to dress his favourite daughter and bring her out into society,
he doesn't buy fashionable boots, but wears his everyday ones," I
thought, and I was moved especially by the square toes of those
boots. It was apparent that at one time he had danced quite well, but
now he was rather stout, and his legs were no longer sufficiently
supple for all those elegant, rapid steps he was trying to perform. All
the same he twice circled the room quite deftly. And when after
quickly planting his feet apart, he rejoined them again and, albeit a
bit heavily, fell to one knee, and when after smilingly adjusting her
skirt which he had caught, she circled round him quite smoothly,
everyone loudly began to applaud. After standing up with some
effort, he tenderly, lovingly embraced his daughter's head, kissing
her forehead, and brought her over to me, thinking that I had been
dancing with her. I said that I was not her partner for the mazurka.

' "Well, never mind, dance with her now," he said, smiling
affectionately and placing his sword in its sheath.

'Just as it happens when after one drop has flowed from a bottle,
the contents then flow forth in gushing streams, so the love for

Varenka in my soul released all the pent-up potential for love in my soul. I loved the hostess in the diadem with her Yelizaveta Petrovna bust, I loved her husband and her guests and her servants, and I even loved the engineer Anisimov who was now feeling a bit peeved with me. And towards Varenka's father with his everyday boots and caressing smile just like hers, I experienced at that moment a certain rapturously tender feeling.

'The mazurka ended, the host and hostess summoned the guests to supper, but Colonel B. refused, saying that he had to get up early in the morning, and bade them farewell. I was beginning to fear she would be taken away too, but she remained with her mother.

'After supper I danced with her the quadrille she promised me, and despite the fact that I seemed to be infinitely happy, my happiness kept on growing and growing. We did not speak of love. I did not even ask her or myself whether she loved me. It was quite enough that I loved her. And I feared only one thing, that something might spoil my happiness.

'When I got home, I undressed and began to think about sleep, but then realized that sleep was completely beyond me. I was holding in my hand the feather from her fan and the glove she had given me upon her departure, when she was getting into the carriage and I helped her mother to get settled and then her. I looked at those objects and without closing my eyes saw her before me, now at that moment when to choose between two partners she was trying to guess my quality and I heard her dear voice as she said, "*Pride*, right," and joyfully gave me her hand, now at that moment after supper when she was sipping a glass of champagne and looking somewhat distrustfully at me with her caressing eyes. But most of all I saw her dancing with her father, smoothly circling around him, as she surveyed with pride and joy for both him and herself the admiring spectators. And as I unconsciously linked them together, I was overcome with a soft, tender feeling.

'I was living at that time with my now deceased brother. In general my brother neither cared for society nor attended balls; moreover he was then studying for his final examinations for graduation from the university and leading a very regular life. He was asleep. I stared at his head buried in his pillow and half covered with his flannel blanket and I started to feel lovingly sorry for him, sorry that he did not know nor share that happiness which I was experiencing. Our household serf Petrusha came in with a candle and wanted to help me undress, but I didn't let him. The sight of his sleepy face and tousled hair touched and moved me. Trying not to make noise I walked on tiptoe to my room and sat on my bed. No, I was too happy, I could not sleep. Furthermore I was warm in the heated rooms, so instead of taking off my uniform, I went into the hallway, put on my overcoat, opened the front door, and went quietly out onto the street.

'I had left the ball after four and about two hours more had passed since I got home and sat for a while, so that when I went out it was already light. The weather was typical for Butter Week: it was foggy, the snow which was saturated with water was melting on the roads, and there was dripping from all the roofs. At that time the B. family lived at the edge of town next to a large field at one end of which was a parade ground and at the other a boarding school for young girls. I crossed our deserted lane and walked out onto the main road, where I began to encounter passengers and carters with firewood so weighed down on their sleighs that the runners were scraping the road. And the horses, rhythmically swaying their soaked heads under the glistening shaft-bows, and the cabbies covered with bast matting, thudding along in their huge boots beside their cabs, and the houses on the street, which in the fog appeared very tall—all this seemed to me especially dear and meaningful.

'When I came to the field where their house was, I saw something huge and black at the end of it, in the direction of the parade ground, and from there I heard the sounds of a fife and drum. The whole time my soul was still full of song and every now and then the tune of the mazurka still resounded in my ears. But this was some other kind of music, harsh and unpleasant.

' "What's this?" I thought, and I took off in the direction of the sounds along the slippery, trampled path in the middle of the field. After walking about a hundred paces, I began to distinguish through the fog a number of black people. Obviously, soldiers. "Must be manoeuvres," I thought, and along with a blacksmith in a soiled apron and sheepskin coat who was walking in front of me and carrying something, I moved closer. Black-uniformed soldiers were standing in two rows opposite each other, holding their rifles at their feet and remaining motionless. Behind them stood a drummer and a fifer who kept on repeating without stop that same unpleasant, shrill melody.

' "What are they doing," I asked the blacksmith who was standing next to me.

' "They are beating a Tatar* for desertion," the blacksmith said angrily, as he looked intently to the far end of the rows.

'I started to look there too and between the rows caught sight of something horrible approaching me. What was approaching me was a man, stripped to the waist and strapped to the rifles of two soldiers who were leading him. At his side in an overcoat and cap there was walking an officer whose figure seemed familiar to me. His whole body twitching, his feet tramping through the melting snow, and with blows raining upon him from both sides, the man being punished started to move toward me, now toppling over backwards, with the non-commissioned officers who were leading him by their rifles pushing him up, now falling forward, with the non-commissioned officers who were trying to keep him from falling pushing him back. And ever at his side there walked with a firm, bobbing step that tall officer. It was her father with his ruddy face and white moustache and side-whiskers.

'With each blow, as if in astonishment, the man being punished would turn his face contorted with suffering toward the source of that blow and baring his white teeth would keep on repeating certain words. Only when he got quite close did I make out those words. He did not speak them, but sobbed them out: "Have mercy on me, lads. Have mercy on me, lads." But the lads had no mercy, and as the procession came right up close to me, I saw the soldier standing across from me take a decisive step forward and swinging his stick with a whirr smack the Tatar across the back with all his might. The Tatar jerked forward, but the non-commissioned officers held him back, and a similar blow fell upon him from the other side, then again from this side and again from that. The colonel was still walking right alongside and, now looking down at his own feet, now at the man being punished, he took in deep gulps of air, puffing out his cheeks and then slowly letting the air out through his protruding lips. As the procession passed the place where I was standing, between the rows of the soldiers I caught sight of the back of the man being punished. It was something so motley, wet, red, and unnatural that I could not believe it was the body of a human being.

' "O Lord," uttered the blacksmith who was standing next to me.

'The procession began to move into the distance, but the blows kept on falling from both sides on the stumbling, writhing man, the drums kept on beating, the fife kept on piping, and with that same firm step the tall, stately figure of the colonel kept on moving right alongside the man being punished. Suddenly the colonel stopped and rapidly approached one of the soldiers.

' "I'll teach you to go easy on him," I heard his enraged voice. "Are you going easy on him? Are you?"

'And I saw him strike a frightened, puny, weak soldier in the face with his powerful, suede-gloved hand, because the soldier had not struck the Tatar's red back powerfully enough with his stick.

' "Get them some fresh willow sticks!" he shouted, as he looked around and caught sight of me. Pretending not to know me, he quickly turned away with an ill-tempered, menacing frown on his face. I was so ashamed that without knowing where to look, as if I had been caught in a most shameful act, I lowered my eyes and hurried away home. All the way home my ears rang now with the beating rolls of the drums and the piping of the flute, now with the words, "Have mercy on me, lads," now with the self-assured, enraged voice of the colonel shouting, "Are you going easy on him? Are you?" And all the while in my heart I felt an anguish that was almost physical to the point of nausea, so that I stopped several times, feeling that I was about to vomit all that horror that had entered into me from that spectacle. I don't remember how I managed to get home or into bed. But no sooner did I start to fall asleep than I heard and saw everything all over again and sprang right up.

' "Obviously he knows something that I don't," I thought with the colonel in mind. "If I knew what he knows, I would understand even what I saw and it wouldn't torment me." But no matter how much I thought about it, I could not understand what it was the colonel knew, and I managed to fall asleep only toward evening and then only after going over to a friend's and getting completely drunk with him.

'So do you think that it was then that I decided that what I saw was a wicked thing? Not in the least. "If it was done with such assurance and deemed necessary by everyone, then they must have known something I didn't," I thought, and I tried to find out what it was. But no matter how hard I tried, I could not find out what it was, not even later. And since I couldn't find out, I couldn't enter military service, as I had formerly wanted to, and so I didn't serve in the military nor in the civil service and have been quite useless, as you can see.'

'Well, we know how useless you've been,' one of us said. 'It would be better to say how many people would be useless, if it hadn't been for you.'

'Well that's just sheer nonsense,' Ivan Vasilyevich said with genuine vexation.

'And what about that love of yours?' we asked.

'My love? From that day on my love began to fade. When she would grow pensive with that smile on her face, as she often did, I would immediately remember the colonel on the parade ground and it would become somehow uncomfortable and unpleasant for me, and so I started seeing her less. And finally my love just came to an end. And so that's the kind of thing that happens and that can change and direct a person's whole life. And you say . . .' he concluded.

EXPLANATORY NOTES

The Snow Storm

3 *Don Cossack ... Novocherkassk*: the Don Cossacks, so named because they were settled along the Don River, were known for their bravery and love of freedom; they were often pressed into service for the Tsar. Novocherkassk, a city in the Rostov province in south-western Russia, served as the capital of the Don Cossack region.

4 *verst-post*: a road-post marking distance. A verst is 3,500 feet (1.06 km.).

5 *troikas*: a troika is a sledge pulled by a team of three horses.

8 *artel*: a voluntary association of workers which had a manager, was contracted as a unit, and divided its earnings among its members.

15 *beetle*: a wooden paddle-like instrument used by women for washing clothes by beating the water from them after they had been rinsed in lakes or streams.

19 *arnica*: a medicine made from a mountain tobacco plant.

20 *Kalmyk territory*: the Kalmyks are an Islamic people who at this time lived as nomads in the plains and foothills of Dagestan.

Lucerne

32 *Murray*: John Murray published a series of 'handbooks for travellers', in this case obviously a guide to Switzerland.

crooked bridge: the Hofbrücke, which was removed in 1852.

35 *Tuileries*: the French royal residence in Paris, adjacent to the Louvre. Destroyed by arson in 1871.

36 *Tyrolese*: Tyrol is an alpine region in western Austria and northern Italy.

38 *Aargau*: a canton in northern Switzerland, bordering on Germany.

40 *à la Mousquetaire*: a large protruding feather, as worn by 'the three musketeers' in the novel of that name published by the French writer Alexandre Dumas (*père*) in 1844.

45 *republican laws*: the laws as expounded in the constitution of the Republic of Switzerland (1848), which included various limitations on wandering beggars.

48 *Sevastopol*: here Tolstoy is drawing on his own experience in the defence of Sevastopol, the major battle of the Crimean War (1853–6), a war which the Russians lost to the allied forces of England, France, Sardinia, and Turkey.

51 *Chinamen*: in 1856 the Chinese arrested some opium dealers travelling on an English ship. The British, interpreting this as an insult and humili-

ation, retaliated by bombarding the Chinese fleet at Canton and then seizing and ransacking that city, killing many of its inhabitants.

Arabs: after the colonization of Algiers, the French army attacked and killed a number of mountain tribesmen who resisted despite the odds.

Jew: in 1857 there was a conflict between Turkey and Naples, because Naples would not recognize a Turkish envoy since he was Jewish.

Plombières: the solitary walks of Napoléon III in this resort town were considered a sign of his distance from Parisian politics and thus of the 'freedom' of the French in the upcoming elections.

52 *in India*: the British were trying to attract workers from among the Chinese men who had settled in India, but these settlers usually came without their wives, intending to return home. The House of Commons proposed levelling a special tax on such 'settlers'.

Africa: Tolstoy is here being ironic about the French methods of colonization.

human race: Tolstoy is mocking the discussions in the French and British press in 1856-7 of a possible 'general union of European nations', in order to create 'a single family of all humanity'.

Three Deaths

55 *calèche*: an open carriage with facing passenger seats and an elevated coachman's seat joined to the front of the shallow body. The word comes from the Czech *kolesa*, meaning wheels or carriage.

60 *Fedka*: a diminutive form of Khvyodor, as is Fedya. Khvyodor is a peasant dialectal pronunciation of Fyodor, the Russian form for Theodore (Gr. 'gift of God').

65 *'I congratulate you, my dear'*: because the reception of communion was relatively rare and marked by special preparations, it was customary to offer the communicant congratulations.

66 *'Thou hidest . . . for ever'*: Psalm 104: 29-31, in Russian Psalm 103.

Polikushka

68 *commune*: peasants traditionally lived in a village community presided over by a council of elders. The Russian word (*mir*) extends in meaning from 'commune' to 'world', 'universe', and 'peace'.

69 *feast of Pokrov*: a feast in honour of the protection (*pokrov*) and intercession of the Mother of God, 1 October (OS).

70 *three hundred roubles*: for such a fee it was possible to buy a substitute for military service.

72 *Polikey*: the formal name for Polikushka, which is a more intimate form, not without a touch of condescension or contempt.

75 *trave*: a frame or enclosure of bars in which a restless horse is placed to be shod.

76 *Wage . . . zu träumen*: 'Dare to err and dream,' a quotation from 'Tekla', a poem by Johann Christoph Friedrich von Schiller (1759–1805).

78 *Ilyich*: peasants often referred to people by their patronyms alone, as here.

86 *Ilya*: the formal name for Ilyushka, who is also called later in the text Ilyukha.

87 *mischief*: to escape service men sometimes mutilated themselves, for instance by cutting off their trigger-finger.

89 *samovar*: a special kettle with a charcoal stove underneath, used for heating water for tea.

91 *assignation roubles*: a type of paper currency issued officially from 1769 to 1843. One silver rouble was equal to 3.5 assignation roubles.

92 *kvas*: a mildly fermented drink made from grain.

93 *cares for*: this translates the Russian *zhalko*, a word that conveys an important emotion related to the Russian Christian understanding of 'love'. It appears in this text in various forms, including the verb *zhalet'* (in peasant language, 'to love'), and is translated variously: 'be sorry for', 'take pity on', and in relation to money 'begrudge'.

110 *abacus*: a wooden frame with rows of movable beads commonly used in the East for arithmetic calculation. They are still in use in Russia.

115 *Julia Pastrana*: a bearded lady who in the 1850s travelled around Russia along with albinos and other 'marvels of nature' in a kind of circus troupe.

122 *head shaved*: on being conscripted a man's head was partially shaved to make desertion more difficult

Strider

133 *assignation roubles*: see note to p. 91.

148 *troika*: see note to p. 5.

151 *host . . . hostess*: in the Russian original the words for 'master' and 'mistress' (*khozyáin, khozyáyka*) are the same words also translated here as 'host' and 'hostess'.

samovar: see note to p. 89.

beard à la Napoléon III: a stiletto beard—a narrow goatee from the lower lip to an inch or so below the chin—combined with a long horizontal moustache waxed straight at the sides.

152 *incrusté*: inlaid with various woods to create artistic patterns.

157 *versts*: a verst is 3,500 feet (1.06 km.).

God Sees the Truth, But Waits

161 *versts*: see previous note.

samovar: see note to p. 89.

troika: see note to p. 5.

163 *Cheti-Minei*: the great *Menologion* or *Saints' Calendar* compiled by Makary, Metropolitan of Moscow (d. 1563). This collection of saints' lives, which had various redactions, was popular among the Russian people.

164 *man of God*: an honorific appellation derived from the saint's life 'Aleksey, Man of God', popularized by the 'spiritual poem' (*dukhóvny stikh*) based on the story as told in the *vita*.

The Notes of a Madman

170 *bonds*: government bonds given as payment to owners of serfs at the time of the Emancipation in 1861.

versts: see note to p. 157.

171 *samovar*: see note to p. 89.

Where Love Is, God Is

179 *wanderer*: a person who left everything worldly and wandered about living 'as the lilies of the field'. A characteristic type of Russian Orthodox piety.

Troitsa Monastery: the famed Troitse-Sergieva Lavra outside Moscow, founded by St Sergy of Radonezh (d. 1392). It is still a functioning monastery and the site of the Moscow Theological Academy.

180 *man of God*: see note to p. 164.

judgement: this Russian proverb, *Ne nashim umom, a Bozh'im sudom*, is also cited by Platon Karataev in *War and Peace* (IV. i. 12).

181 '*Unto him . . . likewise*': Luke 6: 29–31.

'*And why call . . . great*': Luke 6: 46–9.

182 '*And turning . . . with ointment*': Luke 7: 44–6.

samovar: see note to p. 89.

183 *upside down*: turning the glass upside down was the customary sign that one had had enough.

190 '*I was . . . took me in*': Matthew 25: 35.

'*Inasmuch . . . unto me*': Matthew 25: 40.

The Devil

192 *desyatins*: a *desyatin* equals 2.7 acres.

201 *Institute*: a boarding school for the daughters of the gentry, in which great attention was paid to the manners and accomplishments of the pupils.

209 *'envelopes'*: an 'envelope' was a small mattress with a blanket attached, on which babies were carried about.

217 *samovar*: see note to p. 89.

221 *troika*: see note to p. 5.

229 *zemstvo*: an elective district for local administration; established in 1864 and abolished in 1917.

232 *live like this*: the alternative ending, printed here at the end of the story, replaces the text at this point.

236 *trial by jury*: trial by jury was introduced in 1864, along with other liberalizing measures, such as the *zemstvo* mentioned earlier. In the beginning juries tended to be extremely lenient on the prisoners.

Father Sergy

240 *Tsarskoe Selo*: a suburban village outside St Petersburg where the great tsar's palace designed by the Italian architect Rastrelli was located. It was here that the elite school attended by the famous poet Alexander Pushkin was established. The village is now called Pushkino.

Mary's: the English form of the name, printed here in Cyrillic, is used (*Meri*).

242 *Institute*: see note to p. 201.

Nevsky: Nevsky Prospekt is the main street in downtown St Petersburg.

243 *feast of Pokrov*: see note to p. 69.

Paissy Velichkovsky: the Ukrainian monk (1772–94) who founded a monastic commune on Mt. Athos, which he later moved to Moldavia. He is responsible for the re-establishment of the Hesychastic tradition of meditation in Moldavia, Ukraine, and Russia. In Russia this led to the great spiritual revival of monasticism in the nineteenth century.

246 *iconostasis*: the screen of icons that separates the inner sanctuary from the *solea*.

247 *klobuk*: a tall cylindrical-shaped headpiece with a veil at the rear, worn by Orthodox monks.

amvon: the raised area in front of the Holy Door at the centre of the screen of icons that separates the inner sanctuary from the *solea* (the equivalent of the Roman Catholic 'sanctuary').

north door: one of two doors, on opposite sides of the screen of icons, that lead from the *solea* into the inner sanctuary. The north door leads into the 'chapel' where the priest prepares the bread and wine at the beginning of the divine liturgy.

angelic image: a monk was said to be an 'image of an angel'. Here it is used ironically.

249 *Butter Week*: the last week before the Great Fast (i.e. Lent), during which one fasts from meat but not dairy products. In the Great Fast neither meat nor dairy products are eaten.

troika-party: see note to p. 5.

bliny: the traditional pancakes served with butter and sour cream during Butter Week.

250 *pirozhki*: small bun-like hors d'oeuvres usually filled with sautéed sauerkraut or ground beef.

252 *analoychik*: a lectern (*analoy*) on which service books were placed. The narrator here adds a suffix to the word that makes the reference ironic.

254 *'Lord . . . a sinner!'*: this prayer, the so-called Jesus Prayer, is the mantra-like prayer used in the hesychast tradition to help create the meditative state.

255 *arshins*: an *arshin* is 28 inches (71 cm.).

260 *the parable of the unjust judge*: Luke 18.

261 *versts*: see note to p. 157.

262 *wanderers*: see note to p. 179.

263 *'Forbid them . . . unto me'*: Matthew 19: 14.

267 *'Lord . . . troubles me'*: a variant on the common morning prayer said at home. Tolstoy himself often cites it in part in his own diary prayers.

278 *servant of God*: in Orthodoxy this phrase is used sacramentally (at baptism, matrimony, and burial) as the sign of one's true identity.

After the Ball

281 *any circles or any theories*: the 1840s were in general a time when 'circles' of philosophically minded students abounded. They gathered to discuss mainly German idealism (Schelling, Hegel, and Fichte) and French utopian socialism. Such philosophy with its potential for 'free thinking' and especially its speculation about alternative views of governance was considered subversive by the highly autocratic regime of Nikolay I, which in 1848 even closed the departments of philosophy in the universities.

Butter Week: see note to p. 249.

Yelizaveta Petrovna: Empress of Russia from 1741 to 1761.

282 *my quality*: the ritual of choosing a partner required the guessing of a pre-established 'quality', a kind of secret code name based on a moral virtue or vice.

Alphonse Karr: French novelist and journalist (1808–90), whose works combined sentimentality with wit. He has been immortalized by his famous epigram apropos of the revolutions of 1848: 'Plus ça change, plus c'est la même chose.'

good son of Noah: after the flood Noah became a farmer and planted, among other things, a vineyard. He once got drunk on the wine he produced and lay down naked in his tent. His son Ham saw him and told his two brothers Shem and Japheth. They entered the tent backwards and covered their father's nakedness with a cloak (Genesis 9: 20–4). Thus there were two 'good' sons, not one as Ivan Vasilyevich believes.

283 *style of Nikolay I*: Nikolay I, who ruled from 1825 to 1855, established a strong military rule which shaped the temper and fashion of the times.

287 *Tatar*: a Turco-Mongolian people, mainly nomads known for their military system and ferocious warriors, who acquired wealth through raiding and tribute. The word tends to be used to describe various Mongol peoples.

The Oxford World's Classics Website

www.worldsclassics.co.uk

- Browse the full range of Oxford World's Classics online

- Sign up for our monthly e-alert to receive information on new titles

- Read extracts from the Introductions

- Listen to our editors and translators talk about the world's greatest literature with our Oxford World's Classics audio guides

- Join the conversation, follow us on Twitter at OWC_Oxford

- Teachers and lecturers can order inspection copies quickly and simply via our website

www.worldsclassics.co.uk

American Literature

British and Irish Literature

Children's Literature

Classics and Ancient Literature

Colonial Literature

Eastern Literature

European Literature

Gothic Literature

History

Medieval Literature

Oxford English Drama

Poetry

Philosophy

Politics

Religion

The Oxford Shakespeare

A complete list of Oxford World's Classics, including Authors in Context, Oxford English Drama, and the Oxford Shakespeare, is available in the UK from the Marketing Services Department, Oxford University Press, Great Clarendon Street, Oxford OX2 6DP, or visit the website at www.oup.com/uk/worldsclassics.

In the USA, visit www.oup.com/us/owc for a complete title list.

Oxford World's Classics are available from all good bookshops. In case of difficulty, customers in the UK should contact Oxford University Press Bookshop, 116 High Street, Oxford OX1 4BR.

A SELECTION OF OXFORD WORLD'S CLASSICS